DAMAGE CONTROL

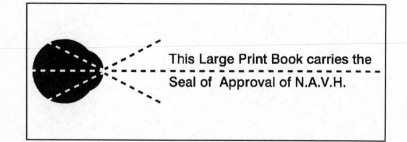

This Large Print Book carries the
Seal of Approval of N.A.V.H.

DAMAGE CONTROL

DENISE HAMILTON

THORNDIKE PRESS

A part of Gale, Cengage Learning

Detroit • New York • San Francisco • New Haven, Conn • Waterville, Maine • London

Copyright © 2011 by Denise Hamilton.
Thorndike Press, a part of Gale, Cengage Learning.

Thorndike Press® Large Print Thriller.
The text of this Large Print edition is unabridged.
Other aspects of the book may vary from the original edition.
Set in 16 pt. Plantin.

LIBRARY OF CONGRESS CATALOGING-IN-PUBLICATION DATA

Hamilton, Denise.
    Damage control / by Denise Hamilton.
      p. cm. — (Thorndike Press large print thriller)
    ISBN-13: 978-1-4104-4299-4 (hardcover)
    ISBN-10: 1-4104-4299-3 (hardcover)
    1. Women public relations personnel—Fiction. 2. Politicians—California—Fiction. 3. Scandals—Fiction. 4. Teenage girls—Fiction. 5. Female friendship—Fiction. 6. Los Angeles (Calif.)—Fiction. 7. Large type books. I. Title.
PS3608.A68D36 2011b
813'.6—dc22   2011033256

Published in 2011 by arrangement with Scribner, a division of Simon & Schuster, Inc.

Printed in the United States of America
1 2 3 4 5 6 7 15 14 13 12 11

This one's for the perfumistas
and in memory of Hélène Hamilton
(1920–2011)

In my dreams, Anabelle Paxton and I are still friends and that summer night in Playa never happened. I am married to her brother, Luke, and we live in a Spanish house overlooking the Pacific. Anabelle and her husband live down the street and each morning our kids walk down the sandstone cliffs to surf before school, just as we once did. There is sand on the floorboards and art on every wall, and at night, our big unruly tribe gathers around the mesquite grill and someone strums a guitar.

And no one is dead.

For two years during high school, the Paxtons were my life, the sun around which I revolved. They taught me a new way of seeing. For them, there was no barrier between wanting something and getting it. They simply made it happen — with their money, connections, and magnetic personalities. Their confidence was contagious, inspiring me to reach for a future I'd never imagined before. In many ways, they made me what I am. That's why despite everything that came later, I owe a debt to that family. And I wish things could have turned out differently.

PROLOGUE

Summer 1993

The party was in the Jungle, not our usual scene at all, just a bunch of clapboard beach shacks in Playa del Rey, leaning drunkenly under the crescent moon.

Luke went on ahead while Anabelle and I stopped under a palm tree for a lip gloss boost. Above us, something rustled, but when I looked up, it was only dead gray fronds trembling in the breeze. The air smelled of coconut oil, spilled beer, and Mr. Zog's Sex Wax.

From the party bungalow came hoots and jeers, then the knifing soprano of a girl's laugh. Black Flag blasted from fuzzy speakers. As the song ended, a wave crashed in perfect time just beyond the dunes.

Luke was already on the porch, high-fiving his surf buddies and nodding coolly at the girls.

Luke, our passport to adventure.

It was a mystery to me, in that world before IM and Twitter and Facebook, how he always knew where to show up. I never saw Luke call anyone or make plans. Anabelle believed that her brother and his surfer friends had their own secret language, like the eerie singing that whales use to communicate across vast distances. She said the booming surf was a tribal drum and that if you listened very hard, you'd hear words in the watery rush the pebbles made when the tide pulled back.

Each weekend, we'd pile into Luke's cherried-out '67 Mustang convertible in the indigo dusk and head for Malibu or Hermosa, County Line or Venice, wherever the party was. Luke popped in the latest metal, though he also liked Hawaiian steel guitar, and would even play one of Anabelle's mix tapes if we begged and he was feeling charitable.

Luke drove fast, tires squealing around the curves, laughing as Anabelle and I slammed together in the backseat. We would shriek, our long hair whipping behind us in the warm desert air like fragrant banshees.

The summer we were sixteen, Anabelle dressed in tulle and organza and lace. She wore a ruby stud in her nose and hammered silver bracelets that made Gypsy music when she walked. When she was sad, she'd slip on fairy wings and sit cross-legged on her bed, drinking green tea and sketching out her demons so we could burn them in a ritual cleansing. I'd sprawl on the tiger rug that her grandfather had shot on Kenyan safari, reading *Les Misérables* and trying not to show how happy I was.

I loved Anabelle with an intensity that frightened me. She was my best friend and my only ally in that lunatic asylum known as Our Lady of Corvallis High School, and I knew I'd collapse in abject misery and die if she ever dropped me.

I also knew, despite my social awkwardness, that it was absolutely necessary to conceal these fears. I'd transferred to Corvallis as a sophomore that fall, an entire year after everybody else had met and bonded, so I cultivated an air of enigmatic aloofness for self-defense. This kept the pleated-skirt tormentors at bay, but it had the perverse effect of attracting Anabelle.

It wasn't until years later that I understood how my behavior must have been catnip to her. She was a girl who chased the unattainable, certain that, by virtue of her purity and goodness, she could triumph over all adversity. We didn't yet understand that there are forces in this world that are immutable to change. That see purity and goodness only as things to defile.

That summer, as L.A.'s infamous June gloom turned to firecracker July heat, Luke had finally caved to Anabelle's pleas and let us tag along to the parties he got invited to because he was a Surf God.

And so one night, with Labor Day and school already glittering darkly on the horizon, Anabelle and I picked our way past tangled surfboard leashes and drifts of sand, up the steps to a bungalow in a crowded, run-down part of Playa Del Rey known as the Jungle.

The party was in full swing.

Up close, the music was so loud that the glass in the front windows rattled in time to the subwoofer. The wood porch sagged like a busted trampoline from all the kids hanging off it. Punks, Goths, surfers, glammed-out Hollywood kids, a squad of polo shirts that looked like they'd wandered down from a UCLA fraternity. Lithe tanned girls with kaleidoscope eyes drifting like jellyfish.

Luke disappeared inside with a wave and a grin. That was our deal. He brought us along but he didn't babysit.

"Whoa," said Anabelle, her platform sandal catching on an empty beer bottle. With a gurgle it spun and rolled away. *Spin the bottle.* I caught her arm to steady her and breathed in gusts of Clairol Herbal Essence shampoo.

Anabelle wore a batik skirt with indigo fringe and a sleeveless crop top made of crocheted lace. I wore an ivory satin camisole slip dress with round-toed vintage pumps from Bullock's Wilshire that I'd found at an estate sale in Hollywood.

In the living room, furniture had been cleared away and kids were pogoing in slow motion, as if the music in their heads ran at half speed. Guys leaned against the walls, drinking beer out of plastic cups.

Not knowing a soul, we made our way to the bathroom to check our fabulousness and plan our assault on the evening. I locked the door. Anabelle leaned against the counter, cradled her taut, exposed belly, and frowned.

"I look fat," she told the mirror.

"No you don't," I said loyally (and truthfully). "You're skinny."

"I feel so bloated. I'm about to get my period."

"You can't tell."

Someone pounded on the door.

"Just a minute," I called.

In the mirror, Anabelle's eyes flickered over my dress. "Let's switch," she said. "I have to hide my big fat poochy stomach tonight."

"You're on crack," I said.

But I was already shimmying out of my frock and handing it to her because it was inconceivable that I'd deny her anything. In fact, I was *grateful.* We were the same size, but it was usually me raiding *her* huge closet.

When we were dressed again, I put one hand behind my head, thrust out a hip and vogued, amazed at the foxy stranger who stared back from the mirror. But a flutter of panic rose in my throat. Where was the real me?

Anabelle leaned in and examined our reflections. "We really could be sisters."

I didn't say anything. I didn't trust my voice. I wanted to freeze that frame, to stay in that cruddy bathroom in that halo of perfumed, squeaky-clean, lace-and-satin-and-indigo-batik grrrl love forever.

We were as perfect that night as we'd ever be.

The doorknob rattled angrily.

"Let's get a drink," Anabelle said as we slipped our fabulous selves past a gaggle of scowling girls to the kitchen, where we got in line for the keg.

"You don't want to drink that pisswater."

14

It was a cute blond guy in shorts and a faded Wile E. Coyote T-shirt.

"Got something better?" said Anabelle, giving him the full-on face.

He smiled in appreciation.

"I'm Ivan," he said, his arm already snaking around Anabelle's waist. "Follow me."

He led us back through the crowded living room and down a hallway to the rear of the house, with me clinging to Anabelle so we wouldn't get separated.

He opened a door and we entered a room lit only by flickering candlelight. There was a futon in the corner where a couple lay entwined. Kids sat cross-legged in a circle on the floor, passing a joint.

Ivan shut the door and we sat down. The guy next to me said his name was Dan. He had the most amazing blue eyes and curly brown hair pulled back in a ponytail.

"What about our drinks?" I said.

"Coming right up."

Ivan went into the adjoining bathroom and returned with ice, a bottle of gin, and cans of tonic.

"G&T okay?" he asked.

Anabelle and I said yes.

Ivan's eyes met Dan's. A look passed between them. Almost imperceptibly, Dan nodded. "Sure thing, bro," he said. "I'll behave myself."

Ivan brought four drinks and sat down next to Anabelle. I'd never had a G&T but I could tell he'd made it strong. I sipped, trying not to gag on the oily juniper taste and the bitter tonic that puckered my mouth like I'd sucked a grapefruit. The joint came around and I took a halfhearted toke. Immediately, the smoke expanded in my lungs, making me cough.

"Here," Dan said, handing me my glass.

Embarrassed, I drank. After the first few gulps, I didn't notice the bitter taste anymore.

The room began to vibrate in a way that was not unpleasant.

I tried to focus. Ivan and Anabelle were kissing.

"Want to go for a walk along the beach?" Dan asked, holding out his hand, which shimmered and pulsed before my eyes.

I pushed it away. "I want to stay with my friend."

"It's okay," Anabelle said from a great distance.

There were only the four of us in the room now. Even the couple on the futon were gone. Someone blew out the candles and the air filled with waxy smoke. The room was lit only by the spectral moon.

16

I stood up, but the floor shifted beneath me. I put one foot in front of the other, extended my arms like a high-wire artist, and made my way painstakingly to Anabelle. Proud of my accomplishment, I took a bow and nearly fell.

Maybe a walk was just what I needed to clear my head. I wished Luke would come and find us, but he didn't know where we were.

I tapped Anabelle on the shoulder. She and Ivan stopped making out.

"What?" she said, annoyed.

Ivan let out a sigh.

"I don't want to leave you here all alone."

"She's not alone," Ivan said, nuzzling her neck.

"You sure you want me to go?" I said miserably.

"Yeah."

I felt a hand on the small of my back. "C'mon, babe," said Dan. "A little fresh air will do you good."

Still I hesitated.

"Oh, for God's sake," said Ivan, breaking away from Anabelle.

He began to lay out lines on a mirror.

"It's fi-yunne," Anabelle told me with a walleyed smile. Her lip gloss was smeared over half her face and she looked like a

17

pretty clown. "Nothing's gonna happen unless I want it to."

With reluctance, I let Dan lead me out of the room. The hallway was dark, the light blocked by the silhouette of a big guy with a beer gut who leaned against the wall. I caught a glimpse of his face as he lifted a cigarette to his lips. It was red and bloated, the hairline receding, the nose splotchy with incipient skin cancer. One of the aging beach boys who hovered on the fringes of the scene.

I shrunk against the opposite wall as we squeezed past and reached for Dan's hand.

The air outside was misty-wet, salt spray clinging to my lashes. From beyond the dunes came voices. And the crash of the waves, rhythmic and soothing as a lullaby.

"Going for a walk?" said a guy sitting with friends around the barbecue pit. There were guffaws all around.

"Shut up," Dan told them.

"Should be a good view from there." I pointed to a high dune. The words were clear enough in my brain. But what came out was more like "pshaw."

"I wanna show you the phosphorescence," said Dan. "Lights dancing on the waves. It's magical."

He led me down to the waterline, where it

18

was as beautiful as he said but also darker and more lonely. All of a sudden, I missed Anabelle and Luke and wanted them to be here too. The moon rose higher in the sky. A madness seized me and I began to spin, thinking that Anabelle was right, the pebbles *did* whisper as they tumbled in the tide. I could almost make out the words. But my feet weren't doing what my brain told them anymore. I tripped and fell.

I lay there giggling and making a sand angel. Then the moon was blotted out as Dan loomed over me.

"Oh, you pretty thing," he said. "You're driving me crazy. I've got to kiss you."

He was very beautiful, suspended against the night sky. Then he came closer. His cornflower blue eyes held a sad, rueful look that I wouldn't understand until much later. Not many boys had kissed me at that point in my life, and the possibility usually filled me with breathless giddiness. But tonight there was only a strange, disengaged hunger. Then part of me rose up and left my body. Looking down from the sky, I felt like I was watching a wanton actress play me in a movie. Just before I floated away altogether, the me on the sand reached for Dan.

"Yes," she said, smiling in invitation. "I'd like that very much."

1

August 2009

For years I avoided the beach.

I begged off ocean swims and barbecues, cultivated a wan urban pallor, refused to go west of La Cienega, and sneered with art-school disdain at the hedonism of surf culture.

But two months ago, I started working for the Blair Company. It's the top crisis management firm in L.A., and many of our clients live at the beach. So I spend a lot of time driving up and down Pacific Coast Highway. And I no longer freak when I see the endless ribbon of pale sand and the deep blue sea. In fact, I am especially fond of our sandstone cliffs that rear up for hundreds of feet, trailing purple morning glory and crimson ice plant.

But memory is a tricky thing, and the tiniest detail can set me off. The scent of Coppertone wafting on the breeze. A strobe of sunlight bouncing off a metal wristwatch at white-hot noon. The ka-boom of angry surf when it hits the full, round, terrifying timbre of a cathedral bell.

So I work hard to stay focused, which is harder than it used to be. I'm thirty-two, and that's almost cronehood in this town. My belly's no longer flat, I've got tiny crinkles around my eyes when I smile. And I swear I can feel the synapses sputtering and dying as my zealous gardener brain prunes millions of connections each day.

It's nothing major, but I'm a beat slower to remember the name of a client's daughter, inquire about the health of the family pet. That sort of thing. And there are plenty of eagle-eyed associates stalking the corridors, putting in even longer hours than I. The other day at the caf, I heard one joking about his "vitamin A." Adderall. In a lot of college dorms, it's as common as Wi-Fi.

And I've got to stay competitive.

Steering with one elbow, I fished in my purse for my own bottle. Adderall is a neuro-enhancer, what they call a smart drug, created to help ADHD kids focus. I tapped one out and popped it dry. Fifteen milligrams. I'm not stupid. I don't grind it up or snort it or anything. That's for addicts.

The bottle was back in my purse by the

time I pulled up to the guard station at Malibu Colony.

The security guard checked my name. We went through the verbal do-si-do, and the electric gate slid back to let me pass.

It was high tide, and the waves roared like hungry tigers beyond the great houses that lined the sugar-white sands.

I parked and pulled out a different bottle. Eau de Guerlain: clean, crisp notes of citrus, bergamot, and verbena. Nothing cloying or clobbering that would offend the client or scream *me, me, me.* Just a subtle scent amulet to infuse me with secret grace and power.

The doorbell was answered by a young man in his early twenties. He was dressed in severe black, with hair cropped almost to his scalp. He regarded me with the keenly ambitious eyes of the Hollywood personal assistant.

"Oh," he said, stepping back, as if he'd expected pizza delivery.

As if the guard hadn't just called in my arrival.

I had no time for his little power games, his fluttering hands and mobile features that beamed with slavish devotion at his boss and tyranny toward everyone else.

Even though I fell squarely within the

ranks of hired help, I was expensive and I knew it.

So I leaned against the doorway and threw the attitude right back.

"Maggie Silver. The Blair Company." I allowed myself a tiny, enigmatic smile. "The Holloways are expecting me."

The assistant took my measure. His expression changed. "I'm Xavier, Mr. Holloway's assistant," he said, in a different voice. "Come right this way."

"Thank you, Xavier," I said, wondering why personal assistants never had names like Bill or Mary.

He led me to a living room lined with plate-glass windows that overlooked the ocean. On a deep couch of caramel leather, two men sat talking.

Xavier introduced me, then left.

Trent Holloway stood up. He smiled as we shook hands and I felt the dissonance I always did at seeing actors in the flesh.

Trent was fine boned and willowy in person, hardly the predatory Don Juan in black leather he played on TV. Today he wore faded sweats, tube socks, a white linen shirt, and horn-rimmed glasses that gave him an absentminded, almost scholarly air.

I'd have to remember that.

Flowing white natural fibers that suggest in-

nocence. It's biblical. It's the Resurrection.

It's a powerful media image.

Trent introduced the man on the couch as his manager, then led me to a chair made of steel tubes and leather.

He asked what I'd like to drink, then walked over to the bar. A man of the people — he still made his own drinks.

"I want you to know that she's a lying little tramp," Trent said from behind the bar.

The manager stirred with alarm. "Trent doesn't mean that."

"Furthermore," said Trent, "NBC doesn't care about my side of the story. There's talk they want to write me out of the show completely. And I've got a family to feed."

In the distance, a lone sailboat slid across the horizon. On the sun-splashed deck just beyond the living room, two seagulls fought over a crab, screaming as they tore the flesh apart with sharp, curved beaks.

I crossed my legs and tried to get comfortable on the narrow sling seat. The chair seemed designed for buttless people.

"We've checked with the lawyers," I said. "The contract's airtight and they can't do anything without just cause."

" 'Just cause'? Give me a break!"

Trent slammed down a bucket of ice and

the manager and I both jumped.

"Can we all take a deep breath?" the manager suggested.

"It's rigged, Irv, can't you see? I'm the womanizer who invades their living rooms each Thursday night. The cad who slept with his wife's kid sister in last season's finale. The other day a woman on the street called me a cradle-snatching slimeball. For something that happened on TV! This town's got no idea what's real and what's scripted, and who can blame them when even the reality shows are faked."

I let Trent finish. Then I said, "Mr. Holloway, even if you played an avenging angel on a TV show full of demons, you'd be up against the wall right now as a result of your au pair's allegations."

I paused to let this sink in, then made my voice soft and reassuring.

"That's why you hired us. To guide you through the labyrinth and convey your story to the media and the public. Blair represents the world's top actors, athletes, rock stars, politicians, and CEOs. Our clients come back time and again because we deliver."

"With the fees you charge, I certainly hope so," Irv the manager grumbled.

My pulse was up from the Adderall. The cologne came on subtly, hints of lemon, bergamot, and verbena. I inhaled deeply.

Trent emerged from the bar carrying a tray of drinks and I resumed studying him.

It gave me a thrilling, almost masculine sense of power to stare at the famous face.

I've got a license to stare.

Because in my business, image is crucial.

Any client who comes off as aloof, insincere, scared, or flippant loses in the court of public opinion long before the case ever goes to trial.

So my eyes raked over him, cold and dispassionate. And I saw no deceit in Trent's face, just outrage.

But then, innocence in itself is no guarantee that things will go smoothly.

Sometimes it's quite the opposite.

That's why it's important to "manage" the crisis.

There are two sides to every story, and our job is to make sure the client's version gets told.

We're the number that movie stars have on speed dial when they get caught buying heroin or transvestite hookers on the wrong end of Sunset. We step in when gay male escorts allege affairs with married politicians, and corporate titans get charged with fraud. We tell clients whom to talk to, when to go to rehab, what emotions to show

27

(remorse, sorrow, sincerity, guilt, humility). We're burrowers too, unearthing new facts and pointing out discrepancies. Sometimes we can only limit the damage and orchestrate a public confession, preferably on a national talk show with flowing waterworks. But even infamy has its uses.

Everybody messes up, and most people deserve a second chance.

It's the American way.

And if there's one thing I learned early in life, it's how to clean up messes.

The only difference was that now I got paid.

"Mineral water with lime," Trent said, handing me a glass and giving me that pensive, searching look that set women of all ages aquiver.

He seemed unaware of his magnetism, and I could detect nothing lecherous in his demeanor. But unless he was a total dog, there wouldn't be. Trent Holloway's most important role right then was to *seduce* me into believing he was a gentleman.

We made small talk until we heard the front door open, then close. Moments later, a woman wearing drawstring pants and a tank top appeared. Her hair was pulled back in a ponytail, which made her cheekbones pop exquisitely. She beelined over to the drinks, grabbed the one with a sprig of mint, and threw herself onto the sofa.

"Sorry I'm late," she said breezily. "I nearly rear-ended a jeep on PCH." She took a long pull of her drink. "That's what I get for being high on yoga."

I nodded sympathetically, as if that always happened to me too.

"This is my wife, Boots," Trent said. "She's an actor and she writes bestselling parenting books."

I said I was pleased to meet Boots. I was especially pleased at the sixteen minutes of billable time at $750 an hour I'd just racked up waiting for Trent's wife to show up.

It was their money.

I asked if we might begin, and everyone nodded grimly.

"Good," I said. "Mr. Holloway, we'd like to get you on a late-night talk show this week. We think that's preferable to *Good Morning America,* given your demographic. And *HuffPo* may be interested in a first-person essay. We can write the initial draft, if that's more comfortable. Laying out the facts. Expressing your shock at the betrayal. Your determination to seek justice for yourself and your family."

"Sounds good," the manager said.

"I'm on board," said Trent.

"We *do* feel betrayed," Boots said. "Marie was like family. She had her own bedroom, car, iPhone. We took her to Aspen for Christmas. She had to stay on the bunny slopes with the kids, but come on, it was a free vacation! For her to accuse Trent of this . . ."

Boots trailed off, unable to speak the words *sexual harassment.*

"And the children" — she lowered her voice — "are devastated. We haven't told them, they're too young. Poor lambs!"

Boots got up and threw open a door so I could witness the devastation of the lambs firsthand.

In the family room, a toddler boy and a tween girl sprawled in front of a giant flat-screen TV watching cartoons while a Latina in a white uniform poured veggie chips into a bowl. Xavier was sitting on the floor, looking miserable as he assembled a Hot Wheels track. Despite the sunny summer day, the curtains were closed, the room sunk in bluish shadow.

"Dad?" the boy said, without taking his eyes off the screen. "When can we go jump through the waves?"

A commercial came on and both kids turned hopefully to Trent.

"Anytime. Carmen or Xavier will take you."

"Can you or Mom come too?" the boy said.

Trent grimaced and ran his fingers through his hair. "I've got a script to learn. And there's probably paparazzi camped out on the dunes."

He raised an inquisitive eyebrow at his wife.

"Don't look at me," Boots said. "I've got a spa treatment in exactly one hour. Ekaterina's booked months in advance."

"We're kind of busy here, kids," said Trent.

"That's what you said yesterday," the girl said solemnly. "But it'll be dark soon and then Carmen will say it's dinnertime."

"Where's Marie?" asked the boy, bouncing on the sofa. "Why did she go away?"

"Is *she* going to be our new au pair?" the girl asked, examining me with a practiced eye. "She's prettier than Marie."

"I don't want her, I want Marie," wailed the boy, shoving his thumb into his mouth.

Boots leaned over and squeezed my hand.

"See," she whispered. "She's a home wrecker as well as a liar. That letter!" She shuddered. "TMZ put the worst bits online. I'm ashamed to show my face at their school."

Boots's breath was slightly astringent, sweet, and medicinal. Her glass was empty.

Trent's manager stirred and said, "Her lawyers want $1.5 million or they file suit. This is a bald-faced attempt to extort money from the Holloways after Boots confronted the nanny about some missing jewelry."

Trent nodded vigorously. "Maybe she thought we'd pay to shut her up and settle this thing, but she picked the wrong family. Our lawyer has advised us to countersue for libel."

Of course he did. It's a windfall for him at $700 an hour.

"You might want to discuss that with Mr. Blair," I said. "Marie's lawyers could retaliate by requesting copies of every text message and e-mail you sent to her *and* to each other since she was hired. Those filings are public and the celebrity sites will be all over it."

Boots gasped. "But that's an invasion of our privacy. Can't we ask a judge to seal the records?"

"You can, but he might say no. Either way, it's bound to leak, along with the deposition videotapes."

I watched their beautiful golden faces turn to ash.

"I know we're short on time, so let's continue," I said briskly. The Adderall had kicked in. I was so focused I could have balanced on the head of a pin. "At Blair we like to be out in front, setting the agenda rather than reacting defensively. So I'll need a few things. A list of the jewelry, its total value, and when you noticed it missing. Photos if you've got them, so we can check pawnshops. Also the tape from your nanny cam, as far back as it goes. Security cameras too. Phone records, since you pay her bill. Mileage on the car. We'll want to run histories of any computers she had access to. How about boyfriends? Did she date?"

"I have no idea," Boots said. "But we had ground rules. She couldn't have men over."

"The nanny cam may tell us whether she violated that. Plus whether she drank on the job. Did drugs. Dressed provocatively, behaved seductively around your husband, spanked the kids, lost her temper. Have you played the tapes back?"

The Holloways looked embarrassed. "There were so many and . . ."

I smiled reassuringly. "Never mind, that's what we're here for. I'd like to talk to the children too, if that's okay. Adults assume kids are too young to understand, but you'd be surprised at what they pick up. And you've got smart cookies there. They'll tell us what goes on when you're not around."

Something flashed in Trent's eyes and I wondered if the kids had seen Marie emerging from the master bedroom when Mommy was off on book tour.

"Don't worry, I'll be delicate. And I'm good with kids. You're welcome to sit in."

"Do you have children, Maggie?" Boots asked. "I'd love to give you an autographed copy of my latest book."

I hesitated, because this was a sore spot. "Not yet."

Boots was visibly crushed that we couldn't bond over children. She really, really wanted to give me that book.

"But I'd love a copy, if you have one to spare. I'll share it with my . . . sister. She's got two kids."

Boots said it would be her pleasure and we moved on.

I told them I'd need Marie's full name, address, and social security number to check court files, plus any references she provided.

"You think she has a criminal record?" Trent asked in a tight voice.

"I hope not. But there are sociopaths out there who think people like you make easy targets because you're in the public eye, have money, want to shield your family. You'd be surprised how often —"

My phone began to vibrate. I glanced down. It was the office and coded urgent.

"That's Mr. Blair on the line," I lied smoothly. "I'm very sorry but I've got to take it. If you would please excuse me . . ."

At their dovelike murmurs of acquiescence, I crossed the living room and stepped onto the blond wood deck cantilevered over the sand. The seagulls had gone, leaving behind a single shard of translucent orange shell. For a moment, I stood at the continent's edge, breathing in the briny Pacific as the wind whipped my hair. Then I punched in the phone.

"Maggie Silver."

"We've got a new VIP case," said my boss, "and I need you back doubleplusfast."

My serenity dissolved. "I thought the Holloways were VIP."

"Then this is VVVIP."

"What should I tell them?"

"Use your vast diplomatic skills."

"Should I call you from the car?"

"We'll talk at the office, my lovely bird-of-paradise."

And he was gone.

Blair has a list of code words that everyone has to memorize when they come aboard.

I'd always thought it silly, some James Bond routine. Now I grasped the wisdom of being able to discuss sensitive matters in public — or on notoriously insecure cell phones.

Bird-of-paradise meant someone was dead.

2

I walked back into the Holloway house and announced a change of plans: Mr. Blair wanted me to go down to the Santa Monica Courthouse immediately to check whether the au pair had a criminal record.

Impressed with the speed of the investigation, and unaware that the courthouse closed at five p.m., the Holloways promised to pull together everything I'd requested and we said good-bye.

Bird-of-paradise, I thought, taking PCH's curves like a ballroom dance, Lucinda Williams crooning on the stereo. The day was palm-frond balmy here at the beach, the air caressing as blue velvet, the breakers punching the sand as the shoreline stretched to moneyed infinity. Something shimmered on the edge of my consciousness.

But I wouldn't let it come.

I concentrated on the brown hillside instead of the bonny blue sea. Soon I was passing the canyon with the secret waterfall. It was so secret and magical that it didn't exist most years. Even when a heavy rain brought it to life, it was gone within days.

There were many secret waterfalls in L.A. if you knew how to look. Anabelle used to say that on a full moon, you could cross through the water into other realms. We always wanted to try, but there was a drought the years we knew each other. And then our friendship grew as parched and brittle as autumn leaves blasted by the Santa Ana winds. When the rains finally came, it was too late.

The car clock read four forty-five. I'd never make it home for dinner. Pulling on my hands-free, I called home.

"I'm making burgers," my mother said by way of hello. "It's Nancy Silverton's recipe; the butcher says there's been a run on the thirteen percent fat ground sirloin since the article ran in the paper."

My mother, who was never home when I was growing up, who never cooked anything more elaborate than a frozen pizza, had in her retirement become a gourmet chef.

It rankled. I knew I shouldn't let it bother me but it did, because it was twenty years too late. I needed those meals as a kid. Hell, I needed *her* as a kid, but she was always working. Dad too, but he died when I was fifteen.

I made decent money now, enough that my ex-husband, Steve, and I were able to buy a hillside bungalow in Cypress Park northeast of downtown. The name makes it sound grand, but the cypresses aren't the tall romantic ones in Italy or Greece. They're small and scrubby and grayish green and their numbers dwindle as they fight a losing battle against erosion, drought, and chain saw–happy homeowners.

But I was determined to hang on to the place. We'd bought at the height of the market, so my mortgage was upside down. Once, I'd envisioned which room would become the nursery and where the swing set would go. But we worked long hours and Steve's sales job often took him out of town. On the rare evenings we spent together, he'd retreat into the "nursery" to play video games after dinner, leaving me feeling very much alone in my marriage. When I finally brought up divorce, he agreed without protest. It was only when he moved directly into the home of a female colleague that I learned about the affair.

It's blackly humorous, isn't it? The crisis consultant who can't control the damage in her own life? It's not like I don't try. After the divorce, I added a bedroom and was about to advertise for a roommate when Mom was diagnosed with breast cancer. At the same time, her landlord sold the crappy building where she lived and the new owner evicted everyone.

So Mom became my roommate, which continues to astound and at times horrify me. It worked out okay during the chemo, since I helped care for her. Now that she was fine, I'd hinted that she look for her own place, but Mom wasn't interested. Our roles had reversed, now I was the one who worked late and nagged her to exercise and eat right.

"Save me a burger," I said, my mouth watering. "I just got a new case and you know how that goes."

"Sure thing," said Mom. "But I don't know about the truffle-oil potatoes. Earlyn is coming for dinner and she likes her starches."

Earlyn Spector was the lady next door. She and my mom played gin rummy together. My mom complained about me, and Earlyn complained about the war she waged against the squirrels. It really heated up each summer because the squirrels snuck into her yard and ate the figs and apricots off her trees. I'd been woken up more weekend mornings than I cared to remember by Earlyn banging a wooden spoon against a metal pot in her backyard to scare them away. The squirrels retreated to the safety of higher branches, but they were not cowed.

"I had a doctor's appointment today," my mother said with studied casualness. "They found a lump under my arm."

"Oh?" A wave of anxiety washed over me.

"They think it's only an enlarged lymph node, but they have to do some tests."

"You should have told me. I'd have gone with you."

"You have to make a good impression with this new job."

"I'd make time, Mom. Stuff like this is important."

"So is the bonus you get when a case goes well," Mom said dryly. "It would be nice to put a dent in those bills."

"Let me know when the next appointment is," I said. "And don't forget to save me a burger."

I got the nagging feeling there was something else I needed to do, but then Faraday called, screaming where was I, and I said I was driving up the California Incline and would be shooting onto the Santa Monica Freeway any minute. And the thing I'd been

41

trying to remember flew right out of my head.

Soon I was back in town, where smoke from a massive forest fire boiled in a pyrocumulus cloud above the San Gabriel Mountains. I was headed for a twenty-story building of glass and steel in an industrial park along an unfashionable stretch of Olympic Boulevard in West Los Angeles. No famous architect built it. There were no big-name tenants and no trendy restaurant on the ground floor. Building management shunned publicity, preferring to lease to insurance and accounting firms that kept regular hours. All prospective tenants were told the top five floors were unavailable.

The upper levels were where I worked.

It was here, from a penthouse overlooking Catalina Island, Downtown Los Angeles, and the San Gabriel Mountains, that Thomas Blair ran his secretive damage control empire.

Blair understood the twenty-four-hour news cycle better than anyone else in the business because he helped create it.

The story was on our website, and everybody had to memorize it because it helped to wow clients. In a snarky nutshell, here's how it went:

In 1980, just out of Emory University, Thomas Blair landed a grunt job at a little experiment in Atlanta called Cable News Network. His fortunes rose alongside CNN's, and when he jumped ship a decade later to run the New York offices of PR giant Burson-Marsteller, our founder could already see how celebrity culture was beginning to blur the distinctions between Hollywood and Washington, Main Street and Wall Street.

It was only a matter of time before the rest of the world caught on.

After learning all he could at Burson, Blair gallop-a-trotted out to Hollywood, where he ran publicity at Columbia Pictures. For two years, he cultivated the city's wealthy, famous, and fatuous and the journalists who wrote about them.

Finally, he was ready.

Leasing a twelve-hundred-square-foot office in the cheapest Westside address he could find — a half-empty building on Olympic — Blair hung out his own shingle. He cared nothing for decor and a prestige address. Most clients preferred to meet at their lawyer's offices or on their own turf, a little power trip that provided the illusion of control as things around them fell apart.

Once the stationery was printed and the

website up and running, Blair contacted old clients and scoured the news feeds for new ones. He clipped stories of high-profile scandals, then e-mailed the besieged CEOs and celebrities to offer his services. He was the guy who pioneered the idea of using game theory and reverse engineering in PR campaigns.

Soon Blair's name was whispered in the city's best restaurants, boardrooms, and bedrooms, his card pressed discreetly into palms. There were plenty of scandals to untangle in a place where giant egos, immense wealth, and dreadful behavior collided with metronomic regularity.

But despite what I told the Holloways earlier today, our bread-and-butter work has never been scandal-ensnared celebrities. That gets the most ink, obviously. And each winter the Hollywood studios hire us to create PR campaigns so their films will win Academy Awards. But the bulk of our work is a lot more humdrum — corporate PR for firms that are merging, going public, or restructuring after bankruptcy.

As Blair expanded, he began to hire associates from the world of politics, journalism, law, finance, high-tech, and pure academia. He looked for people with hungry eyes, drove them like Third World donkeys, and rewarded them with such magnificence that few ever left. Half our VPs have been here from the beginning.

Several years ago, Blair bought the entire building and set about fortifying his empire. He brought in his own security and janitorial staff and wired the building with the best technology Silicon Valley had to offer.

Blair made himself available to clients and media 24/7 and expected the same of us, which could be stressful when the phone rang at three a.m. on a family vacation. You might even say it helped break up my marriage. But by that time, most of us were addicted to the lifestyle or so in debt we couldn't afford to quit anyway.

At the parking entrance, I showed my ID to the guard (sometimes it seems I spent half my day running security gauntlets), then drove down several levels to a kiosk, where I inserted a key card and waited for the electronic arm to admit me into the secure area reserved for Blair employees.

My heels clicked on the slick cement, and a free-floating anxiety kicked in. I hated these subterranean structures, with their buzzing fluorescent lights, their shadows and hidden alcoves. It was silly, of course. The Blair building has impeccable security.

I was in much greater danger out on the street.

At the employee elevator, I held my ID under a light that scanned the bar code before opening the door. There was supposedly a secret elevator somewhere in the bowels of the building that whisked media-shy clients directly into the conference room on the twentieth floor.

But maybe that was just a rumor.

The elevator shot me to the fifteenth floor, where a woman got on, carrying a salad and a fruit smoothie from our cafeteria, which is run by Arnold Schwarzenegger's former chef. There's also a free espresso bar and energy drink machine to keep employees focused.

We exchanged hellos and she exited at the sixteenth-floor gym, where we can earn financial incentives for working out twice a week. I had yet to don workout gear, but the possibility existed aspirationally.

When the elevator pinged again, I stepped out onto the seventeenth-floor lobby of the Blair Company. Despite the leather couches, the artwork, and the latest magazines scattered along the coffee table, the lobby was mostly for show, as was the handsome young man named Patrick seated behind the desk. Few clients ever waited here; it was anathema to everything that Blair stood for.

"Hullo, Ms. Silver. Working late?"

"Afraid so, Patrick. How are you?"

"Tired. I was up late last night finishing a paper."

Patrick was a graduate student at UCLA's English Department and I enjoyed getting book recommendations from him. As I walked past, I pulled a paperback from my purse and tossed it onto his desk. It was an L.A. werewolf novel he'd loaned me called *Sharp Teeth,* written completely in verse.

"Thanks," I said, walking to a side door. "It blows away all other werewolf novels."

I punched a security code, submitted to a hand scan.

Patrick nodded thoughtfully. "Barlow writes in the grand epic style, like the classical Greeks. If Ovid was reincarnated as a Hollywood punk, he might create something like this."

I waited for the biometrics to recognize me. "Being a werewolf would be so cool," I said, "even though I realize it's just a sexual metaphor."

"Fangs, claws, fur," said Patrick. "What's not to like?"

"There are days when fangs would definitely come in handy," I said as the door

47

buzzed and I stepped through. "Hope you get some sleep tonight."

Patrick waved and the door snicked shut behind me.

This floor and the eighteenth were where most of our business took place. Vice presidents had corner offices with ocean views, associates had smaller offices with inland views, and the admin staff clustered in the middle with no views at all. I wasn't sure what happened on the nineteenth floor, which was filled with computers and high-tech equipment and black-clad people who came and went at all hours. The twentieth floor was the private domain of Mr. Blair.

I checked my cell phone mirror for smeared lipstick and put on my game face. Then I squared my shoulders and walked down the hallway to Faraday's office.

3

Jack Faraday was sitting at his desk, leaning back, feet up. His secretary, Allison, was just leaving, staggering under a foot-high stack of files and legal documents. At the table, Samantha George and Matt Tyler, two associates, bent over their laptops, typing furiously.

Seeing me, Faraday stopped midsentence. "Finally!" he said. "Sit down, Maggie."

Faraday was in his fifties, tall and muscular, with a pale Irishman's florid complexion and strangely arched eyebrows that gave him a look of perpetual astonishment. He spoke slowly and eloquently, savoring each word before he spit it out. In the time I'd known him, he'd been abrasive, sexist, complimentary, patronizing, helpful, and irritable. It was whispered he was once in the CIA, a rumor that Faraday cultivated while making clear the subject was off-limits. I'd heard him screaming at subordinates behind closed doors and I didn't want to get on his bad side.

"A little review, for Maggie's sake," he said now. "You all signed confidentiality oaths when you started. That means nothing you learn here is to leave this office. Are we clear?"

"Yes," we chorused obediently.

"Good. Our new client is a U.S. senator. He's got a wife and grown kids, spent years in business before entering politics, and has been touted as a candidate for vice president in the next election. This afternoon a female aide in his Los Angeles office was found murdered."

I glanced at my colleagues, who gazed at Faraday with the rapt attention of loyal bird dogs.

"Let me remind you of protocol. You must copy the senator's attorneys on all sensitive correspondence. That includes e-mails, texts, or memos you send to anyone at Blair, the senator's people, *and* anyone else connected with this case."

Faraday turned to me. "And why is this necessary?"

"I know," I mumbled.

"Because," said Faraday, unfazed, "copying the lawyer makes the correspondence a privileged document between the client and his attorney. And that means it stays out of the court record."

We nodded impatiently. There was something different about Faraday's face today, his mouth maybe, but I couldn't put my finger on it.

"Lawyer-client privilege does not, however, shield the client in the event of a serious criminal investigation," Faraday continued. "I don't believe that's an issue here." He paused. "But if in doubt, please do not fire off a text or discuss it on your mobile. Save it for face-to-face. Is that clear?"

"Yes," we chorused.

Faraday took his feet off the desk.

We stood.

"Separate cars?" I asked, not relishing another drive across town.

"The client is waiting in the conference room."

My eyebrows rose. "We're not meeting in his lawyer's office?"

"He appreciates the extra privacy and anonymity we can offer him at this difficult time," Faraday said. "And turn off your BlackBerries. Nothing annoys a client more than feeling he lacks your full, undivided attention."

We fell into line behind Faraday like ducklings. I'd rarely seen him so wound up.

Usually he just briefed me and handed over the file; the need for discretion went without saying. I also wondered what I was doing here. Unlike some of my colleagues, I had no experience in politics.

In the elevator, Faraday punched a keypad and we rose heavenward.

We exited into another world.

Thomas Blair may have once settled for a no-frills office, but success has a way of changing things.

Here in the penthouse suite, the travertine marble came from the same Italian quarry that supplied the Getty Center on its exclusive Brentwood hill. We stepped onto sumptuous Persian carpets and marveled at the Diebenkorns and Hockneys and Ruschas that hung from the walls. Beyond the picture windows, Los Angeles sprawled from purple mountain majesties to shining sea.

A giant saltwater aquarium took up the middle of the room. It teemed with tropical fish and dead-eyed sharks that roamed in endless hunt. The metaphor was inescapable: This is a place of power, a place with teeth. And the carnivores are on your side.

In the conference room, four men in suits huddled at a huge wood table that could have been pillaged from Beowulf's longhouse.

Two more men stood at the panoramic window, their backs to us, heads bent in quiet talk. The taller one wore an expensive charcoal suit. His colleague was in shirtsleeves with red suspenders, his posture slightly deferential. Charcoal Suit must be the senator.

A bank of TVs below the ceiling played CNN, MSNBC, Fox News, and C-SPAN. Faraday grabbed a remote and switched most of them to local stations, keeping the sound muted. The anchors moved their pretty plastic mouths as the inset screens cut away to a freeway chase and evicted homeowners. I watched along with everyone else, but not even the bottom crawl mentioned a senator or a dead girl.

Everybody was now seated except for the two honchos at the window. Red Suspenders rested his arm on Charcoal's back and murmured something. Then he glided to the table, his movements sinuous, his deep-set eyes darting as he assessed us and scanned for hidden threats under the table, behind the curtains, in our pockets.

Suspenders' face nagged at me. But then, I'd met so many men just like him — type A power brokers in tailored suits, Italian shoes, and hair strategically blow-dried to hide the bald spot. Maybe I needed to up my Adderall dosage.

Charcoal stared out the window a moment longer. Then he turned in profile, one hand across his eyes, massaging his temples so the top of his face remained obscured. Thick wavy graying hair fell below his collar. *No bald spot for him!*

He and Red Suspenders must be related. But Charcoal was taller and broader and his jawline well-defined. Red Suspenders was more spindly, with shoulders that sloped and a chin that receded. His clothes didn't hang as well. He looked like a potter's first, fumbling effort to cast a figure in clay. Charcoal's eyes were still obscured by his hand, but I was seized with déjà vu. I *knew* this guy.

A panel in the teak wall slid open, revealing a door, and Thomas Blair walked through, followed by an aide.

I'd met Blair only once, during my final job interview. He was a big guy who made a big impression — black, hawklike eyes, large blade of a nose, a smoothly shaved head and close-cropped black beard, full pink cheeks glowing with ruddy health. He wore a black suit with a mandarin collar and shoes of buttery leather so soft they seemed woven.

Blair's aide set out the boss's things: a PDA that looked like it was made of titanium, a notepad, several fancy pens and mechanical pencils. The movements were spare and ritualistic and somehow soothing instead of pretentious. Then he left, gliding the door shut with a whispered click.

Blair moved toward the window where the senator stood and the two titans shook hands.

"I could have gone with a political PR firm in Washington, Mr. Blair," the senator said in a deep, modulated voice that I'd heard before, probably on TV. "But a *New York Times* reporter once told me you're the best. Says he e-mailed you at three a.m. over a holiday weekend asking about some obscure court document. Five minutes later you sent him a detailed answer. And I remember thinking, that's the man I want if I ever get in a jam."

"Thank you, Senator," said Blair. "Your colleagues on both sides of the aisle speak highly of you. That bipartisan goodwill will be a great asset in the coming days."

Blair's voice was low and melodious and he radiated serene confidence.

It was said that Thomas Blair fed off chaos. As situations grew more tense, his movements slowed and his pulse dropped. He seemed to command time itself as he retreated deep inside, searching for the Zen path that would lead his clients away from the precipice and to safety. His focus was almost autistic savant in its intensity. If it was an act, it was one that played well on the cool medium of TV.

But I knew that damage control, like magic, could be all about misdirection. And if modern wizards cloaked themselves in Eastern mysticism instead of pointy hats and flowing capes, did that make it any less of an act?

As the two men finally took their seats, I stared at my enigmatic boss, trying to figure out what made him tick. Then I turned to the senator and something pressed against my memory banks and I had to look away and grip the underside of the table.

Blair nodded to Faraday, then leaned back in his chair and closed his eyes.

"Senator," said Faraday, smoothly taking the baton, "let me introduce our crisis team. Matt Tyler, Samantha George, and Maggie Silver. Folks, this is United States Senator Henry Paxton of California, our new client."

The senator looked around the room, summoning his best professional smile.

"It's a pleasure to meet everyone," he said.

"It's a great honor, sir," said Tyler.

"Lovely to meet you," said Samantha.

The senator's eyes moved quizzically to me, but I stared at my hands. I was incapable of speech, my brain a numb, buzzing blank. His face, his voice, his name. His dishwater blond hair had grayed, he'd trimmed his luxuriantly shaggy eyebrows, put on a few pounds, and he moved with a new gravitas.

But it was him, and I had to struggle to keep from blurting out, "Henry!"

4

There was an uncomfortable pause as everyone waited.

"It's a real pleasure, sir," I said at last.

Then Faraday took over, speaking in the silky tones he reserved for important clients.

I studied my notepad, examining the senator from behind lowered lashes. I didn't think he remembered me. How could he reconcile the sleek young woman in this corporate penthouse with the coltish kid in glasses and with unruly hair who was once his daughter's friend? I hadn't gone back to using my maiden name, so Silver would ring no bells. When he last saw me, I was Maggie Weinstock.

And then the world tilted and I *was* Maggie Weinstock, fifteen years old and sitting awkwardly at the Paxton dinner table with a linen napkin on my lap.

Miranda Paxton was serving white asparagus as Henry decanted a bottle of wine. Anabelle had warned me I'd be expected to discuss art and war and politics, and nervous sweat had pooled under my arms. Reaching for my glass, I saw the ruby liquid refract through cut crystal and marveled at the complex taste on my tongue.

By the second glass, I was describing the immaculately restored midcentury modern home where we lived in Encino, an upscale neighborhood on the Valley's southern edge. When Henry inquired pleasantly what my parents did, I continued my carefully rehearsed script. My mom ran a hospital nursing department and my father, who'd passed on, was a screenwriter.

"Really?" Miranda regarded me dreamily, chin propped in hand. "What studio did he work for?"

"Monogram."

Just as I'd expected, Miranda looked puzzled.

"It was a B studio that cranked out films in the 1950s," I explained. "My dad was a lot older than my mom."

"Did he write anything we might have seen?" Henry suggested with affable interest.

"Probably." I shrugged. "But he used a pseudonym. He was very idealistic as a young man. He never told me the titles. Said they were no-good trashy pulps."

I took a languid sip of wine. "I guess he took those secrets to his grave."

Anabelle's brow furrowed. Luke put down a forkful of lamb couscous and examined me with new interest.

"Fascinating Hollywood history, and so close we can touch it," Miranda Paxton said, her smooth, cool fingers gliding along my arm. "Henry and I grew up in the Northeast, a very different world. It's a pity we never got to meet him. We're so sorry for your loss, Maggie, and we want you to know you're always welcome here."

I picked at my couscous and felt I might burst into real tears at the loss of this noble, talented, and completely fictional father. The truth: Dad worked in an airplane parts factory and liked to drink until he passed out.

"Thank you," I said softly.

The next day at school, I realized my whoppers would crumble to tabloid dust if Anabelle probed even the tiniest bit. To my puzzled relief, she never did. Nor did she push to visit me in "Encino."

Maybe it was a little Westside snobbery kicking in, and she was unable to conceive of a world more interesting than her own.

Or maybe she just considered everyone's parents irrelevant at that juncture in her life.

Whatever the cause, I was too busy with precalc and my new role as Anabelle's confidante to worry long. But I did check out some library books on Hollywood so I could entertain the Paxtons with a few anecdotes if the occasion came up.

I'd always been a quick study, but now I was learning how to *frame* a narrative.

Even though I wasn't old money like the Paxtons, I'd cloaked myself in something more valuable and intangible here on the Coast — the nostalgic glamour that gilds all tales of lost Hollywood.

And then I was sitting in the Blair conference room once more, struggling to compose myself and stop the vivid, warm flush I knew was staining my cheeks. Faraday was speaking and Senator Paxton was jotting down notes. He didn't remember me, I realized with relief. But it had nothing to do with my ugly duckling transformation.

U.S. Senator Henry Paxton had more important things to think about.

Which brought me back to what I'd been wondering since I realized who our new client was.

Why had Anabelle's father hired the city's

top damage control firm?

Was it just a prudent step for anyone in the public eye these days?

Or did he have something to hide?

Paxton introduced his staff. Red Suspenders was his brother and chief adviser, Simon Paxton. Bernie Saunders, the senator's PR director, had pale skin and red hair. Neil Bernstein, dark, handsome, and going to fat, was his chief of staff. The green-eyed, slightly fey man with wire-rimmed glasses was Paxton's lawyer, Harvey Lambert, and he would tell us more.

"There's bound to be media speculation once they connect the dots," Lambert said, explaining why he'd counseled his good friend and golf buddy Henry to hire a crisis management firm.

"The tabloids will come sniffing around, and they're brutal. Politicians, movie stars, it's all fair game when a beautiful young woman linked to a wealthy and powerful man is murdered."

"*Was* she beautiful, Harvey?" Faraday asked dryly.

Lambert held Faraday's eyes but said nothing.

For a moment, the room was silent. Blair seemed asleep.

"Yes she was," said Senator Paxton. "A

lovely, lovely girl. Turned heads aplenty."

Lambert shot Faraday a significant look.

"I see," Faraday said slowly.

I saw too.

I saw that Henry Paxton might be skilled at navigating the cutthroat, bruising battles of Congress, but he needed to be coached and protected from himself. If he spoke truthfully and from the heart, his words would be twisted and used against him.

The PR redhead spoke next. "I don't care what anyone says. Hiring a damage control firm is a huge mistake. It suggests to the public that we've got something to hide." His voice grew petulant. "And we don't."

Lambert frowned but said nothing.

Saunders's next words were for Senator Paxton alone.

"Please, sir. It's not too late to walk away. My staff and I are perfectly capable of handling this internally. Haven't we weathered the CIA oversight committee hearings? Your brother-in-law's insider stock trades? The health-care gaffe? Our people can do everything Blair can, without the notoriety and the high price tag."

Simon Paxton put up a hand to silence him.

"No one's denying your brilliance, Bernie," he said. "But this is about us tapping into a very specific skill set. Crisis management is what Blair *does.* They are the pros."

"Then let me go on record and say that no good will come of it and I am opposed."

"Objection noted and overruled," Simon Paxton broke in smoothly. "My apologies to the Blair team for subjecting you to this turf war. Bernie, we need your cooperation."

The senator shot Bernie Saunders an apology, and the fraternal dynamic grew clear. The senator was the good guy. His brother was the hard-nosed enforcer.

Saunders shot the Blair camp a look of cold loathing. "You've got it, sir," he said sulkily.

"Thank you, Bernie. All right, Neil, please brief us." Simon Paxton drummed his fingers on the table.

"The victim is Emily Mortimer, twenty-three," Neil Bernstein said.

He swallowed, struggling to compose himself. Then he continued.

"Personnel records show that Emily Mortimer came on board June 27 of last year as a summer intern in our Washington office after graduating from Loyola Marymount University in Los Angeles. Her job was to develop the senator's social networks. Twitter, Facebook, MySpace, YouTube, whatever the hell tube comes next. By November she was new media director."

Bernstein's head dipped. "Emily was well liked and professional. She was a workaholic. She had a low-level security clearance. Two nights ago, she attended a fundraising dinner at the Beverly Hills Hotel. Her tablemates say she got a call halfway through. Soon after, she made excuses and left, saying she wanted to turn in early. She never made it into work yesterday and didn't return calls or e-mails, which was unusual. The cleaning lady found her at home this morning when she let herself in. Police say she'd been dead about twenty-four hours."

Blair opened his eyes. "Any sign of forced entry?"

"Don't know."

"Does the building have security cameras?"

"Police are checking the lobby and parking structure."

"Who was the call from?"

"We don't know."

"The cops will get her records from the phone company," Faraday said.

I examined the Paxton camp for a tell. Except for the senator, they were jumpy as cats. Was it dismay at realizing that the inner workings of their office were about to be thrown wide open? Or something else?

"Do we know the cause of death?"

Bernstein shook his head.

"Was she sexually assaulted?" I asked.

Faraday gave me a thoughtful look.

"Don't know," said Bernstein, his lips disappearing into a straight thin line.

"Anything missing? Purse? BlackBerry?" Faraday asked.

Again, Bernstein didn't know.

I realized I was massacring my cuticles. A nervous little tell of my own. Placing my hands on the table, I nodded sagely, as if murder was something I dealt with on a regular basis.

Harvey Lambert cleared his throat. "Ah. The fund-raising dinner isn't quite the last anyone saw of Emily."

He glanced at the Paxtons. The senator stared fixedly at his notes. When Simon Paxton gave a terse nod, Lambert continued.

"Henry has informed me that he met with Emily Mortimer two nights ago around ten p.m. at the Bryson, a hotel bar near Macarthur Park."

The only sound was the gentle burble of a water pump in the aquarium.

Blair's eyes had gone slitted. Bernie Saunders wore a look of shocked and queasy fascination. So he hadn't known.

Anticipating what would come next, I tried to hide my surprise. I'm not naïve. I know that wealthy and powerful people often have secrets. But this was Henry, whom I'd grown up with, who adored his children and his wife and had a rosy future in politics. It was completely out of character that he'd throw it away for a roll in the hay.

Or was it? I wasn't sixteen anymore. I was an adult in a profession where scandal, crisis, and disgrace were everyday occurrences. My job had taught me that people don't always act rationally. In fact, given the right circumstances, they're capable of almost anything. I could no longer make assumptions about the man sitting across from me. Years ago, he'd been a father figure and a role model to me. Now he was a stranger.

"The senator met Emily Mortimer at a hotel bar? So perhaps he sent the text after all?" Faraday suggested, hands folded over his stomach.

"No, sir," Lambert said. "The senator most emphatically did not send Emily a text that night."

We waited for Lambert to elaborate. After a moment, he went on.

"The senator had a meeting with Emily Mortimer scheduled at two p.m. But he ran late, so they made impromptu plans to meet up later. Isn't that right, Henry?"

The senator nodded.

"When they got to the bar, Senator Paxton and Emily Mortimer each had two drinks and she briefed him on how to make his Twitter postings more personal and humorous. Together, they posted several tweets in this lighter, more casual vein. Do I have that correct, Henry?" Lambert asked solicitously.

"Yes," said the senator. "You can check the, erm, tweets. We finished up by eleven thirty. Then we said good night and went our separate ways."

I glanced at Thomas Blair. His eyes were fully open now, focused on something far away that none of us could see.

Faraday rubbed his jaw. "So the doorman, the parking valet, the security cameras . . . there would be witnesses that you left separately?"

Paxton winced. "I'm afraid not. The valet brought my car and I drove Emily to her car. She'd parked a few blocks away and the neighborhood can be dicey late at night."

"Senator Paxton dropped Emily Mortimer off at her vehicle before midnight," Lambert picked up. "He waited while she started her car. Then he drove home. His wife will attest that he woke her up at one thirty getting into bed."

Blair stirred. He regarded the senator, his eyes seeming to glint and reflect light like a cat's.

"Don't you have a driver and a car to take you around?"

Lambert pursed his lips and nodded vigorously. "Good point. Yes, he does. And most days, he uses them. But the senator enjoys taking his own car occasionally when he's home in L.A. It's nicer than anything the government provides."

Blair's chin was propped on his hand and he stared out at the night sky like he was mapping the Horsehead Nebula. "And Tuesday was one of those days," he mumbled into his hand.

"That's right," said Lambert.

"Any witnesses when the senator dropped the girl off?"

"It was deserted," Paxton said. "I remember being glad I'd insisted on driving her."

"So there's almost a two-hour gap between the time you dropped her off in Mid-City and your wife noticed you were home in Santa Monica?" Blair pressed.

"I was downstairs watching TV for a

while," Paxton said.

"Does your home have a security system that would have recorded your arrival time?"

"We do, but my wife hates it so it wasn't on."

"Did you make any calls on your cell phone during that time?"

"No, I did not."

Paxton's lawyer spread his hands. "So there it is, folks," he said with faux cheer. "You can see why we brought you in."

"Was this night meeting with Emily Mortimer on the senator's calendar?" Faraday asked.

"We've already told you it was a spur-of-the-moment thing," Simon Paxton said sharply.

"Does he often meet aides after hours in bars? The media's going to have a heyday."

"The senator enjoys getting out in his district," Bernstein said. "Architectural preservation's a little hobby of his and the Bryson is a historic Art Deco landmark. I've met him for drinks at a dozen nightspots in the last two years."

Faraday leaned forward. "But you're not a pretty young girl and you're not dead."

I glanced at Blair, but he'd lapsed back into a comatose state.

"I object to what you're implying," Lam-

70

bert said, half rising from his seat.

"Sit down, Harvey," said Faraday. "You're not in court."

He turned to the senator. "Sir, there will be hard questions asked. They will delve into your personal life. You know that, or you wouldn't have hired us."

Paxton nodded.

"In order to draw up the best strategy, we need to know all the facts. So let me ask you, sir, with all due respect, is there anything else that we here at Blair should be aware of?"

The entire room held its breath as the unasked question percolated through the air.

Paxton held Faraday's eyes without faltering.

But my boss didn't know Henry Paxton the way I did. He didn't know the stubborn look that crept across Henry's face when faced with something he didn't want to discuss. Like the time Anabelle and Luke asked him about Vietnam atrocities like My Lai. Or the night the police picked Luke up in Carpinteria for trespassing onto private property to get to his favorite surf spot.

But I'd spent two years practically living in Henry Paxton's house. I knew the look. And I saw it bloom across his face.

"You want to know if we were having an affair," Paxton said.

Faraday grimaced and nodded almost apologetically.

"No, we were not," the senator said through clenched teeth.

I let out my breath. A rush of fresh oxygen seemed to fill the room.

Paxton's eyes glowed with candor and sadness. His hands lay on the table, loose and relaxed. He was calm, in control.

"Do you honestly think I'm stupid enough to drive off with her in front of witnesses if we were having an affair? Or if, God forbid, I meant to do her any harm. This is just ridiculous!"

"Sir!" said Bernstein, appalled. "No one here is suggesting . . ."

"That's all right, Neil," the senator said. "I'm not offended by Mr. Faraday's questions. But I would never jeopardize the trust of the American people or the love and respect of my wife, Miranda, and our wonderful children, Anabelle and Luke. And I refuse to believe that even my political enemies would stoop to make hay out of this sorrowful occasion."

Tyler shot me a look that said, maybe they won't, but their surrogates on the blogs, websites, and talk shows will be attacking his character and demanding his resignation within hours.

If Faraday thought so too, he gave no sign.

"Thank you, Senator," he said smoothly. "That's what I need to know."

Lambert steepled his fingers and looked at Faraday. "So? What's the plan?"

Faraday put both hands flat on the table. Then he addressed Henry Paxton.

"The next twenty-four hours are critical. You are a public figure, Senator, and you need to explain to the public in your own words how close you were to Emily Mortimer and what happened the night she was killed. I realize that even public figures have private lives, and you don't need to tell everybody everything, but because of what has transpired and the rumors that are going to swirl, it is essential for you to address this. You don't want to be seen as lying and you don't want to be seen as dodging the topic. So my advice to you is: *Own the story.* Tell the truth, with full sincerity and conviction. Then I'd like you to get on the phone with the *New York Times,* the *Washington Post,* the *Los Angeles Times,* and the *Wall Street Journal.* The rumors and innuendos will fly, so brace yourself. But you have an opportunity to change them into truth if you tackle them head on. You need to get this behind you so you can get back to governing our fine nation."

"All right," the senator said in a resigned voice.

"What about the police?" Saunders asked.

"At this point, the senator isn't required to speak with them. But I think he should. And I'd like him to tell the authorities exactly what he just told us. The bar meeting is troublesome, but there's no way around it, he was seen with the girl."

Faraday pursed his lips. "Have you called Emily's parents to offer your condolences?" he asked the senator.

Paxton's eyes filled with resigned dread. "I was going to do that tomorrow."

"Perhaps you could pay them a personal visit," Faraday said. "We'll alert the media."

"I refuse to turn this tragedy into a circus," Paxton said.

"It's already a circus," Faraday drawled. "That's why you hired a ringmaster."

"We'd better get their okay first," I said, pleased to have something intelligent to add. "It could backfire on us if the family refuses to allow TV cameras into the home."

"On second thought, let's bring them to the office to pick up Emily's belongings and Senator Paxton can offer the family his condolences on camera." Faraday turned to

Paxton's men. "Maggie will go fetch the parents. She's got an excellent bedside manner."

Bernie Saunders flipped through a manila file. "The Mortimers live in Valencia, near Magic Mountain. They're retired, in their late sixties. Wife doesn't drive. Husband can't, he's got macular degeneration, according to what Emily told a staffer."

"Well done," said Faraday with false bonhomie. "You ever need a job, come see me."

I rolled my eyes inwardly. Faraday's affable and open demeanor was a mask. He cloaked himself in approachability to disguise his utter impenetrability.

Bernstein put his face in his hands and groaned. "It won't work. Henry's got a press conference tomorrow morning at nine to announce the latest on the Financial Crisis Inquiry Commission."

"But that's excellent." Faraday beamed. "Why?"

"Because it gives you an opportunity to address Emily's murder publicly while going about business as usual. The news will be out and the press conference will be mobbed. You can express sorrow for Emily's murder and sympathy for her family. We'll get the parents up on stage and the three of you can make an emotional appeal for the public's help in catching the killer."

Henry Paxton stared at Faraday with revulsed fascination.

"We need to sew up those parents," Faraday went on. "Maggie will suggest that Blair represent them — pro bono of course. No one should have to deal with reporters camped out on their lawn at a time like this. Now, let's hear more about this Financial Crisis Inquiry Commission."

Bernstein said, "Henry chairs a bipartisan committee that is working with a congressional commission to investigate the financial meltdown."

Senator Paxton took over smoothly. "There are suggestions of bribes and kickbacks to elected officials. The recent bankruptcy of industry leader JTM Financial Services and the sudden willingness of its directors to point fingers means that the public may soon learn more. But unless they get a larger budget to hire more staff, the commission is limited in what it can accomplish."

"Was Emily Mortimer privy to any of these financial briefings?" I asked.

"No," snapped Neil Bernstein, the senator's chief of staff. "I've already explained that Emily Mortimer was director of new media."

"It's a legitimate question, Neil," Paxton said mildly.

"You told us the dead girl had a security clearance," Faraday said, running a finger along the table.

"Not high level," said Bernie Saunders. "This is getting way off track."

"That's right," Faraday said in mollifying tones. "Senator, we at Blair often find that there is more — or less — to a story than meets the eye. We plan to set up a truth squad to monitor all press mentions. Within twenty-four hours there will be hundreds of stories online and in print. We'll review each one, and when we find a mistake, we call up the reporter and tell them, casting ourselves as crusaders for journalism ethics. Our goal here is to reframe the discussion and stress your bona fides, Senator: years of patriotism and service to your country. Valor and bravery. The war injury. The Congressional Medal of Honor." Faraday allowed himself a tiny smile. "And we will use righteous indignation at anyone who suggests you were sleeping with your aide."

"You gonna get him on Conan or Letterman?" Simon Paxton asked.

"What for?" Faraday said. "It's very tragic

that Senator Paxton's aide was found murdered, but no one's accusing him of anything. He should appear sympathetic but not defensive. That would just raise questions."

"What about Twitter?" I said. "Should the senator address his aide's murder through social media?"

Bernstein wrinkled his nose in distaste. "Too frivolous."

"Twitter is a neutral medium, it's how you use it. Look at the Iran protests, the Mumbai terrorist bombings."

"Let me think about it," said Faraday. "But first, we'll draft a statement for the old media."

"Way ahead of you," said PR man Bernie Saunders. He pulled a paper from his briefcase, got up, and handed it to Faraday with a flourish.

As he leaned forward, I caught a whiff of his cologne.

It was a scent called Kouros that assaulted my nostrils like a Mike Tyson punch. If Satan wore cologne in hell, it would be Kouros.

Faraday skimmed the press release. "Has this gone out?"

Saunders shook his head, releasing another gust, and I put my hand discreetly to my nose. Amazingly, no one else in the room seemed to mind.

"So no one's talked to the press yet?"

"We know better than that," Saunders snapped.

"It's good," said Faraday, holding the statement between his thumb and forefinger like a soiled diaper. "But we don't need all these details. The tone we're aiming for is magisterial sorrow."

"But . . ." spluttered Saunders, who thankfully had gone back to his seat.

Faraday handed me the paper. "New draft, please, Maggie. Well-regarded employee, etc. . . . My prayers and thoughts go out to the family . . . difficult time . . . I and everyone in my office are cooperating fully . . . hopeful that authorities will resolve the case soon . . . justice for Emily Mortimer and her family, etc."

Faraday looked up. "We'll have the senator sign off on any quotes, of course," he assured the room.

"This is how it starts," Saunders said darkly.

"That's enough, Bernie," snapped Simon Paxton.

He leaned over and whispered in the senator's ear.

Saunders immediately began whispering

in the senator's other ear.

What a snake pit the senator's office must be, I thought, with staffers constantly back-stabbing one another and jostling for position. Emily Mortimer was a newcomer to this cutthroat world. Could it be she'd made a powerful enemy?

Paxton listened to both sides, then brought the power struggle to a close by saying, "Mr. Faraday, you may proceed."

Saunders pounded the table.

The senator looked annoyed. "They're the damage control experts, Bernie, and we'll do what they advise."

"Thank you, Senator," Faraday said smoothly. "We prefer the term crisis management. It's more neutral."

Bernstein's phone beeped and he looked down, then swore.

"The LAPD want to interview the senator tonight."

Faraday rocked in his chair. "Tell them he's happy to oblige — tomorrow. It's late and we're still getting our ducks in a row. How's that statement coming, Maggie?"

I hit several keys and handed the laptop to Faraday, who tweaked a few words, then passed it to the Paxton camp.

"Looks good to me," Paxton said.

"Great." Faraday beamed. "From now on,

please refer all media inquiries to us. They can call twenty-four/seven."

He slapped down business cards like he was dealing a hand of poker.

"And make sure none of your people tell the press 'no comment.' "

"Why shouldn't they say that?" Saunders demanded.

Blair smiled disdainfully. "Because when you say 'no comment,' it suggests that you're hiding something. We want the senator to tell his story first, get it out there in a controlled way, with our spin."

"I think we should ride it out," Saunders said.

"The Internet abhors a vacuum," Blair said. "If you don't talk, others will, and within hours you'll have an electronic echo chamber of gossip and innuendo. And that will be what people remember. It will float through the Internet forever. So we always comment. And we tell the truth. Or at least we don't tell lies. Please make sure your staff understands that."

Everyone nodded.

I caught Senator Paxton studying me. I'd forgotten that politicians were trained to remember faces.

So much for hiding behind my laptop.

I'd been made.

Faraday's phone buzzed just then and we all looked over. My boss squinted at the LED readout, then took the call.

"Thanks," he said after twenty seconds, thumbing it off.

Simon Paxton glared, baleful at the interruption.

"My apologies, gentlemen. That was our computer whisperer. He can crack any code, retrieve any deleted file, find anything that's ever floated on the Internet. He's been monitoring the political and celebrity websites. Nothing so far and" — Faraday tapped his watch — "let's hope it stays that way until bedtime."

"Bedtime?" Simon Paxton frowned.

"The end of the East Coast nightly news shows. It could buy us until morning."

"I see."

"We'll know more as soon as my electroboy gets hold of Emily's records from the office computers."

Paxton looked nervous.

"Wouldn't the police see that as tampering with potential evidence?"

Faraday smiled.

"Remember those laws about a worker's expectations of privacy in the workplace? As Emily Mortimer's employer, you have every right to examine any and all correspondence that occurs on U.S. government computers, phones, or other electronic devices. We're not going to wipe the files, but we are going to exercise that right.

"Moving on," he said smoothly, "did Emily Mortimer have any friends or colleagues we should look at? Had she received any threats? Gotten into any arguments? Maybe with constituents?"

The chief of staff threw up his hands. "Everything you can imagine flows through the senator's office, from UFO sightings to immigration appeals to crazy dames who send him proposals of marriage. It's a lot to sift through."

"But you're not aware of anything negative directed personally at Emily Mortimer?"

"No."

"What about boyfriends?"

The chief of staff checked his notes.

"She had an on-again, off-again boyfriend named Jake Slattery. The receptionist said they often argued. No one on staff seems to have met him."

"I hope the police interview this fellow," Senator Paxton said. "Isn't that what they always say?" He looked around. "That the husband or boyfriend did it?"

A silence descended.

"That's one theory," Faraday said.

"She was a wonderful girl. Smart, a fast learner. Reminded me of my own daughter."

To my horror, U.S. Senator Henry Paxton now pointed at me.

"And don't think I don't remember you, Maggie Weinstock Silver." He shook his head. "I'm sorry we have to meet again in such unpleasant circumstances."

5

U.S. Senator Henry Paxton seized my hand and shook it vigorously. "It's good to see you."

"It's good to see you too."

The meeting was over and I stood there uncertainly, wondering how to navigate this murky new terrain between crisis consultant and family friend.

"Both the kids are finally back in L.A.," Paxton was saying. "Luke's a prosecutor and Anabelle's a stay-at-home mom. Her husband's been a calming influence. But now he's the one who needs . . ."

A shadow darkened Paxton's brow. "I was always sorry when you and Anabelle lost touch. How have the years treated you?"

His eyes went almost imperceptibly to my ring finger. Self-conscious, I tucked my hand behind my back.

Alarmed by our tête-à-tête, the senator's chief of staff walked over. "Henry, if I might have a word," said Bernstein, wedging himself between us like a sheepdog who smells a wolf.

"Yes, yes. So many official things await me. But this is important too," he said. Impulsively, the senator pulled out a Montblanc pen, jotted down a number, and thrust it at me.

"Anabelle's in Palos Verdes. I know she'd love to hear from you."

And with that, they hustled him away.

In the hallway, Faraday's eyes glittered at the paper in my hand.

"Come with me," he said.

Fletch was sprawled on the couch in Faraday's office, noodling on his laptop as we walked in. He had hair like straw, pale skin, ropy, gym-worked arms, and tiny black eyes behind round glasses. I'd seen him around but we'd never spoken.

Now I detected a faint accent I couldn't place.

"Jake Slattery lives at 435 South Orange Grove in the Fairfax District. He's got . . . hold on," Fletch said, flipping through screens, "exactly $2,317 in his bank account and looks like . . ." He pressed a few keys and scrolled up. "His Visa shows a purchase of a plane ticket, earlier today, to Mexico

City. Open-ended return."

He looked up and grinned. "Want me to drop by his place? Check for a bloody glove?"

"Do we even know Emily's cause of death?" I asked.

"It's possible," continued Fletch, "that Slattery left an electronic trail to mislead the police. He could still be holed up in L.A. I'll need to check the airline's passenger manifest."

He bent over his keyboard once more.

I said, "Maybe the police are interviewing Jake Slattery right now and we're all jumping to illegally gained conclusions."

"Get out of there, Fletch," Faraday said.

"If you say so, boss."

Fletch winked at me. His fingers scurried along the keyboard like long pale spiders.

"You're going to the senator's office," Faraday told him. "Please shut the door behind you."

"So what'd the senator give you?" Faraday asked with a conspiratorial lilt after Fletch left.

It hit me then that Faraday knew all about my relationship with the Paxton family. Somehow, the bastard had found out.

Which meant I wasn't sitting here because of my hotshot PR skills. I'd been brought onboard solely because of my *connections,* because Faraday wanted an inside pipeline to the senator.

"Damn it, Faraday," I said, "did your operatives put together a dossier on me when I applied for this job?"

"We can't afford to hire whack jobs," my boss said mildly. "We check out all prospective employees."

The idea made me supremely uneasy.

That's an invasion of our privacy, Boots Holloway had complained this afternoon.

Suddenly, I knew exactly how she felt.

"All the way back to high school? Give me a break."

Faraday tapped a pencil. "We just did, Maggie. Mr. Blair himself suggested you for the Paxton team. A friendly face to inspire trust and confidence."

He gestured to the note. "And look, it's already paying off."

"It's just his daughter's number," I muttered. "He wants me to call her."

"A fine idea," said Faraday.

I scowled and shoved the paper in my pocket. Tonight's events had stirred my curiosity. But I didn't want to be played like a marionette. I wanted to call Anabelle when I was good and ready.

"It's a little late," I said stiffly.

"Tomorrow will be fine," said Faraday. "I've asked Allison to bomb your in-box with stories about the senator so you can get up to speed. But right now, Tyler's taking you to meet one of our cop sources."

"Wouldn't I be more useful here tonight?"

Faraday flipped through a stack of papers.

"Tyler is a brilliant strategist, but he can get a little . . . overeager. He has, at times, stretched the boundaries of propriety."

"You expect *me* to keep him in line?"

"That shouldn't be necessary. He's already been warned: no cowboying. Do you have any other questions, Maggie? I'm happy to take the time to answer them."

Faraday smiled. He was at his most deadly at these moments, when his voice grew softly solicitous, his manner ultrapolite.

I shook my head.

Faraday pulled a photo out of a manila envelope, slid it across the desk. "The senator was right about Emily Mortimer."

I leaned in and saw a serious girl with shoulder-length blond hair. Her eyes stared steadily at the camera, as if confronting it. Her mouth was large, her lips full and mobile. She looked very young.

"His kind?" Faraday asked slyly.

"I wouldn't know if he had a kind."

"Do the Paxtons have a happy marriage?"

"Since you've obviously snooped so extensively into my past, you know I haven't seen any of them in ages. So I have no idea whether Senator Paxton has a happy marriage. Not that *that* ever has anything to do with it."

"Speak from experience, do you?" Faraday's voice was playful now.

"You'd like to get something like that on me, wouldn't you? Well, sorry to disappoint you. But it sounds like you think the senator hasn't told us everything."

Faraday's face was inscrutable.

"Go see the daughter," he said. "Make nice. And let me know what she says."

"If you think Senator Paxton is lying, then why did we agree to represent him?"

"I didn't say he was lying. Maybe he's getting a raw deal and he needs our help. You know Blair's a soft touch for the underdog."

"I've noticed. Especially underdogs with deep pockets."

Faraday grew thoughtful. "Even if he did sleep with her, adultery's not a crime in this country, last I heard."

"But murder is."

I stopped, appalled. What was I saying? That I believed Anabelle's father had killed his aide?

"Senator Paxton says he's innocent and

we believe him. In this country, people are innocent until proven guilty and that's what keeps us in business."

I heard a Windbreaker zip. Matt Tyler was standing in the doorway.

"Ready?" he said.

6

Tyler drove east on Olympic.

I stared at the neon skyline, how the downtown skyscrapers clustered around the glass-crowned U.S. Bank Tower like chessmen protecting an embattled queen. At seventy-three stories, U.S. Bank was the tallest building west of the Mississippi. Pretty brave for an earthquake zone.

Tyler switched to 6th Street, the car swaying and sashaying through the leafy old homes of Hancock Park.

I recalled a long-ago tiki party that Anabelle had taken me to around here. She'd introduced me to a delicate blond boy and we'd necked in a sea-green pool while chlorine steam rose around us. He was Anabelle's second cousin, pale and beautiful as a tubercular swan. Later, I heard he'd OD'd on heroin at Raji's.

"Where are we going?" I asked.

"Secret location," Tyler said.

I rolled my eyes in the dark.

Tyler was about my age, with slim hips and a swimmer's broad shoulders. He had a wide, open face anchored by a classic Roman nose and was one of those men who never lose their boyish enthusiasm for skullduggery and secret codes. His loafers, khaki pants, and rumpled, button-down shirts screamed preppie, but in my limited dealings with the guy, I'd also noticed a subversive humor that suggested not all his edges had been buffed smooth.

It took awhile before I realized Tyler's car radio was tuned to a Spanish-language station. I reached out to switch it.

"Hey now," Tyler said. "I like to listen to the DJ banter. Keeps my Spanish from getting rusty."

"That's impressive."

Just then a Lady Gaga song came on. I listened to see how they would translate *bad romance* into Spanish, but Tyler quickly changed the station. "Ugh, what a caricature."

"But she's in on the joke. All those fabulous costumes and killer voice and irresistible pop hooks. As Courtney Love sang when we were kids, 'I fake it so real I am beyond fake.' I admire Gaga's audacity."

Tyler snorted and shook his head. "Chicks

93

are weird."

But he put the song back on and I thought I saw his fingers tapping to the beat.

"You think the old goat killed her?" he said as it ended.

"Who?" I said, still seeing the video in my head, Lady Gaga's machine-gun breasts firing at the smoldering skeleton on the frilly white bed, a cigarette dangling between her lips.

Tyler was silent.

"Senator Paxton is hardly an old goat," I said, annoyed. "But no, I just don't see it."

"So maybe Paxton's wife did it. She found out they were having an affair and decided to off her rival."

I laughed. "Doubtful. I know the family, Tyler. I went to school with Paxton's daughter. They're not capable of murder."

Tyler's upper lip curled. "Everyone's capable of murder if you give them the right reason."

"Or the wrong one, I guess."

We contemplated this as the big Spanish houses flew by in the moist green dark.

Water rationing had begun in L.A., the first step in our slow devolution back to a dusty Mexican pueblo. But the people in these big homes seemed determined to defy the law; from every direction we heard the whispered hiss of lawn sprinklers.

"Faraday wants me to reconnect with Paxton's daughter," I said after a while.

"You sound unsure about that."

"We had a falling-out senior year in high school. I haven't talked to her in years."

"You young people and your feuds," said Tyler.

"I'm serious. It about killed me. I felt like an Aztec sacrifice whose heart is ripped still beating from my rib cage."

"That's a bit dramatic."

"Don't you remember what it was like at sixteen? Everything so raw and close to the surface." I paused. "Naw, maybe not, you're a guy."

"Everything was raw, all right," said Tyler.

"Okay, sex too. The most tantalizing mystery of them all. But we wanted love too. We obsessed over it. We were inseparable, you know. We followed the same bands, studied together, ate exactly the same things. She held my hair back in a grotty club toilet when I barfed after too much Jack Daniel's. But she changed. And then she went back east for school and I stayed here, at UCLA. I heard she married some trust fund guy and they moved to Berlin. She was going to paint and he'd write at night after his bank job, financing the reconstruction of Bosnia. I remember thinking they were a twenty-first-century Scott and Zelda. And being very jealous."

"But remember what happened to them — she went crazy and he drank himself to death."

A premonition seized me and I laughed it off.

"Well, they're back in L.A. now, living in Palos Verdes, so I guess they're doing okay."

He gave me a jaundiced look. "I guess you'll find out soon enough. So fill me in, Silver. What's your story?"

I told him I'd been a flack since college, when a work-study job had landed me at UCLA's external relations department. I liked the problem-solving part of the job but was so shy I could barely answer the phone. Luckily, a raspy-voiced PR veteran had taken me under her wing.

She told me, "Nobody cares about you. They've got bigger things to worry about. So just pretend you're playing a role. Think Katharine Hepburn in the old movies. Brisk. Competent. Cool and poised.

" 'But I'm not any of that,' I protested.

"She cocked her shellacked blond head, blew out a lungful of cigarette smoke and leaned in so I could see the freckles on her leathery chest. 'So what?' she said. 'Nobody can see inside you. If you project confidence, over time you will become that person. Guaranteed.' "

I turned to Tyler. "And damned if she wasn't right.

"After graduation, UCLA offered me a full-time PR job. I moved up the ranks and eventually landed at UC San Gabriel, where they made me a vice president. It was a sleepy place until a scandal hit our Reproductive Clinic. We had a Paraguayan doctor who'd patented a fertility procedure with incredible results. Couples flew in from around the world to get a miracle baby. He was written up in *People.* Then the lid blew off."

"I remember that," said Tyler. "Wasn't he shuffling the eggs and using his own sperm?"

I nodded. "It was a PR nightmare. Everybody blamed everyone else and the parents started suing everything that moved."

"Epic fail," said Tyler. "I don't envy you. Angry parents are the worst."

"Well, that's what I thought at first. But then something kicked in and I realized I liked the challenge. I represented the university and we'd been swindled by this guy too. So I got all fired up about getting justice for my school. And I started to enjoy the hurly-burly of the media, the horse trading, dealing with lawyers. I guess that makes me one sick puppy."

Tyler just grinned and made a right turn onto Western Avenue.

"The school gave me a fat promotion after that, but ungrateful wench that I am, I jumped over to Sitrick and he put me to work in the dotcom mines, representing twenty-three-year-old billionaires in trouble."

"Why'd you leave Sitrick?"

"Thomas Blair offered me more money. Now, could you please tell me where we're going?"

Tyler shot me a conspiratorial smile. "The murder scene."

"Emily Mortimer's apartment?" I said, aghast. "Count me out, dude. We're crisis consultants, not private eyes."

Tyler leaned back against the headrest. "At Blair, we believe in being proactive."

"Yes, of course," I said impatiently. "And we do our own investigations. But this is foolhardy. Won't the crime scene be roped off?"

Tyler pulled out an LAPD press pass. A younger Tyler with shaggy hair and aviator glasses stared back at me.

The laminated tag read: "Matthew Tyler.

Staff Writer, New Times Los Angeles."

"Didn't that paper fold years ago?"

Tyler winked. "Sure it did. But I still know some cops. That's why Blair hired me. He likes journalists. We know how to work a story."

"Trust me, Faraday doesn't want you doing this."

"He wants results. He doesn't care how I get them."

I considered asking him to drop me off so I could get a cab back. But the city wasn't exactly crawling with cabs at this hour. Or any hour, really. No, I'd wait in the car and call Faraday. But then I remembered my boss's admonition about cell phones.

We parked off Normandie and Tyler led me past necking teenagers, homeless men in doorways, and squat brown women balancing woven baskets of laundry atop their heads. A taco truck parked in an alley advertising Kogi Korean BBQ Tacos was drawing a lively crowd.

Emily Mortimer lived in a 1920s Art Deco apartment building called Hawksmoor that had once been grand. Its frosted glass entrance was emblazoned with a wrought-iron hawk, its wings spread in flight.

A cop stood guard just outside. More cops were inside, checking ID before letting residents through.

I tugged on Tyler's arm. "Let's go back to the car. We'll find a pay phone and you can call your cop source."

Instead, to my horror, Tyler threw off my arm, strode up to the cop, and held out his press pass, thumb blocking the paper's name. "Media," he announced. "Who's working this case?"

"I'm sorry, sir," said the cop, "but I'm going to have to ask you to keep moving unless you have business inside this building."

"Is Detective Lewis here?"

"I wouldn't know, sir."

"How about Perez?"

"All questions are being handled by Media Relations. Sir, you need to stand back."

Tyler retreated down the block and I pushed through the crowd to catch up, pleading with him to leave.

Instead, Tyler stepped behind a palm tree and pulled out a pair of binoculars. Stealthily, he trained them on the tenant mailboxes. Then he told me to wait there and walked across the street to a convenience store.

To hell with this, I thought, pulling out my cell phone to call Faraday.

Just then a TV van jumped the curb and screeched to a stop, almost running me over. Two cameramen climbed out and began to unload gear. The cop walked over to tell the van to move.

Tyler reappeared with a quart of milk in a brown bag and whispered, "Quick now!"

He grabbed my arm and steered me inside the lobby.

"I'm sorry, sir, ma'am," said a cop inside. "This is a crime scene. You can't go upstairs unless you have proof that you live in this building."

Tyler looked stricken. "What happened?"

"We're not releasing that information right now. But tenants are in no danger."

"Glad to hear it."

I looked longingly at the door.

"It's okay, honey," Tyler said in a worried tone. "Didn't you hear him say it's safe?"

"ID, please," the cop intoned.

"Hey, babe, did you bring your ID?"

"No," I said, tugging and shooting him rusty dagger looks. Any moment now, we'd be revealed as imposters and hauled away by the police. We'd both lose our jobs. The bank would foreclose on my house and my mother and I would be out on the street. Despite myself, I gave a muffled sob.

"The premises have been secured. It's okay, ma'am," said the policeman, misinterpreting my fear.

"She's worried about the baby's nighttime

feeding," Tyler said, holding up the carton of milk. "The movie just let out and we've got to relieve the sitter."

"Name and apartment number, please," said the cop, flipping pages on a clipboard.

"Garland. 7B," Tyler said without hesitation.

The cop found the name and frowned. "He already came in."

I thought I might hyperventilate. Damn Tyler and his stupid plans. I opened my mouth but found I couldn't speak.

Tyler had no such problems. "That was my brother," he said easily. "His wife kicked him out so he's staying with us."

The cop squinted at us. "Then why didn't he relieve the babysitter?"

"He's no good with kids."

The cop got out his phone. "I'm calling 7B. He can come down and identify you."

I sidled closer to the door. I'd run like hell once I hit the sidewalk. Let the cops chase me. I'd tell them it was all Tyler's fault.

The elevator doors opened and a Latino family walked out, leading a pit bull puppy on a pink sequined leash. At the same time, the on-air talent from the van and her camera people marched in. The pit bull broke free and ran to the TV reporter, jumping up and trying to lick her. The reporter screamed.

In the ensuing commotion, I darted out the door and down the sidewalk, not stopping for two blocks. Tyler was right behind me.

"Don't you ever do that to me again. That was beyond stupid. You could have gotten us arrested."

"It almost worked."

"And what were you planning to do once we got up there?"

"I told you, I know people," Tyler said, smiling.

That infuriated me until I realized he was smiling at a man in a sport coat walking by, talking on a cell phone.

"Sinclair," Tyler called softly. "Hey, Sinclair, what's up, buddy? Ain't parking a bitch?"

The man in the sport coat gave Tyler a suspicious once-over that I could only describe as coppish. He flipped his cell phone shut and approached. After a quick nod, Sinclair said, "Let's walk."

We stopped in an alley next to a Dumpster that overflowed with putrefying trash.

"Jesus," said Sinclair, wrinkling his nose.

"Cloud cover," Tyler said. "No one'll bother us here." He bounced on his toes and grinned at me. "Not so eager to leave now, I'll bet."

Then he lowered his voice and asked Sinclair, "What can you tell me about Emily Mortimer?"

Sinclair pulled out a pack of cigarettes and lit one. The tobacco crackled as he inhaled. For once, I didn't mind. The smoke disguised the garbage reek.

"What does a high-octane PR firm care about a murdered girl?" Sinclair said, blowing out smoke.

"We've been hired by her employer," I said.

Sinclair's eyebrows went up. "Ah, yes. The esteemed senator."

Tyler looked around nervously, but the only eavesdropper was a large brown rat that stood on its hind legs, chittering atop the bags of trash.

Relax, buddy. We're after a different kind of trash.

"Our client wants to nail this scumbag as much as you do," Tyler said earnestly. "But his political enemies are already sharpening their knives. And the media will manufacture a scandal if they can't uncover one. Any details you have would help us."

Sinclair shook his head like he didn't know why he let himself get talked into these things.

I thought I knew. It was green.

"Off the record?" Sinclair said. "She was found naked in bed. She'd been strangled with a scarf. No sign of forced entry. Her purse and BlackBerry are missing."

"Go on," said Tyler.

"I'm keeping strict accounts."

"Like always. Now tell me something that won't be in the LAPD press release."

"Ziplock bag of prescription pills found in her bed stand. The coroner'll run some tox panels, but we won't know anything for a few days."

"My employer will show his usual gratitude," said Tyler.

Sinclair threw down his cigarette and ground it underfoot. He inclined his chin several blocks over. "They won't let you upstairs," he said.

"I'm good," Tyler said.

The detective walked off, crunching on broken glass. The sound echoed down the narrow alley.

Tyler took out his cell phone and stared at it, considering. He flipped it shut.

"We better go back to the office."

He walked off quickly. I ran to keep up, stumbling as my heel caught in a pothole.

"So Blair pays him to pass on information?" I asked.

Tyler turned. "Not at all. Mr. Blair hires off-duty policemen to provide security at concerts and parties that he organizes for clients. Detective Sinclair's brother-in-law owns a private security firm."

"Isn't that illegal?"

"It's perfectly legal. Your twenty-thousand-dollar signing bonus was legal too. Did you appreciate that, Maggie? Did you buy yourself something nice? Treat your family to a Mexican cruise? Put a down payment on a car?"

My palms began to sweat. I was still on probation. And I'd already spent the bonus to pay Mom's oncologist. Though I wasn't about to tell Tyler that.

Two months into my job at Blair and already my mind was walling itself off into compartments. But it wasn't just me; the whole company was honeycombed with secrets. Should I tell Tyler why Faraday had wanted me along tonight?

I said, "Faraday told you to play everything by the book tonight, and you took a huge chance back there that almost back-fired horribly."

Tyler dismissed my concern with an airy wave.

"He always says that. Gives him plausible

deniability. But he doesn't care."

"He's a control freak. Of course he cares."

"So touching, this innocence of yours."

Tyler made his thumb and forefinger into a gun, then playfully shot me.

"Pow-pow," he said, tilting up his hand and blowing off imaginary smoke. "It's dead now. Buried and gone. Welcome to the real world, Maggie."

He smiled like our boss, which reminded me that Faraday had done something to his mouth. His teeth, shiny and straight and . . .

"Did Faraday whiten his teeth?"

Tyler nodded. "Just the two in front."

I flashed on Faraday's crocodile smile.

Why hadn't I seen it before? What else did I know that my brain couldn't dredge up?

"He ought to shell out the dough for the rest," I said. "It looks weird. I mean, the guy's in the image business."

"Go ahead. Break the news to him."

"Not me." I shuddered.

I still thought Tyler was a dick, but our close call back there, or maybe my furor afterward, had torn down some wall. We were less competitive and more chatty. And I still had so many questions about Blair.

"That guy Fletch," I said. "He seems really bright, but a little Asbergersy, don't you think?"

"Our own feral youth. You know his story, right?"

I shook my head.

"He's from Ukraine. One of those adoptions that didn't work out. By seventeen, he'd bounced through twelve foster homes and racked up ten arrests for hacking. Somehow, he landed in the Big Brothers program, which is a charity that Blair does pro-bono PR work for. Faraday got involved, took a liking to the kid, and lined up a lawyer who got everything expunged from Fletch's juvenile record."

"Out of the goodness of his heart," I said.

"He does have one," Tyler said. "Faraday got Fletch an internship here doing computer security and Blair's generous tuition reimbursement paid for college. He never left. I don't think he could work anywhere else. You'll notice Faraday keeps him far away from paying clients."

"About those clients . . . how does Blair know whether some celebrity really beat up his girlfriend or some hedge fund manager really ran a Ponzi scheme? Or does he not care, so long as he gets paid?"

"Mr. Blair operates purely on intuition and gut feeling."

"You can't run a PR business on that New Age bullshit."

Tyler shrugged. "Blair said no to Michael Jackson and O. J. Simpson. Last year he turned down Kim Jong-il."

"That North Korean lunatic who shoots off missiles and starves his people? Gee, that must have been a tough call."

"The Dear Leader himself. And Blair made sure everyone knew it. Great free publicity. But he *was* impressed they'd heard about him all the way in Asia."

Tyler nodded in approval. "Mr. Blair is a corporate visionary. He saw something in us that nobody else did, and he's molded us into the elite of the business. But he demands absolute loyalty. Your first allegiance is to Blair now. Don't forget it."

"You make it sound like a cult."

And indeed, Blair often struck me less as a twenty-first-century firm than a Machiavellian fortress where brilliant and impenetrable strategies were drawn up. An aroma of clannishness wafted about the office. Although it was never discussed out loud, some of our colleagues treated damage control as an aesthetic sport rather than real life where people's lives and reputations were at stake.

Tyler laughed. "Damage control is like any other business. It runs on favors and the greased wheels of personal relationships."

He cocked his head. "I'm sure Senator Paxton would know exactly what I'm talking about."

Again I saw the senator in the Blair conference room, his shaggy head bent, his brow furrowed. I wanted to do right by Anabelle's father, to finally prove my worth to the Paxton family. And I wanted to keep my job. And later, when I thought back, I realized that this was where I began justifying things to myself, until I was in so deep that I had no idea where the truth lay anymore and it was too late to break free.

Back at the office, Faraday debriefed us.

"Good work you two," he said, when we finished.

Tyler shot me an I-told-you-so look.

"Strangulation, scarves, nudity, and pills," Faraday mused. "I think I can do something with that."

"The coroner's going to do toxicity tests and check if she was sexually assaulted," Tyler said.

"Looks like our girl may have led a double life," Faraday said, lost in his spin. "We want to stay sympathetic while distancing her from the senator. Maggie, grab a cup of coffee if you need it. Then draft me a new statement about how shocked and dismayed

Paxton is. The cops won't be able to keep this under wraps for long."

"Yes, sir."

I looked at my watch: 11:05 p.m.

"The purse and the BlackBerry make me nervous," Faraday said. "You know I *hate* getting broadsided. Tyler, find out who owns the lease on Emily Mortimer's apartment. Then check if she had a criminal record. Drug bust, maybe?"

"Wouldn't the government security check have turned that up when she was hired?" I asked.

"It's like the airports. Stuff slips through all the time. Okay, folks, I'm writing the senator a memo outlining what we've learned. Let's meet back up in fifteen."

Tyler and I were at the door when Faraday said, "Maggie, c'mere a minute."

I shot Tyler a look and walked over.

Faraday rolled his chair back and spun around so his eyes met my breasts. When I'd started at Blair, I'd wondered whether my boss's mentoring had ulterior motives. Maybe Tyler wondered too, because he leaned against the doorway, arms crossed and waiting.

"This is about to get very ugly," Faraday said. "I'll be counting on you to keep a cool head and come to me if you hear anything from the Paxton clan that could affect the case."

"Yes, sir."

"Dis-missed."

I had to brush past Tyler on my way out. He turned to watch me walk away. And I couldn't help it. I swung my hips and gave him a show.

Soon, I heard the clack of keys, loud and rapid as gunfire, issuing from my boss's office.

Faraday was using a typewriter.

When we reconvened, Faraday handed me a manila envelope. "Do you remember how to get to Paxton's house?"

I glanced at the address. Villa Marbella, Temescal Canyon Road. Yes, I remembered.

"Did Tyler behave himself tonight?" Faraday asked in a casual tone.

I hesitated. Did my boss already know, and this was some loyalty test?

"He didn't get us into any trouble," I said carefully.

"Glad to hear it."

As I walked away, I wondered why I was covering for a guy I barely knew. Maybe it was because as much as I disapproved of Tyler's tactics, I resented even more Faraday's attempts to get me to rat out a colleague. Was my boss now grilling Tyler on *my* performance? Was that the real reason he'd paired us up? Eight weeks here, and already I was growing paranoid.

7

The big boulevards were wide open tonight, the caffeine and Adderall clasping hands to sing a duet in my veins. Snug in my metal cocoon, I exulted in the rare beauty of speed. All around me, house lights winked out like snuffed candles until the city slept and only the streetlamps remained, wreathed in marine fog.

The houses grew bigger and the landscaping lush as I entered the coastal foothills of the Santa Monica Mountains. I remembered these hushed green streets, the jacaranda trees that formed a canopy overhead each spring and showered us with fragrant purple rain.

Memories flooded me: the tart pulp taste of homemade lemonade, the taut feel of salt water drying on sunburned skin, the smoky tang of barbecued potato chips, the skunky-sweet smell of reefer and patchouli incense — the scent markers of adolescence.

And other things too: orange blossoms, black leather zipper jackets, Tiffany lamps, candlelight, heavy gold bracelets, full-bodied oaky red wine, chandeliers, cashmere, black coffee, dark bittersweet chocolate, Spanish brandy.

Long before I met Anabelle, I'd cultivated a rich fantasy life, fueled by books like *A Little Princess* and *The Secret Garden.* When reality grew too dreary, I'd escape into a world of sumptuous courts, lost princesses, and castles overlooking the sea. It was so real that I felt the silk and lace undergarments against my skin, heard the rustling of taffeta and velvet ball gowns, saw the sun sparkle off the diamond pendant between my breasts. Maybe that's why it didn't seem strange when I stepped through Anabelle's looking glass. Her world aligned so perfectly with my inner landscape that it felt like coming home.

But I'd kept my distance the first time Anabelle tried to draw me into her orbit.

I couldn't tell her that the real reason I wouldn't be joining her family at their weekend place in Catalina was that I had to sober up my father for his night shift and cook dinner for my mother, who worked two jobs.

One afternoon when I was fifteen, I tiptoed into the bedroom where Dad lay snoring and found exactly $7.93 in his wallet to go grocery shopping. I couldn't believe it, he'd gotten paid the day before. Sitting at the kitchen table in my blue-and-gray plaid skirt and white blouse, I studied a stack of unpaid bills and came to a decision.

I changed out of my uniform and into my clingiest dress, put on heels and heavy makeup, grabbed my Polaroid camera, and teetered over to the neighborhood bar where Dad spent his spare time.

At Dad's watering hole, I cajoled a half-crocked patron into buying me a martini for my twenty-first birthday. He even snapped a picture of me having my first legal drink. Bottoms up, baby!

Then I walked into the manager's office, slapped down the Polaroid, and explained who I was. I told him that unless he banned my father for good, I'd notify the Department of Alcoholic Beverage Control that his place sold booze to kids.

The manager looked like he wanted to kill me, but he agreed. It didn't stop Dad from drinking, of course, but it did slow him down some. And I learned that while I couldn't always solve my problems, I could limit the damage if I thought long and hard and desperately enough.

I likened it to the controlled burns that firefighters here in L.A. use to clear brush and prevent deadlier fires from destroying hillside neighborhoods. My methods weren't always ideal, and they wreaked their own devastation, but they kept me alive.

The city was subdued and wary in 1993. The L.A. riots had erupted the previous April, and many people had moved away, including Anabelle's best friend, Charlotte, which must have left her lonely and at loose ends. Then suddenly my dad dropped dead of a heart attack. When I returned to school after the funeral, listless and hollow eyed, Anabelle must have sensed the chink in my armor. Or maybe she just felt sorry for me. Holding up two tickets, she asked if I wanted to go to the PJ Harvey concert at the Hollywood Palladium that weekend. She'd bought them months ago for herself and Charlotte.

Soon we were doing our homework together and bonding over our shared passions for Tori Amos, John Keats, and the German Expressionists. We talked on the phone five times a day and spent weekends watching old gangster movies, eating two-pound bags of peanut M&Ms, and playing dress-up, Anabelle styling her long blond hair like Veronica Lake in *The Blue Dahlia* while I was Barbara Stanwyck in *The Lady Eve*. I loved the cool whitewashed rooms and dappled turquoise pool of her Spanish house in Temescal Canyon, Villa Marbella. It was a universe removed from the stifling apartment above a North Hollywood alley where my mom nagged me incessantly to keep up my grades so I wouldn't lose my scholarship.

Until I met the Paxtons, I'd never heard of houses with names. And I hadn't imagined that parents could be witty and charming and, most of all, relaxed. Anabelle's parents embraced a policy of benign neglect toward their children. They traveled frequently, collected modern art — Anabelle's mom made strange feminist sculpture — and insisted we call them Henry and Miranda. Oh, and Henry was a Vietnam War hero, with an award from the president to prove it.

As my friendship with Anabelle deepened, life with my mother grew less and less real. A kind of seasonal affective disorder set in each time I returned to our apartment, where the trash cans rattled in the alley at night and a homeless drunk mumbled himself to sleep.

By then I was lightening my hair with Sun-In and growing it out to look more like

Anabelle's. A thrill went through me when ancient, birdlike Madame Louvray mistook me for "Mademoiselle Paxton" in French class. Sometimes I fantasized that the Paxtons might adopt me so Anabelle and I would be real sisters and I could live there with her and Luke forever.

Luke was a year older than we were, tall and lean with razor-cut hair that the sun bleached to spun gold. He'd been at an East Coast boarding school when Anabelle and I first became friends but had returned home for senior year because he missed L.A. and his friends.

On nights when I slept over, I found myself listening for the rumble of his Mustang in the driveway and lingering in the upstairs hallway, hoping to "accidentally" run into him. But actual Luke sightings were rare. More often, I nourished myself on the skunky weed smell that seeped from under his closed door and the muffled music and laughter that told me he was in there with friends.

I didn't risk telling Anabelle how I felt. My own position in her life was still too precarious. And something else held me back — Anabelle herself veered between wild affection for her brother and sisterly disdain. What if my confession made her jealous? Or disgusted? What if she told Luke and he merely found me pathetic?

One Saturday morning when the yeasty aroma of pancakes roused Anabelle and me from our beds of lazybones, we found Luke at the stove in his board shorts, already back from a dawn surfing expedition.

He turned, spatula in hand, and in the morning light, he looked like an angel from an illuminated manuscript. A ridge of golden hairs marched up his belly, fine grains of sand nestled within.

Unthinkingly, I reached out a hand to dust them off.

Laughing, he twisted away.

"They'll be off the griddle in a sec, hungry girl," he teased.

I hurried to the coffeepot to hide the blush that was stinging my cheeks because Luke refused to see me as anything other than his little sister's dork friend.

But Luke was right about one thing — I was hungry that summer, filled with a ravenous need that threatened to consume me. And as the Paxtons moved through their lives of burnished ease, I studied them like a mathematical algorithm that I might apply to my own life. I wanted to be just like them. I even dreamed of them, though I must confess it was Luke that I dreamed of most often. Gorgeous, unattainable Luke.

Traveling purely by instinct now, I slowed at a giant eucalyptus tree. The driveway was just where I'd remembered it, half obscured by a giant bougainvillea. The wrought-iron gate with its fleur-de-lis pattern was open, the Paxtons anticipating my arrival. I turned in and drove past the row of Spanish lampposts that illuminated the rolling grounds, the spreading oak trees, the wooden chicken coop, the rusty jungle gym that had been old when I first saw it. The familiar sculptures and artworks I'd seen reproduced in books and magazines.

I wound the last few hundred feet to Villa Marbella, a rustic two-story home that had always reminded me of a Tuscan farmhouse (not that I'd ever been to Tuscany, mind you). The tires crunched as I drove onto the gravel and killed the engine.

I dug into my purse and pulled out a mini bottle of perfume, Serge Lutens's Féminité du Bois. Tart plum and sweet, spicy woods, but light and shimmery too. A secret talisman. I dabbed my wrists and felt the scent wreathe me. I was a girl knight donning armor, mounting my horse, lowering my visor as red ribbons trailed behind.

Invincible.

I walked up the flagstone path to the thick, wood front door bound with black iron straps.

It was spooky, I could almost hear New Order fading on the car stereo, doors slamming, then the slap of our leather slave sandals as Anabelle and I raced inside. I felt awkward and sixteen again, the straps of my backpack digging into my shoulders as textbooks jostled inside.

I rang the doorbell. Far away, an owl hooted mournfully. A man opened the door and stood, pooled in shadow, his hair reflecting gold in the porch light. A lurch of vertigo, then a crashing time skip.

"Luke?"

A light flipped on and the shadow stood revealed. A tall man with light-blond hair in his early twenties. Not Luke, who'd be in his midthirties now, I realized with a shock. And had his own house somewhere, just like me.

I thrust out my hand, introduced myself, and apologized for arriving so late.

"Jeff Canin with the senator's L.A. office," the young man said. "And it's fine. We were expecting you. Please come in."

I stepped into the foyer. I remembered the floor tiles. They'd been hand-painted in

Mexico from a design created by Miranda Paxton.

I lifted my eyes, determined to banish these cluttered memories, but the past was a minefield exploding behind my eyes. There was the wrought-iron balustrade along which we'd wound tinsel at Christmas. The fifth stair from the top creaked. Upstairs to the left was Anabelle's room with its canopied bed, porcelain lamps with fringed shades, carved wood furniture. Anabelle had melted a purple candle on my *Al Green's Greatest Hits* record and we'd watch it spin on the turntable, growing dizzy with the revolutions, with the kaleidoscope of unlived life that lay before us.

"Please wait," Jeff Canin said, and disappeared down the hall.

I examined the photos on the walls. Faded Kodachromes of the Paxton family lined up on skis, the snowy, pine-tree mountains and startling blue of Lake Tahoe behind them. The Paxtons tanned and wearing leis on a Hawaiian beach. There was Henry — here, in his own home, it felt weird not to call him Henry — in his air force uniform, receiving an award from the president after his plane was shot down. Photos of the Paxton kids with beloved family pets, long laid to rest. My eye went to a photo of me and Anabelle in mortarboard and robes at high school graduation, arms slung around each other, clutching our diplomas. I felt obscurely pleased to see us there, frozen in time.

Suddenly, voices drifted from upstairs. From the Paxtons' master bedroom, to be precise. Too low to make out, though I thought I heard the clipped diction and sibilant tones of Miranda.

Not wanting to be caught eavesdropping, I moved to the wood coat-rack, where I could swear the same umbrella and L.L. Bean jacket with the plaid hood had hung fifteen years earlier.

This house had been a refuge when I was in high school. But tonight, the familiar terrain had turned murky. Was I a family friend, a hired hand, a spy, or some weird mix of all three? How should I act? Where did my loyalties lie?

The voices grew louder. I could hear occasional words now.

"I won't have it," came the impassioned voice of Mrs. Paxton.

"Now, Miranda," said the senator in a wheedling, pleading tone, and then the conversation grew inaudible.

Then all of a sudden Paxton's voice rose. "It's the lesser of two evils. At this point, we've got no choice."

Miranda Paxton began to make soft, stifled sounds. It shocked me to think of her crying. In my memories, Mrs. Paxton was forever elegant, steely, and unflappable. What had happened to this family?

And then Jeff Canin was standing in the foyer, frowning as if I'd done something wrong. When all I'd done was wait where he told me.

"The senator will see you in the den. Please follow me," he said. As if I didn't know where the den was! But I followed him down the hallway.

There were photographs on the wall I'd never seen before.

It was a gruesome procession of Miranda's artwork — blank-eyed mannequins posed in torn and mangled designer dresses sporting livid black eyes, decapitated limbs, blood-smeared knives protruding from chests. Miranda's art had always been edgy, but it had grown more transgressive since I'd seen her last.

It was funny, really. Critics expected to meet some edgy, chain-smoking bohemian, so they were shocked and titillated by WASPy, blueblood Miranda and fought over themselves to praise and analyze her work. Miranda's art illustrated the Jekyll-

Hyde nature of women. It was full of Harpy-like fury and self-hatred. It commented on the violence perpetrated on women by men, society, and high fashion. And Miranda just smiled, sphinxlike, and refused to answer questions.

"Ah, there you are."

The senator stood in the doorway, looking as fresh and composed as if he'd just showered and had his morning coffee. There was no hint of the argument he'd just had with his wife. His features were relaxed and in control. Simon Paxton hovered at his elbow, looking haggard, a living Dorian Gray portrait that absorbed all his brother's stress and age.

I handed Henry the envelope. He opened it, scanned the typed pages, and gave it to Simon. The senator's brother read them quickly, said, "I'll take care of it," and left.

Henry stared thoughtfully at the door.

"I don't believe you know my brother, Maggie. He was already in Washington when you and Anabelle were in high school. He's my right-hand man, handled my campaign three years ago when I ran for the Senate."

"Yes, sir."

The senator gave me a genial look. "Look, um, Maggie, why don't you call me Henry?

That feels more natural."

"Yes, sir. Henry, sir. I'll try."

"Goodness! Well, call me whatever's comfortable." He rubbed his chin. "I was startled to see you in that conference room. But I'm glad you're working on my behalf. It makes me feel I'm in good hands. But I'm sorry to keep you up so late. Your family must not appreciate that."

"It's all right," I said, realizing it was the wrong time and place to explain that I had neither husband nor children.

Miranda saved me the trouble. She swept into the room and took my hands, saying, "Maggie Weinstock, how lovely to see you. I was so delighted when Henry told me you'd be working with us. May I get you a drink?"

I demurred, saying I was happy to see her too.

Some women grow more handsome with age, and the blossoming of Miranda's artistic career had given her an assured confidence in manner and dress that I hadn't remembered. Her flowing indigo silk kimono jacket with carved ivory buttons screamed restrained money, exotic travel, and good taste. She wore hammered silver earrings, and her hair, once blonde like her daughter's, framed her face in soft wisps of silver.

"Anabelle will be so thrilled," Miranda said. "She's often talked about you and wondered how you're doing."

But she'd never picked up the phone. That's okay, I hadn't either.

"I've often thought about her too," I said. "We had some good times."

And some bad ones.

"Well," Miranda said brightly, "I suppose we can catch up later. Right now, I know that you people have important work to do. But, Maggie, you're always welcome here."

And with that, she was gone.

Jeff Canin brought a pot of coffee. Behind him came a tall, attractive man, the cool night air still clinging to his suit. His wavy dark-blond hair was combed straight back off his forehead just like his dad's and he moved with an athlete's grace.

And this time, it really was Luke Paxton.

Age had brought a pleasing maturity to his features. He had a few crinkling laugh lines, but his eyes were still blue as buffed sea glass, his teeth white against tanned skin.

It was also clear that Luke had no idea who I was.

He hurried to his father and their heads bent together.

". . . whatever help and support I can offer," I heard him say.

"Thanks, son." Henry placed a hand on Luke's shoulder.

Then Luke lowered his voice and asked something about the police.

"Not yet," Senator Paxton said, turning to me.

"I've been advised to hire a damage control firm, and I've done so," he said. "Blair is the best there is. One of their associates is here now. I think you may recognize her."

Luke pulled back. "Why would I recognize her?"

"Because it's Anabelle's old friend, Maggie Weinstock."

For a moment, Luke's face showed his struggle to absorb this news. His eyes roved over me. Then he gave a wry smile and he clasped my hand in his large, smooth dry ones.

"Well, I'll be darned. Little Maggie. Look at you, all grown up. You're even prettier than you were in high school."

Gosh, Luke, I didn't think you'd noticed.

There was a time when I would have been overjoyed to hear such words. Now I felt only the awkwardness that time and distance sow among people who once knew each other.

"You're looking good, Luke. Still surfing?"

He nodded. "My job's pretty high stress, it helps me unwind."

"He's a deputy district attorney in the L.A. office," said Henry Paxton, with the unmistakable pride of a father whose progeny have given him some shaky years. "On the fast track. Maybe a judgeship in his future."

"Dad," said Luke, "this isn't about me. Don't you have a lot to prepare for tomorrow, which" — he looked at his watch — "officially began forty-five minutes ago?"

"Thanks for bringing the package, Maggie," said Henry Paxton, dismissing me. "Go home and get some sleep. We're all going to be busy tomorrow."

With a round of good-byes, and Luke's eyes following me as if he was still trying to puzzle out the changes that time had wrought, I left.

I was pulling up to my darkened bungalow when the nagging feeling I'd had earlier returned and I realized what I'd forgotten. The week before I'd met a man through work and we'd made plans for tonight. Our first date, and I'd stood him up. I lowered my head onto the steering wheel and moaned.

8

The Emily Mortimer murder coverage was in full throttle when I woke up. Shots of her and her Koreatown apartment, footage of Senator Paxton, endless chatter about the once-elegant neighborhood's long slide into gangs and crime and attempts to regentrify.

I slipped out of bed and began the morning ritual: coffee, shower, dress, hair, makeup, perfume.

Smells have always affected me profoundly. One of my first childhood memories was rubbing crinkly geranium leaves on my arms from the bush at the end of our alley. I loved the spicy, exotic oil it released on my skin.

But it wasn't until I started hanging out at Villa Marbella that I really got into scent. There, at Miranda's vanity table, I discovered that perfume was a key, unlocking a door I didn't know was inside me.

Today, my own vanity table overflows with

bottles from Steve and lovers before him, plus fragrance I've scavenged from estate sales and discount bargain bins. Some are brand-new; others approach a balsamic vinegar reduction, labels faded with age. There are antique Lalique bottles of clear glass, frosted ones with carved stoppers, handblown glass suggestive of female curves, cheerful dimpled bottles, elongated towers, and modern flasks with clean, utilitarian lines. A perfumed cityscape whose sculpted beauty never failed to moved me with pleasure.

Today it was Frederic Malle's Iris Poudre with its powdery floral dry-down. Nothing brassy, exotic, or heavy. It matched my lavender twinset, pearls, and low heels, and would convey muted sorrow and sympathy to the Mortimers.

Then breakfast: yogurt-topped granola, multivitamin, and cognitive enhancer.

A tech client had introduced me to Adderall's wonders. As our second meeting stretched past midnight, he'd handed me a pill, and I have to confess that the allure of a "smart drug" was irresistible. Who didn't want to be more intelligent, even for a few hours?

"It doesn't make you smarter," said my billionaire client, who'd cofounded an Internet portal, "but it lets your wetware work at optimum capacity for sustained periods."

Soon I felt a serene and objective state that I can describe only as *mindfulness.*

This was accompanied by a sharpened mental focus, heightened concentration, and an improved memory. A generally more evolved cognitive state. As the meeting ended and I stood to go, the client tucked the bottle of pills into my purse.

The next time I had to work late, I popped one and loved the way it razored my focus. In the competitive, deadline-driven world in which I moved, it was the miracle drug. Blair had never been nine to five, and when something big broke, it was about how much we could squeeze into a twenty-four-hour work cycle. Those first hours were all-important.

Maybe I'm kidding myself.

In my family, alcoholism is the great white shark lurking just below the surface. Pills seem rather benign. But I do worry. People used to say I looked good. Now they wonder if I'm eating right. When this case is done, I'll taper off, even though it might mean feeling thick and fuzzy for a while.

I live in a transitional neighborhood, as the realtors say, and each morning I'm glad my car windows are still intact. Despite its name, Cypress Park is a hilly neighborhood. The lots are steep and strange, with narrow, winding streets, bare hillsides, and terraced gardens that put me in mind of Southeast Asia. And the residents? Some keep chickens, and many have dogs. There are big Latino families, elderly white widows, yuppie couples, Hollywood prop people, and your assorted boho bric-a-brac that can't abide tract homes or condos. In Cypress Park, we see coyotes and deer from our decks and killer views of downtown. So even though Steve and I had bought at the top of the market, which left me with an upside-down mortgage I'm trying to renegotiate, I loved my little house.

In the car, I monitored news and talk radio, which was abuzz with the Emily Mortimer story.

I considered the Paxton stories I'd read last night in bed, laptop propped on my belly, schooling myself on the man I'd known only as my girlfriend's father.

Henry Paxton had been an air force pilot in the Vietnam War and won the Congressional Medal of Honor. After the war, he'd run a consulting firm, working with companies like Boeing that vied for defense contracts. Paxton had always been active in Democratic circles and won election to the state Senate on his first try. Four years later he was elected to the U.S. Senate. In Washington, he quickly developed a reputation for deal making, getting warring sides to reach compromise and ram bills through.

He sat on several committees — unusual for a junior senator — and was known as the "eyebrows of justice" for his crusades on behalf of veterans' benefits and, more recently, reform of the banking industry.

It shocked me to realize how ignorant I'd been. I kept up with the news as part of my job, but the flow was so relentless that the baleen of my brain often filtered out stories that didn't affect my clients.

So while I'd known about the senator named Paxton, I'd never connected it to my high school friend. I guess that showed what a good job you can do of forgetting something you've made up your mind not to remember.

There was no traffic driving north to Valencia, all the cars were headed into the great, smoggy metropolis.

Plugging in my hands-free, I called the man I'd stood up last night, feeling buttery flies of apprehension. Waiting on hold, I recalled how we'd met.

One of my first cases at Blair had been figuring out how to promote a $1,500-a-plate fund-raiser at the Beverly Hills Hotel for an Afghan women's charity founded by a group of influential Hollywood wives.

Thomas Blair knew several of the wives — he'd represented them in nasty divorce cases. So when the gals hit him up for some free publicity, he agreed and the event landed on my desk.

There were two weeks to go and half the tickets remained unsold. The Hollywood wives were growing desperate. Then, at our second meeting, I noticed all the surgically enhanced faces in the room and had an idea.

What if the organizers threw in a free Botox or collagen treatment with each ticket purchase, to be carried out in luxury hotel suites directly after the luncheon?

The Hollywood wives were skeptical until I presented them with a list of plastic surgeons who'd agreed to donate their time. As I suspected, they'd jumped at the opportunity to meet wealthy women who might become clients.

One of the doctors was Dr. Rob Turcotte. He had sandy hair, an easy smile, and a thriving Westside practice. He also spent two months a year in Third World countries, sewing up cleft palates and other birth defects for poor villagers.

He bought me a drink at the hotel bar and

I listened to his tales of trekking through malarial jungles to operate on impoverished children. Rob was funny, laid back, and self-deprecating. When we said good-bye, he asked me out. I didn't tell my mom, who had the annoying habit of considering any unattached male who got within a twenty-foot radius as a potential son-in-law.

Dr. Turcotte kept me on hold for five freeway exits. When he came on, his voice was cordial but frosty.

"Maggie! What happened?"

I explained that an emergency at work had left me tied up until midnight.

"You could have called. I waited an hour at the café."

"I'm sorry, I was so focused on work that I forgot. Besides, I have only your business card."

"That's no excuse, the service can always page me."

"You're right."

For a moment I drove in silence. I knew I should ask if he wanted to reschedule, but the words wouldn't come. I'd forgotten how to do this. It had been such a long time.

"Should we try again?" Rob Turcotte asked at last.

"I'd like that."

"If you can find a night when you're not

working."

We made a date for tomorrow, at nine p.m. Surely the Paxton case would have calmed down by then.

Three cars and four news vans were parked in front of the Mortimer home when I pulled up. I ran the gauntlet, ignoring the babble of questions. Was I a family member? A detective? Was I with the senator's office? Could they get a statement?

When I rang the bell, a bloodshot eye appeared at the peephole.

"Maggie Silver, the Blair Company," I said. "I believe Mr. Faraday spoke to you last night."

The eye was removed and the door opened. I slipped inside and the door slammed shut.

"Jesus," said a middle-aged man wearing a wool cardigan. "It's like a siege out there. Don't we have enough to deal with?"

His wife appeared. She had Emily's blond hair, now streaked with gray, and a small, trim figure. The figure didn't match the face, which was blotchy and swollen.

Mrs. Mortimer offered me a cup of coffee, and although it was the last thing I wanted, I smiled and said that would be wonderful.

After inquiring how I took it, she returned with a china cup and saucer and I took a dutiful sip.

I didn't think I'd be offering anyone coffee if my child had just been murdered. I'd be lying in a crumpled heap on the floor. Or loading a shotgun. Or maybe both.

"Did you work with Emily?" Mrs. Mortimer asked politely.

"I'm afraid not," I said. "Though I understand she was a lovely girl. I'm with the public relations firm that Senator Paxton hired in the wake of what's happened."

"PR?" echoed Mr. Mortimer. "I didn't realize . . ."

Either there had been a complete breakdown in communication, or Emily's parents were so unhinged that they'd forgotten.

Mrs. Mortimer's lips curved down. "Well, if that isn't just like a politician. Wouldn't want this reflecting poorly on him."

"It's not like that," I said. "The senator is just being . . . prudent."

"What do you know about it?" Mrs. Mortimer said, her reddened nostrils flaring. "You didn't know my daughter. You didn't care about her. All you care about is making that . . . man look good. Well, let me tell you something. Don't go putting him on a pedestal. Don't go thinking he's so high-

and-mighty. That's what my daughter thought, and look where it got her. If he had any decency, he wouldn't be hiding behind some fancy PR firm. No offense to you, miss, you're probably just a flunky like our Emily. Oh, John!"

Mrs. Mortimer collapsed, sobbing, into her husband's arms.

I excused myself to use the bathroom. I'd give them a few minutes to compose themselves. I also wanted to consider what Mrs. Mortimer had just said.

In the hall, I passed a study. My eye was drawn to a table with a framed photo of Henry Paxton with Emily Mortimer. They wore sleek professional smiles, as if they'd posed for the shot, but there was a curious intimacy to their posture. Had they been carrying on an affair despite the senator's denials? Did Emily's parents know? Is that what accounted for my chilly reception?

When I returned to the living room, the Mortimers were ready to go to meet Senator Paxton and retrieve their daughter's belongings.

"There's an alley out back," Mrs. Mortimer said. "If you pull up, we can dash out and be on our way."

When I emerged onto a side street moments later with my precious cargo, I noticed a housepainter sitting in a parked truck with a ladder strapped to the back. The man's face nagged at me; it was familiar.

As we passed, he averted his face, and in that quick, evasive gesture, I remembered where I'd seen him: Blair headquarters. A repairman, I'd thought at the time, noting his engineer boots and work belt hung with tools, his shambling gait. In that office filled with sleek, polished people, he stuck out.

What was he doing here? What, exactly, did the senator have to hide?

And what kind of company was I working for?

Soon we were winding through the upscale malls and housing developments of Valencia and back to the freeway. On I-5, we joined the workday shuffle, moving in fitful starts. The car filled with a tense silence.

Tyler would have cajoled all sorts of strategic information from Emily's parents by now.

"What did you think of Emily's boyfriend?" I asked at last.

"We never met him," said Mr. Mortimer. "I didn't get the impression it was serious."

For a while, we drove in silence.

"I hear Emily was a real wiz at new

technology," I tried again after a few more miles.

"Look," said Mr. Mortimer, "I don't feel like talking about our daughter right now."

"I understand," I said quickly, "but the media is not going to let up. They are going to camp out on your sidewalk and ambush you each time you come out. They are relentless and cruel. I know, I deal with them every day. And so, on behalf of Blair, I'd like to offer my services as a 'family spokesperson.' At no cost, of course. It would give you some breathing room and create a buffer. There's no need to subject yourselves to a pack of aggressive reporters right now."

"What's the catch?" said Mr. Mortimer.

"No catch. You refer all calls to us or put a forwarding number on your phone and we take care of everything."

"I'm sure you people would like that," Mrs. Mortimer exploded. "Who knows what kind of shenanigans Senator Paxton was up to with our daughter. Like that other girl who was murdered, that Chandra Levy."

Chandra Levy was a pretty, young Washington, D.C., intern who'd disappeared while out for a jog in Rock Creek Park. She'd been having a secret affair with the congressman from her home district and, naturally, he came under suspicion. But eventually her body was found and a career criminal was charged with the crime. Not that I wanted to get into that with these bereaved parents.

"Senator Paxton is hardly —"

"I think your senator doesn't want us talking to the press because he's got something to hide."

"That's not true," I said, braking as traffic stopped. "But I wonder what makes you think that."

"Our daughter was a moral young woman," Mr. Mortimer said. "She knew right from wrong. But a girl like her, raised to believe the best about everyone . . . to feel that serving her country in this way was a patriotic honor . . . a girl like that might be easy to manipulate, especially by someone older, someone in a position of power and authority."

From the backseat came the sounds of Mrs. Mortimer sniffling.

"Do you have any proof that Emily and the senator were involved?" I pressed, needing to know.

"If we did, why would we tell you?" said Mr. Mortimer. "You work for him. You'd just twist our words."

"We'll save it for the police," Mrs. Mor-

timer said tartly. "They're coming this afternoon."

"And our lawyer," Mr. Mortimer added.

I knew this was just an afterthought. If
they had a lawyer, he'd be sitting between
us right now.

Mr. Mortimer turned on the car radio and
a notorious drive-time talk show came on.

"There's a rumor drugs were found in her
nightstand," one of the hosts said. "Maybe
she liked the Michael Jackson sleep aid. A
little propofol to numb her out."

"It could have been female Viagra." The
other host sniggered.

"A twenty-three-year-old babe? What does
she need that for? I bet it was meth. To stay
awake through those boring speeches in
Congress."

With a strangled cry, Mr. Mortimer
punched off the radio.

"Let's get one thing straight," he said,
poking me with a thick, work-roughened
finger. "Our daughter was not a drug addict. She didn't even take aspirin when she
had a headache."

"I'm very sorry you had to hear that
disgusting filth," I said, glad that the traffic
required me to keep my eyes on the road.

Was Faraday behind this whisper campaign? Had the plan to discredit Emily Mor-

144

timer and distance her from the senator's clean-cut image started with an anonymous "police" leak about mystery drugs found in Emily Mortimer's bedside drawer?

We inched toward the cause of the traffic slowdown — a multicar collision. People stood on the shoulder, talking into cell phones, inspecting damage, gesticulating widely. Two people were still inside the smashed cars, heads flung back, while firemen bent over them. We crawled past and then the traffic opened up and we shot forward.

"People have no decency," Mr. Mortimer said through clenched jaws.

"You think the drugs were planted?" I said, to keep him talking and deflect his anger.

But Mr. Mortimer's outburst seemed to have exhausted him. His shoulders drooped and he sagged against the seat and didn't answer.

When we pulled up to the senator's office on Wilshire Boulevard, the press was swarming along the sidewalk. The news media plus the tabloid paparazzi that appear like sharks when they smell celebrity blood. The story had just jumped the tabloid divide.

"Here," I said, handing the Mortimers an

oversized atlas, "cover your faces."

And then they were crowding the car on either side, shoving cameras to the window, setting off flashes as I maneuvered into the underground lot.

Soon I ushered the Mortimers into Paxton's office.

Within moments, the media had reassembled inside like a drifting protoplasm. The press conference began. I fetched coffee for the Mortimers. When I returned, Faraday was watching the monitor, looking pleased.

"He's an orator in the old-fashioned sense of the word, launching his words like rough-hewn boats into the stream," said my boss, who was no slouch himself.

Taking me aside, Faraday instructed me to position the Mortimers next to the senator once the press conference ended so the cameras could get a good shot at Paxton looking "presidential" comforting the parents.

The reporters were asking Paxton to define his relationship with Emily Mortimer, the rumors that she was found naked, that she was a drug addict, that Paxton had been seen in her company late on the night she was murdered.

The senator confirmed the late-night

meeting with his aide and parried the accusatory questions with grace and goodwill. Yes, he'd spoken to the detectives. No, he couldn't be more specific, the police had asked him not to discuss details of the case due to the pending investigation. No, he would not respond to hearsay.

"Jeez, folks, last week all you did was harangue me on the banking inquiry. Don't you want to hear how that's proceeding?"

A chorus of questions followed.

The senator's face eased, as though he'd stepped onto firmer ground. He looked energized and engaged.

"One at a time. Betsy, you're first."

"There are rumors that the commission you're working with has subpoenaed records from twelve individuals high up in the regulatory chain of command. Can you release the names of those subpoenaed and what you've learned?"

"That is correct and no we can't, Betsy."

"Is the AG's office preparing indictments?" asked a male reporter.

"It's too early to say. However, we are finding evidence of troubling ties among federal regulatory officials, banks, and lobbyists on the Hill."

Paxton was inundated with shouted questions. He said the committee's work would

147

continue through the fall and it was too early to discuss specifics.

Neil Bernstein, the senator's chief of staff, now bustled over to the podium.

"All right, folks, last question."

"When will your report be finished, sir, and will it name names?"

As Paxton embarked on a politician's nonanswer, I sensed the Mortimers growing uneasy at the call-and-response, the senator's jocular tone, the stylized theater of politics.

A Paxton aide came scurrying out. "It's time. Bring them up."

And then Mr. Mortimer balked.

"I'm not going to do it," he said, his jaw setting.

Immediately, Faraday was at the man's elbow. "It's your opportunity to go on national television and ask for help in solving your daughter's murder," he said, his voice at once sympathetic and coaxing. "Somebody out there saw or heard something. Your plea will move them to go to the police."

"No thank you," said Mrs. Mortimer, like she was declining a cucumber sandwich.

Even as I cursed the loss of our photo op, I admired their refusal to become part of the spectacle.

"Great," whispered Bernie Saunders, his forehead beaded in sweat. "It's going to blow up in our faces. I knew it."

Faraday pulled me aside, already scribbling. "Go up there, smiling, and give him this note. Then back the hell out." He handed me a piece of paper.

I walked across the stage into a sea of lights. I slid the paper on the senator's podium, then walked away. The reporters' faces quickened with hungry interest.

Paxton never faltered. As he finished explaining an arcane point of the banking scandal, he opened the note and scanned it.

"Folks, I'd hoped to have the Mortimer family here with me for this next announcement, but they have chosen to deal with their grief in private."

Paxton looked into the sea of faces. "I understand and respect their feelings. And I share their pain. And that's why I'd like to announce that our office is putting up a fifty-thousand-dollar reward for information leading to the arrest and conviction of Emily Mortimer's killer."

A surprised murmur rippled through the crowd.

"California's broke," came a cynical voice. "Where's the money coming from?"

"Good question, Bruce. And never fear,

it's not coming from Uncle Sam or Uncle Cal. The money is being provided by a trust, set up by my family, in recognition of the high esteem in which Emily was regarded by myself and all of our staff."

There was a buzz of approval.

"What about the rumors of Emily Mortimer's drug use?" asked a tabloid TV reporter.

"I have no knowledge of that," Paxton said.

"Could you tell us when and where you saw her last?" a male voice from the back shouted. "And whether she seemed tipsy or high?"

"The gentleman must have come in late. But for all those who slept through their alarm, I'll repeat that the LAPD asked me not to discuss specifics of the case," Paxton said, to a sprinkling of laughter. He made a show of gathering up his papers. "Thank you all for your time."

Paxton's look of composure dissolved as he walked offstage. He looked suddenly old and tired.

But he went straight to the Mortimers and extended his hand.

They hesitated. Then their innate decency took over and they shook.

"My deepest sympathies to you both,"

Paxton said, as a camera flashed in the wings, unnoticed by the Mortimers.

It was the woman I'd seen in the elevator yesterday with a salad and a smoothie. She shot off several more frames, then examined her film and smiled. And I knew that within the hour, a "compassion shot" of the senator consoling the Mortimers would be distributed to every news outlet in the country.

"Emily was a valued member of my staff and a wonderful human being," Paxton said.

Mr. Mortimer looked like he might cry. Then slowly anger got the upper hand.

"Our daughter is dead and you're out there exploiting her murder for political gain."

"On the contrary," said Paxton. "It's a nightmare." His voice faltered. "And it's only begun. I . . ."

It was almost uncanny how Faraday materialized at his side. "The senator's overwrought," he said. And he led Henry Paxton away.

Within moments, Faraday was back, talking quietly and earnestly to the Mortimers.

He gestured for them to wait a moment, then walked over to me.

"Please go collect Emily's things while I talk them into representation."

"Good luck," I said skeptically.

"And hurry back, I don't want them wandering around shooting off their mouths to the press."

I glanced at Bernie Saunders, who was looking distinctly reptilian, as if he'd been up sick all night. A light had gone out of his eyes. I almost felt sorry for him.

A staffer showed me to Emily's cubicle, where two detectives were loading her personal belongings into boxes. Soon Faraday and the Mortimers joined us. Seeing a knitted blue scarf, Mrs. Mortimer gave a cry and snatched it up with such alacrity that one end of it slid across my cheek.

I caught a whiff of cool citrus and herbs. Intrigued, I breathed in more deeply, trying to identify it. I wanted to bury my nose in it. I'd smelled this fragrance before. What was it?

"We gave her that last year for Christmas," Emily's mother said, cradling the scarf against her cheek.

"You'll get everything back in due time, ma'am," said the detective, his voice low and sympathetic. "I'm sorry, but right now, we've got to impound everything for the investigation."

Mrs. Mortimer's hand trembled as she handed back her daughter's scarf and stared blindly out the window.

Mr. Mortimer stood stoically, patting his wife's hands and looking lost.

The Mortimers were silent on the drive back to Valencia, locked in private thoughts.

When I pulled up to the alley behind the house, Mr. Mortimer extended his hand. "I look forward to working with you, Ms. Silver," he said.

I shook hands and tried to hide my surprise.

"Your Mr. Faraday impressed us greatly," Mrs. Mortimer said.

Her husband nodded and regarded me sternly. "He's managed to keep his integrity in this soul-sucking business. You can learn a lot from him, young woman." He clicked his tongue. "He told us why he can't quit. Such a shame."

I nodded, but my bewilderment must have shown.

Mrs. Mortimer touched my hand. "Don't tell me you didn't know that his wife has early-onset Alzheimer's? Well, please don't let on. We've all got our crosses to bear. But at least Mrs. Faraday led a full life, unlike our Emily . . ." Her voice wavered. "Oh, John, I'm going to start up again. We'd better go inside. I'm sorry, dear. Thank you for driving us home."

■ ■ ■ ■

When I got back to the office, Tyler handed me a menu and asked if I wanted to order in Thai food.

"How much do I owe you?" I asked forty minutes later in the lunchroom.

"You can get the next one," Tyler said, tucking into his pad thai.

"Really, it's okay," I said.

"Relax, Silver." Tyler cocked his head. "Maybe I *want* you in my debt."

"Why's that?"

"So you'll say yes when I suggest a drink after work."

Suddenly Tyler was very busy picking tiny but diabolical Thai chilies out of his food.

Surprised, I put down my fork. "Are you asking me out?"

"Maybe I'm considering it."

"Ah, I get it. You're being facetious. You probably have a girlfriend anyway. And her name is Muffy or Buffy or Cricket. And she played lacrosse in school, while you crewed. That's how you got those broad shoulders."

I bit my tongue. Now he'd know I'd been checking him out.

"You've been checking me out," Tyler said.

I shrugged. "Hard to miss."

154

"My girlfriend's name is Diane," Tyler said.

For some reason, my heart lurched.

Tyler got up and walked to the fridge. "But we're kind of on the outs."

"Sorry to hear it," I said, between bites of Thai salad.

It was chili-hot, spiked with tiny dried shrimp, fresh coconut, bean sprouts, peanuts, mango, and lacy purple onions. It was hard to feel sorry before such a creation. The heat of the chilies, the creamy sweetness of the mango, the fresh lime dressing. Each bite was totally addictive.

Tyler returned with two fruit sodas. He slid one across and I took it as a peace offering.

"I hear Faraday locked up the Mortimers," he said.

"Yeah, with a big fat lie. He told them his wife has Alzheimer's, when I know for a fact he's not married."

"It's his ex-wife, and she does have Alzheimer's," Tyler said.

I chewed on that for a moment. "Maybe so, but there's still something strange going on. When I went to pick up Emily's parents this morning, there was a guy waiting at the curb who looked familiar. Have you seen that repairman who walks around the office sometimes in overalls, he's got a toolbox?"

Tyler was suddenly very busy slurping up his pad thai.

"Does he work here?" I persisted.

"I don't think so," Tyler said, rocking back on his chair. "Maybe he does odd jobs for the firm from time to time."

"How odd?"

Tyler didn't say anything.

"Well, I could have sworn he was parked outside the Mortimer house this morning when I drove off with the parents. He was dressed like a housepainter."

Tyler shrugged elaborately. "Maybe if Blair can't throw him enough business, he moonlights as a painter."

"I got the distinct impression he was waiting for us to leave."

"I think you've been working too hard," Tyler said. "You're starting to see things."

"He's got a lantern jaw. And droopy eyes. And he turned away as we drove by like he didn't want to be recognized."

"Forget it. You didn't see anything."

"But . . ."

"Maggie." He placed a hand on my wrist. I glanced down and he quickly removed it.

"You're not listening. Forget it. What you saw. Or didn't see. Or thought you saw. Understand?"

But I was stubborn and didn't like being wrong, and so his meaning filtered down only slowly.

And when it did, I stood up, my appetite suddenly gone, the bite of scrumptious salad I'd just taken turning to straw in my mouth.

"Hey," said Tyler, friendly and jovial once more, "if you're not going to finish your salad, can I have it?"

I'd barely sat down at my desk when the phone buzzed.

"Have you called Anabelle Paxton yet?" Faraday asked.

"Haven't had a chance."

"Take your time," Faraday said, in a tone that meant do it immediately.

"And, Maggie? I'd like to stage an event where the media can shoot Senator Paxton with his wife and kids. Something that would humanize him better than a thousand of our words. The senator's not sure about dragging his kids into it, but perhaps you could use your influence. Anabelle will want to do all she can for dear papa, hmm?"

Already, Faraday was using me as a back-door conduit into the family.

I felt like such a tool.

Again, I wondered how much he knew

about my tangled history with the Paxtons. There was one secret from those days that I vowed would stay buried. It wasn't relevant to the Emily Mortimer case. It was Anabelle's business and nobody else's.

"Sure, I'll talk to her," I said, "but it will be awkward since —"

"Of course, you have to do it in a way that feels natural," Faraday broke in smoothly. "But I know I can count on you. You're silky-smooth. The Holloways were impressed the other day in Malibu."

Now he was playing *me,* the shameless dog.

"Except I haven't had a minute to work on their case," I said.

"I've asked Tricia Coogan to follow up," Faraday said. "I need you to concentrate on Paxton right now. Tyler's been monitoring the media and he'll brief us in ten minutes. My office."

He rang off and I noticed my phone light was blinking. I hit Play.

"Hello, this is Fred Sentier. I'm a reporter and I'd like to speak to Senator Paxton as soon as possible. His office gave me this number."

Whom do you work for and why didn't you speak to him at the press conference?

"It's about the Emily Mortimer case,"

Sentier continued. "I've got information that will interest the senator." There was a nasty chuckle. "It certainly interested me. I need to hear from him by four p.m. or it will be too late."

I hit Replay. I hit it five times.

Then I picked up the phone machine and carried it into Faraday's office, where Tyler and Samantha and Fletch were just sitting down around the table. Faraday was standing at the whiteboard, sketching out a time line of the Mortimer murder. He had a red marker in his hand and his glasses were low on his nose like a distracted college professor.

"You need to listen to this," I said, plugging in the phone.

When Sentier's voice died away, I said, "Is that a threat I hear?"

"He's going to go to the police," Tyler said glumly.

"No he isn't," said Faraday, "because then he'd lose his exclusive. The cops put out a press release and everyone's got it."

"Then he's going to throw it online at four," I said.

"He wants to confirm it first," Tyler said. "It's a better story if the senator comments."

"He didn't say who he worked for."

"The name's not familiar," said Faraday, "and I know every hack in town."

"Let's find out," said Fletch, flexing his fingers.

"What if it's blackmail he's after, not a scoop?" I said uneasily.

"Call him and set up a meeting" — Faraday inclined his head to the phone — "so we can find out."

"Right now? Here?" I said, struck with sudden stage fright.

Faraday slit his eyes at me.

I picked up the phone and dialed.

Fred Sentier answered on the first ring. He sounded out of breath or excited, and he balked at meeting with an underling. Maybe he thought he'd be ushered instantly into the senator's presence like in a movie. I explained that Paxton was meeting with LAPD detectives and would be tied up past four, whereas I could personally deliver Sentier's message to the senator once I had more details.

Grudgingly, Sentier agreed and we set a rendezvous for Pershing Square downtown, in an hour's time.

My hand trembled as I put down the phone. Faraday was grinning. "Well done."

"Frederick Sentier is a reporter with the *Washington Post*," Fletch announced, look-

160

ing up from his ubiquitous laptop. "Suburban Metro, not the National Desk. I've just
pulled up a slew of his stories. School board
elections, zoning wars in Northern Virginia,
penny-ante stuff."

"No wonder I've never heard of him," said
Faraday.

"Then for sure they're not putting it online until they can confirm it," said Tyler
triumphantly. "The *Post* is not going to risk
getting egg all over its face."

Faraday pushed out his lower lip.

"I don't like this. What's he doing so far
from home? I want you to be careful, Maggie."

9

I got to Pershing Square early and ducked into the Biltmore Hotel for coffee, ogling the Art Deco architecture, the crystal chandeliers, the b&w photos of movie stars that lined the walls.

When I got back to Pershing Square, I saw a few shabbily clad people, some office workers eating snacks, and a bum snoozing on the grass. A black man in a button-down shirt and khakis stood on the sidewalk, scanning everyone.

"I'm Maggie Silver. Are you Fred?"

The man looked around, as if fearing he might be overheard, but everyone was minding their own business. He nodded. We walked to a bench and sat down.

"Got some ID?" he asked.

I took out my driver's license and my Blair ID. He studied them, frowning. Behind Sentier, a blond man with a suitcase and horn-rimmed glasses moved into view. With a shock, I recognized Fletch. What was he doing here?

"I need to get with the senator," Sentier said.

There was a sheen of sweat on his skin and his eyes shone with adrenaline.

"How about showing *me* some ID?" I said.

He extracted a *Washington Post* press pass from his wallet. The ID matched. When Sentier shoved the wallet back in his pocket, I saw a gleam of metal.

I jumped to my feet. Fred Sentier had a gun. Anyone could print out and laminate a press pass. It didn't mean anything. I wanted to run to Fletch and disappear with him into the downtown crowds, but if I did, I'd never find out what Sentier knew. And then how could I face Faraday? It was pathetic, but at that moment, I was more afraid of Faraday than getting shot.

Sentier saw my alarm. He pulled the gun out to give me a better look and I shrank. "Chill," he said. "This is for *my* protection. What I've got's gonna blow the *lid* off this story."

From across the square, Fletch shot me a questioning look. Almost imperceptibly I shook my head.

Our little dance had also caught the attention of a homeless man who'd been lounging on the grass. He got to his feet, pulled a bag of bread out of his knapsack and began to walk toward us, scattering crumbs every few feet.

Sentier hissed in exasperation and put the gun away. "Will you please come back here? I won't hurt you."

Fletch watched but kept his distance.

The man with the bread walked past very slowly. Sentier watched him, his face scrunched up suspiciously.

"If you wanted to talk to Paxton," I said, "why didn't you attend the press conference?"

"And tip off my competition?" Sentier gave me an arch smile. If he had a mustache he'd be twirling it.

"If you've got something, say it."

"I've got proof that the senator and that Mortimer chick were involved."

I tried to keep my voice cool. "What proof?"

"It's for the senator's eyes and ears only."

The pigeons were cooing and pecking at the ground. The man with the bread was coming back. Up close, he lacked the weathered, dirt-caked texture of the chronically unhoused. But maybe he bathed at a shelter. Maybe he'd only recently lost his job and his house, a victim of the mortgage collapse.

My skin prickled with unease. Was he eavesdropping?

"This is a serious allegation," I said. "I need to talk to my boss."

Sentier looked at his watch. "You've got fifteen minutes. The editors are ready to throw my story up on the website." He gave a Grinchy smile. "But of course we'd really like to include Senator Paxton's response."

I walked to the shelter of a nearby tree and dialed Faraday. There was no time to go back to the office and tell him in person. I'd have to rely on a sort of hackneyed code and hope that my boss understood.

The man with the pigeons turned his bag upside down and shook out the last crumbs, keeping his eyes on Sentier. Then he glanced in my direction and walked away. He no longer had the slow, halting shuffle of people who spend too many hours trudging through the city streets. Now he walked with the brisk stride of a man with places to go, people to see. A sense of awful foreboding came over me.

"Faraday," my boss barked in my ear.

"Hey there, it's Maggie. A car almost ran me over just now. The driver is very agitated. He says he's got proof that it's my fault. Says he saw me necking with my boyfriend when I should have been watching the road."

"I'm sorry," said Faraday, mechanically. "That's horrible. So it's a sex thing?"

"Yeah."

"Did you get any details about his insurance?"

"I'm working on it. Problem is, we're running out of time."

"Tell him you'll do what he wants but you need a few more hours. Promise him a sit-down with your insurance agent. He can take photos. If he balks at that, throw in the offer of a *second, unrelated* insurance policy. But in exchange, the driver needs to lay his own insurance on the table. All of it. He can take it or leave it. But if he tries to leave, call me immediately."

I walked back to Fred and explained the terms. Fletch was sitting on a bench now, eating a banana and reading a paper.

Fred grimaced with disgust. "You PR hacks are all the same. Cover and duck, dissemble, get your story together. You're sleazy and despicable."

"Look, I know you're sore because your 401(k) has tanked and your colleagues have all jumped ship to work in *my* profession. Every paper in this country is in trouble and that's bad for all of us."

Sentier's lip curled. "I'd rather starve than work for people like you, hiring yourselves out to the highest bidder."

I had my answer ready. Every new hire had to commit it to memory, it's the damage control mantra for Blair itself.

"Then you should know that ten percent of Blair's billable hours are devoted to pro bono work. We don't toot our horn, but since you brought it up, our clients include the NAACP, Council of Episcopal Bishops, Afghan Women's Clinic, Big Sisters, and Tree People. So our rich clients subsidize the poor ones. Now if we can get back to business, what proof do you have about this alleged affair?"

Sentier looked smug. "I've got documentation and an eyewitness who swears that Paxton and Mortimer spent a night together at the Mission Inn in Riverside in late May."

"Are you sure the senator wasn't in Washington that day?"

He smirked. "It was Memorial Day weekend. He flew home."

"You're still not telling me what proof you have."

Fred Sentier pulled out a piece of paper and unfolded it. It was a hotel receipt stapled to a credit card slip with the senator's name on it. The signature was illegible.

I inspected it. "So he stayed there. This proves nothing. Maybe he spoke at a Chamber of Commerce breakfast."

"The girl was seen in his room late at night."

"What do you mean 'seen'? Were you there? How do you know it was her?"

Sentier stood up, scattering a flock of pigeons that were pecking at the remains of the homeless man's bread. Shoving his hands in his pockets, he said, "I just do."

"If she was in that room, there was a legitimate reason. She handled his Twitter account, for instance, so she needed access. I'm afraid I need something more persuasive than this."

"They ordered a bottle of champagne. The drinks receipt has a date and time. It was one twenty-four a.m."

"Politicians don't keep regular hours and neither do their staffers."

"He's not exactly burning the midnight oil on the campaign trail right now," Sentier said slyly.

"How do you know the senator was even in the room? It could have been someone using his credit card."

"His personal credit card?"

"There could be a million reasons . . . Did you actually see them?"

"Not exactly."

"So you weren't there?" I pounced.

"Not exactly."

"Then why make such an allegation?"

He turned on me angrily. "The waiter who delivered champagne to the room that night was my father."

I blinked.

"He didn't think anything of it at the time," Sentier continued. "But when he turned on the TV last night and saw the dead girl's pic, it jogged his memory. Because she was pretty and her hair was wet from the shower and she was wearing a hotel bathrobe and because she tipped him ten bucks. A waiter doesn't forget that. So he had a pal in accounting pull a copy of the receipts without telling him what it was for. The name and date match."

I shook my head, still unconvinced, or pretending I was. "The *Post* flew you out here pretty fast."

Sentier gave an enigmatic smile and looked meaningfully at his watch.

"Look," I said quickly. "I promise you'll get your interview. But this has got to stay off the Internet. If what you say is true, it's the scoop of a lifetime and a few hours won't make any difference. But if you're wrong, it will blow up in your face and you'll lose your job. And there are none left in journalism, as we both know. I'll brief the senator as soon as he gets out of his meeting and we'll call you with a time and place."

"No," said Sentier. "You already had your time. He gets on the phone right here, right now, or it's going live."

Sentier took out his phone and began to press buttons.

"Wait," I said.

There was triumph in his eyes as he thumbed off the phone and crossed his arms. "Well?"

"Give us a few more hours and we'll throw in information about another of our high-profile clients. Possibly even arrange for an interview."

"Who with?" Sentier was intrigued but suspicious.

"I'll have to talk to my boss."

Sentier licked his lips.

"You repping any pro athletes that got caught doing the nasty like Tiger Woods?"

"I can't give you any specifics now. But we work closely with the press. We like to build relationships that can last years."

Sentier considered. I could see his thoughts leapfrogging into the future, counting up all the stories he'd break, all the promotions that would come his way.

"Okay." He nodded. "But if you burn me, I will kick your sorry ass into next year. And I'm warning you, the story is already written and ready to go. If anything happens to me, they have instruc—"

"Nothing's going to happen to you," I said. "But leave your gun at home tonight or you'll never make it past security."

In the outer lobby of Senator Paxton's Los Angeles office, an earnest young man was explaining why the senator could not see us without an appointment.

"Dear God, give me strength," Faraday said.

He stepped back, dialing on his cell phone, and bumped into a woman pushing an oxygen tank and carrying a file who'd been waiting when we arrived. Documents scattered. I bent to pick them up. The woman thanked me and said she was waiting to talk to the senator about her canceled medical insurance.

My heart gave a little tug — that woman could be my mother.

Faraday said, "Yeah? Well tell him that Jack Faraday is in his lobby and it's an emergency."

Soon a side door opened. As the woman with the medical file squawked in outrage, we were ushered inside. Bernstein appeared and led us down a hallway. We stopped outside the senator's office where a young man sat at a desk, juggling three ringing lines, flashing phone texts, and a computer that beeped with constant new e-mail.

"You can't go in, he's in conference," the man told Bernstein without looking up. "And whoever they are, they don't have an appointment."

"These people are from Blair, and it's an emergency. Put a note under his nose."

The scheduling secretary's eyes flicked over us disapprovingly. In a world where face time with the politician was the most important currency of all, the senator's scheduler was the royal gatekeeper, with the attitude to prove it.

"Very well," he said at last.

A moment later, he emerged from the senator's office and said it would be a few minutes.

Faraday's shoe tapped impatiently. Five minutes later, the door to the senator's office opened and the man himself told us to come in.

Paxton's inner sanctum was decorated like a Ralph Lauren ad, with antique oak furniture and bookcases and a forest-green leather couch. The senator could look out the fourteenth-floor window upon his constituents in the Los Angeles Basin. Framed photos of Paxton's family added a homey touch to the stacks of papers and thick black briefing books prepared by his staff.

Senator Paxton took a seat behind his large antique desk and said, "This better be important. I just cut short a conference call with Washington."

He looked very imposing, with the seal of the United States government behind him as a backdrop, but his voice held a thickness I associated with sleep, and the couch bore the slight depression of a human body.

Was it possible we'd caught the senator napping?

He hadn't even finished his first term in office, and already people were referring to his bright future as a national leader and a star of the Democratic Party. It was hard to believe that my friend's father might someday live in the White House. But this morning I'd heard him speak. He had the politician's gift for inspiring people and making them believe. Would it be enough to get him through this crisis unscathed?

Faraday closed the door, sat, then clasped his hands, pinkies extended, in an almost dainty manner.

"Does the Mission Inn of Riverside ring a bell, Senator? May thirtieth?"

A muscle on the senator's jaw twitched. "Not especially."

"Were you there?"

"I'd have to check my calendar."

"Now listen here," said Neil Bernstein, "you can't come barging in and —"

"Was Emily Mortimer there too?" Faraday interrupted.

The senator looked like he'd eaten a bad fish taco.

"Sir, shall I call Lambert?" Bernstein said.

"That would probably be a good idea," the senator said.

"Nobody's saying anything until the senator's attorney arrives," said Bernstein, pulling out his phone.

"Sir," said Faraday, "right now your house is burning down and I'm here to put out the fire. A *Washington Post* reporter is about to throw the Mission Inn pajama party on the web. We need to head off the journalistic feeding frenzy that will follow. I need the facts, right now, so I can put together a strategy."

"But . . ." said Bernstein.

Senator Paxton raised his hand to quiet his chief of staff.

"Go on," he told Faraday.

"You rented a room at the Mission Inn on May thirtieth. Was Emily Mortimer with you?" Faraday said.

The senator considered the question. "She might have been," he said offhandedly. "She often accompanied me so she could tweet and blog about the events."

"Champagne. Late at night? Does that jog your memory?"

The senator ignored Faraday's tone. "If I recall, Emily had friends who lived nearby and she wanted to visit them. Maybe it got late and she didn't feel like driving home."

I notice that when people lie, they often offer up too much information.

"So Emily Mortimer spent the night at the Mission Inn too?"

"I don't keep tabs on what my staff does after hours."

Faraday sat back. "Don't lie to me, Senator. The two of you were made."

The senator's brow furrowed. He glanced at his chief of staff.

"That's ridiculous," he whispered. "I don't know what you're talking about."

"You're not going to have a job to go back to if you don't get one thing straight, Senator," Faraday said softly. "We've just been broadsided because you lied to me. If —"

"Nobody lied to you," the senator said.

"Lies of omission are just as bad," Faraday thundered, making it clear who the alpha dog in the room was.

I'd seen this performance before, and I always marveled at its audacity, how it balanced on a razor wire of pomp and desperation. Faraday needed to make the senator understand that his fancy title and political power were irrelevant right now. Here in this room, he was just another Blair client in crisis. And he had to listen and do what Faraday said or else his career, and possibly his life as a free man, would be over.

The senator had gone pale. Bernstein's eyes were bugging out. But no one said a word.

Faraday eyed the room like a conquering general.

"As I was saying, you lose all credibility when you're caught lying. With the public and the police." He waggled his eyebrows for emphasis.

"I am not a liar."

"That's exactly what Richard Nixon said before he got nailed for Watergate. So pardon me, Senator, but Maggie just spoke to a reporter from the *Washington Post*. He's got a waiter on record as delivering champagne to your room at the Mission Inn on May thirtieth at one thirty a.m. Emily Mortimer answered the door in a robe. The waiter recognized her when he saw the photo on TV late last night. And yes, he's checked the room number. It matches. And it's your credit card. Your personal credit card."

Paxton looked stricken.

"A story like that worries me, Senator, because I've got a professional reputation to uphold too," Faraday said wearily. "But how can I do that if the media thinks I'm lying? And why am I lying? Because my client has not been honest with me. So listen up. We don't need your business if it means torpedoing our credibility. At Blair, our reputation is all we have. So this ends here. You will get your deposit check back in tomorrow's mail if you don't tell us the whole truth right now."

Faraday stood up, and the only sound in the room was his chair squeaking backward.

I knew I should rise too, but I was frozen to my seat.

The two men stared each other down — the lean patrician and the bulldog Irishman.

"Sit down, Mr. Faraday," Paxton said at last. "I understand your terms and I'm willing to accommodate you."

"Thank you, sir," Faraday said with exaggerated courtesy. He settled into his seat like a priest about to hear confession. "Please start at the beginning."

Paxton's mouth gave a small, rueful twist. "Yes, well, I'm afraid I can't do that alone. I'm sorry to try your patience again, but I need my brother. Please give us ten minutes."

And he walked out, closing the door behind him.

Faraday shifted in his chair. "Now what?" he muttered.

Fifteen minutes later, the Paxton brothers walked in, the senator with his usual confident stride, Simon Paxton looking slightly green. They were accompanied by Harvey Lambert, carrying a suitcase and bristling with purpose.

The senator and Lambert sat down. Simon Paxton stood by the window, staring at a yellow construction crane that was lifting blocks of steel onto a skyscraper skeleton. His hands moved nervously, adjusting his tie, smoothing back his hair, checking things in his pockets.

Anabelle had never mentioned her uncle when we were kids. Was it because he lived back east? Had the brothers been estranged? Maybe I'd never paid attention, just as Anabelle had never inquired about my parents.

It brought home what a hermetically sealed world we'd lived in as teenagers.

Simon Paxton turned to face us. He cleared his throat. "It wasn't the senator in the hotel room that night with Emily Mortimer," he said. "It was me."

The only sound was the faraway shouts of construction workers, the dim clang of metal against metal.

Then Faraday swore. He swiveled in his chair and glowered at Henry Paxton. "C'mon, Senator. You expect us to believe that?"

The senator's eyes went to his brother. Simon Paxton was expressionless, but his voice wavered as he said, "I'm prepared to testify under oath."

Faraday's lip curled in disgust. He ignored Simon Paxton and addressed the senator. "You're willing to sacrifice your brother to keep yourself from going down? It's not going to fly, you know."

The senator's face was bloodless. He opened his mouth but Lambert beat him to the punch.

"It will have to," the attorney said, a sharp edge in his voice. "Because it's the truth."

A numb relief coursed through me. I had wanted so badly to believe that Henry Paxton was innocent. And here it came. The

senator was sprung. It was his weaselly, con-
niving fixer brother who'd been in the hotel
room with Emily Mortimer that night.

Or was this another lie?

"What is your recommendation, Mr.
Faraday?" Lambert said. "How shall we proceed?"

For a long moment, there was silence, as
Faraday examined the brothers. I could
almost feel his nimble brain working, trying
and discarding strategies, poking holes in
the story, testing to make it airtight.

Finally, he said, "I'd like the senator and
his brother to meet with the reporter and
tell him exactly what they've told me. He's
promised to keep the story off the Internet
for now, but we can't stall him forever."

A horrified look had come over Lambert's
face.

"You'd prefer," asked Faraday, "that it
trickles out bit by bit, giving everyone time
to speculate wildly and come to the worst
possible conclusions? While the brothers
deny and obfuscate and trap themselves in
statements that will come back to haunt
them? We need to be out front with this,
setting the agenda. It's the only way. And
after talking to the reporter, you tell it to
the cops."

"We need time," Lambert pleaded.

"Well, we haven't got any," Faraday snapped.

He turned to the senator. "Sir, when did you become aware of your brother's relationship with Emily Mortimer?"

A look passed between the Paxtons.

The senator hesitated. "My brother came to me today, plagued by guilt."

"And you didn't see fit to tell me? Or the police?"

"I needed some time to absorb this news," Henry Paxton said softly.

"Come on, Jack, he learned about it only this morning," said Lambert.

"So pardon my impertinence, Senator," Faraday said, "but did your brother kill the girl too?"

My head shot up, worried that he'd finally gone too far.

Lambert the lawyer rose. "That is completely out of order. Simon, do *not* answer that question."

"I didn't kill anyone. I swear it on my mother's grave," Simon Paxton said.

"What I'd like to hear more than oaths right now is that you have an ironclad alibi for the night Emily was killed."

"Simon," said Lambert, "please tell Mr. Faraday what you told me."

Simon Paxton walked to a chair like a

zombie. He sat down and placed his hands on his thighs.

"I was in Washington, D.C., Monday night. I had a late dinner with a colleague, then took a cab home. My wife and I have a place near Dupont Circle. The security system in the parking garage and my unit should confirm that I was home from one thirty until about eight the next morning. I had a lunch meeting on the Hill, then took a cab to the airport and flew to L.A. I spent last night in our condo in Century City."

"So you couldn't have killed her because you were still on the East Coast late Monday night and early Tuesday morning," Faraday said.

Simon Paxton nodded.

Faraday raised an eyebrow. "Of course, you could have caught an earlier flight. Or come by private plane."

Simon Paxton threw up his hands. "The cops can dig all they want. I'm telling the truth."

"He's telling the truth," Harvey Lambert intoned.

"Fine," said Faraday. "Let's talk about how you and Emily Mortimer met."

"I like to mentor young people," Simon Paxton said. "They have an energy, an optimism that I find invigorating. They're not cynical and jaded. They want to change the world for the better."

Faraday rolled his eyes, but I saw that he was listening intently.

"For a long time, this is how I excused my attraction to Emily Mortimer. I've got a wife I care deeply about. So Emily and I would meet in bars and places where we wouldn't see anyone we knew. We talked about things that were happening at work. She complained about her boyfriend and asked my advice. It was all very innocent."

Faraday asked, "Did you supervise her? Either directly or indirectly?"

Simon Paxton looked up. "Emily reported to Bernie Saunders. I'm not even on staff. My position is completely unofficial."

"Well, thank God for that. Did she come on to you?" Faraday's eyes narrowed as he sought an angle.

"It was . . . mutual." Paxton stared at his hands.

"Was it only that one time, at the Mission Inn in Riverside?" Faraday prompted. "You were working late, thrust into close quarters, had a little too much to drink?"

Simon Paxton hesitated. "There were other times."

"Did it start that night?"

Again, Paxton hesitated. "Yes. We were

there for the opening of a mall. The senator was going to cut the ribbon and give a talk at the Inland Empire Chamber of Commerce. Emily Twittered the whole thing and uploaded photos of the talk and the Mission Inn, where the senator was going to spend the night. It's a beautiful, Spanish Mission–style building. But Henry ended up driving home."

"With the body man?"

I started, but nobody else reacted, so I figured it must be some political term.

"No body man that day," the senator said.

Faraday raised a skeptical eyebrow. "Well, isn't that convenient."

Simon continued. "After Henry left, I stayed in his room and Emily joined me."

"Are you in the habit of using the senator's personal credit card to order champagne?"

Simon Paxton stared steadily at Faraday. "We're brothers. He doesn't mind. We share a lot of things."

Did they share the girl?

"Why didn't you just charge the champagne to the room?"

"Because taxpayers shouldn't be billed for my personal expenses," Simon said between clenched teeth.

"How very noble. Then why not use your credit card?"

"I forgot my wallet at home," Simon Paxton said evenly. "My brother loaned me his MasterCard."

"That's very convenient."

Faraday rubbed his hands together and blew on them. His cheeks were flushed and his eyes were dilated.

"Mr. Paxton, was the affair ongoing at the time of Emily Mortimer's death?"

Paxton hung his head. "Yes," he said, his voice so low it was barely audible.

Faraday took out a cigarette and shoved it savagely between his lips and began to chomp on it. "Jesus Christ," he said, massaging his temples.

"Were you in love with her?" I asked.

I didn't know why this was important. Would it make what had transpired more palatable?

Simon Paxton lifted his head and fixed me with a look that was sorrowful and enigmatic, lambent and rueful. Something passed between us that unsettled me, and I can't explain why, but I felt sorry for him.

"I don't know if it was love. But that girl made me feel alive."

Faraday chomped on his cigarette. Bits of tobacco had come free and stuck to his lower lip.

"When's the last time you slept with her?"

he asked.

"Three weeks ago."

Simon looked at his brother, his eyes begging forgiveness.

"Henry, there are no words to explain how devastated I feel knowing I've damaged your career through my stupidity and selfishness. I know you have to . . . I want you to throw me to the wolves. You've got to distance yourself from me to save your political life. But I want everyone in this room to know I was not with Emily Mortimer the night she was murdered and I didn't kill her. So help me God."

Faraday examined him with clinical detachment.

"I am truly grateful that neither of you has discussed this with the detectives yet," he said. "Because it has kept you from telling any lies. But the cops are going to hammer you both. The media will be merciless. There will be calls for you to step down, Senator. There will be allegations of a cover-up, probing into sordid sexual affairs. Simon's right. He cannot continue as your political adviser."

"My brother made a mistake and is guilty of using very poor judgment," said Henry Paxton. "But he is guilty of no *crime.*"

The senator stretched the word into three

syllables, his meaning unmistakable.

"And I hope my constituents will not hold my brother's affair of the heart against me."

I winced, because of course they would. The senator should have known about the affair and put a stop to it. And the question would fester: Was Simon Paxton taking the fall for his brother?

Henry Paxton ran his finger along a yellow legal pad. "When I was running for the U.S. Senate, my opponent was found to be embroiled in a sex scandal. There is no doubt that it contributed to my election. I remember, back then, promising the people of California that they could trust me to govern fairly and embrace a strong moral code."

He looked down. "I have betrayed that trust."

"I don't know if I'd go that far, Senator," said Faraday, moving into reassurance mode. "But these are going to be the toughest couple of days you've ever faced. We need to hang tight, ride the whirlwind, and hope for no further surprises."

Faraday put his elbows on Paxton's desk and clasped his hands. "I'm going to tell you something now, and please keep it in mind as the media submits you to the stations of the cross."

Both Paxtons nodded eagerly.

"The news cycle is so short today that everything is compressed. You can go from disgraced pariah to rehabilitated elder statesman in less time than ever. Some of these guys, they're already charting their comeback as they admit guilt. Look at Eliot Spitzer, he's writing for *Slate,* doing the round of talk shows. Nobody asks Bill Clinton about Monica's blue dress. The public is more forgiving today. I'm not saying we're there. I'm saying we've got a fighting chance."

But both the girls those politicians dallied with are still alive.

Faraday looked from one brother to the other. They gazed back, wary but game, like athletes after the coach's pep talk.

Faraday tapped the side of his head as if he'd just remembered something.

"Before I go any further, I need to confirm that you would, in fact, like us to represent Simon Paxton in this new matter."

"I certainly think we need to jump on this," Simon Paxton said.

Henry Paxton nodded, and the brothers turned to Lambert.

"That's fine," he said, "but I want a separate spokesperson for Simon."

"That goes without saying," said Faraday.

He got on his phone. "Lydia, could you please find Samantha for me. A doctor's appointment?" Faraday frowned. "Please call her mobile and tell her I need to see her in my office in exactly one hour."

He looked up.

"I am assigning Samantha George to speak to the press on your behalf," Faraday told Simon Paxton. "But she won't make a move without consulting Thomas Blair or me. We'll continue to supervise both cases."

"Maggie, two statements, please. One from Simon Paxton, admitting the affair and expressing remorse. The other from Senator Paxton. He learned about the affair only today. He is shocked and dismayed and has dismissed his brother as political adviser and banned him from the office until this is resolved. He's calling for an inquiry to determine whether any laws were violated."

My laptop was already out, my fingers moving across the keys. The Paxtons looked stunned at the speed with which Faraday was moving.

"I will do whatever it takes," the senator said, "and so will my brother."

"You'll both be asked for DNA samples," Faraday said. "They may want to swab the entire office."

Simon Paxton examined his hands and rotated them. I thought I saw a tremor cross his face. Slowly he nodded.

"Did the coroner say whether Emily had been sexually assaulted?" Simon asked.

"They are not releasing that information," said Faraday, "but they'll be looking for DNA. Maybe she had consensual sex with her killer."

"Dear God," said the senator.

"Has either of you ever been to her apartment?" Faraday asked.

"No," said the senator.

"Never," said his brother.

Faraday surveyed the room.

"The one question every reporter is going to ask is why. Why would you risk your career and your marriage for a roll in the hay with a girl younger than your niece?"

Simon Paxton looked at his hands again. It was unfortunate, seeing as how Emily Mortimer had been strangled.

"I don't know."

Faraday studied him, picking bits of tobacco off his lips.

"Is your marriage in trouble?" he asked hopefully. "Maybe you and your wife were living separate lives? It happens. People grow apart."

Simon seemed to consider, then dismiss

this idea. "No," he said at last. "I love my wife. And I'm sure that when I tell her she'll forgive this temporary . . . lapse."

Faraday looked at me, as if to get my opinion, but I looked away. I didn't know Simon Paxton or his wife.

"You seem awfully sure of that, Mr. Paxton," Faraday said softly.

"Political wives," said Bernstein. "You see it over and over, when these things hit. They're pros."

"Is that how it's going to be, Simon?" Faraday asked. "It's a powerful media image. A vote of confidence that says, he's my man and I'm standing by him and you should too. Our data shows it could be worth ten percentage points to your brother in the polls."

I marveled at Faraday's ability to reduce all human impulses and emotions — even marital infidelity — to raw statistics. It seemed monstrous.

Simon nodded. "She'll do it," he said, with savage confidence.

"She in L.A.?"

"Flew in this morning."

"She may want to have some Xanax handy. It's gonna be a command performance."

I considered that if Simon Paxton's wife

had half of Miranda's sangfroid, we'd be in good shape.

I was on the upstairs landing, carrying a bag of chips back to Anabelle's room when the doorbell rang.

Anabelle's mom, dressed in her tennis whites, opened the door to two policemen who held Luke by either arm. Luke was eighteen and had crashed his car drag racing on Mulholland. His eyes were dilated and he gave his mom a goofy grin.

Miranda Paxton ignored her son.

"Officers, I can't thank you enough for bringing him back. This is really above and beyond the call of duty and I'm ever so grateful."

She turned to Luke and her voice hardened. "Thank the officers, please, then go get yourself cleaned up."

When Luke disappeared, his mother said, "He broke up with his girlfriend last week and has been absolutely despondent. You probably saved his life by bringing him home, officers. And I can assure you that this will never happen again. We're going to take away the car keys and put him in a twelve-step program. Can I invite you inside for a lemonade? It's so muggy outside. I think I'm going to have something stronger. Would you care to join me?"

The officers declined politely and left. When she closed the door behind them, Miranda Paxton didn't go see how her son was doing. She picked up her racket and strolled back into the twilight to finish her game.

"Do you have a problem with drugs or alcohol?" Faraday was asking Simon Paxton.

A hesitation. Then the senator's brother replied, "No."

"How about prescription pills? People can get addicted before they even know it."

Simon shook his head.

"Pity."

Faraday looked around the room. "That knocks out rehab. It's a cliché by now, but it's still a valid excuse. You were high, drunk, you were non compos mentis. Oh, well. Maggie, let's see Simon's statement."

I handed over my laptop and Faraday read it to himself, nodding.

"Yup. It's all here. And most important," Faraday said, reading aloud: " 'Senator Paxton was unaware of my infidelity until I informed him of it earlier today.' "

"Put in that I didn't kill her," Simon Paxton said hoarsely.

"Unnecessary," Faraday said. "We say you're cooperating fully with the police. That's enough."

"I said put it in."

"If that's what he wants, let's just do it," said the senator.

Faraday slid the laptop back and I wrote: "I would like to make it clear that I am innocent of Emily Mortimer's murder."

When I read it aloud, Faraday made a face. "It sounds Nixonesque. He'd like to make it perfectly clear, yadda yadda. Protesting too much."

"Can't you find some other way to say it?" Simon Paxton asked in a pained voice.

"We'll try. Maggie, please draft the senator's statement now, unless he'd like to write it himself." Pause. "No? All right. Senator, while she does that, could you please draw up a list of powerful people who support you or owe you a favor. Your pastor. Your former commanding officer, who's hopefully risen to the rank of general by now. And some congressional colleagues on —"

"What for?" Simon Paxton asked suspiciously. "This is my scandal, not his."

"Your brother enjoys broad bipartisan support," said Faraday. "So we need a Republican as well as a Democrat who'll speak to the senator's honesty and integrity. While he lies low, these people are going to be his surrogates, out there in force, testifying publicly about his character."

The senator swallowed hard. "I was hoping it wouldn't come to that."

"We need to be ready."

The brothers conferred, wrote down some names, and passed them to Faraday.

"I'd like them to do the interview in my office," Harvey Lambert said. "A neutral place."

"Right," said Faraday. "Simon, with your wife at your side, you man up and admit your mistake. You express remorse. Meanwhile, we release both statements and have Henry's political allies ready. The way this breaks is all-important, and the more control we can maintain, the better position we're in. The *Post* will spin it their own way but we'll preempt them. Senator, you will get on the phone with the *New York Times,* the *Wall Street Journal,* and the *Los Angeles Times.* Here are your talking points: You have volunteered to speak to them because you want transparency and openness. You'd like to come clean about your brother. You're very sorry for the Mortimers' loss. And . . . you're cooperating fully with the police."

10

"You really need to cultivate your poker face," Faraday said as we drove back to the Blair Building.

Sick to my stomach was more like it. I plucked at the leather piping upholstery of his Mercedes 450SL.

"Maybe someone who doesn't know the family would do a better job," I said. "I worry that my emotions are clouding my judgment."

"Why, Maggie? You're a natural."

"Except for my poker face." I shook my head. "I used to idolize Henry. The whole family. I grew up with them. When I met Anabelle, my dad had just died and things were bad. I was probably clinically depressed. The Paxtons helped me through all that. I'm here today in large part because they believed in me."

"Then this is a rare opportunity to thank them," Faraday said, "and show them how much they meant to you. It's your turn to believe in Henry."

"If I'm doing such a fine job, why did you send Fletch to shadow me this afternoon? I almost gave the game away."

"Fletch said you kept your cool." Faraday hesitated. "But it doesn't hurt to have backup when we don't know what we were dealing with."

"The whole thing is giving me panic attacks."

"I don't want you to have a nervous breakdown, but I do need you. You provide a link to the family that no one else in the office can. A sense of trust and confidence. Here's what I'll do. I'll give you a break tomorrow, let you work on a different case. But I still need you on Paxton, Maggie Silver. You're my right-hand man."

"What's a body man?" I asked, remembering.

"Not what you think." Faraday shot me a grin. "It's an assistant who accompanies a politician when he travels. He's on call twenty-four/seven, and he makes sure his boss gets to the next gig on time, takes his meds, makes his plane. A body man drives the car, upgrades the hotel room, and orders the takeout. He collects all the gifts and letters handed to his boss and fends off the groupies. And he's got a Sharpie ready for autograph seekers."

"Politicians have groupies?"

"Why not? They're celebrities like anyone else. They're in *People* magazine and on TV."

"Speaking of which, Sentier is waiting to find out when he can interview the senator," I said.

"We're going to stall him until ten p.m."

"Why?"

"Because then it will be one a.m. on the East Coast and everyone'll be asleep."

"They'll put it on the web," I pointed out.

"But it won't break in a big way until morning. It buys us time."

Back at the office, I called home and asked Mom to TiVo *CSI*.

For once, I was grateful for my small, uncomplicated family. If you didn't count alcoholism, premature death, a latchkey childhood, cancer, and divorce.

"I thought you were Earlyn," Mom said. "She's bringing a widower over for dinner tonight. They met when she did that L.A. River cleanup last month."

"Isn't Earlyn afraid you'll steal him from her?"

"Don't be a wiseacre. She's bringing him

for me."

"Is this a date?"

"I don't know," said my mother, her voice suddenly shy and girlish.

Incredible! My own mother went on more dates than I.

"I'm making fried chicken," she went on. "Earlyn is bringing her potato salad. And don't start lecturing me, it's a vinaigrette dressing, not mayo."

"What's the widower bringing?"

"At our age, honey, all he needs to bring is himself."

"Don't sell yourself short, Mom."

"I'm kidding. Virgil's bringing dessert and wine. Or maybe a dessert wine. I can't remember."

"You should try my Aricept. Works wonders."

"Maggie! That's for old people with Alzheimer's whose brains have turned to Swiss cheese."

"So imagine how well it works on someone young and healthy."

"Aren't you a little old to be experimenting with drugs?"

"Experimenting is when you're seventeen. What I do is purely maintenance."

"You need to flush all those pills down the toilet."

I rolled my eyes and said, "And you need to stop sneaking cigarettes with Earlyn. You think I don't see lipstick traces on the butts? No one else around here wears Hot Coral."

"If you think I'd take even one puff after everything I've been through, you're crazy."

I could picture her biting her lip and crossing her fingers as she spoke. The earnest way she'd look at me. As if she almost believed it herself. But I kept quiet. Because cancer trumped everything.

"Besides," said Mom, "you're the one with a problem. Those pills."

"You're not the boss of me anymore, Mom. Sometimes I think you forget that." I hung up before I said something I'd regret.

Muttering under my breath, I typed Fred Sentier's name into Google.

He was twenty-eight, had grown up in Rhode Island and worked for the *Providence Journal* for two years before landing a job in the suburban hinterlands of the *Post*. From his stories, Fred Sentier enjoyed nailing those in power, which didn't bode well for Simon and Henry Paxton. I looked to see what he'd covered recently, but the stories had tapered off several months ago.

I fished around some more and pulled up a blog reference from DCInsider.com, listing a round of recent layoffs. And then I

200

was out of my seat and running down the hall, yelling, "Faraday, Faraday."

My boss shoved a file into his desk drawer.

"The *Washington Post* laid Fred Sentier off in June," I said.

Faraday's eyes shot to razor sharpness. "So who's he working for? What's his motivation? I don't like this."

"Maybe he landed at another paper?"

"In this economy? Not a chance."

Faraday's eyes went to the clock. It was seven thirty p.m. Then he buzzed Tyler and Fletch and Sam in and repeated what I'd learned.

"What if he's not writing a story?" said Tyler. "Maybe his severance ran out and he's thinking blackmail."

Everyone turned to me, and I assured them that Sentier hadn't asked for money.

"Still," said Faraday, "something doesn't smell right. I'm not convinced this weasel is selling the story to his old bosses at the *Post*. He could be up to anything. On the other hand, he could also get hit by a car on his way home."

Faraday's eyes glinted evilly and a sudden chill went up my spine.

He sighed. "But somehow I doubt we'll have such luck."

His computer beeped and he leaned forward to read the message.

"Simon Paxton's wife is on board," he said with satisfaction. "Maggie, call that hack and tell him your boss wants to chat."

I looked at him with surprise. "You don't think I can handle it?"

"It'll look better coming from a higher-up. That's elementary psychology."

I dialed, explained, and handed the phone over. Faraday put it on speaker.

"Good evening, Mr. Sentier. I hope I haven't caught you at a bad time."

He winked at us.

"No," said Sentier. "I've been waiting for your call."

"Glad to hear it. You know I hate to interrupt you guys on deadline. Listen, I have good news. The senator *and* his brother and chief political adviser, Simon Paxton, have both agreed to talk to you. That's right."

He conveyed the details and Sentier immediately began to pump him, asking when the affair had started, whether the senator's wife knew, and if he'd planned to leave her for his aide.

"All of your questions will be answered," Faraday said.

"But I need to talk to him now," Sentier said urgently. "Ten o'clock is too late."

Faraday said, "You think we're going to

blab to the *New York Times* or C-SPAN? Hell, no. It's your story. You investigated this thing and found something everyone had missed. We respect that and we'd like to give you as much as we can. And that's why it's going to take a little time. Some new facts have come to light as a result of your investigation, and we're giving you first crack."

"Tell me about those things," Sentier said silkily.

"Soon enough, Mr. Sentier."

"Look, your girl promised that if I held the story, you'd leak me details on another case."

Faraday's hand went to his collar. He hooked in a finger and tugged at his necktie, loosening it.

"You sure do strike a hard bargain, Mr. Sentier." He paused. "May I call you Fred?"

"You can call me anything you want provided you keep up your end. Now give me something on this second case so I know you're for real."

"Do you ever watch the TV show *Dream Factory* on Thursdays? The one with Trent Holloway?" Faraday said.

"I know who he is."

"Good. We'll talk more tonight."

"I need details now, so I can prepare,"

Sentier said mulishly.

"You'll get them after the Paxton inter-view. You're already running us ragged, Fred. We'll see you at ten. Good-bye."

Faraday hung up, looking pleased.

At nine p.m., Faraday assembled us in his office for final instructions.

We'd just sat down when Fletch gave a strangled yelp and looked up, his eyes wide. At that moment, every line on Faraday's phone lit up.

"It's out," Fletch said. "And it's the lead story on the *National Enquirer*'s website. 'Senator's Love Tryst with Murdered Aide.' "

"Son of a bitch," said Faraday.

He swiveled to pull it up on his screen while the rest of us jumped up to read over Fletch's shoulder.

"U.S. Senator Henry Paxton shared a hotel room one night in May with his beautiful young aide Emily Mortimer, who was found strangled two days ago. Stanford Sentier, a veteran waiter at the Mission Inn of Riverside, said Mortimer opened the door to the senator's hotel room dressed only in a bathrobe and personally signed a hotel chit for a $120 bottle of champagne at 1:24 a.m. Sentier said he didn't realize the intimately clad girl in the senator's room in the middle of the night was the murder victim until he saw Mortimer's photo on TV."

"That scumbag," said Tyler. "He wanted to pump us one last time before it went live."

We read on.

"A spokeswoman said Senator Henry Paxton was meeting with LAPD detectives and would be unavailable for comment until this evening but promised the *Enquirer* an exclusive interview in which he would detail his romantic relationship with the murdered aide."

"The fuck he did," said Faraday, in a cold hard voice that unnerved me way more than his tirades.

"Wonder how much they paid them?" Tyler asked gloomily.

"More than a waiter earns in a year," said Faraday.

For about ten seconds, we were silent, fortifying ourselves for the onslaught. The phones blinked like NASA Mission Control. Computers and BlackBerries warbled and trilled like a bushful of birds. Three secretaries appeared at the door, holding messages and looking concerned.

Faraday ignored them all.

"Tyler, please get me Joe Gunderson of the *New York Times* L.A. Bureau," he said, "if he's not holding already. Tell him he's got an exclusive interview with Simon and Henry Paxton tonight at ten."

Faraday's voice assumed the professorial tone I knew so well. "The *New York Times* always gets first crack," he said. "Even in the Internet Age, the *Times* still sets the political agenda and the TV news shows follow their lead."

A glazed, serene look beamed out of his eyes now, and I thought the stress might have finally pushed my boss over the edge.

"Fred Sentier and the *Enquirer* have made a big mistake," he continued. "They jumped the proverbial gun and got their facts wrong. This is going to backfire and make them even less credible than usual. It's also going to make every news outlet in the country leery of going with a Paxton story that hasn't been vetted and confirmed by multiple sources.

"Maggie, call Lambert and tell him there's been a change of plans and Mr. Sentier is a dangerous loose cannon who's not allowed into the building. We'll fax over a photo. Sam, I want you to go through that piece-of-shit article with a microscope and write a point-by-point rebuttal for Lambert. And get me a list of every Sentier story where the *Post* ran a correction, amplification, or retraction. Maggie, once we get this under control, I want to you write an affidavit describing how he misrepresented himself and pulled a gun on you. We are going to submit this joker to the Wheel of Pain. Not even the *Enquirer* is going to hire him after we're through. Fletch, did your associate get photos of Sentier brandishing his gun?"

Fletch nodded.

I could only sit there in amazement. They might have sent me out to Pershing Square like a canary in a coal mine, but they'd reverse-engineered the entire thing, anticipating everything that might go wrong.

I swallowed. "So what are we going to tell the *New York Times*?"

Faraday's face split into a wolfish grin and he hooked his thumbs into his suspenders.

"The Paxton boys are going to tell them the truth."

11

The law offices of Lambert, Truesdale, Black & McGilvary were in Century City, on land that had once housed a Hollywood movie studio. Lambert's thirty-seventh-floor office overlooked the Century Plaza Hotel, a midcentury monument to concrete that preservationists wanted to declare a city landmark.

By nine forty-five, I sat in a large conference room with Tyler and the senator's people, while Fletch set up lights and fiddled with his video camera.

Saunders had his laptop out, working. Suddenly, he gave a loud "ha."

"What?" said Bernstein, hurrying over.

"Look at this. The senator's gained 20,005 new Twitter followers since this thing broke yesterday. And 9,579 more since the *Enquirer* story went live. That's fantastic, even if half of them turn out to be journalists."

"It's about getting his name out there,"

Bernstein said sagely. "Brand recognition."

"You'll get one hundred thousand more after the *New York Times* story breaks," I said. "Be giving Ashton Kutcher a run for his money soon."

"Who?" said Bernstein.

"That actor married to Demi Moore. He's the Twitter gold standard, with two million followers."

Faraday looked on, arms crossed, foot tapping. "If you all are finished gossiping, perhaps you could listen up.

"As soon as the *New York Times* interview is done," he said, "we're throwing the entire interview up on SupportSenatorPaxton .com."

Paxton's men looked puzzled.

"That's a new one on me," I admitted.

"It was launched earlier today by a group of 'concerned citizens,' " Faraday said, winking. "The senator and his brother need to be able to speak directly to the public, no filters. What you read in the papers and see on TV is a highly compressed and edited product. Sentences can be spliced together to create new meanings. Questions can be dubbed in afterward to make the subject seem shifty or evasive. You lose context. You lose control. And *we don't like that.*"

"Many Americans no longer see the press

as a good thing," Tyler said, "but as a bully with a skewed agenda that needs a public thrashing."

"You should know," I said. "You used to be one."

"Tyler was a very good journalist," Faraday said, "which makes him an even better crisis consultant. It's like prosecutors who switch to criminal defense. They understand the other side."

Changing the topic, he asked, "Maggie, you have those quotes?"

I handed him a press release with statements from religious and political leaders, praising Senator Henry Paxton's visionary leadership and integrity. I'd been on the phone half the evening tracking them down.

The phone buzzed. It was security. The *New York Times* reporter was on his way up with a videographer. Paxton's lawyer walked in and sat down.

It was showtime.

Faraday greeted Joe Gunderson warmly, asking about his wife and new baby. Tall, lean, and bespectacled, with a receding hairline and a neatly trimmed beard, Gunderson wore formal black-tie attire and had clearly been summoned away from another event. He answered politely while fending off Faraday's overtures of friendship.

"I want you to look around and see how many other journalists I invited," Faraday said, segueing smoothly into business. "That's right." He beamed. "You're getting a world exclusive. And that's because I know you and I trust you to tell the truth, and because you work for the best damn paper, not only in America, but in the entire world. The *New York Times* is the paper of record and we wanted to go right to the top to explain things and debunk that *Enquirer* hit piece as a pack of lies."

Joe Gunderson adjusted his bullshit filter. But he also looked pleased. Praise for his paper meant reflected glory for him.

"The story plus video of tonight's interview will go up on the *Times*' website tonight," he said.

"The entire video?" Faraday said in mock surprise.

"They edit it down."

"I see." Faraday caught my eye.

I went to get Simon Paxton and his wife, who were waiting in another room. Simon's wife, Sally, was a pretty woman with shoulder-length blond hair and good skin, but her face had a glazed, emptied-out look.

Gunderson looked them over and his face fell.

"What's this?" he said, suspicious. "The

211

deal was a sit-down with the senator."

"The senator's brother and political adviser, Simon Paxton, has something to say first."

The interview began.

Simon Paxton started out stiff but got smoother as it went on. Off to the side, Samantha George looked relieved. She'd coached him for two hours, shooting videotape so they could work on inflection and facial expression.

Now Simon even choked up as he admitted the affair on camera, glancing at his wife, whose mouth gave a sorrowful twitch. He and his wife loved each other and were entering counseling to repair this rift in their marriage. He declined to answer speculative questions, citing his lawyer's advice, and asked that the affair be treated as a private matter.

When the senator strolled in for his inquisition, he appeared focused and alert, like he'd spent the afternoon at a mental spa.

"Looking good," I whispered to Bernstein.

"It's some ninja skill he's got," the senator's man muttered. "When everyone on the plane wakes up with rumpled clothes and their hair standing up, his suit is immaculate and he's perfectly groomed. I've seen him at Indian reservations in the desert where

212

it's 125 degrees and everyone's coated in sweat and dust. He looks like he's walking around some exclusive country club . . . one that allows women, Catholics, and people of color, of course."

Senator Paxton conveyed such a sympathetic mixture of bewilderment, sorrow, and outrage that even I felt like misting up. When it was over, he shook Gunderson's hand and told the reporter he followed his byline in the *Times* and found his stories incisive and well written.

12

Twenty minutes later, I sat with Faraday, the Paxton brothers, and Harvey Lambert. Sally Paxton had locked herself in the bathroom, where nose-blowing sounds could be heard.

"I think it went well," Faraday said.

Simon Paxton rubbed his eyes. "We'll know when the story goes up."

"The *National Enquirer,* on the other hand, is going to be out for blood. They will stake out your houses, your office, your hangouts. They may try to bribe your housekeeper, your gardener, your wives' hairdressers. They will comb public records, including the quarterly expense reports you file with the federal government. They will look for anything to use against you. You cannot give them any ammunition. Everything you do has got to be strictly aboveboard."

"That goes without saying," the senator said.

"Well, I'm saying it."

Faraday looked around belligerently.

"Maggie," he said, startling me. "Let's see that statement you just drafted."

He read it, then recapped it to the room.

Senator Paxton was calling for an official investigation after his brother Simon had confirmed the relationship with Mortimer. The senator was dismayed and concerned. He'd banned Simon Paxton from his office and dropped him as an adviser. Simon had never been on staff. The *Enquirer* story was false and the senator was demanding an immediate retraction. Simon and his wife would seek couples' counseling.

"Both interviews with the *New York Times* can be viewed in their entirety at Support SenatorPaxton.com," Faraday said, his voice growing hearty. "The senator and his brother urge all interested parties to watch it and decide for themselves. Senator Paxton and Simon Paxton are cooperating fully with the police in the investigation into Mortimer's death and ask for privacy during this difficult time."

I saw nods from around the table. But Faraday raised his head, frowning.

"What is this 'privacy' bullshit? There's nothing private about it. Take that line out."

"Sorry," I said.

Faraday wanted the Paxton brothers to hammer home the same points to the national media in the morning. He needed them available for at least two hours.

"There's something I wanted to run past you," my boss said. "It's a little unorthodox, but it could bring us some positive coverage. The setup goes like this:

"Senator, early tomorrow morning, you find yourself driving along Mulholland, just north of Coldwater. Maybe you went up there to clear your head after all that's happened. A stranded motorist flags you down and you give him a ride to the nearest gas station. At some point he realizes his Good Samaritan is none other than U.S. Senator Paxton, his elected representative. He's blown away. He's so grateful he notifies the media. They ask us to corroborate and after checking with you, we confirm it."

A look of distaste crept across Henry Paxton's face.

Simon looked intrigued.

"You want us to cruise up and down the canyons looking for a stranded motorist to rescue?" he said.

"That could take awhile," Lambert pointed out. "And why wouldn't the motorist call nine one one?"

Faraday leaned forward.

"Because his cell phone ran out of juice."

"You're gonna plant the guy," Simon Paxton said hoarsely.

The senator looked like he'd swallowed a scorpion.

"Look," said Faraday. "This is Hollywood, and it's all theater."

"There are a dozen ways this could go wrong," Harvey Lambert said.

Faraday leaned back. "We've got reliable people." He grinned. "Who's more likely to have their piece-a-crap car break down than an unemployed actor?"

"No," said the senator.

"Henry," said his brother, "let's talk about this."

"Or how about this," Faraday offered. "You're having lunch on the Malibu pier when a suicidal man jumps off. He can't swim. He's drowning. You dive in and save him."

"Absolutely not," snapped the senator.

"Let's revisit this in a few days," Simon Paxton said, shooting Faraday a look of apology.

I regarded my boss with new wariness. *If he was willing to stage such a spectacle, what else would he do?*

The Paxton entourage left. Faraday gathered his files. I knew he was headed back to the office to brief Thomas Blair. It was a nightly ritual, this pilgrimage up to the twentieth floor. Faraday tried to hide it, but we all knew it made him nervous and jumpy. Now he rustled papers with an annoyed air.

"Samantha will monitor the political blogs all night and brief me if anything else breaks. Keep your phones on. I want everyone in the office by five thirty. Samantha, come here, please."

Samantha walked over, sipping from a mug of steaming coffee. Faraday reached into his briefcase and pulled out a small amber container with a white plastic top.

"Give me your hand."

He tapped something into her palm. "Don't take more than one every four hours."

Samantha left.

"None for the rest of you. Tomorrow's going to be brutal and you need to sleep. In the morning, Simon Paxton is going to sit down with the LAPD and get a few things off his chest."

I rode back to the office with Fletch, who told me that a Blair psychologist would play the tape back in slo-mo, analyzing the senator and Simon Paxton's faces and movements for sincerity and honesty. Then they'd coach the two on their next appearances.

"I thought both of them maintained good eye contact," I said.

"Some of it is almost subliminal," Fletch said. "Looking to the right when you speak can suggest deception. A mouth tilted to one side can signal contempt. Some guilty people nod their head, almost imperceptibly as they deny involvement."

"I bet none of that works with true sociopaths," I said.

Fletch was silent.

I thought about how Faraday had warned the Paxtons that their bushes would be crawling with reporters and photographers from the *National Enquirer.* Reporters would also fan out to Valencia.

"I'm glad Faraday sewed up Emily's parents," I said to Fletch. "And the media can't exactly camp out at Emily's apartment and shout questions each time she comes or goes. In some perverse way, the senator and his brother might be in a lot more trouble if Emily were still alive."

"If she were alive, there would be no story," said Fletch.

Because Emily would have kept her mouth shut about the affair.

But what if Emily had gotten tired of keeping

her mouth shut? What if she'd threatened to go public, and someone had decided to get rid of her instead? And now it had backfired, all because of some elderly waiter out in Riverside County?

The thought made my skin crawl.

"Fletch," I said. "You know how Faraday tells us not to discuss sensitive matters over the phone or online?"

"Yeah."

"Does Blair eavesdrop electronically on us at work? Sometimes I get the creepiest feeling."

"If they do, they're perfectly entitled. The law says anything you do on company time is fair game. So I wouldn't browse, say, perfume sites for an hour or anything."

I flushed with alarm. So it was true.

Fletch gave me a sly look. "You got something to hide?"

The previous week, I'd called Mom from work to talk about reports and scheme about how we'd spend my next bonus. That would tell them how desperate I was and give them leverage against me. It made me vulnerable.

"What exactly do you do, Fletch?"

"I'm just a tech guy."

"Earlyn and I are out back, hon," Mom

called from the porch when I let myself in after midnight. "And there's fresh lemonade."

Through the picture window, I saw Earlyn in the wicker chair, dressed in her usual overalls. Mom sat hunched on the porch swing, wearing a scoop-neck shirt and pedal pushers. A scarf held her hair back, which had grown in curly as a lamb's after the chemo.

I poured a glass of lemonade, piled my plate with fried chicken, and joined them. Below us stretched L.A., blinking in jeweled lights. The air was acrid and smoky from fires burning out of control in the Angeles National Forest. But that didn't disguise the cigarettes that Mom and Earlyn had hastily put out.

I'd asked them not to smoke in the house, but the back porch was just as bad because the odor clung to the cushions and eaves and seeped in through my bedroom window. So they acted like guilty teenagers and stubbed them out when they heard my car approach.

Like I can't smell it.

Maybe that's why I wore so much perfume these days.

Mom denied she smokes, but I found the telltale butts when I was sweeping up the fine white ash from the fires. You'd think that having survived cancer, she'd know better. You'd also think that Earlyn — a responsible adult — wouldn't encourage her. Instead, they were engaged in a conspiracy to put one over on me, the dutiful daughter. Sometimes I wondered who the mom was. There were times when I wanted to stick them in separate rooms and give them a time-out.

It outraged me to be put in the position of the enforcer, the nagger, the beggar. Please, Mom, I wanted to say, don't kill yourself. But the only words that came out of my mouth lately were angry, scolding ones. So I changed the subject.

"Where's Virgil the Widower?"

"He went home early."

"Scratch Virgil the Widower," I said, starting my second piece of chicken. It was bad to eat so much late at night, but I was starved and it was delicious.

Earlyn was studying a brochure for an Elderhostel trip to Catalina Island that Mom had signed up for. She'd be gone two whole days and I felt the delirious anticipation of an adolescent left alone for the weekend who planned a blow-out party.

But I only looked forward to having my house to myself.

"Maybe you'll meet a rugged outdoors type on your trip, Olivia," Earlyn said. She turned to me. "Virgil the Widower showed up with a bottle of cabernet for us and a gallon of rum for him. He put a good dent in it too. I wanted to call him a cab, but he insisted he was fine to drive."

My mother reached for a plate of figs and offered them to me. "Fresh from Earlyn's tree."

They were the purple ones, creamy and sweet as honey, with red flesh inside. I ate three.

"Enjoy, because that's the last of them. Damn squirrels. You know how many apricots I got this year? Twelve. That's not enough for one cobbler."

Mom took a sip of lemonade. "Earlyn, I'm dead tired of you bitching and moaning about those squirrels. I'm buying you a BB gun for your birthday."

"Mom!" I said, almost spitting out my lemonade.

"On second thought, let's make it an air-pellet gun like the kids have."

"I've thought of using my hunting rifle on them," Earlyn said.

"Maybe you should get a cat," I suggested.

"Can't." Earlyn sucked her teeth. "Coyotes would carry it off. I'll never forget when

I went walking early one morning and a coyote ran past with a white cat in its mouth."

"What did you do?" Mom asked.

"I ran after it, hollering for it to let go."

"Did it?"

"Yes, it did, Olivia. Dropped that cat right onto the sidewalk. It took off like greased lightning. Guess it used up a couple of its lives that day."

"What about a Maine coon cat?" I said. "I saw one at a client's house once. They weigh twenty or twenty-five pounds, and I bet a couple of them can take on a large dog."

"Wonder how often those turn up at the pound?" Earlyn said. "But I've got to do something. Did I tell you how many apricots I got this year?"

Mom fluttered her eyes at me.

"Oh, there I go, repeating myself. Time for bed," said Earlyn. "Maggie, hon, would you come over with me a minute. I want to show you something."

Surprised, I follow her down the porch stairs and across the backyard. We climbed through the hole into Earlyn's yard.

Earlyn whispered, "Maggie, I know you're upset about the cigarettes, but I want to explain."

I crossed my arms. "Okay."

Earlyn sighed deeply. "Your mother smokes maybe one or two ciggies a day and it's something that gives her great pleasure. She's going through a very hard time right now, she'll tell you about it. And if it calms her nerves or gives her comfort, you can't get mad at her. She's an adult. She has the right to make those choices."

"But it's going to kill her."

"There's a lot of things that could kill her before lung cancer," said Earlyn. "You need to lay off."

I wanted to beat my arms against the fence and howl that she didn't understand, it was my mother, the only family I had left in the world, and I didn't want her to die, and at that moment, I realized that my anger toward Mom wasn't about her at all. It was about me and my fear. That might seem obvious, but to me it was a revelation.

"I promise to ease off," I told Earlyn. "But I won't pretend I approve."

"What did Earlyn want to show you?" Mom asked when I returned.

"Her varmint gun," I said. "I made her promise to put it away."

Then, to distract her, I told her a little about the Paxton case.

"Well, I'll be darned. I voted for him last

225

election."

"I didn't even realize he'd gone into politics," I said. "After Anabelle and I lost touch, I tried to forget about the whole family. But I was doing the math and he must have run for Senate the year Steve and I were in England for his job."

Mom's voice grew sharp. "I never did like that Paxton girl. She was a bad influence on you."

"Mom! You met her only once, at graduation, and we weren't even friends by then. So you have no idea what you're talking about."

I grabbed a bottle I'd carried out from the bedroom.

"What have you got there?" Mom said in an attempt at reconciliation.

"Dune by Christian Dior. Luca Turin, who wrote a fragrance guide, calls it 'the bleakest beauty in all perfumery.' Here, try."

She sniffed the bottle and wrinkled her nose. "It's bleak, all right." She settled back in her chair. "I'll stick with my Charlie. Revlon makes some fine perfumes."

I dabbed on Dune. Immediately, I was transported to a smoky Bedouin campfire in the North African desert. Our camel caravan was trekking to the bazaar, loaded with bags of myrrh and frankincense, cloves, honey, salt, and lemon oil. I love how scent takes me on a magic carpet ride.

"Steve used to buy you all those perfumes," Mom said.

I often think she misses my ex-husband more than I do. What she means is that there's no man to buy me presents anymore. But I'm a liberated woman. I can buy my own damn perfume.

"I was looking online," I said, "and there's a group of perfumistas that meets in L.A. to sniff and swap."

"I doubt you'll meet anyone eligible there."

"Straight men like fragrance too," I said. "What about all those French perfumers? Guerlain, Houbigant, Ernest Beaux of Chanel. They not only had wives and families, they had mistresses too."

"Oh, pshaw," said Mom. "The French are different. And we don't live in Paris."

"Grasse," I said. "That's the capital of perfume. Where they grow the flowers."

I pulled out some Craigslist apartment rentals that I printed out at work. I'd also gotten lists of government-subsidized senior housing in West Hollywood, Fairfax, and Pasadena. Mom qualifies because her pension is so minuscule. The Pasadena apartments are located in the historic Hotel

Green downtown, walking distance to every-thing.

"I've circled a dozen places that look promising. We can check them out together and I'll help fill out the forms."

Mom folded her arms over her chest and stared stubbornly ahead. "My own daughter wants to kick me out. Kick me to the curb and leave me homeless."

Exasperation and anger began a slow boil inside me.

"Mom, the deal was that you'd move in with me so I could take care of you during chemo. That was last year. Look at you. You're healthy as a horse now. Why do you want to live with me? We fight all the time."

"Why, darling girl? Because I love you."

I groaned. "Oh, Mom, I love you too. But I want my space. My privacy."

"Why? So you can bring men home and sleep with them?"

"Mom!"

"Maybe I'll move in with Earlyn. How would you like that?"

Oh, no! Then she'd be next door, peeking out her windows, climbing through the hole in the fence. Nothing would change.

I nodded judiciously, pretending to think it over. "You could do that."

"She's asked me, you know."

"Wouldn't you rather have your own place?" I wheedled. "Like before?"

"Well, I certainly don't want my entire pension going to rent."

"Look, I'm glad I was able to cook and clean and run errands and offer moral support when you were sick. But this was never meant to be a permanent arrangement. You're fine now."

It was at this moment that my mother revealed what she didn't tell me on the phone yesterday. The doctors wanted a PET scan. Maybe even a biopsy. There were concerns.

"I'm sure everything will be all right," Mom said, hunching, and suddenly she was a shrunken little girl with crow's-feet, wrinkles, and thinning hair.

She wouldn't look me in the eye and I knew it was because she was scared and embarrassed and didn't want to beg.

"Oh, Mom." I put my arms around her.

And for a while we just sat there like that. I was filled with two kinds of horror. Because part of me thought, oh no, what if the cancer's come back? What will her odds be this time? What if she dies?

And shoot me now, but another, more selfish part of me throbbed with despair, because now I'd never get my place back or have any solitude or peace. Because even when she was sick, Mom still tried to mastermind my life. And with that, a spark of resentment kindled. I wished my father were still alive. I wished I had siblings to share the burden. I wished everything didn't always fall to me.

Mom watched me closely. "Earlyn will take me in," she repeated.

"You're going to stay right here. You're my mother and I'll take care of you."

"Really?" she said in that breathless, hopeful voice.

On one condition: You have to promise to stop smoking.

I thought this, but I didn't say it because I remembered Earlyn's admonition.

"How big is the lump?" I asked.

"Smaller than a pea. I didn't even notice until the doctor showed me." She took my hand and moved it under her arm. I thought I felt something.

"How soon can they schedule the PET scan?"

"Early next week."

"We'll get through this, Mom."

I hugged her tight. Her shoulders were bony, poking into me. I welcomed this mortification of my flesh.

With cool, dry fingers, she caressed my temple.

Sometimes I wished we could communicate like this all the time. Without words. Then we'd never fight and say mean things and hurt each other.

The wind gusted, blowing ash. It settled on my tightly closed lashes, then rolled down my cheeks in gritty wetness.

And then I understood: I was crying.

13

By six the following morning, I was at my desk, eating a blueberry muffin and rereading the *New York Times* story when the phone rang for what seemed like the hundredth time but was probably only the eighty-seventh.

It was *USA Today.*

"Senator Paxton and his brother are unavailable at the moment," I said, "but we'll be happy to e-mail you a statement they made late last night. And we urge you to visit www.SupportSenatorPaxton.com to see the entire interview with the *New York Times* last night."

I slurped some coffee to wash down the muffin crumbs.

"The *Times* story uses selective quotes that we believe create misconceptions about the case. Senator Paxton put the unabridged interview online so people can decide for themselves, no filters or manipulation."

As I spoke, I typed the reporter's contact information onto my log. Then I e-mailed him our press release, including my contacts.

Faraday was finishing up with MSNBC.

"I've got CNN on line one and *Extra!* on line two," Tyler called out.

I took another call, watching Faraday move around his office, a wire attached to his ear. He seemed calm and intensely focused. A liter of water and a bottle of vitamins stood atop his computer and he sipped coffee from a gigantic cup that said, "I don't get ulcers, I *give* them."

Around noon, the calls slowed to a manageable level.

Faraday popped his head out. "Maggie, Tyler, come in here."

"He looks almost happy," I said as we walked in.

"He likes mixing it up with the bigfaces," said Tyler.

Faraday looked insulted. "It's not about status, it's about the fight. I never feel more alive than when I'm juggling three or four big scandals. It stimulates the creative juices. Do you know how many interview requests I've got here?"

He held up a thick stack.

"Everyone from Diane Sawyer to Leno to

the *Financial Times* of London."

"What's the next step?" I said.

"Tyler, did you get with the LAPD?"

He nodded.

"Do the cops consider either of the Paxtons suspects?"

"They, um, wouldn't say."

"But you asked and they declined to use the word 'suspect'?" Faraday asked testily.

"Correct."

"So you say that. Quote the officer. And send it out immediately."

Faraday gave a ghoulish smile. "We need to feed the beast."

"Will we sit in on the LAPD interviews?" I asked.

My boss shook his head. "The cops don't want us there. Plus it would look weird."

"What about Lambert?"

"Lambert and I will coach Henry and Simon Paxton, but I've recommended they go alone. They have nothing to hide. This is purely an information-gathering meeting. You just heard Tyler. The LAPD does not consider either of the Paxtons a suspect in Emily Mortimer's murder."

He gave us his Stare of Steel, daring us to disagree.

"I've got something else," said Tyler, proudly sliding a copy of Emily Mortimer's preliminary autopsy report onto Faraday's desk. It was stamped confidential.

No one asked how he'd gotten it. Instead, we crowded around like vultures.

Death had occurred by strangulation. There was no indication of sexual assault. Emily had eaten Mexican food for dinner. There was trace alcohol in her blood but she wasn't drunk. Tests also showed the presence of Percocet, a synthetic opiate and controlled substance.

"That's what police found in her bedroom drawer," I said.

"Nice job," Faraday said. It was his highest praise. "I can use this."

"But they also found pill residue in her mouth," Tyler said, reading on.

"Do they think she took one right before she was killed?" I asked.

"Maybe someone dropped it in postmortem and it didn't dissolve all the way," said Tyler.

"The coroner will run tests to see if hair follicles show traces of earlier drug use. But that takes awhile."

Fletch was surfing online, as usual. Now he gave a yelp.

"Borez Milton has a crime scene photo of Emily Mortimer up on his website."

We crowded around. The photo was

blotchy, the girl's face puffy and discolored, her eyes popped out, her tongue purple. It brought home to me that this case, at its most basic, was about a young girl who'd been murdered. And there was no way to spin that.

"If everyone has satisfied their prurient curiosity, let's get back to business," said Faraday.

"Just one more thing," said Fletch, peering at his screen. "Looks like the LAPD has launched an internal investigation into how the photo got leaked. They're going to look into the autopsy report too if you're not careful how it leaks."

"Things are getting nasty," said Tyler.

"You say that like it's a bad thing," said Fletch.

"Back to work, everyone," Faraday said loudly, but when I rose with the others, he told me to stick around.

"Have you called Paxton's daughter yet?"

What, between one a.m. and six a.m.?

I grimaced. "It's been a little busy."

"Maybe you can see her this afternoon."

"This feels creepy, Faraday. What exactly am I supposed to find out?"

"It's Blair's idea, I'm just passing it on. Why don't you give her a try now."

I pulled the number out of my pocket and dialed.

A generic recording came on, asking me to leave a message.

"Hello. This is, um . . . Hi, Anabelle, this is Maggie Silver." I bit my tongue. "Maggie *Weinstock* Silver . . ."

Remember me?

No, that was too corny.

"Your old high school chum. And I don't know if Henry, um, Senator Paxton, told you, but my firm is doing some work for him. Some PR work." I winced. "And he gave me your number. Said I should look you up. And I thought, you know, it *has* been way too long. So here I am . . ."

I stopped, banished the fake chipper tone from my voice.

"And I'd . . . I'd love to see you, Anabelle, or at least chat with you, when you've got a bit of time. That would be lovely. After all these years. So, um. Just give me a call at your convenience."

The awkwardness had left my voice by the time I left my number on Anabelle's machine, replaced by a rush of real emotion. Still, she was going to wonder what kind of dolt was representing her father.

I hung up, my cheeks flushed and hot.

"See, that wasn't so bad," Faraday said,

beaming. "Now, how about putting in a few hours on the Holloway case."

He tossed me a file.

"I had Tricia run out to Malibu to pick up the documents you requested on the au pair. Our girl is Marie Connor. Twenty-three years old. Born in Limerick, Ireland. She signed the standard confidentiality agreement when the Holloways hired her so that's strike one against her.

"Second, the wife found texts she'd sent last year when the Holloways gave her time off and paid for a ticket to Ireland so she could visit her dying mom."

I pulled one out. *Boots, I'm really sorry to leave you in the lurch, you guys are the best and kindest bosses and I'm really thankful for all you've done over the years.*

I looked up. "Exhibit A for the defense, perhaps?"

Faraday grunted.

Next up was a list of the stolen Holloway jewelry, estimated to be worth $150,000. Most of it was still missing. But the cleaning lady had found a ruby ring hidden under a floorboard in Marie's old bedroom.

"Think the kids were playing hide-and-seek?" I said dryly.

"Not a chance, boiled ants."

Shuffling the deck now brought up two

reference letters from Marie's former employers in Limerick. Both praised her as patient, good-natured, and trustworthy. She'd completed a year of nursing classes at the local uni and knew CPR and first aid. She had a way of making scrapes, bruises, and sore throats disappear. She cooked, read to the children, and was an enthusiastic player of board games.

I cocked my head at Faraday. "I want to hire her myself after reading this. And I don't even have kids."

"Uh-huh."

"Too good to be true?"

Faraday shrugged. "The agency says it vets them carefully."

His BlackBerry beeped. He glanced down. "So look into it. And close the door on your way out, I've got *France-Soir* on the line about the Paxton case." He smirked. "The French have the right attitude about affairs of the heart."

But the French also had Georges Simenon, I thought as I slipped out. Simenon was a writer of classic, mid-twentieth-century detective fiction whose dogged Paris police inspector understood how affairs of the heart could turn — given the right mix of motive and circumstance — to affairs of blood.

There are only a handful of motives for murder, after all, and they've been around since the ancient Greek morality plays: money, power, love, revenge.

Which one had claimed Emily Mortimer?

Back in my office, I looked up the telephone code for Limerick. Then I dialed directory information and got numbers for Marie Connor's references.

Mrs. Patricia Highgate didn't answer. The number for Mrs. Elizabeth Burns had been disconnected.

I called the Irish operator back and asked for any Elizabeth Burns in nearby towns. I got one, but she'd never heard of Marie Connor. Had I perhaps confused her with Bethany Burns, her sister-in-law, who had hired an au pair briefly the year before?

I dutifully took down the number and left a message, asking Bethany Burns to call me collect.

The phone rang.

"Did you just call me?" demanded a young woman with a lilting accent.

"Are you Mrs. Patricia Highgate?" I asked. "Or Mrs. Bethany Burns?"

"What'd you say?"

In the background, I heard canned music, tinkling glasses, the roar of a . . . pub?

I repeated the question.

"Oh yer," said the woman, "that's me. Highgate. Who's calling?"

I explained that I was considering hiring Marie Connor to care for my children.

"All the way from Los An-ga-leeze," the young woman whispered to someone. "It's about Marie."

I heard giggles. Then Mrs. Highgate said, "Marie was the finest nanny I ever had. My children loved her. I cried when she told me she was leaving for America."

"Was there ever any hint of improper behavior? Anything missing from your house?"

"None whatsoever," Mrs. Highgate said with a hiccup.

"And what dates did she work for you?" I asked, examining Marie's employment record.

"A couple years back."

"Could you be more specific, please."

"I'm no good with dates. Ever since my car accident. Head trauma."

From the other end came muted laughter.

"And could you verify your address for me, please?"

"What's that got to do with it?"

I explained that it was routine and the woman rattled off a different address from the one on the letter. When asked about the discrepancy, Mrs. Highgate said, "Well, I've moved, haven't I, luv? I've got to run now. The baby's crying. He'll be wanting his bottle."

"How many children do you have, Mrs. Highgate?"

"Too many," she responded, clicking off.

I wondered whether Blair would spring for a visit to Ireland to research this further. I pictured myself lifting a pint of Guinness in a picturesque pub or eating crumbly Irish cheddar on stone-ground wheat crackers as I trooped through the heather after the dissembling Mrs. Highgate, who sounded suspiciously like a girlfriend of Marie's, not an employer.

If Marie had concocted false references, what else had she lied about?

I leaned back, elated. At least one of my cases was going well today.

When the phone rang, I thought it might be Bethany Burns calling back.

"Maggie?" said a familiar voice. "Is this Maggie Weinstock?"

"Anabelle?"

"Oh, my God," Anabelle Paxton squealed on the other end. "It really is you."

And just like that, I was sixteen again.

"Yes," I said, suddenly shy and tongue-tied. "It's me."

"Oh, my God, Maggie! What a way to reconnect. Luke e-mailed me, we're all so grateful that you're working on Dad's behalf. And this horrible thing with Uncle Simon. What a nightmare." She groaned. "Dad's going to need all the help he can get. Gosh, Maggie, I can't believe you're some high-powered PR executive now."

"Well I'm not a vice president or anything, it's a new job." I paused, realizing my words would not inspire confidence. "But I *have* been doing this for almost ten years."

"I'm so proud of you. Tell me, are you married? Do you have kids?"

"I was married, for five years." I gave a flippant laugh. "Steve was a lawyer. Very controlling. We get along better now that we're divorced. How about you?"

Anabelle said, "It's been a long, interesting ride. I'll tell you when we see each other. When do you want to come over?" She hesitated. "I don't want to take you away from Dad's case, but if you're free, how about this evening when you get off work? We're in Palos Verdes."

This evening I had a date. And I wasn't about to forget it.

"How about tomorrow?"

"We've got plans tomorrow," Anabelle

said. "But next week's pretty clear."

I hesitated. Next week might as well be next century as far as Blair was concerned. I wanted to keep my bosses happy. But I also wanted a crack at a love life. Why did I have to choose?

But there was something else too. The past was safely locked away in a pretty little box with a red ribbon. When I thought of Anabelle, she was always sixteen and we were hopeful of what life would bring. But many years had passed. Would we like what the other had become? Would we still have things in common? Could we be friends again? Or was there too much secret history and buried heartache for us ever to be more than wary strangers? Sure, I was curious. But I also worried what might befall my pretty little box of memories.

But now work was forcing my hand.

"Next week seems so far away," I said, trying to make my voice upbeat. "Let's do it tonight."

Dr. Rob Turcotte was in surgery. His secretary asked if I'd like to schedule a consultation.

"No, thank you. Does he have voice mail?"

At least this time I was calling ahead to reschedule. Dr. Turcotte was a busy professional. He'd understand.

"This is Maggie Silver," I said into his machine, "and I'm so sorry because I was very much looking forward to seeing you tonight." I paused. Was this too forward? "But I've got to cancel again due to a work emergency. Look, perhaps we could get together in a few days, when things have calmed down? I owe you a dinner at this point, not just a drink. I'll call you tomorrow and hopefully we can talk in person. Okay, bye."

I hung up, feeling I'd just made a terrible mistake. Then I walked to Faraday's office to brief him, liking the gleam that appeared in his eye, liking the "Nice work" he lobbed my way. To my elated surprise, he said he'd think about a trip to Ireland.

At four p.m., I found myself on the 405 Freeway, passing LAX.

I've always had a love-hate relationship with L.A.'s big, dysfunctional airport.

It was a portal to new worlds and I loved the clothes and smells and languages. But its very transience held the menace of a border town — where fear of lost papers and missed flights and plummeting death clung to wayfarers like spent jet fuel.

Because I'd lived so little when I met her,

it was LAX's glamour I first saw with Anabelle: the airline counters all shiny-clean and white, the crisp cardboard tickets tucked into our purses, the matched set of Louis Vuitton luggage lined up next to my battered black duffel as I accompanied Anabelle and the Paxtons on their Hawaiian vacation.

My mom had worked double shifts to buy my ticket, and the Paxtons were picking up the tab for everything else, relieved, perhaps, that their daughter had a friend to entertain her while they played golf and met friends for dinner.

So that was the dreamtime, the tropical waterfall, coral reef, coconut oil, and turquoise water part of it, Anabelle and I clip-clopping giddily onto the plane in our glitter platforms, our bikinis chafing tender flesh under tight silver Fiorucci jeans.

We were glam Bowie girls all the way, throwbacks to the glitter-rock 1970s. But there was more than a little boy in us too because we didn't want to marry Ziggy Stardust, we wanted to *be* him. So we sipped banana daiquiris by the pool, the sweet foam drying on our Bonne Bell lip-smacked lips, wearing identical Walkmans and singing "Starman" and "Five Years" and yeah, that would have been enough for me.

But I got only two.

Then came the uneasy autumn when the bond between Anabelle and I began to erode like the sandstone cliffs along PCH: slow, silent, inexorable.

And when Anabelle developed a strange new game, I learned the dark side of the airport.

Fall 1993

"Where are we going?" I said, sitting in the car, filled with nameless dread.

"You'll see," Anabelle said, her laughter loud and shrill.

She drove fast and recklessly, grinding the gears of her Jetta, turning every couple of miles to examine me, strands of long blond hair flying into her mouth.

My anxiety mounted as she drove along Jefferson, passing the remains of Ballona Creek, where the Chumash Indians once caught fish and wove river weeds into baskets.

We were headed for Playa del Rey.

She couldn't be taking us there, could she?

To my relief, she turned left at Lincoln and we cruised up the hill, past Loyola Marymount University, then down Manchester, and my anxiety spiked again, but instead of heading down to the beach, she turned left once more and drove into a residential area that abutted the airport.

We were on Sandpiper Lane now. She parked by a chain-link fence. Beyond it lay a no-man's-land. Night was falling, a burned caramel cream puff sunset, redolent of marsh grasses and dusk and sun-warmed skin.

This was a neighborhood with street grids and lights and fire hydrants, but no houses or people, just cracked concrete foundations where homes had once stood.

Like most places of human habitation that lie fallow, it had a strange energy. There were ghosts here, the faint afterimage of lives fractured and uprooted. You could almost see the freckle-faced, sunburned-nosed kids racing bikes down the streets, hear their shouts and laughter. Apron-wearing moms with bouffant hairdos stood on the front porches, calling them in for dinner while aerospace-industry dads relaxed with highballs in Pleather recliners.

But now it was utterly deserted.

"What is this place?" I said.

"They used to call it Palisades del Rey," Anabelle said. "The king's hills. It was the southern end of Playa del Rey. The airport took over the land and displaced hundreds of people."

"It's eerie and creepy," I said, gazing at the sand dunes drifting across the foundations of what had once been prime oceanfront land. The sidewalks were cracked and buckled, overgrown with marsh grasses.

A jet went by, rattling the windows of Anabelle's Jetta. A jackrabbit loped unconcernedly across the empty street. The streetlights still stood, their lamp glass busted. Palm trees swayed like ghostly sentinels in the jet and ocean breezes. The whole development was fenced off by rusting barbed wire and signs that said, NO TRESPASSING, DANGER, DO NOT ENTER.

We watched the sun set over the water and the sky grow purple, then dark blue and velvety black. Anabelle drank sweet Kentucky whiskey from an engraved silver flask and kept urging me to take swigs.

There was something bleak and desperate and headlong about the way her teeth clenched around the flask, turning her pretty face into a snarl.

Each time she thrust the flask at me, I shook my head.

This angered Anabelle. But in my cautious and plodding way, I was thinking ahead.

Stealthily, I confiscated her car keys. One of us had to be sober enough to drive home.

"Isn't it cool," said Anabelle, waving the

sloshing flask to indicate the landscape. "It's like a doomed, forgotten city, right in the middle of L.A. This is what everything will look like after the apocalypse. Then it'll finally match the inside of my brain."

Around me was eerie emptiness. I heard seabirds calling, the revving of the jets, waves crashing. A symphony of heaven and hell.

Anabelle took one last swig and shuddered as the fiery liquid went down her throat.

"Okay. I'm ready." She opened the car door and stepped out unsteadily. "Let's go."

"Where?" I asked, following as she walked up to the fence, her hand trailing along the chain link until she found the section she wanted. She applied pressure and a hole appeared. She pressed against it and climbed through.

"We shouldn't be doing this," I said. "It's illegal."

Anabelle gave me a look of disbelief and laughed. "Lots of the best things are, you know. When are you going to learn that?"

Then she walked off, leaving me on the other side, fingers clinging to the wire mesh.

"Wait!" I climbed through myself and ran to catch up.

"Where are we going? Anabelle, stop. This isn't funny."

Somewhere nearby, there was a runway. I could feel wind as the planes landed and took off, it was that close. But I followed her, out of fear, out of guilt, out of friendship.

"We're going to play a little game."

It was completely dark now, though the powerful runway lights lit up the night like a million moons.

Anabelle's face was in shadow.

"What game? I don't want to. Please, Anabelle, let's go back. You've had a little too much —"

"Don't you want to test yourself?"

"What kind of test are you talking about? And no, whatever it is, I don't."

A plane rolled by, very close, preparing for takeoff.

In the distance, I saw another jet approach. It picked up speed.

"No, Anabelle, don't. You're . . ."

My voice was drowned out by the impossible noise of the jet drawing closer. I felt my eardrums would burst as the jet rocketed by like some great steel monster. The air filled with the choking, sickening industrial stench of jet fuel.

Anabelle darted out across the runway to the culvert and threw herself down, just feet from the runway. She lay on her back, arms folded over her chest like a sacrificial offering to the cruel, steel-nosed gods of the sky.

My shrieks rose with the jet's engine and then a wind whipped me and I clung to the chain-link fence in the dark as it went past, burrowing my face into my chest, beseeching the gods. *No, no no, Anabelle,* I wailed.

When it passed I looked up, terrified of what I'd see. And she was still there, like a corpse, but unharmed.

She got up and walked steadily back to me. Her face was pale, her hair snaking like wild tendrils around her face, her lips compressed into a tight but triumphant line. She held out her hand.

"Come, Maggie. Your turn."

I was backing away, shaking my head.

"You're crazy, Anabelle. I'm not doing that, I'm not . . ." I lapsed into incoherent babble.

"It's like nothing you've ever done before. The ultimate drug. It's a shock to your system, it clarifies and purifies. You're missing out on the high of a lifetime. The buildup of the jet, then the release. Sometimes I come as the plane passes over."

"No thanks," I said. "Anabelle, let's go home. I'll get high with you. We'll play music. I'll tell you a story. Please. Let's get away from here."

I walked back, opened the passenger door, and held it for her.

Anabelle looked serene and I swear there was something postcoital about her now, as if this insane caper had released all the pent-up emotions that haunted her.

She climbed into the seat like an obedient child, yawned, and fell deeply asleep.

When we got back to Villa Marbella, I'd shaken her awake. We sat cross-legged in her room and I asked how she'd learned that game.

"Some guys showed me. They like to smoke sherm, then go down there and play chicken with the planes."

"You shouldn't hang around with guys like that, Anabelle."

"Who should I hang around with? You?" She paused. "But you're so boring, Maggie."

Abruptly, she got up and began to flip through a stack of tattered old records that she kept around, even though she'd replaced them with CDs.

She was right. But if her idea of fun was playing chicken with jets at LAX, I wanted no part of it. Her crazy antics had induced a certain clarity of my own.

"You're really starting to scare me. You've

been different. Ever since . . . I mean . . . can't you see? You've changed."

"And you haven't changed, Maggie. That's the problem right there."

She pulled out Led Zep's *Physical Graffiti* and pretended to read the liner notes. She'd never understood why I haunted the thrift stores, scooping up dirt-cheap first pressings of X and Wall of Voodoo and Patti Smith and John Hiatt as everyone else dumped their vinyl.

I told her it was because vinyl sounded warmer to this analog girl and she'd believed me because the truth wouldn't have occurred to her: I couldn't afford a CD player.

I loved Anabelle. But I was losing her. Ever since that night on the beach, things had changed drastically between us. And there was no one I could talk to. Not Luke, who saw me as the Judas who'd betrayed his sister, even if Anabelle herself didn't see it that way. Not my mother, who'd just forbid me ever to see Anabelle again. And certainly not the Paxtons. It was as if we existed in two separate universes, with no wormhole to connect us. I couldn't tell the Paxtons what their daughter was up to any more than I could tell our teachers. And yet I had to do something. And so my brain ran like a rat on a treadmill, panting, exhausted, unable to get off. I knew things were moving toward some kind of cataclysm. Some kind of rift. But when it would come, and what would be the aftermath, I couldn't have imagined.

Sixteen years later, I shuddered as I drove past the crawling anthill city of LAX. I didn't think kids played chicken on the jet runways anymore. I'm not even sure how Anabelle and her friends got away with it back in 1993. But I knew for certain that 9/11 had ended the days of lax security.

I jumped when the phone rang, but it was only Mom.

She told me the hospital had scheduled the PET scan at two the following day. Earlyn would accompany her. Mom said that was fine; she'd rather have me home when the doctor called her with the results.

I told her to keep me posted and shoved my fears into a dark closet. It did no good to get worked up until we knew more. Instead, my thoughts toggled back to my anxiety over seeing Anabelle after all these years.

She'd sure picked a pretty place to live, I thought, driving through the rolling hills and million-dollar homes of the Palos Verdes Peninsula that juts into the Pacific.

It was a gorgeous afternoon, filled with that limpid afternoon light we get along the wild coast. The road undulated with gentle swells, reminding me of a time when Angelenos still enjoyed a leisurely Sunday drive.

Then suddenly the smooth road grew cracked and buckled beneath my wheels. The terrain was unstable here, and magnificent sea-view homes in Portuguese Bend lay abandoned and condemned, victims of the shifting soil.

CONSTANT LAND MOVEMENT NEXT 0.8 MILES, read the yellow street sign.

USE EXTREME CAUTION.

And here I was, doing the opposite. Driving straight into darkness. Straight into the past.

Back to Anabelle.

How would she have handled Dr. Turcotte, I wondered? Anabelle who'd already been so sophisticated and poised at sixteen, collecting friends as effortlessly as butterflies.

And in the end, discarding them just as easily.

It wasn't only her blond looks, slender frame, and disturbingly pale blue eyes that captivated people. There was a mysterious radiance to her, as if she'd found the secret to life and might share it with you if you stuck around. Anabelle filled people to the brim with exhilarating possibility that paths would appear, doors open, chests unlock, treasure spill forth.

But then one night, the box we opened belonged to Pandora.

And there was no treasure inside, only demons.

I checked the address and pulled up to a house of glass and steel that rose like a futuristic spaceship from the hill overlooking the ocean. A giant bird-of-paradise rose two stories high, splashes of blue and orange against dark green fronds. On the suspended steel balcony, a girl was waving. She wore a dress of gauzy white that set off her tan, and the rays of the afternoon sun illuminated the golden highlights in her hair, creating a kind of halo.

Anabelle.

"Maggie!" she called, in that deep, throaty contralto. "I'll be right down."

My stomach clenched. I smoothed down my tailored skirt and made sure no buttons had popped on my silk blouse. I wanted to look sleek and professional, to impress Anabelle with what I'd become. For her dad's sake, I had to project self-assured confidence and banish the hot jumble of emotions that roiled inside of me.

And so as I walked up the path, I performed a little crisis management on myself and felt the Blair associate slowly gain the upper hand over the sixteen-year-old dork. My low pumps, tailored jacket, and amber teardrop earrings with matching necklace provided the finishing touches to the well-heeled young professional.

When we were young, Anabelle and I wore clothes as fragile armor against the world, investing them with almost talismanic power. We really believed that beautiful things — pleated, ruffled, ruched, beaded, plaited, pearled, bias-cut, hand-crocheted things — had the power to hold back evil and keep the dark at bay.

And for a while, they had.

Inside, a door slammed. I heard the creak of footsteps on the stairs. Then the door opened and Anabelle stood before me.

"Oh, my God," we said at the same time.

There was so much to say, and so much we couldn't ask. Instead I shuffled my feet and lowered my gaze, unable to bear the intensity of her pale blue eyes. Her hands hung at her sides, nails painted a lustrous seashell pink. The fingers of her right hand curled around the folds of her dress, clenching tightly, and I realized she was as nervous as I was.

Reassured, I looked up and for a long moment, we stared at each other. Anabelle was more beautiful than I remembered. Her eyes were large and luminous, almost haunted. The plump fullness of her face had melted away, leaving high cheekbones and angular planes. The peachy perfection of the California Girl had given way to a more profound beauty, tempered by age and all she'd been through.

"Maggie! I can't believe it. You look great!" Anabelle said.

"You do too, Anabelle."

We heard a *slap, slap* on the marble, then a small boy with anime eyes peered from between Anabelle's legs.

"Come in."

I stepped into a cool foyer of glass bricks and followed Anabelle into the living room.

We hugged awkwardly, all elbows and colliding wrist bones and flying hair. I made to step back, but her arms tightened around me and she squeezed hard, and in that moment, through some strange alchemy, it was as if no time had passed and we were best friends again.

The spell dissipated as we broke apart. Anabelle gave a deep, throaty laugh and tousled her son's head.

"This is Lincoln. He's four. Sweetheart,

this is Mommy's friend, Maggie."

"How do you do?" Lincoln asked solemnly, offering his hand.

"It's lovely to meet you, Lincoln," I said. "Did you know that your mother and I were friends when we were girls?"

Lincoln's skeptical look said he doubted his mother and I had ever been girls.

"Hey, buddy, want to jump on the trampoline while Mommy talks to her friend?"

The boy nodded shyly.

"Inez will take you out back."

A young Latina stepped up. She'd been standing so still that I hadn't noticed her.

Anabelle caressed the boy's face as she handed him off to the nanny, and a silent pang went through me.

"Let's get something to drink," Anabelle said.

I followed her, feeling clumsy and nervous. The woman moving with graceful ease through these beautifully furnished rooms had been my friend once. Did we still have anything in common besides memories? I was almost afraid to find out.

We moved into a designer kitchen with a gleaming industrial steel stove. Shiny copper pots and braids of garlic and red chilies hung from the ceiling. Carly Simon played softly on the stereo, and I wondered if Anabelle had picked her to remind me of old times.

"What would you like to drink?" Anabelle asked.

"Whatever you're having."

Something carved and masklike slipped over her features.

"I've been sober for eight years," Anabelle said. "It took awhile, but I finally decided to grow up and became a productive member of society." She smiled. "I have Randall to thank for that."

"Randall?"

"My second husband. He's a captain with the LAPD."

The thought of rebel child Anabelle married to a cop was mindboggling.

"Wait! Last I heard, you were married to a banker named John."

Anabelle's face darkened. Her fingers stroked a bowl of peaches and plums.

"John is long gone. And good riddance."

"I'm sorry. Henry didn't tell me."

"It's a long and sordid story."

"You don't have to . . ."

"But I do. It's part of my recovery." Anabelle sighed. "And really, you never know what the bad is good for. If I hadn't gone through all that, I'd never have met Randall."

"Really, Anabelle. If it makes you uncomfortable . . ."

"It's okay."

She pulled a jar of sun tea out of the fridge.

"John and I never should have gotten married. We were too young and too alike. But we did and he got a job in Berlin so we moved there after the wedding." She laughed ruefully.

"There was a lot of heroin flooding into the city from the Balkans because the war had disrupted the old trade routes. We got caught up in it."

A man walked into the kitchen and poured himself some iced tea. Tall and well built, with black hair, ruddy skin, and brown eyes, this had to be Anabelle's husband.

Anabelle ran to him, twining her hand in his.

"Randall, this is Maggie. We went to high school together. Maggie, meet my darling husband. I owe my life to this guy."

Randall thrust out his hand and almost mangled my fingers.

Macho prick.

With great effort, I restrained the impulse to kick him in the shins.

Anabelle, I screamed inwardly. *How could you marry this guy?* The earth cracked and shuddered as the gulf between us widened.

"Pleased to meet you, Randall," I said.

"Maggie is an old friend who was always a *good* influence." She turned to me. "Remember that time we went to the Baked Potato to hear some jazz?"

"Vaguely," I said.

Randall edged away. "Wait, darling," said Anabelle, tugging at him. "I'm telling a story. The waiter went around the table, taking our elaborate drink orders. And when he got to Maggie, guess what she ordered?"

"Beats me."

"A glass of milk."

Randall rolled his eyes.

"The waiter looked us over and promptly asked to see our IDs and that was the end of that. We were all ready to kill you."

I said, "He would never have served us. We were sixteen."

Randall pulled a carton of milk out of the fridge and plopped it on the counter. "Just in case," he said. Then he left.

Anabelle and I looked at each other and collapsed into hysterical giggles, which gave me, at least, the much-needed opportunity to vent some nervous steam.

"He arrested me," Anabelle said, when we'd wiped the tears from our eyes and calmed down.

"What?"

"I was starting to tell you when Randall walked in. After my first husband left me for some junkie model in Berlin, I moved back to L.A. I thought the sunshine would help me get clean. Instead, I got busted at Fifth and Main, trying to score."

"By Randall?"

"Crazy, huh? Dad hired a good lawyer and I did Betty Ford and got off with probation. When I got back to town, Randall started calling and coming around. I was so thick, I thought he was checking up on me, like a probation officer. Until finally one day, it was like, duh!"

She crossed her eyes and slapped the heel of her hand against her forehead.

She'd married her rescuer.

I stared through the French doors at an azure pool whose tile reflected the sky. Bougainvillea and banana plants grew riotous. Tall, graceful frangipani hung over the water. A dog slept on a patch of grass, surrounded by toy cars, balls, a jungle gym, and a swing set. Lincoln jumped silently on the trampoline while Inez sat on a lounge chair, hands in her lap, watching. Did she have four kids of her own back in El Salvador, or wherever she came from, being raised by her mother in a concrete shack with a dirt floor? Did she ever imagine her own kids swimming in that pool?

"We keep the pool at eighty degrees year-round," Anabelle said. "It's saline, with reverse ionization."

"I'm glad to hear it," I said, trying to recall high school chemistry.

"So what about you? Dad said you're pretty high up at the Blair Company."

Should I tell her the truth — that I was just an associate vying for promotion in a firm of charismatic cutthroats? Would she think less of me?

I paused. Anabelle had called Henry Dad. This was the girl who'd called her parents Henry and Miranda when we were still in high school! I'd been very impressed by such sophistication and resolved to try it at home. But my attempt to call Mom Olivia had been immediately shot down.

"I'm not your friend, I'm your mother," she'd said archly. "And that's what you may call me."

Did Anabelle need a father more than a friend now that she was in her thirties and a parent herself? Had sophistication melted away with age, leaving a little girl lost?

I explained that my life hadn't been nearly as exciting or dangerous or glamorous as hers. As usual, I felt like a sand-colored tortoise next to a crimson fox. And I felt obscurely cheated. Because Anabelle had danced on the edge of the knife, then returned to the wealthy life of ease that was the Paxton birthright.

"It's not like my biological clock went off," Anabelle was saying, "but Randall wanted kids so I went along. But now that I'm a mother, I understand, for the first time, why parents will do anything to protect their children. I mean, I could easily kill anyone who tried to hurt Lincoln. It's like this dormant instinct that blooms, a pregnancy chemical. So I worry, because I know what's out there. When I think back to some of the things we put our parents through . . ."

She gave me a rueful smile and changed the subject.

"Isn't it gorgeous here? The house belonged to a disciple of Richard Neutra who was married to a 1950s Italian film star. She used to stare out at the ocean and mourn her lost beauty."

She laughed, but there was something forced in it.

This house, with its aggressively modernist lines, its cold steel and glass geometry, was the polar opposite of Villa Marbella. It

266

was an unambiguous statement that Anabelle had rejected the past. In a house like this, rigor and discipline ruled. All straight ninety-degree angles and man-made materials, where Villa Marbella sprawled and curved like a languorous courtesan.

But the big house, the landscaped gardens, the pool, the toys, the elegant furniture, the full-time nanny. Surely it didn't come from an LAPD captain's salary? I wondered how Randall felt about relying on his wife's money.

Anabelle grabbed the remote and Carly Simon's voice grew louder, the aching melancholy of "Boys in the Trees." Back in high school, Carly Simon had pierced to the heart of my confusion about boys and sex. I felt guilty too, "though no one was at fault, frightened by the power of every innocent thought." Sex was like some kind of powerful, uncontrollable magic, whereas I wanted to kiss and pet and be held. But my fantasies mostly faded out after second base.

"We damn near wore the grooves off that record, didn't we?" Anabelle said, her eyes turning inward, far back in time.

Carly sang:

Last night I slept in sheets the color of
     fire
Tonight I lie alone again and I curse my
     own desire

As the last chords died away, Anabelle muted the sound and we stared at the black slate tiles, surprised at the intense emotions the words still aroused.

"How's Luke?" I said at last. "I saw him at the house, but it was late, we didn't get to talk much."

My very own boy in the tree.

"He's okay," she said. I got the feeling she was waiting to see if I'd inquire further.

When I didn't, Anabelle said, "He had to sell some stocks recently, got caught in the upside-down market. And he broke up with a girlfriend not too long ago and it's hit him hard." She gave a short laugh. "I guess she left him, and Lover Luke isn't used to that."

"That's too bad."

But somehow, I couldn't work up much sorrow for Luke's lost love. In fact, it was great timing, as far as I was concerned. But I kept my thoughts to myself.

"Do the police have any idea who killed Dad's aide?" Anabelle asked.

Just then, Randall appeared again. The LAPD captain stopped in his tracks.

268

"Emily Mortimer?" he said.

Anabelle nodded. "Dad's hired Maggie's firm to represent him until this blows over. She's a crisis consultant."

Randall gave a short, tight nod, as if this news reinforced his negative impression of me. He leaned against the granite counter.

"So you're the meddlers who are making it hard for our detectives to do their jobs."

"That's not —"

"Randall," Anabelle interrupted, "this is my friend. And since when is that case even in your jurisdiction?"

She turned to me. "Randall's a captain out at Devonshire. The Valley's a whole different ballpark."

"When I found out that murdered girl worked for your dad, I started asking around," said Randall. "Unofficially, of course."

"You didn't tell me that," Anabelle said with forced brightness.

He shrugged. "That's because there's nothing to tell."

I felt the word "yet" hovering in the air.

We watched with rapt fascination as Randall shook pretzels into a bowl. Tucking it under his arm like a football, he said, "Have a nice visit," and left.

"Randall and my father don't always see

eye to eye," Anabelle said. "You'd think being vets would have brought them together — Randall was among the first U.S. troops into Afghanistan after nine/eleven and Dad was a pilot in Vietnam. But I guess it doesn't work that way."

Unsure of what to say, I focused on the designer kitchen, the Sub-Zero fridge.

"And it's not because my parents paid for all this," Anabelle said, misinterpreting my gaze. "LAPD captains actually make good money, and Randall's been consulting for an upcoming cop show, *Rookie.* Mom and Dad helped us with the down payment, but Randall doesn't want to take any more money from them. He says we need to pay our own way."

"That's just terrific," I said, walking to the French doors that opened into the backyard.

Something was wrong. Anabelle was too eager to convince me of her marvelous life and wonderful new husband.

The sun was setting in tangerine-lavender–red licorice sherbet. I suggested we sit outside to watch the dusk come on. Anabelle followed me out without looking at the sky — it must be like wallpaper to her by now. The dog, a Lab mix named Bangs, wandered over to say hello.

"Oh, I almost forgot." I pulled a glass vial

out of my purse. "Chergui, my new favorite. I made you a sample. You've got to try it."

Anabelle flinched. "What is it?" she said guardedly.

She thinks I'm offering her drugs.

"It's 'fumes, honey," I reassured her. "Just like old times. Remember how we'd raid your mom's vanity table, spraying and dabbing until we smelled like a punk rock bordello?"

"Vaguely."

"And that old Guerlain I loved so much, Vol de Nuit, that I wanted to snort up my arm?"

Anabelle placed my vial on the table, where it rolled to the edge.

Would it fall onto the grass? Would it break? Anabelle studied the hand-lettered vial like she was trying to decipher a message from a long-extinct civilization.

"It's very nice of you to bring me your latest discovery," she said at last. "I haven't thought about perfume in years."

Abruptly, she rose and walked to the end of the backyard and I followed. Below us the sea crashed and roared. Just past the fence, a spiky green plant grew out of the sandy cliff. Its creamy white flowers with purple-tipped edges were beginning to open. They glowed in the dusk, giving off a cool lemony fragrance.

"Datura innoxia." Anabelle reached through the fence and plucked a flower. "Also known as moonflower, thorn apple, jimsonweed."

With a dreamy look, she lifted the delicate, trumpet-shaped bloom to her nose.

"Isn't that toxic?" I asked.

"The witch's weed?" Anabelle nodded. "Known to induce hallucinations and visions. The gardener wants to pull it out, it's very invasive, but I love its shamanistic history. Sometimes when things get bad, I come out here and . . ."

In the dusk, the pale moonflower glowed with an atavistic beauty.

Anabelle sighed. "But it's a fleeting vampiric beauty. By noon, they're wilted and forlorn."

"You feel an affinity to them?"

She shrugged her shoulders. "Oh, look, a luna moth."

A giant jade moth with swallowtail wings dipped and soared. Anabelle ran after it, laughing, trampling the datura underfoot. But instead of heady fragrance, I smelled manure.

Anabelle wrinkled her nose and checked her espadrilles.

"Ick! I stepped in dog poop." She pulled off the offending shoe. "Argghh. I just

272

bought these."

But I was staring at Anabelle's foot. The Band-Aid couldn't cover the red inflammation in the webbing between her second and third toes.

"Cat pounced on my bare foot," she said, catching me staring. "I'm afraid it may be infected."

Could my friend be using again? Had her husband found out? Did that explain the unease I sensed?

As these thoughts ricocheted around my head, I massaged my neck.

"What's the matter?" Anabelle said, misinterpreting my frown.

"Oh, I um, woke up with a crick. Must have slept wrong."

She smiled in sympathy. "Those can be so painful."

"I'll be okay."

She placed her hand on my wrist. "I'll get you something, just in case it gets worse."

We walked back into the kitchen and Anabelle ran upstairs. I heard her slamming drawers. Taking advantage of her absence, I walked around the kitchen, inspecting the tile floor for the telltale food and water dishes that would tell me a cat lived here.

I didn't see any.

"Randall, honey," Anabelle called down,

"where's that Percocet the doctor gave you when your back went out?"

Anabelle's husband came out of the den and stood at the foot of the stairs.

"Check my bedside table," he called up.

"It's not there."

"Then I don't know, honey."

Seeing me, Randall came into the kitchen.

"So," he asked in a low, falsely jovial voice, "did Anabelle give you an earful out by the pool?"

"About what?"

"Me."

Anabelle began to walk down the stairs, complaining that the pills had disappeared.

Wordlessly, I shook my head at Randall.

Anabelle's husband tucked his hands under his arms and shot me an enigmatic look. "All I'm saying is, don't believe everything she tells you."

When I played the conversation back later, I wondered why I hadn't paid closer attention to the signs. Why did a shadow cross Senator Paxton's face when he mentioned Randall. Why had Anabelle lied about the cut on her foot? And why, despite her insistence that life was grand, did Anabelle seem so dreadfully unhappy? I was so busy convincing Anabelle about my successful life that I failed to see the cracks widening in hers.

That night, Mom and I avoided talking about the PET scan. She was cranky and snippy, and I refused to engage with her. It's ironic. A disease like cancer should have brought us closer. But it only heightened what was already there. We were still the same two people.

I got my laptop and Googled LAPD Captain Randall Downs.

Randall was a veteran cop who'd started his career in an area with heavy gang problems. Some of his colleagues had been accused of staging home invasion robberies to rip off drug dealers and coerce sex from prostitutes, but Randall had not been implicated. In fact, he'd recently been promoted and transferred to Devonshire Division for his role in an undercover operation that convicted an L.A. drug kingpin who laundered money through legitimate businesses.

Still uneasy, I googled the TV show *Rookie,* but turned up nothing. I wondered whether I'd be defending Anabelle's husband from accusations one day. And what about the sore between Anabelle's toes? Is that why she hadn't tried to renew our old friendship? Because there were too many messy questions?

I turned off the computer and stood at my window. The moon was waxing, almost full. Dark clouds scudded across the sky and a warm wind whipped the curtains. A mockingbird began to sing. With its full-throated warble echoing in my ears, I got into bed and pulled up the sheet.

14

"I hope I'm not calling too early?" said a male voice.

I lifted my head, propping my chin up with my elbow. I squinted at the digital clock: 6:30.

"No, no, I have to get up. Who's this?"

"It's Rob Turcotte. I just got back from my morning run. Look, I'd like to talk to you."

Suddenly, I was wide awake. "Gosh, I'm so sorry about last night."

"Well, I just wonder, is this your way of saying you're not interested?"

"Not at all. I'm just incredibly busy with this new job." Pause. "So, you want to try to get together for a meal?"

There was a long silence.

"Hello?"

"I guess we can give it one more try. But, Maggie?"

"Yes?"

"Last chance. After this, the stars don't align, you know?"

There was much excitement in Faraday's office when I got in. Tyler's cop source had called, saying they'd traced Emily Mortimer's cell phone to a tenement in Koreatown. We turned the channels to local news with anticipation, but there was nothing new.

"All right, folks, let's keep it moving. Tyler, see if you can get an update."

When Tyler left, Faraday turned to me. "How'd it go with Anabelle Paxton?"

I flushed. "It was really just personal stuff, us catching up."

"Tell me every little thing." Faraday settled back in his chair.

And even though I felt squeamish, I sat there and recounted the visit. Faraday was interested in Anabelle's child, in her relationship with her husband, in how she viewed her father.

"We didn't really talk about the case and what her dad and uncle may or may not have done," I said. "Anabelle loves Henry and believes what he's told her."

"And the son-in-law's a cop, is he?" Faraday said.

"Yeah." I frowned. "I didn't really like him that much. He seemed a bit pompous. Said he was asking around about the case, making unofficial inquiries."

This seemed to interest Faraday very much. "And how was he going to do that?"

"We didn't get into it."

"And how was his investigation going?"

"He said there was nothing to report," I said, glad when Faraday changed the subject.

"And how would you describe Anabelle's relationship with her dad? Close? Distant?"

"Distantly close," I said. "She calls him Dad now, which is interesting. In high school he was Henry. Maybe she needs a father now that she's an adult herself."

"I understand she's had some substance abuse problems?"

My mouth dropped. "What does that have to do with anything?"

"Maybe nothing, maybe something. We like to know all the angles, we like to stay informed."

"This conversation makes me feel like a traitor, like I'm supposed to spy on them and report back to you."

Faraday leaned forward. "I'd never want to put you in an uncomfortable position. But we're trying to learn as much as we can. You know we always conduct our own independent investigations. And we've learned that sometimes when you throw unrelated facts in the mix, patterns emerge."

He saw that I wasn't convinced.

"Come on, Maggie, why are you so protective? She doesn't need it. She's the kind of poor little rich girl who floats along without a dollar in her purse because she knows there's always someone waiting to buy her a drink, pay for a meal, slip her past the velvet rope, make the bad stuff go away. You and I aren't like that. We're scholarship kids. We've had to fight hard for everything we've ever gotten."

"How'd you know I had scholarships?" I said, annoyed. It was none of his business.

Faraday gave me a coyote smile.

Just then his computer beeped. He glanced down.

"*HuffPo* is taking the Trent Holloway piece but they want it by three p.m.," he said. "Seven hundred fifty words. Can you get me a draft in an hour?"

I glanced at my watch. It was almost noon.

"Sure," I said, swallowing hard.

"The tone is personal. He's upset and outraged. He feels betrayed. His only concern is for his family."

"Got it."

At my desk, I tried to empty my mind. Then I wrote:

A former employee has made false allegations against me after my wife, Boots, and I confronted her about $150,000 worth of jewelry that went missing from our bedroom. This employee demanded that we pay her $1.5 million or she would file a lawsuit accusing me of sexual harassment. This is a cold-blooded attempt to extort our family and damage and humiliate not only my wife and me but our two young children. We are not going to pay hush money so she will go away. We feel betrayed by her accusations and we vow to fight back.

My computer beeped.
"How's it going?" Faraday queried.
"Fine," I wrote back.
I counted the words, then wrote more. Fifty-five minutes later I hit Send and got some coffee.
When I returned, there was a message waiting.
"Nice work. It's off to Holloway and his lawyers for approval. Go grab some lunch."
But I had other plans.
I needed something to wear on my date and wanted to check Le Boutique.
I found the most amazing things there —

designer dresses, plein air paintings, Art Deco mirrors. There was a magic about the place. With the regularity of the tides, it tossed up what I needed, often before I knew myself. And the prices couldn't be beat.

Le Boutique was a thrift store. Like many women I knew, I struggled to make ends meet. Blair didn't provide a clothing allowance, but I was expected to look neat, trim, sleek, and professional at all times. So, frugalista that I am, I waited for sales and then splurged on basic black and good bras.

But I would have frequented Le Boutique even if I had money. The giddy pleasure of finding something cool for next to nothing gave me a buzz that was akin to a drug.

At the counter, I browsed the jumble of cheap jewelry and asked to see a box of perfume.

It was called Chaos by Donna Karan and smelled smoky, sweet, and spicy. I said I'd think about the $29.95 price tag (pretty steep for the thrift store).

"Too exotic," I told the clerk as I left ten minutes later, the clothes racks having proved a disappointment.

Back at the office, I found the fragrance had dried down subtle and intriguing — a warm essence of cinnamon and cardamom, musk and lavender. It conjured up South-east Asian bazaars, aromatic oils, harems, Arabian genies emerging from lamps to grant wishes.

On impulse, I Googled it.

Chaos was discontinued and highly sought after, selling on eBay for hundreds of dollars. Sniffing my wrist again, I revised my initial opinion. Now I could appreciate its complexity. Shallow and easily swayed, that's me.

Calling the thrift store, I gave them my credit card number and asked them to hold it, fretting about the unbillable minutes I'd just wasted.

But who doesn't love a bargain?

Besides, if I sold it on eBay, I'd have money for Christmas.

I was leaving the thrift store with my new fragrance when I noticed a man at the plate-glass windows, contemplating a display of baby furniture. He'd also been there when I walked in, but in my hurry to buy the perfume, I'd paid him no mind.

He was about fifty-five, with a comb-over, clad in brown slacks and a corduroy jacket that must have been murder in this heat. Somehow, I didn't think he was in the market for baby furniture.

"You like perfume?" he asked.

I gave him a stony stare and kept walking. I liked to keep my thrifting private. It didn't go with the image of the fancy PR executive.

"Ms. Silver?"

I turned. "Who are you?"

He stepped closer and pulled out a badge. "Oliver Goldman, U.S. Attorney General's office."

"I-I haven't done anything illegal."

"I've seen you on TV. You work for Blair."

I wound the bag handle tighter. "What do you want?"

"We're interested in your employer. Their name keeps popping up in a criminal investigation."

"I don't know what you're talking about."

"Yeah, I know." He smiled. "You just do damage control on the Emily Mortimer murder."

"What are you getting at?"

"We're pretty sure Blair does more than straight crisis consulting."

"That's news to me. What else do they do?"

"Blair is a high-powered outfit, known for getting the job done. They are relentless on behalf of their clients, and vindictive bastards when they perceive a wrong. They're also very creative, always pushing the limits of the law. We suspect that Blair is breaking the law and engaging in criminal activity on behalf of clients. Perhaps even federal conspiracy, in the case of a major player in the banking meltdown. You don't want to get mixed up in anything illegal on the Paxton case, Ms. Silver. It would blacken your name and destroy your career."

"I would never . . ."

"But there's a lot we still don't know. That's why the government is very interested in keeping lines of communication open. You can help us."

"Even if I knew anything, why would I risk my job and breach client confidentiality?"

Oliver Goldman rolled forward and bounced on the balls of his feet.

"Because when indictments come down, you'll want to be on the right side."

"What exactly are you insinuating?"

"I'm just warning you. Remember what I said, stay in touch. Here's my card. You can reach me at this number day or night."

Without even thinking, I took it, then said, "Why would I want to reach you?"

"Because our work is going to intersect down the line. Don't hesitate to use that number if you feel overwhelmed or run into trouble. We can protect you."

"Are you saying I'm in some kind of danger?"

He gave me a shrewd look. "You have no idea what you're mixed up with, do you?"

"I have a pretty good idea that you're on a fishing expedition."

"You're a nice girl, I can see why Blair hired you. Bet he keeps you far away from the black ops."

"I have no knowledge of anything like that."

"Keep your eyes open," said Oliver Goldman. "And don't do anything you'll regret. Remember, we're watching."

"Come in," said Faraday, looking up at my knock.

"Something very strange just happened," I said.

Faraday's glasses slipped down his nose and he peered over the frames.

"What is it, Maggie? Sit down." His voice was warm and smooth as twenty-year-old scotch. "Has Anabelle called with something interesting?"

"No, nothing like that. I was coming out of a . . . store after lunch and this guy stopped me. Said he was with the U.S. District Attorney's office."

Faraday wrinkled his nose. "What did he want?"

"He knew my name and where I worked. He said Blair's name kept coming up in investigations his office was doing into criminal conspiracy."

Faraday was suddenly very alert. "What did you tell him?"

"I didn't tell him anything. It wasn't a long conversation. I got away as quickly as I could."

I looked up, expecting an explosion. But Faraday's face had relaxed.

"We get accused of black PR," he said. "It's usually our competitors who spread those rumors. Engaging in a little black ops themselves, accusing us of industrial espionage, smear campaigns, defamation. It's just sour grapes."

"He also hinted that Blair had done illegal things on behalf of a client who played a major role in the bank industry meltdown. And he seemed interested in the Paxton case. He specifically mentioned Emily Mortimer's murder."

Faraday's face was unreadable. "The senator is a powerful politician who is tackling one of the most explosive and divisive issues of our day, and that's the banking collapse. Some unscrupulous people have

287

made millions of dollars in recent years. Many more lost their homes, their jobs, their savings. It's natural for emotions to run high and for people to point fingers. As to Emily Mortimer's murder, let the feds investigate all they want. They won't find anything illegal because there's nothing to find. Do you understand?"

"Yes."

"All right. Did this Goldman guy ask you to cooperate with his investigation?"

"Yes, but I told him I wouldn't."

"Did he threaten you in any way?"

"No."

"Did he ask you to wear a wire?"

"No."

"Did he give you a number where you could contact him?"

"I threw it into a Dumpster," I said, not mentioning that I'd memorized it first.

Faraday studied me. Then, apparently satisfied, he said, "I can't tell you how pleased I am to hear about your loyalty. I will inform Mr. Blair and tell him how well you handled yourself."

"Thank you."

"You are not to speak to this investigator again. If he makes contact, I want to know about it right away."

"Okay."

I took a deep breath. "Now I've got a request."

He gave me a wary look. "Yes?"

"I'd like you to take me off the Paxton case."

Faraday blinked. "Because this government guy freaked you out? He cannot compel you to do anything. You are not breaking any laws."

"I know. I just can't deal with it anymore. I sit there in the Paxton house and I feel like I'm being split in half. I'm supposed to be their friend, but I can't just be normal because I'm too busy figuring out how to spin everything they say. It's giving me an ulcer. I can't eat, I can't sleep. I feel like I'm going to have a nervous breakdown."

"I need you to give it a few more days. Will you do that for me?"

I looked up. Miserable, I nodded.

Then I stood to go.

"Henry's counting on you, as a spokesperson and, even more, as a family friend. And so are we. You won't let us down, will you, Maggie?"

I thought about how the Paxtons had taken me into their home when I was sixteen and introduced me to travel, art, and culture. How Anabelle's friendship and the family's boundless confidence had helped me become the adult I was today. No, I wouldn't let the Paxtons down. And then there was Mom. She depended on me. If I lost the house, we'd be back living in a dismal apartment over an alley somewhere, right where we'd started. But this time she'd be a lot older, and she might be very sick. No, I wouldn't let down my mom either. And mostly, I wouldn't let myself down.

And so I assured Faraday, "You can count on me."

I sloped back to my office and sat at the computer, trying to look busy.

What if Oliver Goldman was right? What did I really know about the rough-and-tumble world of Washington politics and Senator Paxton's investigation into the banking scandal, which mostly happened behind closed doors?

And what did I know about Blair, other than the cases that I personally worked on? The nature of client confidentiality ensured that my colleagues did not discuss their work around the water cooler — how could they when they were sworn to secrecy?

When Faraday buzzed me an hour later, I was nervous as a rat at a cat show.

I slid into a seat across from my boss and

then Tyler walked in, bustling with importance.

"The LAPD raid was a bust. They sent a bunch of heavily armed guys to the apartment and found a couple of Korean teenagers using Emily Mortimer's BlackBerry to Skype with friends in Seoul."

"Where'd the kids get the phone?"

"Claim they bought it off a guy on the street."

"Do the cops believe them?"

"They're checking it out. The kids barely speak English and they're scared shitless. They never heard of Emily Mortimer."

"It's a big break for the cops," I said. "They can check her list of contacts, everything sent and received, and who called her the night she was killed. Remember she left her fund-raiser dinner early."

"Maybe it was the senator confirming their meeting."

"His level of intimacy on the phone might be illuminating," I said.

Tyler said, "The phone's been wiped. But LAPD's forensics people will try to retrieve it, if they don't get records from the phone company first.

"But the big news," continued Tyler, sticking his chest out like a peacock, "is that the coroner says Emily Mortimer was five weeks pregnant."

Faraday flopped back in his seat. "Jesus," he said, "can it get any worse?"

"Sure," I said. "If the senator or his brother fathered the baby."

"LAPD's already got their DNA samples. They'll do paternity testing," Tyler said.

"Do they need special permission for that?" I asked.

"I don't know. But Lambert is going to have an absolute cow," Faraday said.

He typed the attorney's name into the recipient field, then cleared the screen.

"I'd better use a typewriter," he said. "The police haven't announced this yet."

"I can deliver it to the Paxton home if you'd like," I said.

I gave him a reassuring smile to show he could count on me. But inside, I was already strategizing. I'd drop the memo off, make sure nothing at Villa Marbella needed my attention, then leave early and hightail it home to see how Mom was doing. Right now, she needed my support more than the Paxtons.

Faraday pursed his lips and considered. "That's a swell idea."

15

The coral trees were in bloom along San Vicente Boulevard, dense clusters of spiky red flowers jutting from the ends of branches. Red seed pods littered the grassy median like explosions of blood.

Soon I was ringing the doorbell at Villa Marbella.

The maid led me into the senator's office, where he sat at a rolltop desk, reviewing his mail and jotting down notes with a blue cartridge pen. Several reports lay scattered on the desk.

I saw now that he was on the phone. "Okay, Neil," he said, "consider it authorized."

He signed off and swiveled in his office chair to face me.

"Oh," I said, stepping back. "I thought . . ."

I bit my tongue, shocked to see Simon Paxton sitting at his brother's desk. I'd thought that Simon was no longer advising the senator on politics.

I'd thought he was supposed to stay away from Henry.

I'd been a fool.

Simon was dressed all in black. With his prominent nose, hunched shoulders, thin flyaway hair, and pouchy circles under his eyes, he resembled a beaky, disheveled raven.

"Yes?" he inquired, frowning.

"I've, um, got a package for the senator."

"I'll take it." He extended his hand, but something in his proprietary tone made me dig my heels in.

"Mr. Faraday said to deliver it personally."

"Well, he's not here right now, so you can't deliver it personally," Simon said in a mocking tone.

For a moment, we stared at each other. I'm not sure who showed more distaste.

Then Simon stood.

"Come this way." He walked into the hallway. The passage was cool and shadowed, the iron sconces along the wall casting dim, watery light.

This side of the house faced a row of towering eucalyptus trees that screened out the light, even at high noon. Now a crepuscular dusk seeped in over the open windowsill and pooled in the corners.

In these close confines, I smelled Simon's aftershave and something more sharp and acrid. We entered another room and he gestured at a carved wooden desk.

"You can leave it there and I'll lock it. No one will touch it."

Simon brushed past me, and opened the middle drawer. I slid the envelope inside.

"You feel quite comfortable here at Villa Marbella, don't you?" Simon Paxton said with distaste.

I wanted to tell him that Anabelle and I were old friends and I knew my way around the house blindfolded. But I kept quiet.

Simon's eyes darted to the door, as if measuring the distance.

I wondered who else was home. I sensed in him the desperate caginess of a fox as the hounds close in. He moved toward me.

"I thought Mr. Faraday asked you to stay away until this is resolved," I said with a bluster I didn't feel.

Simon stopped. He stood perfectly still.

"That's right. My noble senator brother can't risk associating with an adulterer and possible murderer."

He raised his arms and I couldn't help but flinch.

"Then why are you here?" I said.

He cocked his head. "Certain matters still require my attention."

He saw my expression.

"Nothing illegal. But for instance, Henry likes to run his four-hundred-dollar Beverly Hills haircuts through my credit card so they don't show up on his quarterly government reports. Journalists and political opponents seize on silly things like that, especially coming from a self-proclaimed man of the people."

The mockery in his voice was unmistakable.

"Where is Henry?" I asked, suddenly uneasy.

One eyebrow went up. *Henry?*

"The senator."

"You ask a lot of questions, *Maggie.* That's not part of your job description. You ought to stick to your job. It would be a lot safer for you. We do, after all, pay your salary. We could have you taken off the case at any time."

Be my guest! Perhaps you'll have more luck than me convincing Faraday.

Simon Paxton pursed his lips. "A complaint in the right place and you could be out of a job altogether. And it's a tight market, even in the damage control business."

A shadow passed over my heart. Why did he hate me so much?

It rolled off him in waves. Was it because he'd been forced to take the fall for his guilty brother and now his own reputation lay in tatters?

He stepped closer, and involuntarily, I stepped backward. He glanced at the fireplace, where his eyes lingered over the iron poker and coal tongs. I took another step back and tripped over a footstool.

Simon Paxton laughed. "We're being defended by rank amateurs," he said. "They sent a girl to do a man's job."

"What girl is that?" The light switch flipped on and Henry Paxton stepped into the room.

"Good heavens, who's that crawling on the floor?"

The lamp glow illuminated me as I struggled shamefacedly to my feet.

"It's your . . . *damage* girl, Henry," said Simon Paxton. "It seems she's tripped."

"What's going on here?" the senator asked. "Are you okay, Maggie? You look like you've seen a ghost."

I was incapable of words.

"Simon been giving you a hard time?"

Gratefully, I nodded.

"He's very displeased about this turn of

events. But when we're dealt such a hand, we must play it as best we can."

He bounced on his heels as I retrieved the envelope and gave it to him.

"Ah," Henry said, "my Blair care package. Thank you, Maggie."

"They want you to read it right away."

"Let me walk you out," said Henry.

His shoes crunched on the gravel, hands clasped behind his back, his big leonine head bowed.

After the darkness inside, the sunlight was almost blinding. A silver moon hung in the daytime sky.

Henry looked around, master of all he surveyed.

"I miss this so much when I'm in Washington. Being able to walk in my garden, watch the seasons change. It's lovely on a sunlit day. But it's also beautiful at night. Hushed and green and shadowed, the elms and sycamores with their black silhouettes. Rather eldritch, don't you think?"

"Yes, sir." I paused, looked around. "There's a new development, sir. Emily Mortimer was five weeks pregnant."

He stopped. His face showed no surprise. He either knew, or he was a master at disguising his emotions. But surely this wasn't the time to hide behind a mask?

"Maggie," Senator Paxton said gravely, "I've spent my whole life building a safe world for my family. Making it impenetrable. With money. The best schools. A stellar reputation, a respectable career. And now, in these last few days, I find everything I've worked so hard for threatened with destruction. I'd do anything to protect it. I hope you understand that."

"Yes, sir."

"You know there's been talk of my running for higher office."

"I've heard that. Yes."

"There are only so many times in a man's life when that door cracks open. And when it does, he's got to take the opportunity and push his way through, because the chance might not come again. And if we succeed," he said, putting a hand on my shoulder, "I could use a bright young woman like you on my team. Think of the possibilities, Maggie. The sky's the limit. We could ride this thing all the way to the White House."

It was intoxicating to listen to him. I thrilled at his inclusive "we," of being part of a winning team, of the frank enthusiasm and excitement in his voice. It was clear why both ordinary citizens and party leaders saw him as a rising star.

"There's nothing that could stand in my way," Senator Paxton was saying. "I simply won't let it. Do you understand?"

"Not really, sir."

He sighed. "You're young. Youth is careless. Youth thinks it's immortal. And age is left to pick up the pieces."

"Is that Shakespeare?"

He smiled and opened my car door. "No. It's Henry Paxton."

The doctor called at seven thirty with the results of the PET scan. Mom and I were moving food around our plates, neither of us able to muster an appetite.

I watched her face as she took the call and knew that the news was not good. I got up and put my hand on her arm. Her flesh seemed bony and loose, like a bird's.

"He wants to move forward with a biopsy," she said as she hung up.

She looked at me apologetically, like it was her fault, and her mouth creased.

"He says the PET scan was inconclusive. A biopsy will allow them to rule out malignancy one hundred percent."

And if it doesn't?

The words remained unsaid between us.

"How quickly can they schedule that?"

"He said it should be in the next six

weeks. They have to get the authorization and put through the paperwork."

I imagined a malign flower blooming inside her, its tentacles reaching out to taint surrounding tissue. Every day might count if the mutated cells were hitching rides in her bloodstream, moving through her body, looking for new organs to lodge in.

"What can I do?"

She looked up. "I suppose you can call the insurance company, try to hurry them along. But I can do all that, if you're busy."

"If we both hammer away at them, maybe it will move faster."

Mom sighed and asked if we could talk about something else for a while.

So I brought out my pretty, faceted glass bottle of Donna Karan, told her the story, and spritzed the fragile stem of her wrist.

"The perfume website I like says sandalwood, cardamom, cinnamon, paduk wood, agarwood, saffron, clove, amber, musk, sage, lavender, chamomile, and coriander. I'm not even sure what several of those are."

"I think you should keep it."

"But we ought to be saving money right now, not spending it. What if your insurance balks at paying for some of the tests or . . . treatments? Remember last time, we had to battle them for those antinausea pills,

301

and even then they paid only half."

"Thirty dollars or three hundred is not going to make a difference in the long run," Mom said. "If it makes you feel rich as a duchess, keep it."

16

The next morning I placed a drop of my new perfume on each wrist when I got dressed.

It was intimate on my skin, warm as sable, cool as a monsoon breeze, and I marveled at its almost alchemical ability to transform me. I wasn't a twenty-first-century crisis consultant, I was Cleopatra, welcoming Marc Antony to her bed. I was Tzu Hsi, the Chinese concubine who schemed her way to empress. I was Josephine Baker, dancing naked on a Paris stage.

"I like that, what you're wearing, Silver," Faraday said, sniffing the air at our morning meeting.

Tyler grabbed my arm and planted his nose against my inner wrist, sniffing like a bloodhound. For a moment, his chin scraped my sensitive skin, sending electric sparks up my arm and down the center of my body.

"Tyler, it's my duty as a supervisor to remind you about our sexual harassment policy. Knock it off."

We were reviewing the latest media on the Paxton case and making lists of whom to contact with corrections and amplifications. Faraday was especially incensed at a *Los Angeles Times* reporter who'd suggested that Simon Paxton was taking the fall for his brother.

"Sam, I want you to comb through that story, looking for misspellings, factual inaccuracies. Titles, dates, anything. We're going to get him," he said, rubbing his hands together.

We also discussed the latest on the LAPD investigation.

"Emily Mortimer's boyfriend is still MIA," Tyler said. "He moved out of his apartment two months ago, left no forwarding address."

"Job?"

"Until late last year, he worked for a venture capital firm in Marina del Rey. They downsized his ass, but it wasn't personal. They got rid of the entire real estate division."

"What address did he give them?" I asked. "He'd have to provide that for his severance and COBRA health care."

Tyler flipped through some papers. "A post office box in Culver City."

"Is LAPD staking it out?"

"We can't wait for him to surface," Faraday said. "I'm going to sic Fletch on this and see what he comes up with."

Tyler laid on the horn and cursed.

We were south of downtown, stuck in a massive traffic jam in the middle of the day. Crackheads wove in and out of the stalled cars, begging. USC students pedaled blithely past giant potholes and blocked-off lanes. Tired, sweaty, annoyed people stepped off the curb and peered into traffic for exhaust-belching packed buses that never seemed to come.

"From street level, Los Angeles sure looks like a Third World country," I said.

"This city is doomed." Tyler was in a foul mood because his car A/C was out.

He leaned forward and the back of his sweat-soaked shirt peeled off the seat with a wet suck.

"The schools are getting worse, the police force is being slashed, everyone's out of work, no one's got medical insurance. And it's gridlock twenty-four hours a day."

I nodded. "For me, L.A. is like a bad boyfriend I can't break free of. Every time I start packing, it lures me back, promising it will try harder this time." I sighed. "When it gets miserably hot like this, I remind myself what temperate winters we have."

"That's working real good for you. Is that sweat beading on your upper lip?" Tyler said. *He'd been looking at my lips.*

"It's not just me, everyone's hot and miserable today," I said, "but they're out there hustling. They know the government's not going to bail them out. So they're going to roast a goat in a pit and sell some dang tasty *birria* tacos on the corner until the health department shuts them down."

"Stop it," Tyler moaned. "I'm hungry and you're torturing me."

We were due downtown at the office of Paxton's lawyer at two p.m. and had decided to grab lunch first at a food mall near Grand and 36th called Mercado la Paloma that was short on ambience, long on taste, and easy on the pocketbook.

Settling on a Peruvian eatery called Mo-Chica, we slaked our thirst with exotic drinks that we got from huge glass bottles on the counter.

I chose a violently purple drink made of Inca corn. Tyler got a sunshine yellow passion fruit *liquado*. As the sweat dried on our skin, a Japanese waitress took our order in

Spanish-accented English.

Outside Mercado la Paloma, the streets were a wasteland of mirage-inducing heat, trash, pawnshops, strip malls, and greasy smells from fast-food joints. Inside, it was cool and clean and industrious and humming with the homey, satisfying vibe of people chowing down.

"I wish they could clone Mercado la Paloma and put one in every neighborhood," I said, between bites of a dish made of chicken, walnuts, egg, and potatoes.

Tyler chewed in ecstasy, swallowed, and shook his head. "You think these mom-and-pop places could afford the rent in West L.A.? Uh-uh. That's why they're here."

After lunch, we walked to the next stall and bought *nieves,* ice cream studded with swirly chunks of *guayanaba* and *coco.*

In the parking lot, Tyler called over a guy pushing a beat-up cart and bought a baggie full of mango slices and chili salt, joking all the while in his fluid, colloquial Spanish.

The seller, a small, bowlegged man with deep creases in his face, waited hopefully to see if I'd buy one too, then accepted his dollar, tipped his hat, and rolled off, ringing his bell in search of more customers.

At two p.m., we waited in Harvey Lambert's

immaculate office while police detectives interviewed Henry Paxton for the second time. The detectives wouldn't say what new information they'd learned to prompt this meeting.

The senator walked in to debrief, looking shaky. He said, "They found Emily's purse in a Dumpster about a mile from her apartment. No cash or cards. That's all they told me."

Faraday asked me to ride back to West L.A. with him.

We had a new case, a pro athlete named Artemio "Art" Salazar who'd been accused of rape. My first task was to set up a meeting with the athlete, his manager, and his attorney.

I called from the car.

Salazar's manager told me the athlete was in Amarillo visiting his mother and would be back in two days. Salazar's attorney said his client was at a training facility in Denver. I suggested they get their stories straight, explaining why Salazar had to tell his story before anyone else did. The attorney promised he'd talk to his client and brief us at two o'clock the following day in his office.

Faraday, who was listening in, looked unhappy.

My old-school boss liked to sit down with clients.

If they were good speakers, if they were sincere and sympathetic, we trotted them out before the cameras like prize ponies. If not, we coached them, then set up limited press. Everyone has a narrative, they just need to learn their story arc.

Face-to-face meetings with clients also allowed us to probe more deeply, gathering information to construct a better defense. In some cases, we told the lawyers that unsavory facts should be admitted and dealt with up front because they'd eventually leak out, making the client look sneaky and deceitful.

But we didn't always get the access we wanted. Some clients were too distracted or messed up or checked out. In those cases we met with their lawyers and managers, who told us only what they wanted us to know. It looked like Art Salazar was going to be one of those.

Back at the office, I read up on our new client.

Salazar was a Mexican-born, Texas-raised pitching phenomenon who'd signed with the Dodgers last year in a $60 million deal. He hadn't talked to anyone since a waitress at a Cleveland hotel had accused him of luring her up to his room under false pretenses and raping her. A tall, sinewy athlete with green eyes, café-au-lait skin, and a soft-spoken manner, Salazar had dated Britney Spears and a long string of Hollywood "it" girls. Last year, he'd set the celebrity world agog and stoked the hopes of regular girls everywhere when he married his high school sweetheart from Amarillo, a pretty, lynx-eyed teenager who still lived at home. They'd recently become the parents of trip-lets.

After doing my homework, I made a few calls to Mom's insurance company and her doctors. I also scoured the Internet for any upcoming medical trials for promising new breast cancer drugs. Plan for the worst, hope for the best, that's my motto.

When I headed out for my date that evening, Faraday was in his office, talking into his Bluetooth. He gave me an inquisitive look and glanced at his watch, as if to say, "I have seen you and taken note of the fact that you're leaving the office so early."

Only in the Blair universe was nine p.m. considered early.

I drove east with the windows down, enjoying the evening breeze on my bare skin. But by the time I hit La Cienega, I was sweating. Reluctantly, I raised the window and put on the air. I wasn't in coastal L.A. anymore, where ocean tradewinds cooled the land. Five miles inland, a different L.A. began. The inhabitants here also looked to the Pacific for inspiration. But against their backs, they felt the hot dragon breath of the desert sprawling sixty miles to the east.

Soon I hit the Pico-Union district, an old, densely populated barrio south of MacArthur Park where Central Americans and Koreans jostled for space.

I was headed to a homey Cuban place called El Colmao. Like so many of L.A.'s best ethnic restaurants, its substantial delights hid behind a no-frills strip mall in a graffiti-plagued downmarket neighborhood. These places had to be good — there was just too much competition.

In front, vendors with pushcarts roamed the sidewalks, selling tacos, *paletas,* and fresh papaya on a stick.

Illuminated in the sodium light of the streetlamps, they looked like a tableau out of a nineteenth-century Jacob Riis photo of New York's Lower East Side, where peddlers and ragpickers roamed the streets, selling everything but WASP forebearers.

I'd initially suggested a tapas bar, but I was happy that Dr. Turcotte preferred the garlicky juices of El Colmao. The guy had a Beverly Hills practice but his heart was with *la gente* in the barrio. Already I could see us trekking through the jungles of El Salvador, packs strapped across our backs, as we made our way to the remote village where he'd tend to the sick while I would . . . I wasn't sure what I'd do, but I loved the idea of such an adventure.

It was easy to spot him amid the crammed booths and tables. He was the only blond.

"Hi." I slipped into the red booth across from him, my palms suddenly slick with sweat.

"You made it!" said Rob.

"I'm sorry about last time."

"No worries. Don't you love it here? I think I could live off the smells alone. And the chicken is extraordinary. With *moros y Cristianos y plátanos.*"

"Yum," I said, noting how the Spanish flowed off his tongue. For some reason, that reminded me of Tyler. Firmly, I pushed my colleague to the back of my head and concentrated on admiring Rob's tan, muscular forearms. His face was open and pleasant and symmetrical, the skin smooth and ruddy. I wondered if he'd had any work done, and if I'd ever know him well enough to ask.

It occurred to me that Rob and I were polar opposites. He was all about using cutting-edge technology to create a beautiful exterior while I'd embraced smart drugs to tweak and improve my cognitive function on the inside, where no one could see. Cosmetic *neurology.*

The waitress came and we both ordered Jamaica, a purple drink made of boiled flower petals.

"Rough day?" he asked, giving me a pensive look.

"We've got a couple of big cases and I'm a little stressed."

"Anyone I'd recognize?"

"I'm not supposed to talk about it." I smiled apologetically. "Violating client confidentiality, all that."

"Will I read your name in the paper or see you interviewed on TV?"

"You might. What about you? Operated on any movie stars lately?"

"Touché." He grinned.

Even though we were white-collar professionals, we were still in the service industry.

The chips and salsas arrived — an emerald green tomatillo, a chunky tomato one, and a smoky, brickred one with charred chipotles.

"So tell me about your next medical mission," I said between bites. "I want to live vicariously."

He was planning a trip to a refugee camp on the Thai-Burmese border. Malaria was rampant. Snakebite was a constant problem. Malnutrition. Infant mortality. There was almost no prenatal care; folic acid supplements were unheard of, so cleft palates were a problem. There were plenty of wounds to sew up as well.

Rob was enthusiastic about his work and damn sexy, with that explorer's tan. He was flirting with me.

"I almost gave up on you, Maggie. Figured you were just shining me on. I mean, we're both busy, but sometimes you just have to make time. Or it sends the wrong signal, you know?"

"I'm sorry. But I cleared the decks this evening. We can eat in peace."

"I don't believe it. Maybe you should turn off your phone."

"I'll put it on vibrate."

The food arrived and we tucked in. The chicken was all lime, vinegar, and garlic juice goodness. The plantains were hot. The yucca, which is often too starchy for me, was tasty. The *moros y Cristianos* an inspired blend.

I was on my fifth bite when I heard buzzing. My phone skittered across the table.

I looked down. It wasn't the office, I saw with relief.

"Whoever it is can wait," I said as the phone finally went quiet.

But the call had killed our relaxed mood. We made desultory small talk, both of us avoiding looking at the phone that sat on the table like a little black bomb about to go off.

"Oh, hell," I said, reaching for it. "I'll put it away."

Just then it vibrated in my hand and automatically I answered.

And immediately realized what I'd done.

I glanced up at Rob. His brow furrowed and his eyes darkened like a tropical sky before a storm.

"Hello," said a voice in my ear. "My lawyer said to call you. So I can tell you what happened." The voice had a lilt not unlike the restaurant patrons of El Colmao.

My heart thrummed, then sank.

"Sure," I said. "Thanks for calling. Is this Arte . . ." I glanced up at Rob's stormy eyes and remembered about confidentiality. "Who's calling please?"

"Art Salazar. I'm on my way to my lawyer's office. Meet me there in twenty minutes."

I took a deep breath. "I thought you were in Amarillo. Or Denver."

"No, I'm right here. Okay. You have the address?"

"I know where he is," I said.

I made one last attempt to salvage my romantic summer evening. "I thought we were going to meet your attorney tomorrow at two?"

"This is getting done *now.*" The phone in my ear clicked off.

Rob put down his fork.

"Um," I said. "That was a very important client."

The doctor's eyes narrowed. "Aren't they *all* very important clients."

"Some clients are more important than others."

"You can deal with it tomorrow, right?"

"I'm afraid I can't. I have to be at a lawyer's office in twenty minutes."

Quickly, greedily, I shoveled in another three bites.

Rob wore a look of disbelief. "You're kidding."

"No. I'm sorry."

"It's almost ten."

"The news cycle runs twenty-four hours."

I put my napkin on the table.

"I don't like this any more than you do," I

said. "But I have to go. I have this all-consuming, high-pressure job and basically I'm on call all the time if something breaks. And this is a big one. It's something you've seen on ESPN, in the paper."

I hated the pompous way I sounded. Important, high-pressure job. As if his wasn't.

"This is it, Maggie. I've given you three chances."

"I know. And I've already apologized profusely. Maybe we could have another meal next week, when this case is under control," I said.

"Why bother? By then you'll have a new emergency. And our meal would end the same way."

"Not necessarily."

"Don't kid yourself. You're a slave to your job. You're on this ridiculous treadmill and life's passing you by."

"Thanks for the lecture, Doc, but right now, I've got exactly fifteen minutes to get downtown." I got a twenty-dollar bill out of my purse. "Let me give you some money toward the meal."

"No."

I laid it on the table. "Then please buy some refugee kid a dose of antibiotics when you get to Myanmar."

He looked at me for a long moment. Then he shook his head.

"I like you, Maggie. But I can't live this way."

"You don't have to be so mean, I'm just trying to make a living."

My phone chirped, and despite myself, I glanced down. "HOPE YR ON WAY TO AS LAW OFFICE," Faraday texted.

"See," said Rob Turcotte. "Even now, when I'm trying to have a serious conversation with you, you can't focus."

"I'm a horrible person. It was nice knowing you."

I shouldered my purse and made my way blindly through the Formica tables filled with families relaxing over late-night dinners.

From behind me, Rob yelled, "Call me if you get downsized and decide you're ready to get a life."

It was after midnight and Mom was asleep by the time I got home, so I went out back and sat in the glider, rocking pensively. A head poked through the backyard fence, followed by a pair of shoulders. Then Earlyn crawled through the hole and advanced toward me. She held something in her arms.

"I thought I heard you come in," said Earlyn triumphantly. "Look what I've got."

The thing in her arms squirmed and I realized it was alive. She sat down, pulling it into her lap. It was a cat. A very large cat. Tawny and luxuriously furred. It had large tufted ears, a ruff of fur around its neck, large whisker pads, and a long fluffy plume of a tail. And large green eyes that regarded me with solemn intelligence.

"Jesus Christ, Earlyn, have you captured a bobcat?"

"This is Smokey," Earlyn said. "I got him at the Maine coon rescue."

"Hello, Smokey," I said, petting him. His fur was soft and thick and his motor started up immediately.

"He's a love," I said.

"Yes, he is," Earlyn said. "I've been scouring the Internet, looking for one of these guys. Got him off a family in Artesia. They're moving to Singapore and can't take him. And when I got home with him tonight, there was a message on my machine about another one. So I'm driving up to Ventura tomorrow. I'd like Smokey to have a companion."

"What you gonna call the second one?"

"Bandit. Get it?"

An image of Burt Reynolds flashed through my head. "Smokey and the Bandit."

Earlyn nodded. "I can't believe it. Two cats in one day. When it rains, it pours."

"That is so true. With men as well, I think. I've gone months without anyone so much as looking at me, and now there may be several possibilities on the horizon," I said, suddenly feeling the need to confide in someone.

"Your mother will be thrilled."

"It's like they can smell that someone else is interested. The first is a doctor, but he wants someone who can give him undivided attention, and my work gets in the way. The second is a colleague who's been throwing some interesting vibes my way."

I made a face. "But I don't trust him. He's too much of a wheeler-dealer." I hesitated. "And there's a third guy. He's lemon meringue pie-in-the-sky à la mode gorgeous and I've had a terrible crush on him since high school. Tall, blond, tanned lawyer surfer. Wonderful family." I paused. "At least I used to think so. They've been having troubles lately."

"Date them all, honey. Enjoy yourself. You're young."

"Only from your perspective, Earlyn. I'm thirty-three."

"What I wouldn't give to be thirty-three again. You know, I feel younger now than I did at fifty-three and even thirty-three, when I was so preoccupied with raising my family. But this old body . . ."

"You're young at heart, Earlyn."

When I tiptoed down the hallway twenty minutes later, Mom's reading light was back on. She was in bed, a Charlaine Harris book propped on her chest. Mom had always been an insomniac and a reader. Now she was bingeing on vampires.

She wore a frilly cotton nightgown and I couldn't believe how young she looked. She was sixty. By my ripe old age of thirty-three, she was already married, a mother, and working two jobs.

Now she scooted over and patted the covers. "Come here and tell me about your day."

Soon I was nestled in the warm hollow where her body had just lain.

I figured she'd bring up her illness when she was ready.

"Got a new case today, Mom. Art Salazar."

"He that athlete raped some girl?"

"Well, that's the question. Salazar says it was consensual."

"I heard his wife just had triplets. He's probably not getting any at home."

"Mom! When did you become such a

brazen hussy?"

"When did you become such a prude?"

My face fell. She reached out and touched my arm. "I shouldn't have said that, hon. It's not true, anyway."

But she'd hit a nerve and I started to sniffle. "Sometimes I'm afraid I'll never feel a man's arms around me again. It scares me."

I didn't want to tell her about my botched date.

"Of course you will," Mom said soothingly. "You're beautiful and funny and smart and kind."

For some reason, that just made me more melancholy. "Thanks, Mom. But I work around the clock. Look, it's after midnight. Again! How will I ever meet anyone this way?"

"At work, maybe?" Mom said. She slapped her book closed. "Now tell me about this baseball player. They're all overgrown kids, you know. They're paid to be aggressive on the field and they're indulged and pampered and showered with money and they never grow up. Raping girls! He could get any girl he wants, good-looking guy like that."

"Salazar says the girl came on to him."

"Oh?"

"We just met with him, in his lawyer's office. Luckily for us, he's the poster boy for clean living. When his teammates go out carousing, he stays in the hotel and Skypes with his wife. On the night in question, he says the waitress at the hotel restaurant struck up a conversation when she brought his salad. Said her eleven-year-old nephew idolized him and was there any way she could get an autographed baseball. Salazar said the best he could do was an auto-graphed photo. She said she'd come up to his room to get it when her shift ended."

"Uh-oh," said Mom.

"So at eleven fifteen she walks into Sala-zar's room. He asks for the nephew's name and signs a photo: 'Dear Brandon. Stay cool and live your dreams. From your pal, Art Salazar.' He hands her the photo, and from there, the stories diverge wildly. Salazar claims she started kissing him and pretty soon they moved to the bed and had consensual sex."

"Uh-huh," said Mom.

"The girl claims that Salazar threw her on the bed and raped her."

"Did she scream? Did anyone in the other rooms hear any signs of a struggle?"

"The girl said she feared for her life. Sala-zar's six two, a professional athlete. She's five three and weighs one hundred ten pounds."

Mom made a clicking sound with her teeth. "In my day, if you went up to a guy's room, you were asking for it." She looked at me. "So what do you think? Did he rape her?"

I stretched out, feeling the nubby chenille of the bedspread through my silk blouse, and recalled the meeting.

Salazar's attorney had been fidgety and nervous, like he was on coke or something. He kept interrupting his client to say, "What Art means is . . . What Art's trying to say is . . ." until Faraday turned to the attorney and asked him to please shut up and let the guy talk.

But he'd done it in Spanish. Then he'd looked at Salazar and winked, and that broke the ice.

After that, the baseball player opened up. Salazar seemed filled with anguished guilt for betraying his wife. He'd been deliberate in his choice of words, backtracking at times to correct himself as he described what happened. The story didn't seem pat or rehearsed. He was very specific about some details, while Faraday had to prompt him about others.

There was none of the coiled grace, the laser intensity that I'd seen on TV clips of

Dodger games. Salazar was strikingly hand-some, but I was struck more by his angry bewilderment. Sitting in a high-backed chair in his attorney's plush office, he looked like a small-town boy who'd been plucked up by fate and deposited into a different dimension.

"My wife," he groaned at one point. "The mother of my children. She curses me and hangs up each time I call."

"Here's what you do," Faraday said. "Tomorrow morning, you go down to Beverly Hills and you buy the biggest diamond you can find. You have them wrap it in a fancy box, then you get on a plane and fly home. You get on your knees and you apologize and promise it will never, ever happen again."

A ray of childlike hope lit up Salazar's eyes. "You think she'll take me back?"

We all nodded.

"She's got three babies and she wants them to have a father," I said.

"And you tell her the truth, that the girl set you up," Faraday said. "One of my staffers did a little research and this girl has a history of mental instability. She dropped out of college. Spent time in psych wards. Drifted for several years before landing this job. This isn't the first time she's made a rape accusation. The previous time, the police declined to make an arrest. So it was like a loaded gun, you walking into her waitress station that night."

Now I watched the shadows move across the coved ceiling and considered my mother's question: Was Art Salazar guilty of sexual assault? How could anyone not in that room ever truly know what had happened?

"I think he cheated on his wife," I said. "But I don't think he raped the girl."

I explained what Fletch had dug up.

Mom was silent for a moment. Then she said softly, "Maggie. Do you ever think about the girl who made the accusation? The possibility she might be telling the truth?"

"Yes I do. But you're the one who pointed out that she went up to Salazar's room late at night. She put herself in a vulnerable position. Was that wise? I mean, I'd never do something like that."

But I had, at sixteen. I'd been naïve. Stupid. Trusting. Me and Anabelle, in Playa del Rey.

Later, as I tossed and turned in my own bed, the aroma of night-blooming jasmine invaded my room, thick and cloying as fog. In the Angeles National Forest, an inferno was raging, adding the barbecue smell of smoky ash. Up in the canyon, a coyote yipped. Several more answered, their high, lonesome cries veering into shrieks as they closed in on something.

The smell of panicked skunk wafted slowly into the room.

Behind closed eyelids, I saw the skunk turning in desperation, saw the leering muzzles reflected in the whites of its eyes.

Jasmine with its carnal, charnel-house reek. Skunky animalistic musk. Bonfires that rained ash flakes and rust. My brain supplied the salt sea tang and, once again, I was back on that beach in Playa del Rey where part of me would always remain, when the true face of the world was revealed to me at sixteen.

17

August 1993

I came back to consciousness, shuddering from a nightmare where dark shapes moved below the surface, waiting to devour me. Already their icy tongues lapped at my feet.

The sand was cold beneath me. Fog blanketed the dark beach. The invisible sea crashed and hissed and I cried out, scooting back as waves surged over my legs. How had I gotten here? My mouth felt sour and dry, my head buzzed with static. There were voices nearby, the red cherry of a cigarette. If people were that close, why didn't they help? An image came, unbidden. I was running through the dunes with a guy. David? Darren? Dan!

"Dan?" I called.

"She lives," said a voice.

"Dan went back to the house. But I say, not so fast. Mermaids like you don't wash ashore every night."

There was coarse laughter.

"Only every other night. When there's a par-tay."

Another wave came. I crawled farther up the beach and hunkered on all fours.

"Help me," I croaked.

The voices grew silent, but I felt them in the darkness, like disembodied spirits, watching. Their breath quickened, the air tightened in anticipation. I grew afraid.

I scrabbled upright, kicking sand as I edged away, bleating more loudly as my voice returned. I looked around but the beach was empty.

I began to scream.

From up by the house came an answering shout, then a flashlight playing across the dunes.

"Over here," I called, staggering toward the light.

And then Luke was running to meet me.

"Maggie! What happened?"

His panicked eyes switched from my face to my clothes and back in disbelief.

I looked down. My breasts hung out of Anabelle's lacy top, encrusted with sand and salt water and God knows what else.

Luke was already whipping off his shirt and draping it over my shoulders. "Are you okay?"

Mortified, I tugged the sides of Luke's shirt together and tried to make my trembling fingers push the buttons through.

"Let me," he said, averting his eyes and doing up the shirt. "Now talk to me, Maggie. What happened?"

"I went for a walk on the beach with a guy named Dan. The last thing I remember was lying on the sand looking up at him. He was going to kiss me."

Then it hit me, and I felt very stupid. "The drinks. They were spiked."

"Aw, Christ. Did anything happen? I mean, did he . . . ?" Luke broke off.

Gingerly, I ran my hands over my body. I still had my panties. I slid my hand inside, feeling for wetness, for blood, but there was only damp, chafing sand.

"I don't know. It doesn't feel like it. But I was passed out. I mean, he could have done anything . . . anyone could have."

I leaned into him, sobbing.

His arms wrapped around me. And all the oomph went out of me. My legs buckled. I clung to his neck and he swept me up like I was made of goose down instead of blood and bone and cartilage.

His arms were warm and strong, and he smelled like bleached cotton and barbecue smoke and sharp rye bread. And that part

330

was just like I'd imagined so many times in my dreams. But what followed was not.

His voice rose, urgent and muffled against my shoulder. "Are you sure nothing happened? It's important that you tell me. Please don't be embarrassed."

"I'm okay," I said in a small voice.

"Good." Luke breathed heavily, then gave a loud moan. "Where's Anabelle?"

"Back at the house."

"She wasn't with you?"

"She wanted to stay with this guy Ivan," I said, trying to piece the shards of the evening back together. "They were making out in a bedroom."

He gripped me tighter and began to jog uphill, back to the house.

"Why didn't you stay with her?" he demanded between gulps of air.

"She didn't want me to."

"Come on, Maggie! You're her best friend. How could you leave her?"

He was huffing now from the exertion of carrying me. And from anger.

I was glad I couldn't see his face.

"I don't know," I wailed. "She practically ordered me to leave and I was feeling so strange and floaty and my brain wasn't working right."

Luke jogged faster.

"And when Dan and I left the bedroom," I went on, "there was this creepy old guy in the hallway . . ."

I didn't get a chance to finish.

Luke's arms went slack and I tumbled unceremoniously onto the sand.

"Oh, Jesus," he said. "I've got to get up there."

And he was sprinting away.

I started to cry.

Still running, Luke turned and shouted, "Don't cry. It'll be okay."

But that just made me sob harder, because it wasn't okay.

Sitting there on the damp sand, I knew that something had ruptured. A crack had appeared in our world, sucking us into a black abyss. Nothing would ever be the same again.

There were dozens of kids on the ocean deck, smoking and drinking and talking, and they barely looked up when I stumbled in.

"Hair of the dog?" said an older guy by the keg, taking in my disheveled state and offering me a beer. I ignored him and walked inside, finding my way to the bedroom where I'd left Anabelle.

Someone had kicked the plywood door

open and it hung by one hinge.

Inside, Luke had Ivan up against the wall. Anabelle lay huddled on the futon, grinding her face into the pillow. Luke seized Ivan by the collar and lifted him straight up.

"Let go," screamed Ivan, trying to wriggle free.

Luke kneed him and flung him down. "That's for my sister."

Ivan crawled away, making a strange, inhuman sound. For a moment, he crouched, panting in the corner.

"Chill out, man," he said at last. "Your sister's fine."

Luke crossed the room and bent over Anabelle.

"What happened?"

Anabelle's face was streaked with tears and her eyes were dilated. Her pretty dress was hiked halfway up and a viscous white substance trailed along her inner thigh. As Luke touched her shoulder, she turned her face away.

"And the Barracuda got his taste." Ivan smirked. "So everyone's . . ."

Luke leaped up, running at Ivan. "You animal. I'm going to kill you."

"But, Luke," Ivan whined, cowering.

Luke began to kick him methodically. "Shut the fuck up, asshole."

Three guys who looked like beach volleyball players appeared. Two pinned Luke's arms back and the third hustled Ivan out of the room.

"You wanna fight, take it outside, yo," said one.

The volleyballers threw Luke into the wall and left. He landed with a thud and slid down. For a moment, he sat with his head lowered. Somewhere out front, a car started, revved, and tore off.

Luke reached for the overturned mirror where Ivan had laid out lines a lifetime ago. A speckled residue dusted the glass. Luke ran a finger along the mirror, lifted it to his mouth, and licked it.

"Shit."

"What?" I said.

Luke didn't answer.

With great gentleness, he scooped up Anabelle in his arms. "Belle," he said, and his eyes filled with hurt confusion. "I'm sorry."

"Come on," he told me curtly. "We're getting out of here."

We walked out, me trailing behind like usual. Luke deposited his sister in the backseat and covered her with a Mexican serape from the trunk.

For a moment he stood there, staring at her. He ran a hand through his golden hair,

muttering, "What now? What do we do?"
Then he leaned over and cradled Anabelle's
chin. He tapped lightly on her cheek.

"Anabelle? This Ivan guy. Is he the one
who . . . ?"

Slowly, Anabelle shook her head.

"Okay. It wasn't Ivan. But you can identify
who did this, right? You want to call the
police, report what happened? We'll go
straight there."

Anabelle shook her head again.

"What about you?" Luke turned to me.

"I-I don't think anything happened to
me," I said, still fuzzy from the drugs. Luke
rolled his eyes like I was the village idiot.

"What I mean," he said, "is would you be
able to ID the guy to the police? For Anabelle's sake. She may be too out of it to
remember."

He examined me, and in that moment, I
knew that he despised me, that he held me
responsible for everything that had happened.

If I hadn't left Anabelle alone, she
wouldn't have gotten raped. And we
wouldn't be standing here right now, our
lives cracking into fragile eggshell pieces.

I struggled to shake free of the mental fog.
Could I pick Ivan and Dan out of a police
lineup? The roofies had melted their faces

335

into carnival fun house fragments.

"Ivan and Dan," I said. "Yeah, maybe. But I don't know their last names."

Luke sighed with exasperation.

We were driving now, me cuddled around a comatose Anabelle in the backseat, the soft woven serape pulled over both of us.

"Not Ivan and Dan. The guy in the hallway. Did you get a good look at him?"

For a moment, I stared stupidly at the back of Luke's golden head. Then I understood. And the thought of that degenerate aging beach boy violating my gentle, ethereal friend sickened me beyond words.

"The Barracuda?" I asked.

Luke said nothing. His mouth tightened and a muscle along his jaw twitched.

I took a deep breath. "It was dark. I saw only half his face, in the light of a match. I don't know if I could identify him, like, in a police lineup."

Luke groaned.

"I think we could both identify Ivan," I said carefully.

"He took off, didn't you hear his car?" Luke said bitterly. "And I doubt his name is really Ivan. As to the Barracuda. . . ." Luke's voice trailed off in despair. "I think he's some kind of drug dealer, if it's the guy I'm thinking of. I've never actually met him, but his reputation . . . he likes young girls. He likes to get them hooked so he can . . . Oh, God! I *knew* I shouldn't have let Anabelle talk me into this."

I leaned forward to touch his shoulder. "We begged you to take us to parties. We were relentless."

"You're just kids. You think it's all cool glamour. You have no idea what goes on. I should have watched out for you. I should have known better. I should have warned you." His voice rose in despair and he punched the dashboard.

Even through my haze, I realized what an uphill battle we faced. Anabelle and I had been drugged. We'd make unreliable witnesses. Ivan would say Anabelle had kissed him willingly and asked me to leave. If questioned, I would have to confirm this. Who could say Anabelle hadn't engaged in consensual sex with Ivan and the Barracuda and anyone else who'd wandered in?

And the questions wouldn't end with Anabelle. I imagined the defense lawyer cross-examining me, asking why I'd agreed to walk down to the dark dunes with Dan. Why I'd left my friend alone in a volatile situation. Was it because I was a slut too?

And then there was Corvallis. People would whisper and judge us as we walked by. Everyone knew Catholic girls were *the worst.*

I dreaded facing my mother. She'd be sympathetic, but I could already see the disappointment on her drawn, overworked face. She'd pull the plug on my friendship with Anabelle. She was already suspicious of the time I spent there; she'd heard that the Paxton kids ran with a fast crowd. If I had just stayed in the Valley and come home at a decent hour, none of this would have happened. And now my senior year was about to start. I had college applications to fill out. Scholarships to hunt down. I had to study and focus as the last difficult lap came into sight.

We were on the 405 now, instinct sending Luke hurtling home to Villa Marbella. In the dead of night, cars shot past leaving liquid traces in the air.

Miranda and Henry were in Washington, D.C., for some kind of political fund-raiser, which at the beginning of the evening had seemed like a lucky break for us. Now I just wanted to climb upstairs, crawl between the covers, and forget this night had ever happened.

"Maybe we should ask Anabelle what she wants to do in the morning?" I said.

My voice rose in Valley Girl lilt, turning

the statement into a question, hoping he'd disagree. Because even then, I wasn't strong enough to defy Anabelle's wishes by myself.

But I need to say this too: I was a coward.

"You sure?" Luke's voice radiated concern. And something else. A tinge of relief, perhaps? He was the one who'd brought us here. He was Anabelle's older brother. He should have been looking out for us.

I watched Luke's face in the rearview, the moon and headlights glinting off the white teeth in that tanned face, his eyes tense and uneasy, glancing from me to his sister to the road and back again. Trying to decide. Gauging me, what kind of a witness I'd make, if it came to that. And whether to tell his parents.

Slowly, I nodded. "I think this should be her call."

"Okay." Luke let out a long breath. He turned to look at Anabelle, whose head lolled back against the seat, eyes closed.

"It's my fault, more than anyone's," he said, his voice wavering.

"It's not any of our faults," I said mechanically.

But I breathed with selfish relief that he didn't hate me or blame me after all. Then something struck me.

"Luke, if Anabelle was snorting coke at

that party, wouldn't it have counteracted the roofies? Why's she still so out of it when I'm okay?"

Luke's upper lip twitched.

"That wasn't coke. It was heroin."

18

At our morning meeting, Fletch slunk into Faraday's office. He looked pasty and rat-bit, like he'd been up all night and had slept under his desk.

He said, "You wanted to find Jake Slattery."

Faraday stood half out of his seat. "You got him?"

Fletch looked down, unable to bear the eye contact, much less scrutiny from three pairs at once.

"I got something," he mumbled, opening his laptop. "Lot G. Long-Term Parking, LAX."

I felt the familiar tingle up the back of my neck at the mention of LAX. Anabelle was lying in the culvert, shaking, as the jet passed within feet of her prone body. So many booby-trapped places.

"What?" Faraday exploded.

Fletch twitched and grinned like the cat

that ate the meth canary.

"I love patterns," he said. "In nature they're a thing of beauty — golden ratio, seashell spirals, pi. Apply them to what I do and they can be exquisitely revealing. Consider Jake Slattery's credit card bills. There's a pattern to the charges. Most of them occur near the airport."

"Maybe that's where his new job is?"

"He doesn't have one," Fletch said, his Adam's apple bobbing. "But he shops at Trader Joe's in Westchester. Drinks at the Sky-Hi on Sepulveda. Buys his gas at an ARCO station on La Tijera, near Randy's Donuts — that's the place with the fifty-foot-high brown donut you can see from the 405 Freeway. They make a killer glazed. Anyway, he's also been paying one hundred fifty dollars a month for long-term parking at LAX Lot G since June."

"I don't get it. Is it cheaper than street parking?"

Fletch shook his head. "There's no in-out privileges. It's a onetime deal. But the credit card went dead a week ago, right after Emily Mortimer was killed. No new transactions posted."

"He's using cash," Tyler said.

"Or he's got cards under a different name," I said.

"Well, the interesting thing is that the two previous months' fees for parking were posted on his card July 2 and August 1. And it's now almost September."

"You think his car is still there?"

"He drives a blue Honda Odyssey mini-van," Fletch said, scratching his head. "I've got his license plate."

"Well done," said Faraday. "Tyler, Maggie, get over there and take a look, will ya? On your way back, stop at Randy's and buy Fletch a dozen glazed."

So much for giving me a break from the Paxton case.

But I didn't protest. It sounded awfully exciting, and perhaps even borderline dangerous.

Faraday said, "Now let's hear some theories about why his van's at a long-term lot in LAX."

"He ditched it because there's evidence inside?"

"He killed Emily and then somebody killed him and left his body inside."

"Shouldn't we call the police?" I said, feeling queasy.

No one bothered to answer.

The jets screamed and shrieked like Nazgûl,

darkening the sky as they came in for landings.

I shivered and forced back the spectral image of Anabelle in the LAX ditch. That had ended a long time ago. Anabelle had survived and conquered her demons. I didn't need to worry or freak out anymore. Besides, we were a good mile from the runways.

Lot G was off Imperial Highway, surrounded by other parking lots and expressways where thousands of cars whizzed past every day. It was a perfect example of hiding in plain sight. What would it be like to work here? I wondered, driving a shuttle bus filled with people nervous about making their flights, the entire lot juddering each time a plane swooped past.

We drove up to the gate of Lot G, took a ticket, and entered.

At the office, we asked about long-term parking. You had to pay a month in advance.

We thanked the counter lady. Then, armed with Jake Slattery's license plate, we cruised around looking for vans. The farther into the depths of the lot we got, the more beat-up cars we saw. Then the RVs and campers started.

Some were festooned with bicycles and camping gear and plastic vessels to hold water. It looked like people were living in the airport parking lot. There must have been more than a hundred RVs and campers clustered on the far fringes.

"Look." Tyler pointed to a life-sized ceramic dog in front of one camper. From inside another RV, a real dog barked. One camper had laid down a tiny Astroturf lawn surrounded by a white picket fence. Another had a semicircle of plastic chairs. Did people relax here with drinks, late at night when the crowds melted away and jet traffic slowed?

We found the van.

Excited, we called Faraday. He told us to watch from a discreet distance before making contact.

For an hour, we sat and watched. And waited.

There were no signs of life.

Slowly, we approached and knocked.

There was no answer.

We tried again to no avail, then struck up a conversation with a bearded man who poked his head out of the camper next door. He said he didn't know anything, but twenty bucks made him remember that his neighbor had taken off on his bicycle that morning.

Tyler peeled off two more twenties to buy

the man's silence when Slattery came back.

We parked far enough away not to draw attention and close enough to monitor who came near the van. For two more hours we sat in Tyler's vintage BMW 2002. Faraday told us to stay put and call him immediately if Jake Slattery returned.

But Slattery didn't show. Eventually, stuck in such close quarters, the talk turned personal and I learned Tyler had grown up in Inglewood.

He grinned. "People who aren't from here are always surprised to meet a native. But we're really not that rare."

"They like to think it was just tumbleweeds and dust before they arrived. A handful of Mexicans riding burros and Chumash gathering shellfish along the coast."

"Do you remember going to the beach as a kid and finding sand dollars and whelks and clams and pointy spirals? Now you're lucky to get one lousy cowrie."

"It's the same with butterflies," I said. "I used to sit in my friend's overgrown yard and see monarchs and swallowtails and painted ladies and buckeyes and so many others I didn't even know the names of. I was a nut for butterflies."

I looked up, suddenly self-conscious, but

346

his eyes met mine in silent understanding and I knew that he too mourned the passing of these tiny, jeweled creatures.

When Faraday called, it startled us both.

Tyler recapped the stalled stakeout, then handed me the phone.

"I need you to put in some time on Hollywood-Graystone this afternoon, so take a cab back, Tyler can handle it," Faraday said.

"What about Salazar?"

"I've got a few people working it."

Back at the office, I made calls to bands, agents, caterers, and event planners to make sure all systems were go for the gala party that we'd put together for the Hollywood-Graystone Hotel on Sunset Strip.

They'd hired us after the notorious rock star Magnus Rex had OD'd in the penthouse suite. We'd done all the usual things to make it clear the Art Deco hotel bore no responsibility for the death. We even unearthed records confirming that hotel security had called 911 and sent its on-site physician to the room moments after the cleaning lady found the body, cold and stiff with rigor mortis.

Once the investigation was over and the hotel cleared of any wrongdoing, I'd gotten creative. Instead of downplaying the death,

I suggested that management play up the notoriety and turn the penthouse suite into a glam, rock-and-roll bordello shrine to Magnus Rex (birth name: Sherman McCoy). It had been my idea to invite psychics and ghost hunters to the top floor, carrying steampunk equipment to scan for restless spirits.

Of course we'd alerted the media.

To nobody's surprise, the ghost hunters, who'd been plied with free rooms and booze, reported sighting a glowing, ethereal presence that couldn't be captured on camera. A bellboy had felt a rush of cold air when he'd gotten off on the wrong floor by accident, and patrons reported lights that flickered on and off around midnight (the coroner's estimated time of death). There was also a guest's laptop that had switched inexplicably to a YouTube clip of Magnus Rex.

All the hubbub had stirred up TV interest and a producer had dispatched a reporter and camera crew to investigate the supernatural activity as part of a ghost-hunting reality TV show. They'd be filming the party we'd set up to celebrate the official reopening of the suite, which had been rechristened with the dead singer's name and now cost triple the old nightly rate.

Already the hotel was booked six months solid with fans, looky-loos, and tourists who wanted a taste of Hollywood rock star glamour.

Gotta keep those billable hours coming.

As the sun began its nightly plunge into the western sea, Tyler strolled past my office.

I threw off my headphones.

"Did he show? Did you talk to him?"

Tyler turned away. "No. Faraday brought me back."

I wrinkled my nose. "That's stupid. What if Jake Slattery returned and you missed him? What if his neighbor spilled the beans and scared him off for good?"

"Don't worry, champ. I didn't leave until my replacement arrived."

"Who's that?" I said, curious.

"I don't know his name."

19

Several hours later, Tyler and I found ourselves leaving the office at the same time.

In the elevator, office etiquette reigned once more and our conversation was perfunctory and stilted.

In the car, I sprayed on Mitsouko by Guerlain. I'd scored a tiny bottle on eBay awhile back, but didn't dare wear it at the office. Created by Jacques Guerlain in 1919, Mitsouko was one of the original Orientals: a sweet, spicy, leathery, mossy fragrance with hints of peach and oak. Happily, I inhaled the scent of World War I ending, the Roaring Twenties, flappers and pearls, expat American writers sitting in red velvet chairs at Les Deux Magots mooning after beautiful French courtesans.

As I drove out, I saw Tyler bent over the open hood of his car.

"What's the matter?"

His face was glum. "I don't know."

"Need a jump? I've got cables."

"We can try," he said dubiously. "But I replaced the battery in June."

I pulled alongside and Tyler hooked up the cables. The car started. It coughed and rumbled like a tubercular ward, then died.

"Shit," said Tyler.

"You have Triple A?"

"No."

"You going to have it towed somewhere?"

"Viken can look at it tomorrow." He saw my puzzled look. "He's one of the daytime security guys. Armenian. Used to be a mechanic in Beirut. Those guys know their German cars."

"You're going to leave it here?"

"Yeah."

"Want a ride home?"

He looked up, considering. "That's okay, I'll jog."

I examined his clothes, his leather shoes. "Dressed like that? Are you crazy?"

He pointed to a gym bag in the passenger seat. "Got my gear. And I don't mind. It's a great way to see the city. You should try it sometime."

"Where do you live?" I asked, surprised.

"Hollywood." He gave me a loopy grin.

It was infectious. I grinned back.

Then I leaned over and flung the passenger door open.

"Get in," I said. "It's on my way home."

It felt strange to be in a car with Tyler and not be driving somewhere for work. There was a relaxed, almost playful air between us. Like we'd ditched school to play hooky.

Tyler lived way up Beachwood Canyon.

I followed his directions through the rustic stone gates of Hollywoodland, past the little coffee shop and dry cleaners, until the road grew winding and narrow.

As we pulled up to Holly View Drive, I saw two pairs of amber eyes reflected in the headlights. I flipped on the brights and they came into focus on the terraced hillside. Two deer, unperturbed by our presence. They checked us out, then bent their heads again to graze.

"Look," I said, enraptured.

"Rats with hooves," said Tyler. "They're after my tomatoes. I want you to know that I'm sacrificing a significant portion of my fall harvest for your gawking pleasure."

Somewhere below, a car backfired. With a fluid motion, the deer melted into the darkened hillside.

"Aw!" I said.

"They'll be moving on to my side yard for

their second course. Come on, I'll show you."

We got out of the car and, for the first time, I looked at Tyler's house. Up at the top of the bluff, a large villa was silhouetted against the night sky.

Unlocking the gate, Tyler ushered me into a rickety elevator. He pressed a button and the elevator began to rise.

"We could have taken the stairs," he said, "but there are two hundred twenty-seven of them and I figured with those high-heeled sandals . . ."

I glanced down, surprised he'd noticed. Locked in this tiny moving capsule, the space between us felt suddenly hot and intimate. I wondered what would happen if it stalled and we were trapped inside. It didn't seem like such a horrible thought.

The elevator clanged to a stop and we stepped onto the porch of a large Spanish house with a smaller house off to the right. The property was perched on a cliff that overlooked the L.A. Basin, giving a full view of the downtown spires.

Holly (wood) View Drive indeed.

At the very edge of the cliff, a pool glittered cerulean blue.

Tyler pointed to a neatly tended garden of staked vegetables. "I figured the deer would be munching my corn, but they've skedaddled so I won't need my shotgun."

"You don't have a shotgun!"

"Don't be so sure."

"Mr. Tough Guy," I scoffed.

"I also have a very sharp shovel. Comes in handy for killing rattlesnakes."

I glanced down and did a little two-step in my open-toed sandals.

Tyler shrugged. "The first time I found one, I called the Department of Fish and Game. I figured they'd put it in a bag and relocate it. But a guy came up and killed it. 'Dude,' I said, 'I can do that all by myself.' "

I nervously scanned the yard.

"We get tarantulas and scorpions too," Tyler said slyly. "Don't worry. I sweep the place clean every morning. Throw the scorps over the cliff."

The idea of scorpions and tarantulas raining down on unwary homeowners below made me flinch and laugh at the same time.

"I'm scaring you off," Tyler said.

"It's late. I should go."

"Will you stay for a drink? I've got a thirty-year-old Laphroaig that a grateful client gave me. It's the least I can offer you for driving me home."

Tyler took my unresisting arm and led me to an outdoor table sheltered by a grape arbor. Fat purple fruit hung in tantalizing clusters between emerald leaves.

During the day, the arbor would keep out of the worst of the sun and filter the light. At night, the pale moonlight cast a ghostly glow, diffused through the green and purple. The moon was almost full, illuminating the L.A. basin like a giant spotlight.

Above La Crescenta and La Canada Flintridge, the fires still raged with apocalyptic greed. Here in Hollywood, the sky was a peaceful dark velvet blue, the breeze warm but not stifling.

Tyler brought out a bottle, two glasses, and a plate of cheese and crackers. I almost didn't recognize the lanky figure standing before me in khaki shorts, flip-flops, and a black Iggy Pop T-shirt. He'd changed.

"Full disclosure," said Tyler. "This heap isn't mine. I rent the guesthouse."

"Who lives in the big house?"

"A woman named Dina Schwartzman. She was a screenwriter and her husband was a big director. He's passed on."

"I hope this isn't going to end like *Sunset Boulevard,* with you floating facedown in the pool."

Tyler chuckled. "Dina was never an actress, but she *is* a force of nature. She and her husband were bona fide card-carrying

Hollywood Communists. They made a lot of movies here but fled to Paris in 1951 when they got subpoenaed during the blacklist. They lived in Europe for years, hanging out with Picasso and making films with Costa-Gavras and Fellini. Dina came back a few years ago when her husband died. She's eighty-two and likes having me around."

"Is she a recluse?"

"Hardly. She gets flown to film festivals all over the world because she's one of the last remaining blacklisters. She's in Trieste this week or I'd introduce you."

Tyler poured two fingers of the amber liquid into cut-crystal glasses and we touched glasses and drank. The scotch had a rich peaty, smoky, sweet taste and lit me up inside. I took another sip. The liquor radiated outward from a sweet spot near my lower belly.

"What will your girlfriend say?" I asked, the liquor loosening my lips. "Diane. Wasn't that her name?"

Tyler looked at me in surprise. He pursed his lips. "I just made that up. I don't have a girlfriend."

"Hmmm." I slid my glass around on the wooden table.

Tyler poured us another scotch. Then he

went around the table lighting candles, moving with an assured grace and ease. The office seemed a million light-years away. For a moment I fantasized what it would be like to live here with Tyler, watching the sunset as the aroma of grilling fish and chicken came off the barbecue. I'd be climbing out of the pool, beads of water clinging to my skin, slicking back my hair as I wrapped a towel around my waist. Tyler would be bringing out a bottle of wine and a freshly tossed salad so we could eat al fresco.

He finished lighting the candles, then stood behind me, flicking his lighter aimlessly.

"Maggie?"

I turned and at the same time he leaned down and his lips grazed my ear.

"Oh," I said softly.

Then he angled his shaggy head and inclined his face toward mine and then we were kissing. His lips were full and soft and warm. He stumbled and braced an arm against the table, kicking aside a chair as he moved in closer. Then he wrapped his arms around me and pulled me to standing as he continued to kiss me. My arms went up around his neck.

For a long time, we stood together while the moths beat and fluttered and threw themselves against the glass lamps. The sky grew dusky blue as the moon rose higher and the downtown skyline lit up like a Christmas tree.

"You smell fantastic," he whispered at last, gathering up my hair and sniffing my nape. His warm breath tickled the fine hairs on the back of my neck and made me shiver with longing.

"Mmmm," I said, smiling and rising up on tiptoes to press myself against him like a cat.

"Maggie," he said at last, "let's go swimming."

"I-I . . . I didn't bring a suit."

"S'okay. Neither did I."

We slipped off our clothes and dove into the cool water. I surfaced, tingling with pleasure, moving weightless through the dark water, suspended over the city lights.

I dove back underwater and swam the length of the pool. I felt like a mermaid released back into the sea. The air smelled of lemon oil and honeysuckle and the persistent woodsmoke of the fires that were destroying the Angeles National Forest. Tyler surfaced beside me and our bodies entwined as he gripped the smooth tile edges of the pool with one hand. He felt slick and cool and hard against me.

The moon was high overhead, a harvest moon, and I breathed in sharply as it illuminated Tyler's upper body. A gigantic tattoo draped like a shawl over his shoulders and back. It was green and red and blue and black, nestling so perfectly under his shirt that I'd never suspected. I wriggled free and swam around to get a better view.

"Tell me the story of how you got this."

"It's the emblem of the marine squadron my grandfather was in during World War II. We went to a tattoo parlor in downtown Milwaukee, where he lived, and got them together the year before he died."

With butterfly fingers I traced the vines and eagle wings, the scrolled words.

"It's beautiful."

He turned to face me. "You're beautiful. Come here, I want to feel you."

I swam in. "I'm here."

"I want to get even closer."

I put my arms around him and he put his hands under me and lifted me up. And we tried. The movies make it look so easy, but water really does get in the way. Finally, Tyler climbed out of the pool and threw a towel down onto the grass. The air was warm and caressing and I lay down and he knelt next to me, touching all my secret places.

When he entered me, I gave a little gasp and clutched his slick, wet shoulders. The stars wheeled across the sky and the moon looked down on us, so huge and luminous that it made me want to cry.

"I've got to get home," I said, several hours later.

We stood in front of the open refrigerator, tearing strips of roast chicken off the bones with our fingers. We were starving, trembly, gluttonous.

"Jesus, Silver, that was amazing. I had no idea," Tyler said.

I reddened. "I didn't either," I said, wrestling the top off a pint of chocolate mocha almond swirl ice cream.

There's something about a hit of gooey chocolate fudge that really enhances a sex buzz, I thought, licking the spoon dreamily. Then I rinsed off my spoon, handed Tyler the ice cream, and collected my clothes.

I thought about calling him Matt or Matthew instead of Tyler, now that things had changed between us. I tried it out in my head, but it sounded flat and wrong.

Tyler sat on the kitchen counter and watched me dress.

"Just like that?" he said.

"What?"

"You're leaving?"

I nodded.

I wondered if he'd try to stop me. But he just shrugged and said, "Okay."

We didn't kiss good night. We were shy and nervous around each other, jumpy as cats again. I said good-bye. He squeezed my hand.

"Until tomorrow, then. At the office," he added, as if he found it hard to believe.

I told him I'd take the stairs this time.

He followed me across the grass and stood there hesitantly.

"I'll walk you down," he said.

"That's okay," I said, already eight steps down.

I paused and turned. "One thing you should know about me. I'm terrible at good-byes."

"Hello, then," Tyler called down. "Hello hello hello."

The canyon took up his cry, amplifying and ricocheting his voice as I made my way down in the lavender dark.

"Ello llo o oh ohhh."

20

I was showered and at work by eight the next morning.

Faraday was already in, talking on the phone with the door closed. His tie was loosened and his eyes bloodshot. Empty coffee cups and plastic food containers littered his desk.

He waved absently as I walked past. I wondered if he'd gone home. Feeling like he might need an energy boost, I went to the cafeteria and returned with two coffees. After a quick knock on Faraday's door, I walked in to deliver the fresh rocket fuel.

Faraday looked up with annoyance, then motioned me to leave.

I placed the coffee on his desk, thinking that no good deed goes unpunished, when I heard a familiar voice on the other end of the line say, "You've got to *do* something."

It was Luke Paxton.

Thank you, Faraday mouthed, shooing me away.

Wondering what new crisis had erupted, I walked back to my desk and scanned the wires. I was still puzzling it out when Faraday summoned me back.

He was on a different call now.

"You know what I'm wondering, Rick," he said into the phone, winking at me. "Why aren't the cops pounding the pavement to find Jake Slattery? Yeah, Emily Mortimer's boyfriend. Her *spurned* boyfriend. Let's just suppose Slattery learned that Emily was stepping out on him with Simon Paxton. He might have flown into a rage. He might have even killed her. Now there's a motive for you. Jealousy. The old if-I-can't-have-her-then-no-one-can. That's right, Rick. Jake Slattery is the wild card. He's the cipher in all this. Where is he? Why did he run? What does he know? Our clients, by contrast, have been up front about everything. They are cooperating fully with the police. They have nothing to hide."

He slapped down that line and picked up another waiting call.

Faraday listened for a moment, nodding, then said, "That's exactly right, Carl. You've summed things up beautifully. Now I'm going to tell you something. On the Q.T. A

363

little gift, from me to you. Just because we understand each other and sometimes we help each other out. But you didn't hear it from me, okay?"

A squawk of assent came over the line.

"Okay, Carl, here goes. Ask the cops exactly what they're doing to find Jake Slattery. And ask them about a Honda Odyssey in long-term parking at LAX."

Faraday listened some more.

"I'm sorry, Carl. You'll have to get the rest from them. And we understand each other on this, I hope. Good. Talk to you later, buddy."

He killed that call, then told me to sit down, a broad smile on his face.

"The cops don't know anything about an Odyssey at LAX," I said.

"They do now." He played with his earpiece.

"You and Tyler did excellent work yesterday. But I wasn't thinking things through when I sent you two to LAX. What if the guy had a gun? What if he took you hostage or threatened to blow himself up?"

Faraday shook his head. "We're crisis consultants, not a SWAT team. And we were in over our heads. That's why I called Tyler back in. Then I called the LAPD and told those detectives what we'd learned. I said we'd gotten a tip to check out parking spot 749 in LAX long-term parking lot G. That Jake Slattery might be hiding out there. Let them do the dirty work."

Faraday paused, looking pious, looking for praise.

His phone beeped with a text. Faraday squinted. "It's Samantha," he said gleefully. "She's at LAX." He looked up. "A safe distance away, of course. Police cordoned off the lot. They've got the van open, forensics people crawling all over it."

Faraday picked up a cigar and chomped on it.

"I'm feeling optimistic."

Back at my computer, I watched it unfold live. Police had swarmed the van and found it empty. There were shots of burly guys carrying out boxes of evidence.

"Too bad they didn't find the boyfriend dead in his van," said one of the secretaries, dropping a memo into my in-box.

I jumped. Too much Adderall, too much coffee, not enough sleep.

"Sorry, didn't mean to startle you." She lingered, watching the screen. "Isn't that one of your cases?"

I nodded.

"I bet it's a murder-suicide," the secretary

said, "and it's just a matter of time before they find the boyfriend's body."

I stared at her.

And a very unpleasant thought occurred to me.

"That would be convenient for a lot of people, wouldn't it?"

"What was Luke Paxton calling about?" I asked Faraday later when things had calmed down.

My boss snorted. "He wants me to rein in the media vans. The senator's neighbors are having hissy fits because they park on the lawns and urinate into the begonias."

"Want me to go out there and ask them politely? Maybe point out the surveillance cameras mounted on the wall?"

Faraday looked incredulous. "I need you here. Now, tell me what bright ideas you've come up with on the Salazar case."

I'd spent some time brainstorming, and now I sketched out my plan.

"Salazar grew up poor, right? But he's humble. He remembers his roots. He wants to give back to the community. He doesn't know it yet, but for months now, he's been hatching this plan, see, to sponsor a baseball team at an elementary school in a poor Latino neighborhood. We hook him up with the school and he can announce it and give the kids an inspirational talk as the TV cameras roll."

"I like it," said Faraday. "Let me run it by his people. How soon could you line it up?"

"Pretty quickly. I'll start working on it right away."

I'd just gotten an enthusiastic bite from a principal at El Sereno Elementary School when Faraday called me back in.

Samantha George and Tyler were already sitting in chairs. Sam looked haggard. Tyler had his poker face on. It was as if last night had never happened.

"Ladies and gentlemen," Faraday said, "we've got game."

He pointed his remote at the TV and the volume swelled.

The news feeds were reporting that pornographic videos had been found in the van belonging to Jake Slattery. Several showed women being strangled. Just like Emily Mortimer had been. The police said these weren't homemade snuff films; they were professional porn, probably churned out ten miles up the 405 Freeway in the San Fernando Valley, the epicenter of America's adult film industry.

The noose of circumstantial evidence was

tightening around Emily's missing boy-friend.

"This is a significant development," Faraday said. "My disappointment is *non-existent.*"

When he finished gloating, Faraday gave us our assignments: I'd get a comment from the senator and write a press release. Samantha would chase down Simon Paxton for the same thing. Tyler would pump the cops for details.

"It's not looking good for Jake Slattery," I said to Tyler as we stood by the vending machine that dispensed free energy drinks, smart water, and Japanese vitamin infusions.

I wanted to see if he'd bring up last night.

"No," he said, looking morose.

"What?" I prodded.

"Nothing."

But still he looked disconcerted. Then a sudden brain wave hit. Maybe Tyler's demeanor had nothing to do with *us.*

"You wish you'd been there when the cops raided Slattery's van," I said.

"No," Tyler said, but I knew I'd hit a nerve.

"I guess for starters, you didn't have a car. How'd you get to work, anyway?"

"Rode my bike. And Viken's already got

my car sorted. Says it was a loose wire."

"That's good."

For a moment he said nothing.

"It *was* good, wasn't it, Maggie? You doing okay today?"

I nodded.

Then suddenly I remembered something. "Who replaced you on watch out at the airport parking lot last night?"

Tyler glanced around. "Faraday called him back before the cops showed."

"Called who back?"

"I told you yesterday. I don't know his name."

"C'mon, Tyler, you know the name of every single person in this office. You make it your business."

Tyler's eyes darted unhappily. "He's not on staff."

"Who was it?"

"Faraday calls him the Plumber."

An image rose before me. Of a tall, lanky guy in overalls and a work belt.

Now it was my turn to look over my shoulder.

"That's who relieved you at the parking lot? The creep I told you was lurking around the Mortimer house in Valencia the other day?"

"I don't know who was at the Mortimer

house, Maggie. I think you may be imagining things. Last night, Faraday told me to come back to the office when my replacement arrived. And that's what I did."

Tyler walked away and I hurried after him. Why was he acting so weird? Was it because we'd slept together? Or did he suddenly share my uneasiness about this case?

Lowering my voice, I said, "That Plumber guy. He breaks in and snoops, doesn't he? I mean, that's his job. And what if last night, he broke into Jake Slattery's van, not to snoop but to leave something behind? Something the LAPD detectives would be sure to find."

"You mean the porn?"

I nodded.

Tyler nervously licked his lips. "The cops said it was hidden behind a false panel in the van."

I nodded. "The Plumber wouldn't leave it lying around. That would have been too obvious a plant."

I paused, recalling my surprise that Faraday had tipped off the cops. It was out of character. As if he'd *known* that the cops would find something. Something that would incriminate Jake Slattery and distance our client — my friend's dad, U.S. Senator Henry Paxton, and his ever-loving adulterous brother, Simon Paxton — from the murder of Emily Mortimer.

"I think you're way out of line, Maggie," Tyler said, two lines appearing on his brow. "Paranoid, even. Do you really think the Blair Company would do that? Do you think I'd work here if I believed they broke the law and shielded murderers and planted evidence? And if you do, then why did last night happen? And why are you even working here? How can you live with your conscience?"

The air felt fragile, like it might crack apart and shatter. Last night seemed like it had happened in a dream, or a million years ago.

"I don't know what I think anymore. About anything." I glared, willing him to catch my double meaning.

His hand took mine, large and warm and firm.

"I care about you, Maggie. Last night was so . . . magical. Even this very moment I'm finding it hard to concentrate. But . . ."

There's always a but.

"I wouldn't bring any of this up to Faraday," Tyler said.

"I suppose you're right." I turned, chilled by his clear warning.

I wondered if I'd made a mistake by

confiding in Tyler. Last night, he'd unzipped all my defenses. But it was time to put the armor back on.

Would Tyler tell Faraday about my suspicions? How could I find out more about the Plumber without alerting my boss? Did Thomas Blair have any idea that one of his vice presidents might be breaking the law? Or did the directives come from the top floor? I wanted to be able to lay it all out to someone I could trust. Someone who could tell me whether my concerns were legitimate or the paranoid consequences of too much Adderall.

But the Adderall was my big secret. Especially from people at work. Pill-popping drug addicts didn't fit the Blair employee profile. I imagined the disbelief on Faraday's face if I asked for three weeks off to attend rehab. Would insurance even cover it?

What did it matter, anyway? Who had time for rehab?

Not me. With Mom facing the possibility of another cancer diagnosis and expensive medical treatment, my new job, my upside-down mortgage, and now the Paxton case in flux, I couldn't afford to mess up. There was no room for fear or doubt. Everyone was counting on me. But my nerves were stretching like taffy that would soon snap.

"Miss Silver?"

"What is it?" I cried.

A secretary stood behind me. It was the same girl who'd walked into my office earlier. How long had she been here? How much of my anguished conversation with Tyler had she overheard? What if I'd been muttering out loud just now about the Adderall? Would she go back to her desk and write a memo to Thomas Blair?

"Sorry, I didn't mean to startle you. I'm going on a coffee run and Samantha said to ask if you wanted anything."

Tyler was right. I had to get a grip on myself before things got completely out of control.

My brain felt like syrup. God, I needed an Adderall. But what if neuroenhancers were now causing my problem? I couldn't remember the secretary's name. Some kind of flower. Phyllis, Amaryllis? And with that, I had it. Iris! The secretary's name was Iris.

Mustering a smile, I said, "No thanks, Iris. If I have any more caffeine, you'll be able to launch me to Alpha Centauri. But it's awfully sweet of you to ask."

That evening, I got almost to the freeway before I realized I'd left my cell phone charging on the desk. With resignation, I turned the car around.

Ten minutes later, as I waited to turn left into Blair's underground parking structure, I saw a car pull out. Light shone from the security booth, illuminating the two men inside. To my surprise, I recognized Tyler sitting in the passenger seat of a red Nissan Z. His elbow rested casually against the lowered window and his lips moved as he gesticulated with his other hand, telling a story. The driver was smiling and nodding. He too looked familiar.

As the traffic cleared and the Z turned right and roared out of sight, I caught a good look at the driver.

It was the shambling workman, the Plumber.

Tyler had just gotten through telling me he didn't even know the Plumber's name.

I tried to think of reasons he might be sitting in the car of this man who had a knack of turning up whenever there was trouble on the Paxton case.

Maybe Tyler's car was still acting up and the Plumber had offered him a ride home?

No, Tyler had said it was fixed.

The obvious conclusion stared me in the face: Tyler had lied about knowing Faraday's operative. He'd seemed all casual in the car, like they were longtime buddies. They knew each other. They worked together.

There seemed little doubt that Tyler was complicit with whatever was going on at Blair.

Seeing Tyler with the Plumber had sent a charge of adrenaline shooting through my system. Now that too ebbed, leaving me more exhausted, confused, and brain-dead than ever. When I got home, I tumbled into dreamless sleep.

21

Fall 1993

It wasn't like Anabelle and I suddenly stopped being friends after what happened that night in Playa del Rey when we were sixteen.

The next morning, I'd woken up with my head pounding and popped some aspirin. Anabelle was still asleep, tossing restlessly, uttering small, wordless cries. After reassuring myself that she was all right, I went back to sleep and dreamed of a bare concrete cell. I was tied to a chair and a red-faced policeman was shouting, his spittle hitting my cheeks, demanding to know why I'd abandoned Anabelle. When I opened my eyes again it was early afternoon and the shower was running.

Soon Anabelle emerged in a red silk kimono, hair wrapped in a towel. She was shaky and pale, her voluptuous mouth thinned in a tight line. So much for going to the police — the physical evidence had just swirled down the drain.

From the look she gave me, I understood that she didn't want to speak about what had happened.

And so, because I was constitutionally incapable of denying her anything, we never did.

I hung around Villa Marbella as the afternoon unraveled, trying to recapture our usual Sunday groove. We drank coffee by the pool and read the paper, but everything seemed fragmented and made no sense. I listened for Luke's footfall, but the big house was spookily quiet. For a while, I distracted myself by imagining that he'd driven back to Playa del Rey with a Dirty Harry Magnum to blow away those animals (never mind that the perps were long gone).

I kept this revenge fantasy to myself.

Instead, I put on U2's *Zooropa,* whose cool Berlin techno never failed to animate Anabelle. She didn't react. She placed *Madame Bovary* facedown on the chaise longue and stared with blank, sightless eyes at the tropical jungle of her backyard.

For the two of us, who could talk effortlessly about anything for hours, who were never at a loss for words, this new silence held a veiled menace. Since we couldn't talk about what had happened, we found it painful to talk about anything at all.

The shadows lengthened. As dusk fell, the air grew thick with the indolic sweet stench of tuberose.

Like something had died.

"Are you okay?" I asked finally.

She shifted, and the book fell into a puddle.

"Why did Madame Bovary even bother?" She prodded the pages with a lavender-painted toe.

"Killing herself?" I asked nervously. "Or falling in love?"

Anabelle gave a slow, sad smile that about broke my heart.

Then she said, "Please don't worry about me, Maggie. I just need to be by myself for a while."

"Okay," I said, unwilling to linger when I so obviously wasn't wanted. "I'll see you soon."

But still I couldn't leave. I stood there and the words welled up from my heart and got lodged in my throat, piling up unsaid until I thought I might choke on them. Finally, I hugged her. Her body was stiff against mine, her arms limp at her sides.

I got in my beater car and drove home to

the Valley, blasting "Disintegration" by the Cure.

I still visited Villa Marbella after that. Anabelle and I continued to study together and listen to music and hang out. But a zombie had taken over my friend's body. She made the right sounds and motions, but all life and joy had been sucked from her.

Anabelle's parents remained blithely oblivious. Maybe they thought she was trying on a new persona, as teenagers do, and that their doom-and-gloom Goth girl would morph into something new by Thanksgiving.

The demise of our friendship wasn't all dramatic, like in the movies.

The malaise crept in on little cat feet like Carl Sandberg's fog, muffling our voices, blanketing us off from each other, obscuring the path back to what we'd had.

Then daylight savings ended and the world began slipping into darkness. Luke was rarely home, and when I did see him, he kept a polite distance and wouldn't look me in the eye. I wondered if he was trying to track down the guys from that night. But he said nothing and I didn't ask.

Around the time Anabelle showed me how to play chicken on the LAX runways, she began to hang with a girl named Raven who dyed her hair blue black and wore heavy whiteface makeup and rimmed her eyes with kohl. Raven's boyfriend worked at the Viper Room in Hollywood and she'd get us in, but Raven and Anabelle kept disappearing into the bathroom. When the next invitation came, I stayed home.

Still, I told myself that clubbing might be just the distraction Anabelle needed. Her lethargy ebbed as the year drew to a close, replaced by a brassy shrillness. She's just trying to get her bearings, I thought.

The invites to Villa Marbella came infrequently now. In class Anabelle often seemed dazed or hungover, though she still managed to pull A's. Then one night at the Cathay de Grande, I found her in a bathroom stall with Raven, snorting cocaine off the toilet lid. When I told her I was worried, she rolled her eyes and said she had it under control. And she sneered when I declined her offer to get high.

"You're such a *good* little girl. You try to disguise it with your thrift store clothes and your boho music, but deep down, you're all about the money and the big house. I can see it in your eyes. But I've had it all my life and you know what? It's like scooping up water with your hands. When you open them, there's nothing there.

"And this," she said, pointing to the white lines, "is what fills the empty spaces."

"Henry," I said nervously, several weeks later when I'd dropped by to pick up a sweater I'd "accidentally" left behind. "I'm a little worried about Anabelle. She parties all the time."

Henry was in his study. He put down his pen and regarded me with his usual pleasant smile. "She's keeping up her grades," he said solemnly.

"But I get the feeling something heavy is bothering her," I hinted madly.

"Have you asked her?" Henry said sensibly.

I hemmed and blushed and hawed and said, "We're not as close as we once were."

His eyebrows rose inquisitively and I could almost hear him thinking. Maybe our alienation was my fault. Maybe my personality wasn't vibrant enough for his daughter. Maybe I'd come a-tattling to Daddy-O to get revenge on Anabelle for dropping me.

At last Henry said, "She's just got a bad case of senioritis."

"But what if it's more than that?" I persisted.

"I know she's experimenting and trying to

find herself, Maggie. That's normal. Anabelle will be gone in less than nine months.
Off to college." He smiled fondly. "She's
just trying out her wings."

*Big creaking leather wings. Taking her
straight to hell.*

"I appreciate the heads-up, Maggie. And
I'll have a word with her without mentioning your name. But I'm sure everything is
under control."

I turned away. It had taken me months to
screw up the nerve to talk to him. But I
lacked the courage to tell him the whole
truth. Because it would mean exposing my
own complicity in Anabelle's wild decline.
And then Miranda and Henry Paxton would
hate me too and forbid me from ever entering their house again.

And so I thanked him and left.

And maybe Henry did talk to her, because
Anabelle seemed to clean up her act. She
even began dating a surfer friend of Luke's.
And the next thing I knew, Luke began dating Raven.

Clinging to Luke's arm at the senior
prom, they made a striking couple, Raven
pale and luminescent as the moon, while
Luke was a creature of the sun, all blond
hair, golden skin, and blue eyes.

I'd watch the four of them drive off in

Luke's Mustang after school, heads thrown back in ease, lips parted in laughter, as beautiful and glossy and perfect as an ad in a luxury fashion magazine.

And it seemed impossible that I'd ever sat in that car myself.

I don't think I could have borne our estrangement much longer, but soon after that came graduation and everybody scattered.

Anabelle was off to Peru for the summer to build shelters for poor Incas before heading east to Sarah Lawrence. Luke was on a surfing safari in Bali. I was working nine to five in a Van Nuys office, typing invoices to earn tuition money for UCLA. On weekends I scavenged the thrift stores for Chanel suits and signed first editions that I resold to specialty stores for pocket money. My biggest find was a signed first edition of *The Sun Also Rises* that covered my car payment for two months.

Summer passed in a depressed, airless haze. Then college started and I had other things to focus on.

When Anabelle flew home for the holidays and we met at a friend's party, her laughter was harsh, her movements reckless. Still, she hugged me and promised to call. Each night I came home from my temp job and played back the messages, certain I'd hear her dear, familiar voice, inviting me to Villa Marbella.

The previous Christmas, we'd stood at her mother's vanity table, dabbing Caron's Nuit de Noël behind our ears from the ravishing black Deco crystal flask. It was Christmas in a bottle, rich and exotic, all mulled wine and candied chestnuts, green pine with sandalwood and roses and a holiday goose roasting on the horizon. Anointed for Midnight Mass, we'd floated down the stairs in a cloud of scent and black velvet.

Now I could picture the sixteen-foot Christmas tree in the living room, decorated with antique glass ornaments and wooden animals, strung with garlands of cranberries and popcorn. The maid would be in the kitchen, pulling out trays of gingerbread, the family gathered to sip eggnog.

I could almost taste the dusted nutmeg on my lips, hear Bing Crosby crooning on the stereo, feel the rustle of taffeta as Anabelle linked her arm with mine. The memories lodged like glass splinters in my heart, piercing deeper as each day passed.

Anabelle didn't call. We were officially sundered.

22

Now I was ringing the Paxton doorbell again. It was early morning, but the news cycle never sleeps and we didn't either when a case was in play.

I had a box of croissants in one hand and a package from Faraday in the other.

"Why don't you use a messenger service?" I'd asked my boss. "Won't they think it strange that I keep showing up on their doorstep?"

"Every politician I've ever worked with treats his aides like personal assistants and Paxton's probably no different. He wants to see *your* smiling face, not some stranger's."

My boss had been up since five a.m., wheeling and dealing to set up an exclusive TV interview with Simon Paxton. The idea was to put Simon squarely in front of the national media where he would speak with remorse about his affair with Emily Mortimer. The other half of our equation was to keep the senator offstage.

Anabelle opened the door.

"Oh," I said, stepping back, disoriented.

What was she doing here at Villa Marbella so early in the morning?

Anabelle tugged her hair down over one cheek, her eyes reflecting disappointment, as if she'd been expecting someone else.

"Hullo, Maggie," she said.

For a moment, I was sixteen again, awkward and tongue-tied, my nose pressed forever against the window, looking in. Do we ever really lose our insecure, adolescent self, or does it remain locked deep inside, where no one can see?

Then adulthood kicked back in and I noticed something.

Anabelle was already dressed and wore heavy makeup. But even layers of foundation couldn't conceal her swelling, blackened eye.

"What happened?"

Quickly, she withdrew into the shadows.

"Did you hurt yourself?"

"Yeah."

"How?"

"I'll tell you over breakfast."

In the kitchen, Anabelle poured coffee into giant mugs, set the table with linen napkins, and fetched a pot of raspberry jam from the fridge. I walked to the cupboard, reached for a wooden platter from memory — there it was! — and arranged the croissants like petals of a flower around the jam pot.

A shaft of sunlight shone through the bay window above the sink, illuminating the table like some sixteenth-century Dutch still life. How many mornings had I sat at that table, in that very same shaft of light? I felt like a time traveler living simultaneously in two worlds.

"That's sweet of you to bring breakfast," Anabelle said. "Mom and Lincoln are still sleeping upstairs and Dad left hours ago, if you're looking for him." She glanced up nervously. "He was already gone when I got up."

"I'm delivering a package from Blair. Maybe you can call and let him know?"

"Sure."

She got on the phone but handed it to me when she got her father's voice mail. I left a message.

"We'll try again if he doesn't call back. Meanwhile . . ." I stared at my friend's shiner and frowned. "Want to tell me what happened?"

Anabelle poured milk into her coffee from a cow-shaped creamer, then took the engraved silver tongs and plopped in two cubes of sugar.

"I haven't been completely frank with you, Maggie."

"Oh?"

"Sometimes Randall" — she winced, and I held my breath — "has a few too many. You can't believe the stress he's under these days."

"He hits you?" I found my own hands clenching into fists, recalling the tightly wound man in the kitchen the other day.

"I thought he's the one who got you clean? You are still clean, aren't you, Anabelle?" I said, hating the pleading tone in my voice.

Anabelle smoothed her hands over her pants. "I'd be dead in a month if I ever went back to using."

"What about that infected spot between your toes?" I blurted out. "And don't tell me your cat did it."

I hated the inquisitorial tone that had crept into my voice. But I was angry. She'd lied to me. What else had she lied about?

Her lower lip trembled and I wanted to take it all back. Maybe if my husband hit me, I'd seek solace in drugs too. Besides, what right did I have to accuse her, when I popped Adderall all day, which was just a fancy white-collar word for speed. That made me the worst kind of addict — a hypocritical one.

"Okay, Maggie," Anabelle said, her face white. "You want to know how I got that cut? Randall threw a pair of pruning shears at me when I was wearing flip-flops. He was mad that I'd come home late from the gym."

Her words hit me hard. "Oh, Anabelle . . ."

She set her jaw and looked away.

"Can you blame me for making up the cat story? You come over after I haven't seen you in sixteen years. What am I supposed to say? 'Hi, Maggie, this is my husband. He's got a lively temper and sometimes he throws things at me. Punches and garden tools.' " She rolled her eyes. "Yeah, right. Great way to impress my old pal."

"Anabelle, I —"

She put up a hand. "Let me finish. I've had some rocky years. Sometimes I had to look up to see the gutters, that's how low I was. But I climbed out. And I've realized something. Being alive rocks." She gave me a tremulous smile. "I have Randall to thank for that."

Anabelle's diction grew slow and precise. "He'll go months without taking a drink. Then something happens at work and —"

"That doesn't excuse —"

"He's only done it once. Well, twice now."

Her hand crept to her cheek. "And he said he dropped the shears by accident. But last night, I thought it best to pack up Lincoln and come here."

I wanted to condemn Randall. But I knew it would also mean condemning my friend for putting up with him.

"I can handle it. Really. Without Randall, I'd be in some crack house, a strawberry selling myself for a hit. He saved my life."

"But that's no . . ."

She tore savagely at her croissant. "I owe him. And he needs me. He acts strong, but really he isn't. He's a caretaker. It's what gets him out of bed in the morning."

I bit my tongue to keep from saying that any man who hit his wife didn't take very good care of her.

"Last night, I told Dad we decided to drop by after visiting friends in Brentwood. But when he turned on the light he . . . I've never seen him so furious."

The doorbell rang.

"Maybe that's Randall, come to apologize," Anabelle said, a strange, eager light in her eyes.

She hurried to the front door and opened it.

Two men in dark suits stood there. One held up a badge and introduced himself as

Charlie Smalls, an LAPD detective. His partner was John Delgado. Smalls asked to speak to the senator but Anabelle explained he'd already left.

"I'm his daughter," she added nervously. "Is there anything wrong?"

The detective examined her. "You're Anabelle Paxton Downs?"

"Y-yes. Why?"

"Then we need to talk with you too. Is there somewhere we can sit down?"

Anabelle led the detectives into the living room.

"Has something happened to my dad?" she asked, her voice wobbly.

They sat down. I eased out my BlackBerry.

The detective frowned at me. "Are you a family member?"

"She's a friend, and I'd like her to stay," Anabelle said firmly.

In her voice I heard the Paxton imperiousness. But she was also trembling, as if she already knew something was wrong. I pressed my shoulder against hers in support.

"2 LAPD DET @ PAXTON HOME. DVLPNG," I texted Faraday.

"What brings you out so early?" Anabelle asked.

Detective Delgado studied the David Hockney portrait of Miranda that hung behind our heads. Slowly, his eyes settled back on Anabelle.

"Mrs. Downs, I'm sorry to inform you that your husband is dead. He was found shot to death in your driveway early this morning."

Anabelle gave a wordless moan. She began to rock and her hair fell forward into her face.

I put my arm around her and began to tuck a strand of hair behind her ear. Then I remembered the blackened eye and stopped. As my heart expanded in sorrow for Anabelle, my brain considered what this meant: a second murder in the senator's inner circle.

"PAXTON COP SON-N-LAW 187," I texted, using the police code for murder.

"I'm sorry about your husband," said Smalls. "He was one of ours so it hits especially hard. I know it's difficult, but these first hours are crucial, so I'd like to ask you some questions."

"Detective," I interjected, "if my . . . if we could have a few moments."

I'd almost said my client. But Anabelle wasn't my client. She was my childhood friend. Streaky tears were running down her face, carving rivulets in all that foundation.

"We need to get some tissues," I said, standing up.

I wished Faraday would respond so I'd know what to do.

"Go ahead," Delgado said.

Anabelle rose blindly and allowed me to lead her to the bathroom. I locked the door.

Anabelle's shoulders were stooped. Her eyes had turned haggard, her skin blotchy and smeared where the makeup had run.

"Oh, God," she said. "It's impossible. I can't believe . . ."

A niggling thought stirred. Did Anabelle know who'd killed her husband? Should I ask her point-blank? But if she said yes, then what would my obligation be?

As I wondered what my friend was capable of, another part of my brain swung automatically into damage control.

If Anabelle refused to talk to the police, would that make her appear guilty or just prudent? Wouldn't an innocent person be eager to talk to the men charged with finding her husband's killer? Especially the wife of a cop?

Never let the client talk off-the-cuff.

It was a Blair mantra. You sewed it up, you zipped it shut, you dead-ended it and controlled the flow of information.

"I want you to tell the detectives you're too upset to talk right now," I told Anabelle.

Anabelle gave me the strangest look. "Why?"

"Your father's battling for his political life. The murder of his son-in-law, right on the heels of . . . well . . . it's going to give his enemies even more ammunition. You don't want to say anything . . ."

I stopped, about to say "incriminating."

". . . that you'll regret later."

Her jaw dropped.

"I mean in light of . . ." I looked pointedly at Anabelle's cheek.

Her eyes turned flat and cold.

"You really don't know me at all, Maggie, if you think that just because Randall slapped me once or twice when he'd been drinking that I would ever . . . I love him. He's my husband and . . ." Her voice grew husky, then wavered.

How could the daughter of a U.S. senator fail to understand the delicate issues at play? But then, Anabelle had always been stubborn. And something else was going on here, I realized. Shame. Pride. Rebellion against anyone telling her what to do. I began to get an inkling of the grief she must have caused her parents over the years.

My phone rang. Faraday, at last, I rejoiced!

But it was Tyler.

"Hi. How are you doing?"

Lousy, you schmuck. You lied to me about the Plumber. You're up to your ears in some kind of dirty business, and it's too bad I found out only after I slept with you. Well, that's not going to happen again.

"Hi, Tyler. I'm okay. But I can't talk right now."

"Why not?" His voice was lazy, like he was still in bed.

"Big development on the Paxton case."

"What?"

"Faraday will tell you. I'm really sorry. I've got to go."

"No regrets, I hope?"

"Talk to you later." I thumbed off the phone.

"Besides," said Anabelle, "it would look suspicious for a cop's wife not to talk to the detectives."

That was probably true. But even as I sympathized with my old friend, my inner damage controller was busy scrutinizing all the possibilities. Could Anabelle have killed her husband? Perhaps in self-defense? Had she snapped after years of abuse? Could Anabelle and her family have hired a professional killer? The Paxtons were powerful. Wealthy. Used to calling the shots. I was

395

also beginning to get an inkling of how ruthless they might be when pushed to the wall. Senator Paxton himself had looked me square in the eye and said he'd do anything to protect his family.

A fierce look came into Anabelle's eyes. "I'm going back in."

And before I could stop her, she opened the door and walked out.

"I'll be right in. Please wait for me."

I shut the door and called Faraday at work and home. No answer. I imagined him singing in the shower, oblivious.

Swearing, I texted him again. "PAXTON SON-N-LAW SHOT DEAD IN OWN DRIVEWAY LAST NITE. COPS W/ANABELLE P. RITE NOW @ SENATOR'S HOUSE. AM HERE, PLS ADV OK 2 TALK OR TERMINATE?"

Then I opened the door and ran after Anabelle, who sat like death's bride on the living room couch, a box of tissues clasped to her chest.

"Any idea who killed your husband?" one of the detectives asked.

"No."

"Had your husband ever talked about anybody who might have it out for him? Any threats against his life? Disputes? Personal enemies?"

"No."

"Any strange phone calls? Visitors?"

"No. Could you please tell me what you're getting at?"

The cops looked at each other.

"Captain Downs recently supervised an undercover investigation that sent an Arleta drug lord away for a long time," said Smalls. "This SOB is very vindictive. He's sworn to seek revenge, and we believe he may still operate his organization from behind bars. Have you noticed any strange cars parked on your street?"

"No," Anabelle said.

"When was the last time you saw your husband?"

"Last night. Around nine. That's when my son and I left to go visit my parents."

A beat, and then, "It got late and we decided to spend the night."

Delgado rubbed his chin. "Is this something you do regularly?"

"Yes." She pressed her lips together. "Yes, it is."

"Was Captain Downs home when you left?"

"Yes, he was."

"Did anything unusual happen last night before you left."

I kept glancing at my BlackBerry, hoping for a directive, but it remained mute.

Anabelle shook her head.

"I need you to answer yes or no."

Anabelle's shoulders slumped. "No."

"Was he expecting visitors?"

"Not that I know of."

"Nine o'clock at night seems pretty late to go visit your folks all the way across town. Is that what time you usually go?"

"Usually we go for dinner."

"But not last night?"

"That's correct," Anabelle said coolly.

"What made you go?"

Anabelle lowered her head.

I held my breath.

"We had an argument," Anabelle said almost inaudibly.

"And did that argument escalate to physical violence?" Smalls asked, staring at her face.

Anabelle shook her head.

"Mrs. Downs, I'm going to have to ask you to answer —"

"No!" shouted Anabelle. "It did not."

We heard footsteps in the hallway, then Miranda Paxton walked into the room, a silk robe belted over her nightgown, her hair still tousled from sleep. She looked from her daughter to me to the strange men sitting on her couch.

"Anabelle, what in God's name is going on?"

The detectives got to their feet. "Good morning, Mrs. Paxton. We're sorry to disturb you so early, but your son-in-law Captain Randall Downs was found shot to death in his driveway last night. We're trying to establish a few things."

A look of horror crept over Miranda's features. Her mouth twisted and her eyes grew wide.

My BlackBerry chimed. Glancing down, I saw one word: "STOP!!!"

My phone began to vibrate.

I jumped up. "I'm sorry, detectives, but my client's family is unable to continue the conversation at this time."

Anabelle looked at me in fury. "What the hell are you doing, Maggie? Who gave you the right to speak for —"

"Maggie's absolutely correct," purred Miranda Paxton. "I am going to have to ask you gentlemen to come back at a later time." A hint of Long Island lockjaw crept into her voice, which I knew happened only in times of extreme stress.

Anabelle stared from her mother to me. I could see the outrage floating like a thought bubble above her head.

How dare my mother and my pliant old

school friend tell me what to do. Who do they think they are?

"Mrs. Paxton, with all due respect . . ." began Detective Smalls.

I hit Talk and put the phone to my ear.

"Do *not* allow anyone in that family to speak to the cops or the media," Faraday said, his voice skating the edge of hysteria. "Now give me Anabelle."

I handed over the phone. "For you," I said, giving my friend a reassuring smile.

"Officers, could you please excuse us for just one minute," drawled Mrs. Paxton.

She marched to the sofa, grabbed her daughter by the upper arm, and levitated her out the door.

Anabelle's face turned even more pale, then set unhappily as she pressed the phone to her ear and walked to the guest bedroom. "Okay," she said at last and handed me back the phone.

"Lock that family in the bedroom if you have to but keep them the fuck away from the cops. I'll be there in ten minutes," Faraday boomed.

Mrs. Paxton shut the bedroom door, then turned, arms across her chest.

"That Blair man is right," she said. "No one in this family is talking to the police until we speak to Harvey Lambert."

Anabelle looked like she'd gone through Alice's looking glass and was shrinking with every word her mother said. Sad, bereft, and with head hung, a chastised little girl.

Soon we heard a commotion in the hall.

"Young lady, I'll thank you to keep your hands off me. I certainly do have an appointment with the Paxtons. They're expecting me and it's urgent."

The door opened and Faraday burst into the room, the uniformed maid hanging on his arm and trying to tug him back.

"It's all right, Gloria," said Mrs. Paxton, "we are expecting him."

"Mrs. Paxton, you didn't tell me anything about it," Gloria said reproachfully.

"I'm sorry for the oversight. Mr. Faraday, please close the door behind you. Gloria, please bring scones and coffee to the two men sitting in the living room, use the second-best china, if you please, and tell them we'll be out shortly. Thank you so much."

Mrs. Paxton's smile, which was wavering all over her face, vanished the moment Gloria left.

"I'm glad you're here to rescue us from this unholy mess, Mr. Faraday," she said. "We'd best call the senator immediately and ask him to come home."

"He's already on his way, Mrs. Paxton. I took the liberty of calling him. He's heard the reports by now, it's all over the city. And it's just a matter of time before —"

There was a knock on the door.

"Come in," said Mrs. Paxton.

The maid stood there, apologetic. "There's a call for the senator. It's K-CAL. And call waiting keeps beeping too."

"They've made the connection," Faraday said softly.

"What do we do?" Mrs. Paxton asked.

"Maggie, could you please stall them while the Paxtons brief me," said Faraday.

I was already scurrying out the door, following the maid into the kitchen.

I knew the drill.

Engage, without giving anything away. Try to control the conversation. Stay calm, friendly. Appear transparent and open. Make vague promises and follow through with as much information as possible. And if you can't tell the truth, at least don't tell any lies.

"Hello?" I said.

"Mrs. Paxton?"

"No, this is a family spokesperson. Can I help you?"

"Tell the family we're going live at the murder scene in five minutes, detailing possible links between the dead LAPD captain and the senator's dead aide. We need a comment."

I gripped the phone tighter.

"We'd like to cooperate with you and tell you everything we can, but it may take a little time." I hesitated, framing my words. "The family has only just heard the news, and everyone's in shock. Could you please explain what link you're talking about?"

"Four minutes," the reporter said.

"We will get you a comment," I said coolly.

I repeated the same thing to the next three callers, then hung up and ran back to the bedroom.

Faraday had his laptop open and was on the phone to Paxton.

"They want a comment from Paxton or Anabelle in the next five minutes or they're going live at the murder scene saying we refused to answer questions."

Faraday told Paxton we were drafting a statement and would call back.

Despite the early morning cool, my boss was sweating. But I had to admire his unruffled demeanor. A glow animated his features. He twirled his fingers over the keys, then sat back, hands clasped over his belly. "Maggie, please go tell the detectives that Anabelle is too distraught to speak to

403

them. She'll call to set up an appointment once she's composed herself."

"What about the senator?"

"Just go."

The detectives slapped their phones shut as I walked in.

I repeated Faraday's statement.

"We're all on the same side here," Detective Smalls said. "We want to get this guy in the worst way. We take it personally when it's one of ours."

"I'll let Mrs. Downs know. You'll be hearing from her soon."

"Is the senator's wife feeling well enough to talk to us?" the detective asked.

"She can't leave her daughter's side," I said.

"What about the senator?"

"I believe we've already told you he's not home."

"Any idea where he is?"

"No," I said, realizing that Faraday had kept this from me on purpose so I couldn't lie.

The detectives looked at each other. They turned to go.

Delgado said, "You Blair people had better watch your step, or we'll have you up on charges of obstructing a murder investigation."

"I would never . . ." I said. Prickles of apprehension marched up my back.

"You think we didn't notice that shiner?" Smalls said.

"What shiner?"

"We know it's not the first time either."

"I don't know what . . ."

"You may not, but Senator Paxton certainly does. He called the cops on his son-in-law last year, demanding that we press charges for spousal abuse. The daughter wouldn't cooperate, which is all too typical in this kind of case. And the following day the senator changed his mind and wanted the whole thing to go away. Which it did, and that's no easy thing these days. Let's just say pressure was applied. So we'll be looking into whether there was any bad blood between the senator and his son-in-law."

When I returned, Faraday was on the phone, reading the senator his statement. We got his okay, then I called back the K-CAL reporter and read it to him.

Four and a half minutes had elapsed.

The reporter inquired again about a connection between Emily Mortimer and Randall Downs, and I realized he was bluffing. If he knew anything, he would have asked a specific question. I told him this was the best we had right now but to keep checking. I also got his e-mail so we could send him updates as we got them.

Then I called back the other reporters and said the same thing.

Then I went back to Faraday.

"There's a complication everybody needs to know about," I told him as Anabelle and her mother looked on.

"The cops want to know where Anabelle got that black eye and why she spent last night here. They say there's a history of domestic violence. That Senator Paxton called the LAPD last year, wanting to press charges against his son-in-law for beating up his daughter. The next day he changed his mind and the complaint conveniently disappeared."

I paused. "I imagine it's a bit tricky for the cops right now. They want to catch a murderer. But they don't want to smear one of their own as a wife beater, especially a high-ranking officer who's been tragically gunned down. If it comes out that they covered up for Randall Downs by burying the Paxton family's allegation . . ."

A silence descended. Outside, birds chirped and sang.

There were footsteps in the hallway, then Senator Paxton walked in. He hurried over to Anabelle and put an arm around her, whispering something.

Then he looked up. "Harvey ought to be here any minute."

Faraday said, "Now that you're all here, please tell me where each of you was between ten last night and six this morning."

"We were right here," said Mrs. Paxton. "We visited with Anabelle for a while, then went to bed. I think we turned the light out around eleven forty-five, would you say, hon?" Mrs. Paxton asked her husband.

"That's right. I had an early morning breakfast meeting at the Los Angeles Chamber of Commerce. Was up and out the door by six."

The door opened.

"Harvey Lambert," the maid announced, as the Paxton's lawyer walked in.

Faraday filled him in, then squinted at his phone. I saw messages from Fletch and Tyler.

Faraday said, "My people say the cops estimate the time of death as between nine p.m. and three this morning. There was no dew under the body, and that forms a few hours before dawn."

Anabelle gave a wordless cry.

Faraday waited until it died away. Then he said, "So you've all got alibis. Nobody left the house?"

"That's right," Senator Paxton said heartily.

"What if it was a professional hit?" I said, thinking out loud. "A killer hired by someone who hated Randall Downs. Some criminal Downs put away for a long time. The cops said there have been threats." My eyes drifted to Paxton. "But sooner or later it's going to come out that Randall Downs had a history of domestic violence. Someone will leak —"

"That is a private matter," interrupted Henry Paxton. "We all wanted Anabelle to leave Randall. That's no secret. We'd seen the bruises, we'd begged her for years. But she refused. And sure, it infuriated me." The senator threw up his hands. "I felt so helpless. This was my daughter, my darling baby girl, for God's sake. I don't deny that I often wished him dead. But that doesn't mean that I or anyone in this family had anything to do with this tragedy."

"Whoa, whoa whoa." Faraday's face was red with apoplexy. "Henry, I don't ever want to hear those words again. You all have alibis. You were here at home. You didn't like the guy but your daughter's an adult. You deferred to her wishes. Now we're going to go over this thing. I play the cop and you give me your answer. First Henry, then Miranda, then Anabelle. Harvey, feel free to chime in. Maggie, fire up your laptop. You're writing the script."

After an hour my fingers began to seize up so they gave me a break and I slipped out for coffee. My cup sat, cold and untouched, on the kitchen table, a greasy milk skin floating at the top, one bite gone from my croissant. Dust motes danced over everything, the light brighter than ever. A painter would call it *Still Life with Crisis Management.*

I nuked the coffee and stood at the bay window to drink it. I couldn't stop thinking of Anabelle's black eye, of Randall's fist connecting with her cheekbone. My marriage hadn't lasted, but at least Steve had never hit me. I tried to imagine Anabelle's despair, how badly she must have wanted to make this second marriage work. Also how difficult it would be to convince another cop that her cop husband had beaten her up, if she ever did press charges. The fear that the department would close ranks to protect their own, the true blue code of silence.

And also, the humiliation she would have felt telling her parents, her fear that her powerfully connected father might pull some strings or take matters into his own hands. How torn she must have been between her love for her husband and her love for her parents, the need not to sully the Paxton name. Such a lot riding on those narrow shoulders.

Perhaps if I'd tried harder to stay friends, Anabelle would have confided in me and I'd have found a way to help her. That was what I did for a living, after all. And with that thought, my brain looped back to damage control and I tried to assess things with a cool objectivity. Randall Downs had recently put away a drug kingpin. Could that man have ordered the hit from behind bars? Or what if Randall wasn't as clean as he claimed? Could he have been embroiled in corruption that led to his murder? Then there was Randall's comment to us in the kitchen the other day that he was looking into Emily Mortimer's murder. Had he come too close to identifying her killer?

23

When I returned to the command post, a debate was in progress.

"I don't think that's a good idea," said Faraday.

"I insist," said Miranda Paxton with a glacial smile.

"They're not going to let her in."

"Of course they will. She won't tamper with the evidence, will you, Maggie?"

"I never tamper with evidence. What's going on?"

And so I found myself driving to Anabelle's house in Palos Verdes Estates to pick up the family dog, clothes, and personal items for my friend and her son.

Lincoln knew his father had gone to heaven, but kept asking when he'd return. Anabelle feared the boy would be inconsolable without Snoots, the stuffed dog he slept with, so bringing Snoots back was my top priority.

There were police cars and other official-looking vehicles parked out front when I pulled up. The front door gaped open and uniformed officers walked in and out, conferring and talking on phones.

I advanced cautiously and asked to speak to whoever was in charge.

A coroner's chalk outline could be seen on the driveway where Randall's body had lain, the concrete stained and discolored with dried blood, the area cordoned off with yellow police tape. After showing my ID and a hastily scrawled authorization note on embossed Paxton letterhead, I was allowed upstairs for five minutes. A policewoman accompanied me, warning me not to touch anything.

"But I've got to pack clothes and stuffed animals and toiletries."

"You want anything, ask me and I'll fetch it."

Snoots the stuffed dog lay on Lincoln's unmade bed, the covers thrown back, as if Anabelle had plucked the child from sleep. Wearing plastic gloves, the officer examined and squeezed the stuffed animal to make sure no drugs or weapons were hidden inside before allowing me to pack Snoots up. I pointed to clothes in the drawers. Then I consulted my list and added three Hot

Wheels, several Thomas the Tank Engine books, and a Game Boy.

I did the same in Anabelle's bedroom, checking things off — a nightgown and underthings, shirts and pants, a makeup kit from the bathroom, every item inspected by the police officer with the scrutiny of a Soviet-era customs agent.

I knew they feared I'd remove something that might yield evidence about the murderer, but I also thought they were a little paranoid. The last thing I packed was the live dog, Bangs, who cowered, tail between her legs, as if she knew something bad had happened to her master.

I whistled, and she came, sniffing and wagging tentatively. Squatting, I scratched under her chin.

My police chaperone said, "Too bad we can't put her on the witness stand."

"Hello, Bangs," I said, petting her. She stuck her cold nose into my hand and gave me her paw.

The policewoman disappeared, then returned with a leather leash. Bangs's eyes didn't lose their haunted look, but she whined and shivered in excitement.

The cop in charge appeared at the back door and told the policewoman she was needed inside.

"Let me know if you need help getting her in the car," the policewoman said, as she walked away. "I have two dogs at home myself."

I loaded the bags into the car first, then returned for the dog.

Bangs allowed me to leash her up but I had to coax her to leave, and she slunk reluctantly along, giving the policemen a wide berth.

When she stopped to sniff the front lawn, I gave her ample time. I didn't want her to have an accident in my car.

As Bangs completed her reconnaissance under a tree, as if looking for clues herself, a car pulled up next door, an older woman at the wheel. From inside, a small dog barked hysterically.

The woman emerged, leading an elderly asthmatic pug on a leash. The pug tugged and strained to get to us.

I held Bangs's leash tightly, not knowing whether she was friendly with other dogs. Bangs sat and wagged her tail politely as they approached.

The dogs sniffed noses. Then the pug inspected the tree while the woman looked at Anabelle's house with concern.

"What happened?"

For a moment, I hesitated. But it wasn't

414

exactly a secret.

"Your neighbor Randall Downs was shot to death last night in his driveway."

As the woman's curiosity turned to shock, I decided to ask a few questions.

"Did you happen to hear anything unusual?"

The woman clutched a religious medal around her neck and tried to speak.

"He's dead?" she finally said.

"I'm afraid so."

"Who are you? Why are you taking Bangs?"

"I'm a family friend. Anabelle asked me to pick up the dog and get her and Lincoln some clothes and things. What's your name?"

"Verna Pratchett," the woman said. "And I did hear something."

"When?"

"Last night. I've got to tell the police."

She looked down at her pug, who was still sniffing madly. "Hurry up, Brandy."

"What did you hear, Mrs. Pratchett?"

"Well, I was standing right here last night, about ten fifteen, when I heard an argument. *CSI* had just finished and I'd made a cup of tea and was taking Brandy for his constitutional. He always has a good sniff around this tree, it's like a —"

"And what did you hear?" I shifted with impatience.

"I heard two men arguing. One was Mr. Downs. I recognized his voice, he brings my trash cans up the drive for me every Tuesday and we chat over the fence. A lovely man. But he sounded very angry last night, shouting that the other man should shove off and mind his own business. And then the stranger said, 'You're dead meat, Randall.' I couldn't see either of them, you understand. Then Brandy started barking and lunged for a possum and I was so upset to hear such language that the leash slipped right through my fingers. And by the time I caught Brandy and we walked back, it was quiet again."

"And you didn't think to call the police last night?"

"Randall *is* the police. I didn't think he was in any real danger. He has friends over to play poker sometimes, and I hear a lot worse than that. Maybe they have a few." She extended her pinkie and tipped her thumb toward her mouth. "But now I feel just terrible. To think I might have prevented that nice man's murder."

Mrs. Pratchett stared with a queasy horror at the comings and goings of the police.

I tried to think of what else to ask.

"Did you, um, notice any cars you didn't recognize parked in front of the house last night?"

She put a finger to her lips. "There was a big foreign car parked right here, by Brandy's special tree, I remember that. It was a dark color. And newish. Lots of shiny chrome."

"Do you recall the model?"

She got a deer-in-the-headlights look. "I'm not very good with that."

"How about any part of the license plate?"

She shook her head with an apologetic look.

"Thank you, Mrs. Pratchett. This will help the police. So you didn't know he was dead?"

"No! I leave the house very early to babysit my grandson. Brandy comes with me."

The pug had finally completed his examination of the tree and was looking up with that funny little pushed-in nose those dogs have.

Bangs whined.

"I better get going," I said, eager to tell Faraday. "Does Anabelle have your number?"

Mrs. Pratchett wrote it down. I loaded Bangs into the car as Mrs. Pratchett walked to her house.

"Aren't you going to tell the police what you heard?" I asked.

"I'd like to change and put on some makeup first." She primped at her hair. "I expect the TV may want to interview me too. I'd better look nice."

24

I drove back as fast as I could.

Bangs seemed used to cars. She stuck her nose out the window and enjoyed the fresh air. I noticed dog drool on the window and figured I'd be expensing a car wash soon.

I walked in with Bangs, unleashed her and let her out back, then I handed the maid the bags I'd retrieved. When I told Faraday what I'd learned, he groaned and buried his head in his hands.

"Please, Lord, tell me that no one in this family drives a late-model dark-colored foreign car."

"I can check."

I slipped out and did a quick inventory. An old Toyota Camry was parked in the driveway. Probably the maid's car. I peered into the garage and my breath caught. A late-model forest-green Mercedes sat next to a pale blue Prius.

When I reported my findings, Faraday

looked like he might bust a gut.

"Holy mother of Christ," he roared. "Maggie, get them in here. All three of them. Right now. This thing is like a Hydra. You cut off one head and five grow back."

Paxton was the first to stroll in, sucking on a mint and trailed by his chief of staff.

Faraday took one look at Bernstein and pointed at the door. "Out. Now. This is family only."

Bernstein turned to the senator, who gave a slight nod. With reluctance, he stepped out.

Mrs. Paxton and Anabelle arrived together, clutching mugs of tea. Mrs. Paxton looked pale, Anabelle groggy, like she'd been roused from sleep.

"Maggie, please close the door," said Faraday.

"What's this all about?" asked Paxton. "I'm a busy man. And Miranda was upstairs with our grandson."

"Shut up," said Faraday.

Paxton reared back, affronted. "I beg your pardon."

"Why, I never . . ." said Mrs. Paxton. She stood up, fingers worrying the black pearls around her neck.

"Sit down. All of you."

Mrs. Paxton gave her husband a look of entreaty.

"Now," Faraday roared.

Pulling out her skirt, Miranda Paxton sat. The senator rolled his mint noisily and joined her.

"Mr. Faraday," Anabelle said icily, "please remember that you are employed by us and serve at our whim, at least until my parents come to their senses and fire you. I'll thank you to speak in a civil tone."

So Anabelle didn't know, I thought.

"Sit down, Anabelle," Faraday said wearily.

He turned to the senator.

"I don't need this job, Paxton. My professional reputation is at stake here, as well as your political life, though you seem determined not to understand that. So why don't you level with me for the first time since we've known each other and tell me what you were doing at your son-in-law's house last night."

Paxton's face went slack. "I already told you, I spent the night at home. My wife and I went to bed just before midnight."

"A car like yours was spotted in front of your daughter's house. Maggie just spoke to Anabelle's neighbor, a Mrs. Pratchett, who by now has told police she overheard a man arguing with Randall Downs. At some point, they will play her one of your speeches and ask whether that was the same voice she heard threatening her neighbor.

"They will also talk to other neighbors. As soon as they put it together, the police will show up here with questions. So I suggest we go over this now, and you tell me the truth."

I'd been monitoring the TVs — Faraday had ordered two brought in — with the sound muted, flipping through the channels for coverage of Randall Downs's murder. Suddenly, it was everywhere.

"It's out," I said, boosting the volume on Channel 4.

A reporter was standing in front of a house identified as belonging to slain LAPD Captain Randall Downs of Palos Verdes. Next to him stood a nervous-looking Verna Pratchett.

"Breaking news from the murder site, and an interview with a witness who saw and heard suspicious activity when we return from our station break," said the reporter.

After an eternity of commercials, Mrs. Verna Pratchett proceeded to tell the reporter everything she'd told me. But her memory had improved since our conversation. She now recalled a late-model forest-green Mercedes parked out front.

As the news moved on to a dog that could sniff out cancer (I made a mental note to explore that further, for Mom), I muted the sound and waited.

Paxton took his wife's hand and gave her a brief nod. "It's all going to come out, Miranda," he said.

"Did you not hear that?" said Faraday. "It's *already* out. Hear that phone ringing? It's either the media or the cops."

Mrs. Paxton looked like she might cry.

"I know it looks bad," said Henry Paxton, "but I swear to you, I didn't kill my son-in-law."

Faraday raised his eyebrows. "But you did go over there last night?"

Paxton hesitated, then nodded.

"You're right," Faraday roared. "It does look bad. It looks like you killed your son-in-law in a fit of rage because he beat up your daughter. And then you covered it up and lied about it. Why didn't you tell me the truth?"

"Because it was none of your business," Miranda Paxton said, her sibilance coming on strong.

Faraday's mouth hung open in disbelief.

"Let's get this straight, lady. *Everything* you do, including when you move your bowels, is my business until we get this thing resolved."

"Really!" said Miranda Paxton.

"I can't represent you if you keep bobbing and weaving and making everything I say look like a lie."

"I still don't see what this has to do with that aide's murder," Miranda Paxton said icily.

"Maybe it does, maybe it doesn't," Faraday said, "but the senator needs to tell me what happened."

"Daddy!" said Anabelle, who had started to cry.

"It's okay, Anabelle, your father isn't a murderer," said Mrs. Paxton. "Last night after you went to bed, he called Randall to have it out with him. Randall kept hanging up. So Dad drove over to confront him."

"Oh, no," said Anabelle, wringing her hands. "Mom, you and Dad promised you wouldn't interfere."

"I know, honey, but it's gotten out of control. One of these days he's going to put you or Lincoln in the hospital. We couldn't let that happen."

"Mom!" groaned Anabelle. "I'm not a child. You have no right —"

"Anabelle, listen to me. Your father was in the U.S. military. He fought in Vietnam. He knows how war traumatizes people, he's seen it firsthand, some of his buddies . . . God, if anyone knows, it's him. But that is no excuse for Randall to hit you. Randall was coarse and common. We put up with him because he loved you and he straightened you out. But he was not the sort of man your father or I would have chosen for you."

"Can we please get back to the point?" said Faraday.

"If you will allow me these moments with my daughter, I would be *most* grateful, Mr. Faraday."

Mrs. Paxton turned back to Anabelle. "Dad went over there last night to offer Randall a deal: Go into rehab, which he'd pay for so it wouldn't show up on his LAPD file. Or else he'd press charges."

Anabelle lifted her head, curiosity on her tear-streaked face.

"What did Randall say?"

The senator took up the story. "He was drunk, belligerent. He taunted me about Emily's murder. Said a man should get his own house in order before trying to clean up someone else's. Said he'd been asking around, and he'd learned some things. It was the low blow of a mean drunk who wouldn't fight fair."

"I'm sorry." The corner of Anabelle's mouth twitched. "Randall was worse than I'd ever seen him last night. Ugly. Tightly wound, like he was about to explode. It scared me."

"You were right to leave. And you can imagine how his words enraged me. We got into a shouting match, and well, Anabelle . . . I threatened Randall. Said I'd kill him if he ever laid another hand on you. That was wrong, but you have to understand, I've been under incredible pressure with this Emily Mortimer thing. And now my own daughter . . . I love you and want to protect you, and it makes me crazy that I can't. Randall lunged at me and I called him a dirty cop and we scuffled."

"Oh," said Anabelle, aghast. "I never should have come here last night. Then none of this would have happened. And Randall would still be alive and my own dad wouldn't be under suspicion of . . ." She burst into tears again. "I've ruined it for everyone. It's all my fault."

"Stop talking like that," Mrs. Paxton said sharply. "That's the blame-the-victim mentality. You and Lincoln have the right to live with a husband who doesn't lift a hand against you. Who knows what Randall would have done to you, if he was drunk enough to pick a fight with your father."

Senator Paxton cleared his throat. "And if you'd let me finish, what everybody here needs to know is that we scuffled and I stormed out. Randall was alive when I left. He swung at me out on the driveway and missed and almost went down, he was so blind drunk. I got in my car and drove home, ashamed of myself and worried sick for you."

"You baited him, Dad," said Anabelle. "Randall was so sensitive about the dirty cop thing. You always hated him and knew how to push his buttons."

I studied the Paxtons, trying to stay detached from my emotions. In crisis management, we constantly assess what clients say. We have to decide if they're lying, or if their words — on which we base our defense — might come back to haunt us. At times I feel like a dowser, searching for my moral center, trying to align it with the truth, seeking the right thing to do. But in this case, my ties to the family meant I was hopelessly muddled.

Were they lying? They had motive, God knows. They were people who could afford to be careless because they knew there was always somebody else to clean up the messes they made.

Outside, we heard a commotion. I looked through the blinds. At the end of the driveway, cars had stopped. I saw an antenna unfurl.

The media had arrived.

When I walked back inside after speaking to the media, Luke was in his father's office, talking in hushed, vehement tones to Simon.

Seeing me, they fell silent.

"Maggie," said Luke, "what a pleasant surprise."

"She's just leaving," said Simon Paxton.

"Really? At least let me walk you out."

"What brings you out here in the middle of the day?" I asked, happy to see him.

"My afternoon pleading got postponed so I took a long lunch to check in on the old paterfamilias. He doesn't let it show, but it's beginning to wear him down."

"I can imagine."

"And hey, we really appreciate everything you're doing."

"It's my job. I'm sorry it's so awkward for everyone."

"It's not awkward."

I felt his eyes on me. "You were pretty at sixteen, but now you're beautiful. I bet your boyfriend has to beat them off with a stick."

I looked out the window at the heirloom rosebushes Miranda had ordered from a catalog almost twenty years ago, their fluted, pale pink petals edged with crimson.

I thought of Steve, my ex-husband, whom I never should have married. Of Rob Turcotte, the globe-trotting, do-gooding doctor I'd just kissed off for good. Of Tyler, who'd made me dizzy with longing but wary with distrust.

I thought of giving Luke a smart-ass answer, but we weren't in high school anymore and I'd never been very good at that game anyway.

"No boyfriend. No sticks."

"I can't tell you how happy I am to hear that," he said.

After the gloom indoors, the sunlight was blinding. It scorched my pale skin and baked the roses, releasing a perfumed attar oil.

Suddenly shy, I bent over a rose, only to recoil as a black hornet crawled from its pink, secret heart and rose in the air, a ladybug clasped in its dangling legs.

Then Luke was standing beside me. There was a hint of bourbon on his breath, mixing with a fresh soapy skin scent and starch from his ironed shirt.

The hornet flew in circles with its prey.

I shrank back, brushing against him.

Luke flicked his hand, knocking the hornet sideways. The ladybug dropped to the ground and scuttled away and the hornet buzzed in fury.

"Now you've done it," I said.

Luke laughed, removed a shoe, and swatted at the air until the hornet lay crumpled on the ground.

"Any other dragons that need slaying, your highness?"

I shook my head. Luke's close presence. The white, searing heat. The perfumed roses. The sinister hornet and the trapped ladybug. The hatred that had rolled in waves from Simon Paxton.

Then Luke leaned in and kissed me.

I thought I must be having one of those lucid, waking dreams.

I broke away.

It felt wrong. How could it not, under the looming shadow of his family's troubles? This was my client's son. Which made it inappropriate, sticky, and complicated. But Luke was also my sixteen-year-old crush. Scratch that, my unrequited puppy love. Which made it transgressive *and* irresistible.

But I had to be careful. I'd jumped into things quickly with Tyler and regretted it, now that I saw his shady dealings. He might even be dangerous. Whereas Luke was a known quantity. My friend's brother. I'd carried a torch for him more than half my life.

Luke said, "Turns out it's been you, all this time. I was just too stupid to see it."

I stared at the gravel where black bits of hornet lay scattered. Already, ants had come to scavenge the carcass and carry it away.

"I work for your father," I said.

"That won't last forever." He lifted my chin, a bemused smile on his lips.

"I'm a gentleman," he said. "I can wait."

25

I was back at the office, making halfhearted attempts to work but mainly daydreaming about Luke, when Faraday buzzed and told me to come in.

Samantha, Fletch, and Tyler had already assembled. I greeted them, avoiding Tyler's inquisitive eyes.

"I keep reminding Fletch that we work in crisis management, not private investigation, but he's a curious boy," Faraday said.

He turned to the webgoblin. "Tell them what you've learned."

"Emily Mortimer had a checking account and a savings account," Fletch said, legs crossed, one knee bouncing madly. "But I've found a third account. It was harder to . . . access, but not impossible. Last fall, a pattern emerged in this account. Monthly payments. Never a full, round figure but always around $1,000. One month it was $979; the next $1,025."

Faraday leaned forward and licked his lips.

Fletch said, "So I dug a little deeper. It wasn't her paycheck. She didn't have a trust fund. She didn't report any outside income on her taxes, consulting, that kind of thing. So where does this money come from? I've traced it back to a bank in Palau."

"Where the hell is that?" Samantha said.

"It's a sovereign island in the South Pacific. The place has ten thousand inhabitants and four hundred offshore banks, all registered to a single P.O. box."

"So it's a dead end?"

Fletch cracked his knuckles. "I just need more time."

"I can put Maggie or Tyler on it too."

Fletch looked sheepish. "I work better alone."

Faraday looked around the room. "Okay, folks. Who's been paying off Emily Mortimer? And what's she doing for this money?"

"Maybe she's got herself a sugar daddy," Samantha suggested.

"If so, he's gone to an awful lot of trouble to shield himself," Tyler said.

"He's right," said Faraday. "Your average wealthy guy fooling around on his wife wouldn't go to such trouble."

"Maybe not for adultery. But what if he's

already got an overseas account set up," I said.

Fletch nodded. "A politician would have a lot to hide. His marriage wouldn't be the only thing at stake. It would be his career, maybe even a shot at vice president."

"But it was Simon Paxton who had the affair," I pointed out.

"That's right," said Samantha George.

"Maybe the payments were to ensure that Emily Mortimer *didn't* do something," I suggested. "What if she was blackmailing the senator or his brother?"

"About what?" Tyler asked.

Faraday looked very interested. "And they got tired of paying her off? What's your time line on this, Fletch?"

"I'm close to getting the name on the account that issues the checks. But my hunch is that it'll be a shell company. I'll have to find out who it's registered to, then try to track back the names. A lot of these accounts hide their real ownership behind layers of dummy firms."

"Okay, Fletch. Go do the voodoo that you do. But stay within the law."

"Of course," Fletch said, smirking.

Faraday looked like he'd discharged his duty to any microphones in the room. I got a queer feeling in my stomach. Fletch was breaking the law and Faraday didn't care.

"Why are you ignoring me?" Tyler said, following me to the cafeteria.

I picked at my spinach salad and didn't answer.

"Damn it, don't you think you owe me an answer?"

I put down my fork. "I saw you leave work last night."

Tyler looked startled for a moment, then his usual confidence returned.

"What are you talking about? You left before I did. I tried to say good-bye but you had no time for me, remember?"

"I came back. I'd forgotten my cell phone."

At that point, I was so outraged by his deception and my stupidity for sleeping with him that I blurted out everything I'd been thinking.

"Stop lying to me. You were with Faraday's creepy operative. He was driving a red sports car and you were in the passenger seat. The two of you looked like old friends. Why'd you tell me you had no idea who he was?"

Tyler lowered his voice. "Please don't get angry at me. I can explain everything. Viken thought he'd fixed my car, but last night it wouldn't start again. Just when I was getting ready to call a cab, this guy — Stu Nicholls is his name — pulled up and offered me a ride home. I took him up on it."

Tyler kept good eye contact as he told the story, but I still didn't believe him. It was too pat, too convenient. But I was eager to learn more about Stu Nicholls, the mystery Plumber.

"So did you clear up the mystery of what he does for Blair?"

"He calls himself a troubleshooter. Says he's known Blair since his East Coast days and does special projects."

"Uh-huh. And you believed that?"

"Why not?"

"Did he say what he's working on now?"

"No, and I didn't ask. You know we all work on a 'need to know' basis. All I can say is, he seems like a nice enough guy."

"So did you," I said, walking away.

I'd been back at my desk a half hour when Faraday strolled in.

"The text Emily Mortimer got on her cell phone the night she disappeared?" He flopped into a chair. "The police retrieved it but it's inconclusive."

"What does that mean?"

"It's a male voice, muffled, telling Emily

he'll see her later. Then he hangs up."

"Can they tell if it's Senator Paxton's voice?"

"They've done a voice comparison. They don't think so."

"Could it be her killer?"

"If so, he didn't leave many clues. The call was from a pay phone downtown."

"So it's pretty much a dead end?"

Faraday met my eyes. I thought I saw satisfaction hiding behind his. "Seems like it."

He stood up, as if to go.

"Oh, I almost forgot, Harvey Lambert and I think it's a good idea for you to spend the night at the Paxton house tonight to make sure nobody does anything crazy."

"You're kidding me."

"That family is at the breaking point. They don't need damage control, they need a minder. And that person is you."

"I'm supposed to just show up and announce we're having a pajama party?"

"Call Miranda and tell her you've got some press clippings for the senator and you'd like to see how Anabelle's doing. Once there, make yourself useful. I guarantee that before long they'll *beg* you to stay."

"Do I have to sit in the parlor all night with a shotgun on my knees?"

"Don't be a wise guy. You can sleep. But keep your bedroom door open."

"Sounds like a recipe for a good night's rest. And besides, what am I supposed to wear tomorrow?"

"Don't be such a *girl,* Silver." He examined me. "You can go home and change in the morning. Or get the maid to wash out your things. It's not important."

My tail swished. "It is to me. With my luck, you'll stick me on national TV tomorrow morning and everyone will see the sweat stains on my blouse."

Faraday snorted. "At least on TV they can't smell you."

"Hey," I called to his receding back. "How about if I stop at the mall real quick and buy something."

Faraday turned.

"I need you working on billable hours until you head out there. I'm serious, Silver, I better not see any Agent Provocateur brassieres on your next expense report."

He shot me a sly, satisfied smile and swaggered off.

"I bet you didn't think I knew about those bras. I know about La Perla too. I know a lot of things."

On the way out, I pulled up to the guard

shack and asked for Viken. They raised him on the two-way radio and he arrived, holding a chamois cloth.

"Hi," I said. "Tyler from the Blair Company tells me you're a great mechanic and can fix anything."

Viken shrugged. "In my country, I am working for the best garage in all Beirut."

"Well, I've got an MG that's giving me trouble. Would you mind taking a look at it one day this week?"

"I would be happy."

"Great." I nodded. "But I don't want to rush you if you're still working on Tyler's car. I heard he couldn't get it started last night."

Viken squared his shoulders and wiped his hands methodically on his cloth.

"I think you are mistaken. I test-drove it yesterday afternoon. Everything perfect. The engine, smooth like butter."

At seven p.m., I was in the kitchen of Villa Marbella, where the family had gathered, except for Lincoln, who'd already been put to bed with his beloved Snoots.

I got some coffee and sat down. It looked like I'd stumbled into a zombie convention.

"Would you like me to stay here tonight?" I asked. "I could order in dinner, field calls.

439

Be a general girl Friday. So that you can all get some rest."

I fully expected them to decline in their polite way.

"Are you sure we wouldn't be putting you out?" asked Miranda.

When I went upstairs two hours later, I found a spectral presence moving through Anabelle's darkened bedroom, holding a candle that cast dancing shadows on the walls.

She bent over an alcove and a second light appeared, then a third. An offshore breeze blew scented wax throughout the room like a long sigh.

"What are you doing?"

"This suits my mood better tonight than cruel hard light," she said, walking toward me, hands cupping an ivory taper.

She wore a garland of flowers in her hair. With her lace-trimmed nightgown, and the candle illuminating her face, she looked as solemn and virginal as the young girls who filed in procession, voices raised in song, through the cathedral on the Feast Day of Saint Lucia.

She handed me the candle. "You light some," she said.

Then she began to cry. "None of my rituals will make it go away. I can't pretend anymore. But I can't face it either."

"I know," I said.

I lit candles until the room glittered like the boudoir of an icicle queen.

The air filled with the scent of flowers in a sunlit meadow.

Then I tucked her into bed like a child. She looked small and frail in her big four-poster bed, her hair spread out on the pillow like a bedraggled mermaid's. Without makeup, her face was blotchy and red from crying, eyes puffy and bloodshot. The one where Randall had hit her was blooming in evil rainbow colors.

"Oh, Maggie," she said, taking my hand. "What's to become of us?"

I knew she didn't mean our friendship, which seemed deeper, and more mature, this time around, despite, or perhaps because of, everything that had happened. She meant her family, whose carefully constructed façade was crumbling to the ground with each new revelation.

"I'm so sorry, Anabelle," I said. "About *everything*." I squeezed her hand, thinking about Randall, about her father, her uncle, but also about her. Sixteen-year-old Anabelle, sprawled out on a fetid futon in Playa del Rey, grinding her face into the pillow

441

and crying at something lost forever.

And that would always be with us.

"Will you put on some music?" she asked.

"Sure." I rose. "What do you want to hear?"

"Surprise me."

I looked through her old CDs, found *Boys for Pele,* shoved it in and hit Play. Tori Amos sang:

> But threads that are golden don't break
>   easily.

Anabelle's eyes were shiny. "That's true, isn't it, Maggie?"

"Of course," I said, my voice thick.

"Promise you won't leave me."

"I promise."

"But what if I leave you? How can I go on?"

"You have to. For Lincoln's sake. For your parents. For yourself."

"It's like I'm staring into a void. I'm standing at the edge, looking down. And something's drawing me closer. All I have to do is lean over and let it take me. And I want to. I dream about it. A pillowed nothingness. It's what I found so alluring about drugs. Until Randall. He kissed me like Sleeping Beauty, and I came back."

Her voice trembled. "But now he's gone. And I want to go back to that place."

She was scaring me.

"We're all here and we love you. And Lincoln needs you. I want you to visualize backing away slowly from that void. Here, take my hand."

Her grip was cold, smooth, and dry as bone.

"Will you stay here until I fall asleep?"

"I'll be here."

She closed her eyes and passed into sleep within moments. I waited until her breathing became rhythmic and her fingers twitched in an involuntary reflex against my hand, the way Steve's used to do as we drifted off to sleep in the early days, fingers entwined.

Then I stood up and walked to the guest bedroom.

Miranda was putting clean sheets on the bed, bending over, tucking in the corners of the high-thread-count Egyptian cotton.

My brain caught on something and snagged.

Miranda never did housework.

That's what she had maids for. And the maid was downstairs.

As I tried to convince myself that Anabelle's mom wanted to put a personal touch on things to make me feel at home, Miranda straightened.

"There," she said, hooking a lock of hair behind her ear.

"Anabelle's asleep."

"Good. I'm glad you're here, hon."

Miranda gathered the old sheets, then balanced a large cardboard box atop them. Old letters and photos poked out from under the lid, as if they'd been hastily rifled through and stuffed back haphazardly.

"Well, good night, Maggie," Miranda said, and left.

I went about getting ready for bed, washing out my underthings, brushing my teeth, and hanging up my clothes in the large walk-in closet. As I reached for a hanger, I noticed a shelf stacked with cartons of various sizes. There was an empty space where a box had recently been removed; I could see the discolored line where it had sat.

I put my finger down and traced the almost imperceptible rectangle of dust. The space was the size of the box that Miranda had just hauled out.

As I clipped my skirt to the hanger, I wondered what was so important in that box that it had sent Miranda upstairs on the pretext of making my bed. Something she kept on the top shelf of a closet in a rarely used guest bedroom. Was she afraid that I'd wander the room tonight, restless and curious, and eventually make my way to the boxes?

What didn't she want me to find?

I thought about Miranda's studied casualness as she made the bed. Her almost clinical detachment from her family. Could it be that I was missing something obvious right under my nose?

I remembered what Tyler had said in the car as we drove to Emily Mortimer's apartment:

Maybe the wife did it. She found out about the affair and decided to off her rival.

What if what nestled at the bottom of the box Miranda had just carried out was not more letters but evidence of a murder? Or even two? Emily had been strangled, but Randall had been shot. Randall the son-in-law who abused Miranda's daughter. Was there a gun buried beneath the papers in that box? A gun that had recently been fired?

My stomach roiled from too much coffee and Adderall and not enough food. And also from my conversation with Viken in the Blair parking garage, which had confirmed what I suspected: Tyler had lied to me.

Again. Why? I suspected it was because he and the black ops Plumber were engaged in illegal activity on Blair's behalf. Something that could put me in danger if I discovered it. So here I sat babysitting the Paxtons and presenting an earnest, innocent front to the media while the real work went on silently, behind the scenes.

I tried to sleep, but tossed restlessly, fueled by paranoia, fear, and the ebbing chemistry of Adderall. I hadn't slept well in days, which made me pop even more pills at work to stay alert. That in turn fed my paranoia. I tried to calm down and think rationally. It was crazy to think that my employers were engaged in criminal activity or that one of the Paxtons had murdered Emily Mortimer, then Randall Downs, and concealed the crimes. It was crazy to lie here and even imagine snooping in their closets for evidence.

I hated what this case was doing to me. And yet I felt an equally strong compulsion to know the truth. How could I represent this family with a clear conscience when I suspected them of all sorts of malfeasance? I'd never rest until I knew for sure. If what I was about to do was unethical or illegal, well, that was the price to be paid.

Fired up now, I got out of bed and dragged

a chair into the closet. Taking care not to disturb anything, I slid the remaining boxes out. I knew I shouldn't snoop, but I couldn't help myself. I was desperate to penetrate this family's secrets.

There were school photos of Luke and Anabelle, tax forms, fifteen-year-old receipts and invoices, insurance documents. And shoe boxes filled with real shoes. But nothing that might connect Miranda Paxton to murder.

Disappointed and sneezing from the dust, I crawled into bed with a book but soon fell into twitchy nightmare sleep where I stood before the cameras, reading a statement from Senator Paxton that made no sense. The reporters jeered and pointed, and the fat, tattooed cameramen focused their lenses on my chest, until I looked down and saw my breasts exposed in a crocheted lace top, sandy and wet with ocean water.

26

The room was sunk in gray-blue shadow when I woke. Cool air blew in through the open window, bringing the salt tides, the rhythmic hush of waves breaking nearby.

For a moment, I felt I'd come home after a long journey.

Then wakefulness hit, and I wanted to bury my head under the pillow.

Instead, I threw back the sheet and rummaged through the bureau, finding a pair of nylon running shorts and a baggy T-shirt that advertised a local surf shop.

Then I checked on Anabelle. She slept like a child, burrowed under piled-up covers, her breathing muffled and steady in the dove-gray light. How many times had we moved sleepily through this room, gathering our school things, moaning at the alarm that woke us at the "crap of dawn"?

I popped an Adderall, then tiptoed down the stairs and unlatched the front door, slipping barefoot through the wet grass and down to the street. The last news vans had given up and gone home, leaving behind a trail of fast-food wrappers. A coyote loped away with the remains of a hamburger in its mouth.

I walked back inside and stood in the kitchen, thinking about making a pot of coffee. From the bay window over the sink, I could see into the backyard and all the way to the servants' quarters that Miranda had long ago converted to her art studio. The door was ajar. Surely she wouldn't mind if I took a peek? I was curious, about her latest work. Unlocking the back door, I walked down the flagstone path to the studio.

At the door I gave a little knock, not wanting to barge in uninvited if she'd come down here to work in peace while the rest of the house still slumbered.

No answer.

I waited a beat, then stepped inside.

In the dim light, arms reached for me, raking my face. I screamed and put my hands up to shield my head while my bare foot connected with something hard. My attacker made a strange sound and wheeled away, spinning and clattering to the floor. Other shadowy forms loomed in the darkness, surrounding me.

I turned to run out but tripped. As I scrambled to my knees, I felt something smooth and hard. Now another of the shadows was heading toward me. As it drew nearer, I tried to catch my breath to scream, but it was upon me too fast, an elongated arm reaching to grab me.

"Help," I called, scooting backward.

Outside, a gate latch clicked and I heard hushed voices in Spanish.

Beside me, there was a short intake of breath and a muffled curse.

Then the world exploded, blinding me.

When I could finally see once more, the room was ablaze in light. I blinked, trying to focus, and realized I was huddled in a corner next to a collapsed mannequin. The room was filled with a dozen more mannequins in aggressive and kinetic poses, staring out with eerily blank eyes.

Luke stood before me, holding a fiberglass thigh and looking out the window at the approaching gardeners. For a moment, I thought he meant to club me.

"Luke!" I gasped in disbelief. "What are you doing here?"

"Well," he said gravely, lowering the limb, "this *is* my parents' house. What are *you* doing here, slinking around Mom's studio when the only thing up is the surf?"

"Your family asked me to spend the night. I couldn't sleep so I came out here to explore."

Somewhere outside, a rake scratched against hard earth. Metal screeched as a ladder was pulled open. Here in the back forty, away from the sleeping household, the gardeners started early.

We listened to the reassuring sounds and Luke seemed to make up his mind about something. Tossing his weapon to the tile floor, where it clattered noisily, he said, "I came out this morning to see how everyone's doing and catch some waves before work." He grinned. "Instead I find you looking for clues, Samantha Spade."

Were there any to find?

"Your mother's artwork is infinitely creepy and fascinating. I wanted to check it out."

I examined the mannequins. Some had their hands clasped in sorrow, beseeching someone out of sight. Others kneeled in supplication, or lay back with legs splayed in suggestive poses. Their clothes were couture and office and bedroom attire, but always in disarray, torn and wounded. Many had grotesquely swollen lips or extra eyes and teeth, and strange Picasso faces.

"I guess we're both a little jumpy these days," Luke said.

Outside, night was giving up its ghosts. Inside, the studio lighting gave Luke a sickly pallor, his white teeth looking almost skeletal in the sharp planes of his face.

"Sorry, I didn't see your car out front," I said.

"I took the Greek Way. My car's out back."

It was an old joke I hadn't heard in years. I laughed. "You haven't changed a bit."

"You have." He stared with appreciation at my thin, bleached-out T-shirt and I remembered that my bra was hanging in the shower where I'd left it to dry.

"Come down with me to the beach," he said.

"I'm a little too old to sit on the sand and watch you surf."

"I don't have to surf. We'll take the kayak and paddle into the sunrise."

"I'm supposed to stay here and keep an eye on things. The media will be back soon."

"Come on! Live a little! Everyone except Dad the early bird will be asleep for hours. Mommy dearest has her pills and Anabelle doesn't like mornings. No one will even know you were gone."

I thought about it. Would it be a dereliction of duty if my day hadn't even started yet? I'd be back before anyone was awake. I'd have my phone in case of emergencies.

I thought of my aborted date with Rob Turcotte. My ill-conceived and botched affair with Tyler.

Was work always going to take precedence while life passed me by? What could it hurt, going out on the ocean with this gorgeous man who had feelings for me? It would be the most romantic thing I'd done in years.

"I don't know," I hedged, wanting to be persuaded.

"Please come with me, Maggie. It'll just be the two of us, gliding through the Pacific. I'll tell your boss I kidnapped you."

The image was not completely unpleasant, I thought, as I let him take my hand and tug me out.

The air was balmy, the sky lightening to an oyster-shell shimmer.

Luke zipped me into a wet suit on the deserted sand, his breath raising the tiny hairs along my nape as he whispered, "I love the smell of a girl in tight rubber."

The kayak made a pleasing scrunch of sand against fiberglass as it shot into the surf. Cool water lapped against the hull. The only sound was the slow rush of tide, the plash of our paddles, and the call of seabirds.

The air grew warmer as the sun crested

the sea, turning the water bloodred. We were several hundred feet out now, the sun illuminating the sandstone cliffs, panning across palm trees and bougainvillea and purple-red ice plants with the deliberation of a cinematographer.

For once, the beach didn't freak me out. I felt my tension and despair melting as the air grew warmer. Tiny wavelets lapped at the hull, carrying away the fear and replacing it with the promise that all would come around in time.

The marzipan cliffs dwindled as we drifted farther out. A few Lego cars dotted PCH now, surfers bobbing like slick, shiny crows in the waves. This far out, you could see the entire Santa Monica Bay, the white sand like a French manicured nail rimming its edge.

Luke's lazy voice drawled behind me. "I was up late last night watching an old Hitchcock movie and it got me to thinking. Ever consider how easy it would be to kill someone out here? Just hit 'em on the side of the head and over they go, into the drink."

Luke's paddle flashed above my head. Instinctively I ducked. He laughed softly.

"Your perfect surface is beginning to crack."

His arms came around me from behind to

hug me. Suddenly, they tightened painfully.

"Stop," I screamed, trying to break free.

Luke was trying to kill me.

We struggled, and the boat began to rock violently. Luke tried to shove me down, screaming, "Stop fighting me or you're going to capsize us both. Over there," he pointed.

A commotion in the sea resolved itself in a foaming swirl of white water as something rose out of the sea.

I saw smooth, rubbery gray skin, fins, and teeth. Lord, the teeth. And a snub snout and cold, pitiless eyes. The shark breached, torquing in midair before belly flopping with a tremendous splash and disappearing into the sea.

"Paddle!" Luke shouted. "Paddle fast!"

The displaced water was hitting us now, slapping hard against the kayak. I grabbed the paddle I'd dropped while trying to wrestle out of Luke's grasp and rowed with all my strength.

"What the hell was that?" I panted between strokes.

"I think it was a juvenile great white," Luke said, his voice wavering.

Confusion rushed through me. Luke hadn't tried to kill me after all. He'd tried to save me. He'd seen the great white and reacted instinctively by trying to shield me with his body. The painful pressure I'd felt had been his limbs contracting in fear. Hadn't it? I was so flinchy and paranoid that I didn't trust anyone anymore. But I couldn't trust my instincts either, because they were shot to hell.

"Shark," Luke yelled now at the top of his lungs at the surfers bobbing close to shore.

We stroked in rhythm, glancing down each time our oars hit the water, afraid we'd see that gray snout breaking the surface, mouth gaping open with three rows of huge teeth. But the water remained calm.

As we neared shore, the surfers were huddled on the sand, several already on cell phones, watching us anxiously. When we hit the shallows, they ran to pull the kayak in to safety. Someone wrapped a towel around me but I couldn't stop trembling.

"That was amazing," Luke told the assembled surfers. "A fucking great white. Who's going to believe that? We could have gotten killed."

And he laughed uproariously.

We sat in the Paxtons' kitchen wrapped in towels and drinking hot coffee, replaying the scene, describing our glimpses of the great white predator. If that was a juvenile,

I hoped I never saw an adult. Luke seemed energized and filled with strange radiance.

He placed a carton of orange juice and two glasses on the table, then took my hand.

"I'm glad you've come back into our lives," Luke said. "And it feels right to have you here. Anabelle needs the moral support and I . . ."

Miranda walked in, trailing the smell of lavender soap.

"I was hoping you were Lincoln's nanny," she said. "Anabelle's still asleep and that child is driving me —"

She broke off as she saw Luke holding my hand.

"Been for an early morning swim?" Miranda asked.

Then, not waiting for an answer, she said, "You two better get cleaned up before we sit down to breakfast."

I showered, then fished a colorful Guatemalan scrunchy out of a woven basket and pulled my hair back in a sleek ponytail. I threw on a little makeup, then finished my toilette with a second Adderall, admonishing myself that I'd cut back as soon as this case wrapped up.

When I went down to breakfast, Luke had disappeared, and I didn't want to draw attention by asking where he was. I settled for the solace of a chocolate croissant.

Labor Day was coming and things must have been slow, because Henry was working from home.

By nine a.m., I'd talked to Faraday, who told me to stay put, made numerous calls, scanned the papers, and gone to check on Anabelle, who was having breakfast in bed.

She sat propped up on pillows, pale and wan as the Lady of Shalott.

"How are you doing this morning?"

She gave me a rueful smile. "For a moment just now I forgot completely. My brain floated in glorious nothingness. Then everything crashed down again like a fifty-foot wave and I was drowning."

I sat next to her.

"They say that as time goes by, the normal moments stretch out longer and the crashes soften and get shorter."

"I crave that. I want to blot out everything. To feel nothing."

"There are prescription pills . . ." I began.

"I can't take pills. Not with my history."

I gazed at the cozy turret we'd turned into a reading nook and the wooden balcony from which we'd watched the shimmering sea. I'd always felt like a princess here, or at least a lady-in-waiting.

Villa Marbella had been our castle, filled with light and shadow, alcoves and dumbwaiters and secret passageways, and maybe even a dwarf named Rumpelstiltskin spinning straw into gold in a secret room. In those early days of our friendship, it was easy to forget the reckoning at the story's end: Rumpelstiltskin had demanded a child as payment. And only the queen's quick action, carried out by a loyal courtier, had saved her firstborn.

"I could set up an appointment with your doctor, if you'd like to talk to someone who understands these things better than me," I said.

"That's okay." Anabelle sighed.

Wanting to distract her, I recounted our close brush with the young great white in Luke's kayak.

She gave me a strange look. "Luke came by and took you kayaking? Where is he?"

"It was dawn. I think he's left for work now."

"He didn't come up to see me," Anabelle said, with that same mix of petulance and sisterly propriety I remembered from high school.

"Maybe he did and you were asleep."

"You're defending him."

She gave me a searching look, and I knew

459

that now was not the time to tell her there were sparks flying between us.

Instead, I pulled out our high school yearbook and it fell open to a Halloween photo from senior year, Anabelle dressed as a Freudian Slip with her arm around Raven, who was costumed as Death, the cute Goth Girl from *Sandman*. Already, I was MIA from the scene.

I looked up. "Ever hear from Raven?" I asked.

"Oh, my God!" Anabelle's eyes did a weird flutter. "We lost touch ages ago. Sometimes I think about looking her up. It's so easy with the Internet. But I don't know if she's even still alive and . . ." Anabelle was sheepish. "It wouldn't be good for my sobriety if she's still . . . you know . . ."

"I wonder if she's still in love with Luke," I said. "When I heard through the grapevine that they'd broken up, I was afraid she might do something crazy."

Suddenly, I was curious to know what had become of melancholy Raven, who wrote sestinas to Luke in crimson ink mixed with her own tears.

"She and I had a falling-out soon after they broke up," Anabelle said. "I took Luke's side — he *is* my brother, after all — and she couldn't stand it. So that was that."

I shivered in sympathy for Raven. I knew what it felt like to be exiled from the kingdom. Even now, the old insecurities rose like ghosts. I struggled to suppress them and a small demon seized my tongue.

"Maybe you should invite Raven over one evening, and the three of us can eat Doritos and M&Ms and talk about old times as we watch the sun set over the water."

Anabelle nodded but her mouth set in a stubborn line that said she'd do no such thing.

The memories fizzed and bubbled in my head.

"Remember the green flash?" I asked.

She nodded.

The green flash was a rarely glimpsed treasure — an emerald jewel of color that glinted for a second on the horizon as the sun plunged into the sea.

Even though I knew perfectly well that it was an optical phenomenon caused by light refraction, I preferred Anabelle's explanation.

"You used to say it was the naiads, signaling to us from under the sea. You said it was the changeling time, when day became night and all matter was in flux. When the borders between worlds became as porous as the

461

stones we found at the bottom of the ocean cliffs."

Anabelle's eyes tilted back in her head. She was still sitting there, but she was suddenly far away.

"I remember perfectly. Last night I even dreamed of it. The sun was setting over the water and I was swimming out to the green flash so it could take me. I know there are other worlds. There have to be. This one is just too painful."

The hairs on my arms prickled, but there was no breeze.

From downstairs came a gurgling shriek.

We both jumped.

But it was quickly followed by childish laughter and the slap of small tennies on a hardwood floor.

"I know everything's raw and painful," I said, "and that's normal. But this is the world we're stuck in, at least for now. And Lincoln is here. He loves you so much."

Anabelle's hands twisted the sheets. "And I can't face him right now. I want to stay in my room and never come out. Thank God Inez is here, because Mom is utterly useless."

"Give it time," I said. "Your mom, by the way, put fresh sheets on my bed last night."

Anabelle glanced at me with surprise.

"That was unusually thoughtful of her."

"When she walked out of the guest room, she had a box with her. Looked like it was full of old photos and newspaper clippings."

"Yeah, she's been feeling nostalgic lately."

"How so?"

Anabelle shrugged. "I caught her sniffling over the photo of an old boyfriend the other day. From her debutante days. He jilted her. She was waiting for him in the lobby of the Plaza Hotel in New York the night she met Dad. The other guy stood her up, but once she met Dad, Mom didn't care. It was love at first sight, stars, a twenty-one-gun salute. They eloped three weeks later."

"Anabelle, does your family have any guns?"

"Mom bought one a few years back, when she started doing mannequin art. She'd take them out into the desert, duct tape tomatoes to various body parts, then shoot them. It was kind of stupid, if you ask me, but the critics liked it."

My body was humming with so much electricity I thought I might levitate.

"She got rid of the gun, though. Said she didn't want it around the house." Anabelle gave a gruntled snort. "Just those bloody mannequins."

She slid out of bed and walked around

listlessly, moving from her record collection to the window to the bookshelves, running her fingers along the ones we'd devoured as teenagers — Francesca Lia Block, Rimbaud, Baudelaire, Jack Kerouac, Anaïs Nin, even her old *Norton Anthology of English Literature* from junior year that held our favorite Keats poem, "The Eve of St. Agnes."

Anabelle's fingers stopped at a large brown, ugly volume.

"I forgot all about this." She brought over the *Oxford Treasury of World Literature.*

"I don't remember that one," I said.

"That's because it isn't a book, it's a safe. My grandfather gave it to me years ago."

Anabelle turned it sideways, revealing the gilt-edged pages as painted wood. "I wonder if I still have the key?"

She walked to her childhood desk, opened the middle drawer, and pulled out a gold key on a green ribbon. She inserted it and turned.

The book opened, revealing a $2 bill, a bag of grimy dollar coins and Kennedy half-dollars, beaded earrings, a quail feather, a long-matured savings bond, an expired passport, a dented, engraved gold locket, a corsage of rose petals that crumbled as Anabelle touched them, releasing a ghostly perfume, concert ticket stubs for X, Wall of Voodoo, the Clash, Surf Punks, and an amber bottle of prescription pills.

Anabelle picked up the bottle. "Randall's missing pills," she said in wonderment.

"You or Randall must have put them here for safekeeping and forgotten."

Anabelle's nose wrinkled.

"I haven't opened this lockbox since high school." She laughed ruefully. "I'd forgotten it was here. Trust me, I would have cashed out the bond and pawned the coins in a heartbeat back when . . ."

"Then who — ?"

"Someone took the pills from my house and hid them here."

Anabelle unscrewed the plastic top and upended the bottle. Five white pills fell into her palm.

Her mouth parted in surprise. "It was full three weeks ago."

My mind grasped for a connection.

"Anabelle, did you know that the cops found a baggie of prescription pills in Emily Mortimer's beside drawer?"

"Yeah. So what? I didn't know Emily Mortimer. She'd never been to my house. Or here."

Anabelle turned to me. "Unless . . . Do you think Uncle Simon brought that girl to our house when my parents were out of town? And they like, did it in my room, on my bed?"

Maybe it wasn't your uncle who had sex with her.

Anabelle cocked her head. "But how would Emily have gotten hold of Randall's pills? And why would she have brought them here? How would she have known about the fake book, and the key? Besides, if she was a drug addict, she'd never leave her stash here. She'd have it within reach. This I know."

"Has Simon visited you in Palos Verdes recently?" I asked. "A family gathering, perhaps?"

"Never!"

"When's the last time your parents dropped by?"

"Dad was there two weeks ago."

"Did you have the pills then?"

"Yes."

"How do you know for sure?"

"Because a few nights before that, I got Randall a Percocet and a glass of water. He'd just run a ten-K and he'd pulled a muscle." She paused. Her lower lip trembled.

I put my arms around her and we sat like that for a long moment. Then she got up to get a tissue. She blew her nose. "Randall," she said, pressing the back of her hand to her mouth. "I can't believe he's gone."

She heaved a sigh and rubbed her cheeks. "What were we just talking about?"

"How your dad dropped by two weeks ago and that's the last time you saw the bottle in your medicine cabinet."

"Oh, yeah. But you know, it's not like I check the bottle every night. For someone of my disposition, that would be . . . *extremely unhealthy.*"

"Has your mom visited you recently?"

Anabelle gave a short laugh. "She's much too busy making art and playing tennis to spend time with her only grandchild."

"So sometime between your dad's last visit and today, that bottle of pills walked over here by itself."

Anabelle raised her tear-stained face. "What are you trying to say?"

"I'm not sure. But it seems logical to think your dad might have something to do with this. Did he know about Emily's little problem? Maybe he swiped the pills for her but hadn't gotten around to giving them to her yet. So he hid them here."

Anabelle nodded slowly. "Dad knew about the fake book. But he saw Emily Mortimer the night she was killed." Anabelle winced.

"Why wouldn't he have given her the pills then? Besides, they're mostly gone."

"Maybe he was doling them out slowly."

Anabelle said, "I think we need to talk to Henry."

27

Anabelle went downstairs to get her dad.

I looked out the arched window that framed the sundrenched, aquamarine sea. Villa Marbella. *Beautiful Sea.* How many times had I stood here in an adolescent trance, trying to imprint this Impressionist painting onto my DNA?

But the sandstone cliffs crumbled with each passing year. Sharks plied the coastal waters. Billionaires bought up the public beachfront, built mansions, and did everything but place severed heads on pikes to keep the public away.

I was still musing about the shadows that lurk beneath the gleaming surface of things when the senator walked in with Anabelle. When he saw me, he did a double take.

"Hullo, Maggie," he said, slipping on his public face so seamlessly that if I hadn't known his private one I would have thought he was happy to see me.

"If you could excuse us a —"

"She stays," said Anabelle, arms folded across her chest. She leaned against the wall. "Oh God, I don't know where to begin. Maggie, you're the expert."

"I don't know about that. But I'll try. Senator Paxton, I'm hoping you could help us. We're trying to figure something out."

The senator's eyes slid from me to Anabelle, then to the window. "What's this all about?" he asked gruffly.

I pointed to the pill bottle on the bed.

"Two weeks ago, someone removed a full bottle of prescription pills from the medicine cabinet in Anabelle's house. Today she finds that bottle in her old room, hidden in a lockbox she hasn't touched in more than ten years. But most of the pills are gone."

Senator Paxton's mouth turned down. "How very strange. And you're sure it's the same bottle?"

He walked toward the bed.

"Don't touch it," I said. "The police will want to dust it for prints."

Paxton froze. "Dust it?"

"Sure. They're prescription narcotics. Just like the pills the cops found in Emily Mortimer's nightstand. There might be a connection."

"That's ridiculous." He reached for the

470

amber bottle.

"Hmm." The senator picked up the bottle and turned it around. If his prints hadn't been on it before, they certainly were now.

But maybe that was the point.

I wondered if I should call Faraday. But my doubts about Faraday, about Blair itself, grew stronger with each passing day. What would my bosses do with this information? And didn't I owe some allegiance to this family? To at least hear Henry out privately before running off to Faraday?

"Did you take Randall's pills, Dad?" Anabelle asked.

"Well, now," said the senator, evading his daughter's gaze.

"Oh, my God, you did! Why, Dad? Were you going to give them to that . . . that girl?"

Paxton looked stricken.

"I didn't give them to . . . oh, Anabelle. Please forgive me." Her father put his arm around her. "This has all gone so wrong."

Anabelle shrugged off his arm and moved out of reach.

"Maggie, would you mind leaving us?" the senator said. "I'd to talk to my daughter in private."

"No," said Anabelle, hysterical. "I *told* you. She's my friend and I want her to stay. Tell us the truth, Dad."

For a long moment, they stared at each other. The silence grew, swirling around them, arranging itself into monstrous shapes.

"Senator, why did you bring Randall's pills here?" I asked gently.

Paxton reached out to his daughter again, but she flinched and faced the wall. The senator clasped his hands behind his back and walked to the French doors that led out to the balcony. The cool, tiled depths of the pool, the grape arbors, the gaily colored Chinese lanterns, the singing fountain — none of it gave any comfort now.

"Anabelle," Senator Paxton said, "this house has always been a retreat for you and your brother. We've tried to expose you to all the beauty this world has to offer, while shielding you from some of its harsher realities. I guess we can't do that anymore."

He paused and we waited.

Anabelle leaned her forehead against the rose-colored wall, slowly banging it.

"You may recall that I got the Congressional Medal of Honor in the Vietnam War." Henry Paxton sighed. "When my plane was shot down, I parachuted out, as you know. It saved my life but I landed badly. My shoulder was shattered. The surgeons put it back together and I've had a half dozen operations over the years, as you know. There have been times when it's been better and times when it's been worse. But there has never been a time when I've been without pain."

Paxton gave Anabelle a tentative look. He ignored me, but I got the feeling he was playing to me too.

Anabelle had stopping banging her head. She stood very still, forehead pressed to the stucco.

Paxton said, "For a long time the doctors prescribed pain meds, but your tolerance grows, and you need more and more."

I noticed he'd switched to the impersonal pronoun.

"Oh, Daddy, you got addicted."

"That's right," the senator said cautiously.

"Does it still hurt?" Anabelle asked, her voice high and soft as a little girl's.

"Yes. It's hard to admit that. After all, I'm a war hero. A successful businessman. A congressman." He spoke through clenched teeth. "So why can't I whup this one small thing?"

His shoulders sagged. "It really got out of control during the campaign. Sitting in planes and cars and airports. Sleeping on beds that were too soft or too firm. Always on the run. When my regular doctors finally cut me off, I found new ones."

Paxton ran a finger along the window, where a single ray of sunlight fell, illuminating the motes of dust.

"I nearly got caught last year, when one of my Dr. Feelgoods was arrested for supplying drugs to a celebrity who OD'd in the Bahamas. Imagine the scandal if I'd been caught. Your uncle Simon had to fly out to Florida and pay everybody off."

The senator winced at the memory.

"Simon was furious. He threatened to quit if I didn't get it under control. We talked about rehab but it wasn't a good time, politically. I told him I would do it on my own. I have an iron will. I've succeeded at everything I ever put my mind to. How hard could this be?"

A long shudder shook the senator.

"By this time it was getting almost impossible to find doctors to write the prescriptions I needed. But it had its claws in me. I was desperate. I wondered whether I'd have to buy drugs on the Internet like a common criminal. Would it leave an electronic trail?

"One night after everyone at work had gone home, I locked myself in my office to count my dwindling supply and screw up the courage to go online. The door opened and Emily Mortimer walked in. I was so distracted I hadn't locked the door."

He grimaced. "She told me later that she recognized the look in my eyes. Gloating over my little hoard. She'd had a boyfriend with the same problem."

"Jake Slattery?" I said.

"She didn't mention a name. But you can't imagine the relief I felt having someone to talk to. She urged me to go into rehab, but I was too scared. What would voters think? My political enemies would attack me. And the party . . . My name had been brought forth as a potential veep nominee in the next election. How could I torpedo that? And most of all there was you, Anabelle. I feared it could derail your sobriety. I didn't feel I could admit . . ." The senator hung his head. "What a hypocrite I've been."

"Go on," I said. "About Emily. And how she knew your secret."

"I think in some weird way, she felt sorry for me, because when I ran out of pills, she offered to get me more."

"Weren't you afraid she might blackmail you?" I said.

The senator shook his head. "She didn't have it in her. She was a good girl. She *believed* in me and she had contacts in that world through the boyfriend. Eventually it became an unwritten part of her job description."

I put a hand to my mouth as I played back the stricken faces of Emily's parents in the car.

"So Emily Mortimer wasn't the drug addict?" I said. "Those pills in her bedside drawer, they weren't hers, they were yours?"

For a moment, Senator Henry Paxton's eyes blazed like a supernova. Then he nodded.

"That's terrible," I said. "Because we've all heard the rumors that Emily led a secret life — congressional aide by day, low-life druggie slut by night. Yesterday I read online that she was killed in some kind of drug deal gone awry. And I have a horrible feeling that Blair is behind these rumors. A little black op to defame a dead girl who can't defend herself. All to distance Emily Mortimer from you."

"You can't defame a dead person," the senator said, almost reflexively.

"But her parents! They're shattered. Not only is their daughter dead, her reputation is in pieces."

"I'm sorry," Paxton said. "But what can I do?"

You can tell everyone the truth, I thought.

But I wasn't yet brave enough to say it out loud.

"Could Emily Mortimer's murder be connected to the drug deals she did for you?" I asked.

The senator shrunk in distaste and shook his head. "She'd just given me my monthly supply. Besides, she was found naked in bed, not buying drugs in an alley."

"Maybe her dealer dropped by unexpectedly and something happened," Anabelle said slowly. "An addict never has enough. That's why you stole Randall's pills. As insurance. And you hid them here in my old bedroom."

Paxton had the grace to look embarrassed. "I can't exactly keep them in my bedside table. You know how your mother gets into things."

Anabelle refused to be drawn in.

"Maybe Emily and her dealer argued about money and it turned violent," she said. She gave her dad a disgusted look. "My own father! I can't believe we're having this conversation."

"I gave Emily plenty of money each month for the pills," the senator said. "It wasn't that."

"Then what *was* it?" I asked.

The hand on the windowsill clenched.

Henry Paxton pounded a fist against the white wood.

"I don't know."

For a moment, no one said anything.

It wasn't *that,* the senator had said. As if he knew the real reason Emily Mortimer had been killed. Was I imagining things?

But something else had caught my ear.

"Senator, where did the money to pay Emily come from?"

Paxton gave me a cool, appraising look. "It wasn't government money. No one's going to charge me with misuse of public funds."

No, Henry. Just murder.

"May I ask how you paid for the pills, sir? So I can be prepared in case it comes out."

"There is nothing to prepare, Maggie. It was private funds, transferred from an offshore bank account in Palau."

Here was the origin of the secret savings account that Fletch had unearthed.

I wanted to drive away from that house and never return. I'd get to the office and tell Faraday everything and beg him to stop the smear campaign against Emily Mortimer, now that we knew the truth.

But I could already anticipate the answer: Our client was Senator Paxton. Emily Mortimer was dead and gone. Better that she take the fall.

I felt sick.

Paxton pulled an ancient halter top from his daughter's top drawer and methodically wiped down the bottle.

"I'll get rid of these," he said. "I'm sorry you had to find this out, Anabelle."

"Where are you going to get your pills from now?" Anabelle asked.

"Bernie Saunders knows about my little problem. He's working on it."

So that accounted for Saunders's particularly haunted look in recent days. His job now included procuring drugs for the boss.

"And once this all dies down, I promise I'll check myself into rehab," the senator announced.

I wondered if I'd be there too, and we'd wave as we passed in the hallway. The black humor of all this struck me and I suppressed the urge to laugh hysterically.

Instead, I said, "So you're not going to tell Blair that Emily was buying pills for you?"

"I thought I'd made that clear," Paxton said, frowning.

Panicky butterflies fluttered up my throat, threatening to choke me.

"You realize this puts me in an awful predicament," I said.

The senator's upper lip twitched. "I suppose you'll have to choose sides, Maggie."

I buried my head in my hands. "It's like I'm being pulled in two."

Then his hand was on my shoulder.

"Go ahead and tell your bosses if it feels right," he said softly. "You people are already spinning Emily as a sleazy young woman who consorted with drug dealers. You're doing exactly what I pay you for, which is to control the damage and make me look good."

The senator paused. "And I'd imagine Mr. Blair will want to continue that strategy, so long as this doesn't leak." His grip tightened. "There's no danger of that, is there?"

My brain was a hollow, echoing void. I couldn't look at either of them. I studied the floor.

"I'm not going to tell anyone," I said at last.

"Dad's right, you know," said Anabelle, and there was steel in her voice.

I looked at her, mouth agape. *Not you too?*

Anabelle said, "It's important for Dad to distance himself from Emily Mortimer. It's too late for Uncle Simon, but he brought that upon himself. Dad's fired him and hired new advisers, but of course Uncle

Simon hasn't really gone away."

"Of course," I said, recalling Simon Paxton giving orders from the senator's study.

"If the police are investigating a drug link to Emily's murder, all the better. That's a dangerous world — I should know. People die all the time."

And what about your murdered husband, Anabelle? Are you closing ranks as a family about that too? What do the two of you know?

"So can we count on you, Maggie Weinstock?" Henry Paxton asked, with false joviality.

I looked at their sharp, expectant faces.

Finally, I nodded.

"That's my girl," said the senator.

I was sitting downstairs a half hour later when I had an idea.

Opening my laptop, I typed in Raven's name. Within seconds, there she was, my Corvallis nemesis, up on my screen.

Rachel looked great, much better than she had in high school. She'd let her hair go back to its dark brown and she looked toned and healthy. And she was smiling. I couldn't recall her smiling once in four years at Corvallis. On impulse, I went to Facebook and sent her a friend request. Then I read on.

Rachel lived in Echo Park and had a large

shepherd mix dog and was not currently in a relationship. She was a multimedia artist who showed at various Eastside galleries, and she made her living playing Roller Derby on a team called the Dollfaces. When I clicked further, I found that it was possible to buy glossy photos of Rachel, coffee mugs, pendants, and silk-screened T-shirts. The new ones were $17.95 and the used ones were more expensive, topping out at $39.95 for shirts with smears of blood from particularly energetic bouts.

Reading her Twitter feed, I learned that she'd been offered a lot of money to sell her panties as well. She'd just returned from a tour of Japan, where the Dollfaces had battled the top teams of Osaka and Tokyo. Next week, she would fly to Europe.

Suddenly, it seemed important to see Raven before she left town. Maybe she could shed some light on the Paxton kids. I composed a note congratulating Raven on all her success and asking if we could have coffee before she left on tour.

28

The LAPD released its autopsy results that afternoon, which brought the press out to the Paxton home in droves.

And my fears from the day before came to pass as I found myself doing a stand-up outside in my clothes from the previous day that I'd quickly sponged and pressed with a hot iron before walking out. Faraday would have told me to borrow something of Anabelle's, but I'd brought only casual clothes from her home and Miranda Paxton's outfits didn't fit. I could have killed him.

"Seeing as how traces of the narcotic Vicodin were found in Emily Mortimer's body, was there any suspicion inside Senator Paxton's office that Emily Mortimer was using drugs?" shouted a reporter.

"We can't speculate," I said. "Besides, you know that it's a confidential, personnel matter."

"Come on, Silver, she's dead."

"We are not going to get dragged into commenting on speculative gossip about Emily Mortimer's life and death. What I can do for you, ladies and gents, is to read the senator's latest comments."

I launched into Paxton's statement, which I'd drafted, describing his congressional aide as a brilliant, kind, caring employee.

"Was Emily Mortimer carrying Simon Paxton's child?"

"I'm not handling Simon Paxton's case. And I'd like to make it clear that Simon Paxton was not a government employee. He was not employed by Senator Paxton, the U.S. Congress, or any other official agency. He was strictly an informal adviser to the senator. For a comment about Simon Paxton, I can put you in touch with Samantha George." I rattled off her phone numbers and e-mail. "She will be happy to help you.

"What I can say is that every man in Senator Paxton's office — including the senator himself — has agreed to take a paternity test. We are awaiting those results."

Faraday bustled up to the mike and yanked it from me.

"That's all for today, folks. We'll have more as things break. We're doing our best to meet your needs."

Some of the press retreated to upload

video and audio. Others, hopeful of some kind of exclusive if they curried favor, crowded around Faraday.

With relief, I slipped inside the wrought-iron gates and began the long walk back up to Villa Marbella.

I'd never experienced a bigger credibility gap between what I said and what I knew and felt.

29

When day turned to evening, Faraday took pity and said I should go home and get a good night's sleep and a change of clothes.

As I made my way along the hushed residential streets, I noticed a car following me. It was dark so I could see only the headlights, but it kept pace, hanging back at stop signs, then catching up.

Was the Adderall making me paranoid? Maybe I should switch to a newer class of drug like modafinil. I loved the way the name rolled off my tongue, reminding me of an Italian Renaissance painter. The air force offered it to pilots on long missions, so how bad could it be?

I took a quick right, then a left, and the headlights behind me did the same. They were high off the ground, which made me think of a Hummer or Ford Expedition. If the driver was running to the Village for dry cleaning or a bottle of Grüner Veltliner, it wouldn't zig and zag after me. And there were more direct routes to the freeway.

I sped up and the headlights did too. Now I was really spooked. The streets were shrouded in shadow up here in the Palisades, the perfectly landscaped lawns deserted, the houses hidden behind hedges and walls. Someone in a high-riding vehicle could easily force my little Toyota off the road. I'd probably be decapitated if it hit me, the cab plunging straight through my window.

I drove faster, bulleting down Chautauqua, where there would be other cars. Safety in numbers. I made another left and plunged east on San Vicente. The traffic surrounded me now, commuters braking, inching along, talking on phones, tossing bagels to kids in the backseat, cursing the lights. I kept my eyes on the rearview and watched the cars turning right onto Bundy. Was one of them my tail?

Fifteen minutes later, I pulled into the Blair parking lot with relief and killed the engine. I'd meant to go directly home, but what if my pursuer followed me there? I was safe here, protected by layers of security. No one could get to me. I'd run upstairs and grab the Holloway and Salazar files to reread tonight, then drive home after I made damn sure no one was behind me. I was just unbuckling my seat belt when a huge RAM pickup pulled in a few aisles away. Tyler was behind the wheel. He got out and hurried toward the elevator, then stopped, as if seeing me for the first time.

"Maggie!"

I locked my car and walked toward him on shaky legs. "Why are you driving that?"

"Huh?"

Tyler followed my index finger and his face creased into a smile. "It's my brother's. He had to go up to San Francisco for a few days and wanted to borrow my car because it gets better mileage. So we traded. Pretty terrifying, isn't it?"

You have no idea.

"Where are you coming from?" I asked, trying for a jaunty tone.

"Sam and I had a meeting at Lambert's to go over Simon Paxton's case."

My eyes narrowed. "So why isn't Sam with you?"

He looked mildly affronted at my tone. "She wanted to take her own car. What's going on, Maggie? You sound really pissed off."

"Did you follow me here from the Paxton house? Tell me the truth, Tyler."

"Whaaaat? I just told you, I was at Lambert's office for a meeting."

"It'll be easy enough to find out if you're telling the truth," I said, hurrying off.

But not fast enough that I didn't see Tyler shaking his head.

"Jeez," he called. "You better lay off that caffeine."

I hurried on, unwilling to admit he might be right. I also realized it wouldn't be that easy to check up on Tyler. He might have had plenty of time to drive from Century City to the Palisades. But why would he want to shadow me?

"Maggie?" Tyler called. I heard the slap of his shoes. But I was in the elevator already, and as the doors slammed shut on his fine-boned face, I felt a mean twinge of satisfaction.

Upstairs, I sat in the office — still bustling at eight p.m. — wading through hundreds of e-mails and feeling that something had gone very wrong. Feeling fuzzy, I popped an Adderall. Only fifteen milligrams. The mist cleared. I wondered whether Thomas Blair knew what his VP was up to. Hacking into computers, staging publicity stunts, concealing information from the cops. Blair's corporate mantra was "First, tell no lies," but it seemed to me that Faraday and Tyler were violating it daily.

Had Blair signed off on these tactics, or was my boss embarked on some rogue operation that would get us all fired, or worse? Imagine my distress, then, when an e-mail from Thomas Blair appeared on my screen.

Good evening, Maggie. I'm glad you're still here, as I've been meaning to talk to you. Please join me upstairs at 9:25. I'll be in the garden. The elevator code is 4235.

My heart fluttered and skipped a beat. Had I conjured him up like a genie, just by thinking about him? Did he read minds too? How did he know I was still at the office? I turned, my eyes making a complete sweep of the office, almost expecting to see him outside my door, tapping into his PDA. I was looking around my office for hidden cameras when I realized the explanation was much simpler. I was still logged on to the computer.

With that resolved, I bit my cuticles savagely and wondered what Blair wanted from me.

At nine twenty, I walked to the elevator and punched in the code for Blair's penthouse.

Suddenly Faraday was hovering beside me.

"Where are you off to?" he asked with false joviality.

Surprised, I turned. His face was a smooth blank, revealing nothing.

"Blair wants to see me."

A muscle above Faraday's brow twitched. "About what?" he said, gazing out the window as if the familiar smoggy cityscape had suddenly become enchanting.

"I don't know."

Faraday's large, frank eyes swiveled back to me. "Don't say anything you'll regret."

I frowned. "What's that supposed to mean?"

"Consider it a friendly warning."

"About what?"

"Look, Maggie. You're still of great use to us on the Paxton case. Let's keep it that way."

A chill went through me.

What would happen if I stopped being useful? If they knew I'd begun holding back things I'd learned? That I had growing doubts about the Paxton crisis management campaign, the direction of the Emily Mortimer murder investigation, and Senator Henry Paxton himself?

What happened to Blair employees who knew too much but were no longer useful?

491

"Why wouldn't it stay that way?" I said.

He stepped closer. "You think *I'm* bad? Don't let that Zen Buddhist shtick fool you. It's strictly to impress the Hollywood crowd. Thomas Blair didn't get to where he is by fasting and chanting in a monastery. He eats people like you" — Faraday paused — "and me, before breakfast."

The penthouse foyer was lit with warm yellow lights, the fish tanks humming serenely.

I walked toward the sliding wooden doors that opened onto the rooftop meditation garden. An ocean breeze rippled curtains of raw silk the color of flame. The path was lit by candles flickering in iron lanterns.

I walked past bronze Buddhas, pillaged from Asian temples, raked gravel, and waterfalls fed by bamboo aqueducts. All was tranquil. All was serene. But try as I might, I couldn't shake the feeling that danger lurked. Would a hand reach from behind and chloroform me, or inject me with a sedative? Not that I couldn't use a sedative! Would my body be carried down in the private elevator and disposed of like industrial trash?

The path led toward a grotto of volcanic stone flanked by clusters of slender green shoots. Was the stone real, or a papier-mâché prop fashioned by Dream Factory wizards? Overhead, Tibetan prayer flags fluttered like an obedient army. I smelled the salt of the sea and saw the jeweled nighttime necklace of the Santa Monica Bay stretching from the Palos Verdes Peninsula, where Anabelle lived, to the Colony in Malibu, where Trent Holloway fretted over his duplicitous au pair.

Blair was sitting cross-legged in the lotus position, facing the ocean, hands relaxed on his knees. He wore loose, flowing white linen and his feet were bare. His bald head shone like a shiny egg.

It was here, in his aerie overlooking the city, that Thomas Blair retreated to plan his elegant, chesslike strategies.

Despite Faraday's warning, there was something monstrously alluring about him, sitting there like a spider at the center of a web whose tendrils stretched from Hollywood to New York, London to Paris, Moscow, and Beijing. He was omnipresent, barely sentient, and, possibly, immortal. He knew it was human nature to hunger for a savior, one who could reassure us that we were beautiful and wronged and misunderstood, then tell us how to make things right. And the more we paid him, the more we believed.

"*Namaste,* Maggie," said Thomas Blair. "You are welcome here."

On a teakwood table next to him was a glazed Japanese mug steaming with tea and the blue light of a personal electronic device so cutting-edge it looked alien.

"*Namaste,* Mr. Blair."

He gestured for me to sit. I lowered myself a respectful distance away, on a woven mat of pleasing thickness.

"May I offer you tea or coffee?"

"Coffee, thanks."

It was probably a faux pas, illustrating my dependence on Western stimulants, but it seemed suddenly necessary in the Adderall's fading glow.

"It's a very special coffee, grown in the highlands of Indonesia, on an organic plantation where all cultivation is held to the highest standards and the civets are humanely treated."

"Civets, sir?"

"The civets eat the berries of the coffee bush, which pass through the animals' digestive tract, where amino acids and enzymes break down the bitterness of the bean," Blair explained. "The beans are harvested by hand and thoroughly sanitized. The strength of the coffee, the mellowness of the bean, the aromatic essence, it is an extraordinary experience."

You want me to drink coffee from beans found in civet shit?

"Sounds fantastic, sir."

Blair raised his hand.

From the periphery of my vision, I saw a figure detach itself from the wall and disappear into the penthouse. My nerves exploded. I'd walked right past and hadn't seen anyone else up here.

"I hope everyone is treating you well and you have no complaints," Blair said, like I was a guest at an exclusive hotel.

Wordlessly, I nodded.

"Good." He paused. "I thought we might discuss the Paxton case." He inclined his Buddha head, inviting my confidence, inviting me to slice my belly open and wrench out my liver and offer it to him, still steaming, on a stone altar.

And at that moment, I would have done it.

There was something mesmerizing about him, something innate that no MBA school could ever teach.

"The Paxton family has the utmost trust and confidence in you," Blair said. "You must not forget that, Maggie. This knowledge must inform and guide all your actions."

"Well, I'm trying, sir."

Blair closed his eyes in meditation.

"But something troubles you."

Years of Catholic schooling washed over me, the unspoken "my child" hovering in the air, like I was at the confessional, kneeling on the soft leather bench, ready to confess my sins and be absolved.

But that would have been stupid.

"You have some concerns about Mr. Faraday?"

I looked up in surprise, hoping my face wouldn't betray me.

"You fear he may be exceeding the law in his zealousness to defend our client the senator?"

"Why, no, I . . ."

How did he know? Had Tyler told him my suspicions? Iris the eavesdropping secretary? Faraday had been jumpy as a cat downstairs. Was he afraid I'd tell Blair he'd been flouting the law? Or did Blair already know, and this was a test of my loyalty and my ability to keep my mouth shut? What would happen if I told Blair the truth?

"Maggie," said Thomas Blair with infinite patience, "I vet all potential employees before they're hired. It allows me to hand-pick the best. Such as yourself."

I searched his face and saw nothing except

enlightenment radiating toward me, soothing me, encouraging me to tell him everything I knew and suspected.

And I wanted to. I wanted to ask about
the mysterious "Plumber" and explain how
Tyler and I had seen him twice at scenes
crucial to the Paxton case. I wanted to raise
suspicions about the pornography found in
Jake Slattery's van, my fears that an innocent man had been set up to draw attention away from the true killer. I wanted to
describe Faraday's Good Samaritan scheme,
how I'd been followed, the computer hacking, and the withholding of information
from the police. I wanted to ask whether
Blair had ever considered that Faraday
might be a rogue agent, running an unau-
thorized operation from the heart of the
Blair Company. Or whether the founder of
the most highly regarded crisis management
firm in town already knew and approved
and was even directing the operation, from
his penthouse suite.

Instead, I cleared my throat.

"I hope I can live up to your expectations," I said.

Blair's aide arrived with a tray. He served
the steaming civet coffee in a gleaming
white enamel mug. Next to it he laid out
lemon slices and a pitcher of milk and mis-

shapen brown lumps of smoky sugar probably harvested from organic sugar palm
trees by Bengali natives strapped into
ergonomically correct harnesses on the
night of a full moon.

Gingerly, I sniffed the coffee. Not a whiff
of civet polecat musk.

I took a sip. It was nice. Mellow, aromatic.
An upscale joe.

Then I thought of how they harvested it,
pictured grimacing natives poking with
sticks in a pile of steaming . . .

I put my coffee down.

Perception is everything.

I mean, I know that. I'm in the perception
business.

I knew that the beans were disinfected and
sanitized. And that this was probably the
most expensive, exotic coffee I would ever
drink. But I couldn't drink it.

So we waited in silence together, and the
coffee grew cold.

At last, Blair said, "I enjoy these op-
portunities to visit with employees in a
more" — he looked around — "relaxed setting than a corporate boardroom."

He regarded me with benign interest and
I tried my hardest to look relaxed.

"I want you to know, Maggie, that your
work on the Paxton case has already ex-

ceeded my expectations and . . ."

"As a matter of fact," I said, seizing the opening, "I'm so glad you invited me up here tonight, because I was going to ask . . . if it's not too much trouble . . . I ah . . . I'd like to be taken off the Paxton case altogether."

Blair consulted the stars for guidance. Then he said, "It was my idea to put you on this case."

"Mr. Faraday explained that, but in light of recent developments I'd feel more comfortable —"

"You have a nimble and creative mind, Maggie. And you've done terrific work. The Afghan women's charity. The Hollywood-Graystone Hotel. Art Salazar. Trent Holloway's au pair. I'm watching you closely, and I'm very pleased at what I see. When the Paxton case wraps up, I'd like to talk to you about a promotion. You'd make an excellent vice president."

"Sir, I'm not sure what to say."

Was this a bribe?

"I hope you'll say yes. But let's leave this just between you and me for now. And you have my assurance that I'll be watching this case closely. Jack told me about the conflict you've been experiencing, due to your personal ties to the Paxton family. But you can stop worrying about where your allegiance lies. Ultimately, it doesn't reside with work or with the family. It resides within you. Only you can choose the right path."

"Yes, sir."

I knew it was a line, but it played into the part of me that so desperately wanted to believe. In fairy tales. In dream jobs. In happy endings. In noble senators and enlightened PR gurus. Because that was my business, after all. If Faraday and Blair were dishonest, what did that make me?

Blair's aide glided up silently and removed the coffee mug, replacing Blair's now cold tea with a fresh steaming cup.

Sensing my cue, I rose to leave. The papal audience was over.

30

By the next morning, Raven and I were Facebook friends.

She was thrilled and surprised to hear from me and she'd love to have coffee. But she was busy packing for Europe. Was there any way we could meet later today, in Echo Park?

We made plans for five, after I returned from Randall Downs's funeral. I didn't tell her where I was going. If Anabelle had wanted her there, she would have contacted her personally.

I was standing in front of the closet, wondering what to wear, when the doorbell rang. Mom called up that she would get it.

A moment later, she was in my bedroom, eyes alight with excitement. "You better hurry up and get dressed. There's a young man at the door for you. I'll invite him to wait in the living room." *Handsome,* she mouthed, as she hurried out.

Wondering who it could be, I shimmied into jeans and a blouse, threw on light makeup and a spritz of Chanel Gardenia, and hurried out.

Then I froze.

Oliver Goldman was sitting on my sofa with a mug in his hand. Unlike me, he was dressed in immaculate business attire even though it was Saturday morning.

"What are you doing here?"

Oliver Goldman only smiled. "If I'd known your mother made such excellent coffee, I would have come much earlier. I apologize for disturbing you on a weekend, but I'm afraid they're watching you a little too closely at work. I wondered if you've considered my proposal."

"Proposal!" said Mom, lips quivering. "Maggie, you never . . ."

"He's a federal investigator, Mom. He wants me to become some kind of government informant. He thinks Paxton and Blair are in cahoots to cover up the senator's involvement in his aide's murder. I've already turned him down but apparently he doesn't understand the word no."

I turned to Goldman. "The answer's still no, Mr. Goldman. And if you persist in harassing me, I'm going to get a court injunction, forbidding you to get within a hundred feet of me."

Goldman smiled nastily. "Empty threats, Ms. Silver. Imagine what bad PR that would be for your bosses at Blair. If clients knew their damage control people were talking to the feds, they'd drop you in five minutes."

"I'm *not* talking to you."

"If you give us your home number, Mr. Goldman, my daughter could contact you if she changes her mind."

"Mom!" I said, whirling on her. "That is *not* going to happen."

I turned back to the federal investigator. "Please leave. Now."

"You're in danger, Ms. Silver. Two people have already died. I'd like to put you under twenty-four-hour surveillance, but I can't do that unless you agree to work with us and share what you know. In that case, you'd have full immunity when we file criminal charges."

"But I don't *know* anything."

"You think Randall Downs's murder was a coincidence? You think we don't know he was looking into the Mortimer case? These are people who think nothing of killing a high-ranking *police officer,* Ms. Silver. Who are determined to protect their interests at any cost. People die every day in this city. They get hit by cars, run off the road. They

503

OD and have heart attacks and jump off bridges. A slick assassin can make murder look like suicide or an accident."

"Anyone who knows me knows I'd never take my own life," I said.

"Job pressures. A failed romance. A toxic cocktail of prescription pills that shuts down the heart. We can never truly know someone."

"Maybe you ought to consider what he's saying," said my mom, her eyes wide with alarm.

"And maybe you ought to butt out of my business," I told her. "He's trying to frighten and threaten me into cooperating with him. But he's got nothing, not a single detail. And it's because there's nothing to tell. No one's breaking any laws. Mr. Goldman, it's time for you to leave."

I strode to the door and held it open.

Goldman stood up and I noticed for the first time that he'd brought a briefcase, filled, no doubt, with recording equipment and contracts for me to sign.

"You're a wise woman," Goldman said, addressing himself to Mom. "And I hope you'll be able to talk some sense into your daughter."

Just past the threshold, he paused. "Blair has been on our radar for a long time. Many of the clients your firm takes on are incredibly wealthy and powerful, and they think that makes them immune to the rules that everyone else has to play by. There's a reason people pay Blair millions each year, and it's that your bosses are willing to do whatever it takes to get the job done. We need someone on the inside, Ms. Silver, someone who wants to do what's right by her country and make sure the bad guys don't win for once."

I slammed the door in his face.

Then I leaned against it and lowered myself to the floor.

Randall Downs's funeral took place as ash rained down like an apocalyptic warning. It wasn't just me and it wasn't the Adderall; the whole city felt jumpy and raw, teetering on the brink of psychic collapse, while in the San Gabriel Mountains, the Station Fire continued to pump pyronuclear mushroom clouds into the sky.

After telling my mother not to worry, but also swearing her to secrecy about Oliver Goldman's visit — "You can't even tell Earlyn, promise me" — I'd finally donned black linen, low pumps, and pearls and headed out. Even though I'd scoffed at the federal investigator's dire pronouncements, I took them to heart and now they burrowed and festered and bloomed.

His words seemed to confirm my own deep-rooted paranoia about the company where I worked. What if he was right?

I worried all the way down the Harbor Freeway, through Hawthorne, and up to Palisades Episcopal Church, where new concerns took over.

The parking lot was overflowing, including news vans and boxy American models with antennas that suggested undercover LAPD vehicles. Ducking inside, I saw that the Paxtons had not yet arrived. Several senatorial staffers clustered near the back entrance, waiting for the family, just like we'd arranged.

I headed for the sidewalk where the media had set up and explained that the Paxtons would not be making any comments today.

By the time I finished and went inside, the service had started. The coffin was draped in an American flag and an LAPD emblem. With relief, I saw the Paxton family in the front pew: the senator, Miranda, Luke, Lincoln, and the bereaved young widow, Anabelle, her head bent, a black lace mantilla covering her golden hair. Across the aisle, also in the front row, stood a middle-aged man and woman who might have been Randall's siblings.

Behind them stood friends and colleagues, a sea of black police uniforms as the cops came to mourn one of their own. A few reporters had also slipped inside. I sat in back.

Downs's former partner from his squaddie days, Lionel Comstock, with muttonchop sideburns and intense black eyes, gave the eulogy. He praised Randall's service to his country in Afghanistan and his years of unstinting devotion to his job. There was no mention of how Randall and Anabelle had met, just talk of how they'd built a life together and weathered their share of "difficulties."

I nodded. I hadn't liked Randall Downs much when I'd met him. But despite his flaws, he'd saved my friend. If not for him, she might not be alive today.

When the service ended, a phalanx of uniformed cops led by Comstock carried out the coffin.

I joined the flow of people walking out, making a beeline for reporters who were approaching the senator's protective cordon.

I tapped one on the shoulder. "There will be no comments today. Please respect the senator's wishes. This is a private ceremony, and if you persist in your efforts, I will have a police officer escort you to the sidewalk."

This mostly worked, except for one tabloid reporter with lacquered hair, torpedo breasts, and hornet-stung lips who kept insisting it was a free country and she could do what she wanted. I beckoned for assistance and two cops appeared to lead her away.

"Next time we confiscate your equipment," they growled.

The rest of the churchgoers filed out, then I got in line to give Anabelle my condolences. People milled on the church steps, sweating under the August sun in their funereal black. The senator and Mrs. Paxton flanked their daughter as if to shield her, and Luke hovered just behind her holding a solemn-eyed Lincoln.

"Thanks for coming," Anabelle said with a tremulous smile.

She looked so stoic in her simple black sheath and matching gloves, like Jackie O. without the pillbox hat.

"I'm so sorry." I hugged her, then moved on so she could greet other well-wishers.

Suddenly I felt the hairs on the back of my neck prickle. From the top of the church stairs, LAPD officer Lionel Comstock was watching me.

Taken aback, I lowered my head and

fished for my car keys.

When I looked up again, he was making his way down the stairs and through the crowd toward me. I had to stifle an impulse to duck and hurry away.

"I've seen you on TV," Comstock said. "Don't you know this is a private ceremony? What are you doing here?"

"I'm a longtime friend of Anabelle's," I said, summoning up all my dignity.

He inclined his chin. "And I'm a longtime friend of Randall's."

I swallowed my annoyance and stuck out my hand. "It's a pleasure to meet you, Mr. Comstock. Your eulogy was quite moving."

"Thank you."

He hesitated, then shook my hand. One of those cop crunches, but I was expecting it.

"Do the police have any suspects?"

"We don't talk about ongoing investigations."

I nodded. "They wouldn't have you investigate your old partner's murder anyway, I'd imagine. Too close to the bone."

He regarded me with new interest.

"I'm sure they'll be giving your client, the senator, a close look."

"Do they have any leads?" I said, ignoring the jab. "I imagine cops make enemies out

509

on the streets. There must be constant threats on their lives."

"Senator Paxton would certainly like to spin things that way."

"The Paxtons have nothing to hide. They've been completely forthright with the police."

Comstock snorted. "The day I see a forthright politician is the day Hollywood freezes over."

He studied the pavement, scuffed something with his shoe. Then, in a softer voice he said, "As a matter of fact, Randall did have enemies. He led the drug task force that put away Félix Guzmán last year. There was talk Guzmán had ordered a hit, but our concrete canaries wouldn't sing and Randall laughed the whole thing off."

Comstock crossed his arms and tucked his hands under his armpits.

"Homicide will look under every rock until they find who did this. And they will bring him — or her — to justice. And I will help them all I can. Randall Downs was my friend. He was a good and loyal guy. He didn't deserve what happened."

"Nobody deserves to be killed."

Comstock laughed in disbelief. "You should ride along on patrol one night. Change your mind."

"Maybe."

His face grew somber. "Look, lady, I'm here to mourn my pal. That's all."

"You're the one who started this conversation."

"And now it's time to end it."

At the cemetery, Anabelle threw the first spade of earth on the coffin. The wind shifted and ash fell softly and silently over us all, blanketing the dark soil and clinging greasily to our clothes, reminding us of where we'd come from and where we would all return.

31

Rachel, aka Raven, was drinking chai when I arrived for our rendezvous. We squealed and she hugged me as if we'd been best friends in high school instead of frenemies. I guess time congeals all wounds.

Rachel wore a ribbed tank top and cutoff jean shorts and a series of necklaces with pendants and semiprecious stones. Her limbs were toned, with cut muscles, there was a gap between her front teeth, and she sported a tattoo on her right biceps that said "Viva Dollface."

She saw me looking and chuckled. "Viva is my Roller Derby name. I gave up Raven when a boyfriend took my *Sandman* collection after we broke up. So! I looked you up, chica. You're a PR star."

"Not exactly. But it's a living."

"You're one of my friends who made it big," Rachel said. "I was bragging about you last night at practice. Who would have thunk it, back in high school. You were so standoff-ish. A lot of people thought you were stuck up, but I knew that wasn't it."

This came as a huge surprise.

"I was shy and insecure," I said. "And when you started dating Luke . . . and Anabelle hooked up with Luke's friend Graham, the four of you were so beautiful and glowing and perfect. I could only look on in awe."

I hesitated. "It must have been devastating when you and Luke broke up."

Rachel raised one eyebrow. "Why would you think that? I'm the one who broke it off."

"Really! Why?"

She stirred her chai, then looked out the window, where a woman was pushing a double stroller down the sidewalk. We watched the babies roll out of sight.

"Oh, all the usual reasons, I guess," she said at last.

She gave me a strange look. Had she picked up on the caressing way I'd said Luke's name. Maybe she still felt proprietary, in that way some old lovers do, even years later. I decided not to tell her that Luke and I were getting close.

Instead, I said, "Have you heard about Luke and Anabelle's dad?"

Rachel shook her head.

"You know he's a senator, right?"

Rachel looked sheepish. "I don't follow politics. I'm not even registered to vote."

"Well, one of his aides was murdered last week and I'm doing the PR. Turns out that the senator's brother was having an affair with her. But he didn't kill her."

"Wow," said Rachel, wide-eyed. "I guess I was in Japan when all that went down."

"I kind of wish I'd been in Japan myself," I said. "But on the other hand, it's brought me back in touch with Anabelle, so that's good."

Rachel nodded.

"She's gone through some hard times," I said, sipping my coffee.

"Haven't we all, baby. But, hey, live to tell, right?"

"I just came from the funeral for her second husband. He was a cop and was murdered in their driveway."

"No!"

"There are no suspects and it's under investigation."

"That's horrible."

"Yeah. But sitting here with you . . . I realize . . . look, um, something happened to Anabelle one night when we were in high school. I don't know if she ever told you . . ."

Rachel shook her head. Her eyes were curious and sympathetic.

"You hung out with Anabelle a lot back then. When she got so wild."

I paused, remembering Anabelle and Rachel in the bathroom at the Cathay de Grande, snorting cocaine off the toilet lid.

"You used to buy drugs together, right?" I asked.

Rachel pulled back. "On occasion. Why?"

"I don't know. I guess I'm trying to figure something out."

Rachel put her teacup down very carefully. "Anabelle and I had a falling-out too, you know."

"No," I lied. "Over what? Did it have something to do with Luke?"

Rachel looked out the window. "Nah. We just drifted apart."

I asked her twice more as we sat there, but got no further. Either Rachel truly didn't remember or she didn't want to talk about it.

Eventually she put some money on the table and rose to leave.

I sat and finished my coffee, watching her through the plate-glass window as she picked her way through the hipsters and their dogs. From the back, she still looked like a teenager.

Does the past ever really go away? I wondered. Or does it remain inside us, hidden under calluses of age and experience but still affecting everything we do the rest of our lives?

At home, I heated up leftover spaghetti Bolognese in the microwave, then brought it upstairs, fired up the computer, and typed "Randall Downs" and "Félix Guzmán" into the search engine while I ate.

Google is my friend.

Twenty minutes later, I'd downloaded a bunch of stories about how a task force headed by Randall Downs had taken down Félix Guzmán's organization after a year-long investigation that included wiretaps, undercover agents, and surveillance.

The *L.A. Times* had sent a reporter to the high-security pen where Guzmán was being held. Manacled to the wall, clad in an orange jumpsuit, his ankles and wrists chained together, Félix Guzmán had argued that the LAPD takedown was an elaborate plan to frame him, concocted by some crooked cops and an Antelope Valley drug lord named Ricky "Freeway" Ruiz who wanted to eliminate the competition. The prosecution had dismissed these allegations as sour grapes, and no evidence to support that theory had ever been introduced at the trial.

But I wondered.

What if Ricky Ruiz had worked in league with LAPD Captain Randall Downs, giving him information that would defeat his rival and leave him a bigger share of the street-drug market?

Is this where the money for the beautiful house in Palos Verdes had come from? Was Randall Downs's Hollywood consulting gig just a cover?

If so, it seemed to me that there were two possibilities. One was that Guzmán had ordered Randall Downs killed in retaliation for working with his rival to put him away. The second was more speculatory. Once Guzmán was safely behind bars, what would have prevented Ricky Ruiz from putting a hit on Downs, the one cop who knew the truth? A cop who might one day decide to come after Ruiz himself? Downs's murder had all the earmarks of a professional hit, after all.

I wanted to believe that the Paxton family had nothing to do with Randall Downs's murder. Here was a theory that might exonerate them completely.

On impulse, I called the LAPD and asked to speak to Lionel Comstock.

The operator rang through. Maybe the cops were all back at headquarters holding a wake, because I got lucky. After waiting on hold for several minutes, he came on.

I identified myself, apologized for disturbing him, and said I had just one question for him.

"What do you want now?" Comstock asked.

"Was Randall Downs doing consulting for a TV show about cops that was in development? It was something like *Rookie*? I couldn't find any mention of it online."

Comstock hesitated. "Why don't you ask your good *friend,* Anabelle Paxton Downs."

"She doesn't have any details and it will take days to go through Randall's papers and electronic files. Any information you have would be helpful."

There was a long pause. I could feel him weighing whether to continue. I held my breath.

"I'm sorry, but I can't help you. And please don't call me again. Good-bye."

32

The maze glowed with fluorescent lights, lined with empty desks and cubicles. My breath came ragged as I ran. The thing was gaining on me, shrieking in triumph. I felt its hot breath as it closed in.

With a moan I threw off the covers and sat up, my heart pounding. I was covered in sweat. I was safe in bed. But the shrieking was real.

With a curse, I reached for the phone. The clock radio read 3:40 a.m.

"Sorry to wake you, Maggie," said the voice in my ear.

Familiar, but I couldn't place it.

I glanced down. I didn't recognize the number.

"This is Thomas Blair. There's been a development on the Paxton case and the East Coast media are going nuts. I'd like you to come in."

It was the middle of the night in L.A., but

already morning in Washington. I wanted to ask what was going on but knew Blair wouldn't discuss it over the phone. His voice was muffled by street noise.

"Where are you?" I asked.

"In the car, driving in. See you soon."

I rubbed my eyes, wide awake now.

In fifteen minutes, I was backing my car out of the garage.

Blair's middle-of-the-night calls were legendary. This was my first, and in some perverse way, I felt I'd just been initiated into an exclusive fraternity. I wondered if Faraday and Tyler were getting rousted out of bed with similar calls.

The hilly street was hushed and eerie. The lights gave off a ghostly glow. At this deep hour of night, I felt like a trespasser in my own neighborhood. My headlights illuminated a family of raccoons on a porch railing. They froze and stared, their eyes glittering red.

At the bottom of the hill, I waited for the light to turn green and wondered what new challenge we'd face today.

Had the police found a smoking gun linking the senator or his brother to Emily's murder? Was the senator stepping down? Were there calls for his impeachment? Could members of Congress even get impeached?

A car cruised into the intersection. Even through closed windows, I heard the hip-hop music blasting. A window rolled down. I heard a series of pops, like a car backfiring. My car gave several jerks and the windshield exploded. The car sped past, then screeched around and did a U-turn and headed back toward me.

Instinct took over. Ducking, covered in tiny bits of glass, I floored the gas pedal, but my car clunked forward in slow motion, juddering the way it did with a flat tire. Except that this felt like four flat tires.

The car drew closer. The driver wore sunglasses and a baseball cap, and his long, wavy gray hair hung down either side of his face like a witch.

Flinging open the driver's side door, I ran. There was a public staircase about fifty yards away, its entrance shrouded by bushes, that went up the hill to my house. Sometimes I used it as a shortcut when I walked around the neighborhood. I made for it now, running on the balls of my high-heeled shoes.

It was dark on the sidewalk and I ran alongside the shrubbery that lined the road, glad for the cover. When the opening came, I ducked inside and started huffing up the steep stairs.

Below me, I heard more pops, then a car screeching to a stop. The sound of running feet. Did my pursuer know about the staircase? Had he seen me turn onto it? Would he follow?

Up ahead, a chain-link fence came into view. The staircase was blocked. There were orange construction cones and a white sawhorse. The city was doing some kind of work. On either side of me were walled-off residential properties. I was trapped.

Should I scream? That would tell my pursuer where to find me. I looked around. There wasn't enough cover to hide. Only tall skinny palms and cypresses and strange Dr. Seussian trees with long arched petals. I'd have to climb the fence.

Sticking the toes of my shoes in the spaces in the chain link, I pulled myself up. The metal rattled from my weight. Any second, he'd be upon me, catching me like a treed possum. I wanted to glance over my shoulder, but every second counted.

Below me on the street, the footsteps slowed. Bushes rustled as my pursuer pushed aside branches like I'd done. I straddled the top of the twelve-foot fence, the wire ends shredding my pants. I pulled free, kicking off my shoes.

I jumped.

Pain shot up my legs as I landed on concrete. I staggered and ran, the bushes closing in on either side to provide cover. I heard a stifled shout, huffing and running, then the jangle of steel as my pursuer came up against the fence I'd just scaled.

The top of the staircase loomed out of the dark. I was almost there. Above me was another street and a second hillside I could climb to get home. As I ran, I strained for the rattle that would tell me my pursuer was climbing the fence. Could I get out of sight before he caught up?

I hit the top step and glanced over my shoulder. A shrouded figure came momentarily into view. It looked like he was grabbing the fence, or trying to fit something through. A gun? I ran, and he was swallowed into the night.

I was on the street now. There were several houses here, but they were dark. I just wanted to get home, slam the door, slide home the dead bolt, and be safe again.

I forced myself to ignore the pebbles and harsh asphalt that dug into the soles of my feet, pushing myself on, gulping in deep breaths of air. At the empty field, I cut across the hillside, in the open once more, feeling exposed and vulnerable. My lungs burned. My breath came ragged. With one last burst of speed I scaled the hill and found myself on my own street. I pricked my ears for pursuit, for a car that would cruise slowly up the hill in the dark. Nothing. I ran the last hundred yards to my house, ducked around the side and onto the back porch, and reached under the eave for the spare key.

With shaking hands, I let myself in, relocked the door, and pulled all the curtains shut. I ran to the front door to make sure it too was locked and that the living room drapes were closed. Then I stood there, catching my breath. My heart thumped madly. My feet throbbed with a dozen scrapes and cuts.

"Mom?" I called softly.

My mother was still sound asleep, the note I'd written still tacked up on the refrigerator.

I stood in the dark, pondering my next step. The Felix the Cat kitchen clock read four twenty-seven.

I called Faraday.

He answered on the second ring. "Hi, Maggie. What's up?"

Suddenly, I couldn't say anything.

"Has something happened with Paxton?" Faraday said, his voice sharp and pointed.

"I thought so. Did Thomas Blair call you at three forty this morning to tell you to come into the office?" I asked in an increasingly shaky voice, already knowing the answer.

"No."

"Then why are you awake?"

"I wasn't."

"I'm sorry, Faraday. But someone just tried to kill me."

I recounted it, and the whole time all I could think of was that the damned federal investigator had warned me and I hadn't listened.

"I'm going to call nine one one," I concluded.

"Hold on a minute. You sure you're okay?"

"Yeah."

"Good. Let me think this over."

I waited.

"I want to run it by Blair first," Faraday said.

Anger flashed through me. "You want to ask him for permission to report the fact that someone tried to kill me?"

"No, Maggie." His voice was patient. "I want to make absolutely sure Blair didn't call you and this isn't some freak coincidence. Hold on."

Soon he was back.

"It wasn't Blair."

The speed with which Faraday handled this made me understand why reporters on deadline loved working with the Blair Company. Day or night, they delivered.

"Someone set you up. They knew Blair, they knew you were working on the Paxton case. And they were waiting at the bottom of the hill for you."

"Jesus," I said.

My mother, hearing all the commotion, shuffled into the living room, clutching her robe and yawning, her face creased from sleep. With her shorn lamb's head and her blinking eyes, she looked like an old baby who'd woken from a nightmare needing reassurance.

Her eyes widened as she took in my appearance. "What's wrong?"

I put my hand over the receiver. "I'm okay, Mom. It's just work."

Mom went into the kitchen to start a pot of coffee and I took the phone into my bedroom to continue our conversation in privacy.

"We want you to talk to the police," Faraday said. "Then deal with your car and come in. The cops will want to talk to us too, since someone impersonated Thomas to lure you out. But why? You don't know anything that could get you killed."

His voice grew low and intimate. "Unless there's something you haven't told me?"

Oh, Faraday! Where do I start? There's so much. But you're the last one I'd tell right now.

"Nothing."

"You want off the Paxton case, Maggie?" Faraday asked. His voice was silky smooth again.

He paused, and I sensed his supple mind considering whether I'd made up this attack in a dramatic attempt to get off the case.

"Thomas doesn't want your life endangered," Faraday said.

Here was the cold calculus of their equation. Publicity about a little cloak-and-dagger chase added sexy derring-do to the story. It hinted at black ops and Jane Bond intrigue, and might even attract new clients. But a dead employee?

"It wouldn't be very good crisis management if I got killed," I said.

"You want to go back to vetting nannies?"

"I don't mind."

"The Paxtons want you on this case. And there's a bonus if it goes well. When we added Simon Paxton as a client, Thomas Blair renegotiated the contract in a big way. And he passes that bounty on to us. . . . How's your mother doing, by the way?"

Faraday asked.

"Fine," I said stiffly.

"I understand she's been sick."

"Keep my mother out of it. She has nothing to do with this."

"I hope not. We all know how expensive medical care is these days."

I was so furious I couldn't speak. Instead, I weighed the pros and cons. I was scared for my life. But I needed this job. For both my mother's sake and mine. And that meant staying on the Paxton case.

"Don't worry," I said. "I'm in."

33

I took a long hot shower, then ate a breakfast of oatmeal, honey, yogurt, and fresh fruit made by Mom, who fussed and fretted over me. The police came and took everything down, growing annoyed when Mom told them she'd already called a garage to tow my car.

While I'd been in the shower, she'd hiked down to see the damage. Three tires had been shot out and the windshield would have to be replaced, but amazingly my purse was still in the front seat. Further proof that this was no random robbery or drive-by.

The police retrieved the phone number from the incoming "Thomas Blair" call but said they doubted it would lead anywhere.

After they left, I hit Redial just to satisfy my own curiosity. The line rang and rang.

"Anyone can get your phone number," Mom said. "You're in PR. You want to be found."

She was right. My contact numbers were on every press release I sent out. At Blair, we trumpeted our 24/7 accessibility. It was one of our selling points.

For the first time, I began to see the downside. Anyone with my home number could use a reverse CrissCross directory to find out where I lived. They could stake me out, follow me to work, on errands. They could even break in.

"Please keep the door locked when you're home," I told Mom.

"This is L.A., darling. I always keep the door locked."

"The front windows too. And don't open the door to strangers."

"I'm careful."

"I want you to be more careful. The guy who did this knows where we live. And you're home all day by yourself."

"Earlyn is usually around. And that nice Mr. Viner around the corner works at home. I don't understand why you won't invite him to dinner. I told you I'd cook."

"Mom! Earlyn said he's still pining over his wife. And I —"

"Most widowers want to remarry again as soon as possible. You wait too long and someone else is going to snatch him up. Mark my words."

"Mr. Viner's wife has been in the ground three months, Mom."

She considered this. "I guess you're right. We'll give it another month."

"*We* are not doing anything — except maybe buying another dead bolt."

Thankfully, that got her off the subject of poor Mr. Viner.

"I've got my pepper spray," Mom said.

"I don't want to scare you. Just be safe and be skeptical."

"Now you're scaring me. Maybe I should cancel my Elderhostel trip?"

"Please don't. You've been so looking forward to it."

"I feel bad leaving you at a time like this. What else is a mother for?"

"I'd feel worse if you stayed. I'll be fine, honest."

She picked up a flame-orange Descoware skillet. "Just let them try anything. I'll show them." She tried to brandish the cast-iron skillet like a club. Her wrist buckled.

"Put that down," I told her. "You're going to pull a tendon."

34

Tyler was walking toward his car as I drove into the secured parking area. When he saw me, he changed direction and followed, waiting at a discreet distance while I parked.

"Hi," he said when I got out. "How are you?"

"Fine," I said, trying to walk past him.

"Hey, what's with the cold shoulder? Why are you avoiding me?"

"I'm not avoiding you, I'm just busy."

"Like hell." He leaned against a car, giving me a lazy smile. "Look, I know there's a lot going on at work right now that you may not understand, but there are reasons for everything. Most of which I'm not at liberty to discuss. Was it something I said? If so, tell me how I can make it up to you."

I stopped and regarded him. A thought came.

"As a matter of fact, there is. You're tight with the cops, through your LAPD source

Sinclair, right?"

Tyler looked wary. "What about it?"

"There's another LAPD, a guy named Lionel Comstock. I'd like to ask him a few questions, but he won't talk to me. Can you help?"

"Why do you want to talk to him?"

I paused. Would this get back to Faraday and Blair? Would it raise alarm bells? Or would they just see it as me doing my job, collecting as much information as I could to draw up a better PR strategy for our client?

I needed this, and there was no other way.

"Comstock was a friend of Anabelle Paxton's husband. They were partners back in the day. Randall Downs led a task force that put a vengeful drug lord away last year. I want to talk to him about that. The more we know about Downs's work with the LAPD, the better PR campaign we can come up with."

Tyler grasped it immediately. He gave a knowing nod. "Several LAPD cops have been murdered recently in strange ambush situations. Maybe there's a connection."

"Can you call your LAPD pal and get him to convince Lionel Comstock to talk to me? Like, today?"

Tyler thought about it. "I can try. It'll

mean calling in a favor."

"He's not going to talk to me any other way. He's made that clear."

Tyler grinned. "Yeah, we're even lower than the press."

"Thanks, Tyler."

"Is that the only reason you're talking to me? What are you going to do for me in return?"

"I'm going to win the Paxton case in the court of public opinion. That's what I'm going to do for you. And for me. And for Blair. And then we'll all get bonuses and everyone will live happily ever after."

As I walked away, I felt his eyes burning into my back and wondered if I'd just made a huge mistake. I didn't trust him. But there was an inviting light in his eyes that still made me go all warm inside.

"Miss Silver," said a heavily accented voice as I waited for the elevator.

I started. It was Viken the mechanic.

A car horn tooted as Tyler drove past.

Viken turned and waved and Tyler waved back, then drove up the ramp and out of the building.

"That was your friend, Mr. Tyler," Viken said reproachfully. "You did not wave."

"Was that who it was? Gosh, I can't see

anything without my glasses."

"How is the MG doing?" Viken asked.

"What?" I stared at him blankly, wondering if I'd misunderstood through his thick accent, until I remembered the ruse I'd come up with to check on Tyler's car.

I smiled. "Thanks for asking, Viken. I've been giving it some hard thought, and I think I might sell the MG instead of pouring more money into it."

Viken commiserated. "I have an old Aston Martin, so I know. Old cars can be a pit of money."

"Well . . ." I said, eager to get upstairs.

"Not like Mr. Tyler's BMW. Bavarian Motor Works. Precision instruments. I told him last night, why did you tell Miss Silver that I not fix your car right? And he explained that it was a misunderstanding. He said he will tell you that I am a capable mechanic. Then you bring me your MG. I will give you a good price."

"I promise I will if I keep it," I said, relieved the elevator had arrived so I didn't have to tell any more white lies.

As I stepped inside, I thought of something more alarming.

Thanks to Viken, Tyler now knew about my growing suspicions. And that I'd caught him in another lie. This made me uneasy.

Viken and Tyler had spoken yesterday. Last night, Thomas Blair had grilled me in his penthouse suite. Then early this morning, someone had tried to kill me. Now I'd asked Tyler for help in setting up a meeting with Lionel Comstock. I felt like I was being drawn deeper into the web of a malevolent spider from which there could be no return.

When I poked my head into Faraday's office, he broke off a meeting with Samantha George.

"Maggie! Glad to see you. You all right?"

I nodded.

"That must have been so creepy," Sam said. She tossed her hair from side to side. "I would have died."

"You would have done exactly what Maggie did," Faraday corrected her. "You would have thought on your feet and gotten out of there."

"How'd it go with the cops?" he asked, his voice cagey now, something shutting down behind his eyes.

"They asked a lot of questions but it didn't seem to lead anywhere."

"Well," Faraday said, genial once more, "we're happy you're back safe and sound. Have a seat. Sam and I were just discussing the lead goat."

"I'm sorry?"

I really need to cut back on the Adderall.

Sam grinned. "Mr. Blair has a theory that reporters are like pack animals. Someone breaks a story and everyone falls into line behind the lead goat. So we find the reporter who wants to be the maverick, who's itching to stand out from the herd. Faraday calls him up, maybe takes him to lunch, and points out errors or omissions in the media coverage. Maybe even feeds him a new piece of information. And that reporter goes back to his office and writes a story that starts the backlash, or in our case, the rehabilitation. And soon other reporters swing around to follow the pack."

"So who's our lead goat?" I asked.

With an hour to kill before my next telephone interview, I sipped coffee and searched online for more medical trials Mom might be eligible for, but a tendril of unease kept dislodging and floating through my head as I read the complicated medical protocols.

Oliver Goldman.

Faraday had grilled me about the federal investigator this morning, asking if I'd heard from the DOJ man again.

"No!" I said, a little too quickly and

emphatically for Faraday's liking.

My boss grew very still. "Are you sure?"

"No sign of him."

"We believe that the government is trying to recruit someone from inside Blair or within the senator's office."

"How would you know that? Do we have a plant in *their* office?"

Faraday gave me an enigmatic look but didn't answer.

"Why do they think we're doing something illegal?"

"That's what we'd like to know," said Faraday.

I thought back to last night's attack, not twenty-four hours after Oliver Goldman visited me at home. Maybe I should have told Faraday the truth and said I'd shown him the door. What if my boss thought I was cooperating with the feds? Would that put me in danger? What exactly were Blair and the senator trying to hide? Or was it just Adderall-induced anxiety, making me see bogeymen everywhere? I felt like I was playing three-dimensional chess but couldn't see the moves of my opponent.

For now, I'd keep Goldman's visit to myself.

After Faraday dismissed me, I did a few medical searches, e-mailed Mom some promising sites to check out, and wrote her a note saying I hoped she could get enrolled in one of the trials.

Then I thought about Oliver Goldman some more. He'd said the Justice Department was investigating Blair's work for a major player in the banking scandal. Senator Paxton had mentioned a JTM Financial Services. Was there a connection?

I typed in the name.

Immediately, I was swamped by stories about JTM's humble origins, explosive growth, and dramatic crash. There were allegations that directors had secretly sold their stock before admitting the firm was in trouble and had wined and dined auditors, regulators, market analysts, and anyone else who might investigate them. The company CEO was a sixty-two-year-old Greek American from Queens who'd worked his way up from a sales associate and expanded the firm in a dozen risky but profitable directions. He'd been profiled in *Forbes* and *Fortune* as a maverick genius, until the bubble burst and he was revealed as an emperor with no clothes.

As I waded through reams of data, an old story from a PR wire caught my eye. Five years earlier, JTM officials had reassured Wall Street that their purchase of a small subprime mortgage company would allow them to compete in this booming sector of the market and become more profitable. The story quoted a JTM spokesman named Matthew Tyler.

Tyler.

I quickly searched for more JTM stories quoting Matthew Tyler. Nothing.

I don't know why Blair's representation of the now-disgraced JTM Financial surprised me. I'd always known that corporate PR formed the backbone of our company. Firms constantly merged and reorganized and bought one another, and they needed savvy representation on Wall Street. That kind of PR didn't get as much ink as celebrity scandals, but it made us a lot more money. Now the true scope of Blair's activities swam into focus like never before.

What was Tyler's connection to JTM, and what, if anything, did it have to do with Emily Mortimer's murder? No matter how I tried, I couldn't connect the invisible dots. My theories were too far-fetched and preposterous. Blair was a huge PR firm; of course they had clients in every field. It didn't mean anything.

Late afternoon found me at a coffeehouse in Altadena, at the foot of the San Gabriel

Mountains, sitting in a booth opposite Lionel Comstock. The LAPD cop wore wraparound sunglasses and a baseball cap pulled low over his head. He didn't even glance at the colorful paintings on the walls.

"I got you a cappuccino," I said, sliding it across.

"Thanks," he said but didn't touch it.

Comstock clearly didn't want to be here and he liked me about as much as a dog does a mailman. But he'd shown up because Tyler had come through. He'd called up his LAPD source Tom Sinclair, the guy we'd met in the Koreatown alley that first night. And Sinclair had somehow convinced Comstock to meet with me. If money or favors had also changed hands, I didn't want to know about it.

We'd settled upon the Coffee Gallery in these smoky foothills because it was county territory, far away from any LAPD haunts.

I ripped open two packets of sugar and poured them into my coffee. Then I stirred it and took a sip.

"I'd like to get one thing straight before we start. Anabelle is my friend and Randall was your old partner. We're on the same side."

Comstock said nothing.

"I know Homicide is tracking down every

541

lead, and I hope that they look into this
show that Randall was supposedly consulting on, *Rookie.* But I also want you to know
that last week when I met Randall —"

"If you were old friends, how come you
only met Randall last week?"

"We were close in high school. Then we
lost touch. This case brought us back together."

Comstock cracked his knuckles and
looked bored. I could tell he didn't believe
me.

"As I was saying, when I saw Anabelle last
week, Randall mentioned he was asking
around about Emily Mortimer's murder.
And that got me to thinking. Maybe he got
too close to unmasking her killer?"

"That's an interesting theory," said Comstock.

"You have another? Like the drug gang
hit? If there's anything you could tell me
about —"

"I don't have shit," he said. "Neither did
Randall. He was grasping at straws. And
freaking out his wife."

"How so?"

Comstock leaned his elbows on the Formica table. "Maybe you can tell me."

"I have no idea."

Comstock studied me as if trying to make

up his mind.

"Look, I'm doing this because it's what Randall would have wanted. I don't really care about Anabelle or her family or how you've reconnected yadda yadda. In fact, it's a little strange that Anabelle didn't tell her *good friend* that her husband was looking into links between Mortimer's murder and other unsolved L.A. strangulation murders with female victims. 'Cause she knew. Randall said she brought him coffee one night when he was working at home and when she saw what was on his computer screen, she made a strange noise and dropped the cup."

Comstock paused.

"It was the mug shot of a small-time drug dealer who'd been charged with strangling his girlfriend in the mid-1990s. The scumbag was acquitted after a long trial. His name was Stephen Dumbrowski. The vic, Heidi Magellan, was murdered in their Inglewood apartment."

Comstock watched my reaction.

I shook my head. "Never heard of him or her."

"Randall thought Anabelle might have recognized Dumbrowski from her junkie days."

"So you know how she and Randall met?"

Comstock nodded. "But it's not common knowledge at the LAPD. They frown on things like that."

He looked at me and something passed between us. We'd both been entrusted with secrets. While it didn't make us friends, it thawed the icy gulf between us.

I said, "So did Anabelle know Dumbrowski?"

"Randall pressed her, and finally she admitted she'd met him in her party days. She was floored to learn he'd been tried for murder. She'd apparently been out of the country when the trial went down. Randall had a hunch she knew him better than she let on."

"But he never got to the bottom of it?"

Comstock shrugged.

"If you think this is so important, why not ask Anabelle yourself?"

He shook his head. "I'm not a detective and I'm not assigned to the case. There are protocols about these things."

"Have you told Homicide your suspicions?"

He grimaced. "I'm going to. But I'd like to give the detectives something more solid than a spilled drink."

Comstock fired up his laptop and called up a file. He slid the screen around to me.

It showed a police mug shot of a sullen young man holding a booking number.

I felt an icy trickle down my back and swayed in my seat as the memories rose like bile. Immediately I fought to shove them back into the hellish little box that resided somewhere between my heart and my belly.

But for once, I couldn't. I had to go back there, to that night, and figure it out.

And then I was sitting cross-legged on a dirty shag carpet in a bedroom in Playa del Rey. The music was pounding in the other room. A couple lay entwined on the bed and a guy named Ivan in a Wile E. Coyote shirt was mixing G&Ts with date-rape drugs that would knock us out. Then Anabelle was kissing Ivan, and a blue-eyed guy named Dan was trying to tug me to my feet and lead me from the room. And despite the roofies, despite the booze, despite the fact that I'd spent half my life repressing it, I knew exactly who the guy in the mug shot was. I ID'd him instantly.

Comstock leaned forward. "You know this guy?"

But I was very far away.

"It's fi-yunne," Anabelle was saying. "Nothing's gonna happen unless I want it to."

Oh, Anabelle! We'd been young and immortal until the illusion cracked like a shoddy ceramic doll.

"Does he look familiar?"

I squinted and turned toward the voice and slowly LAPD sergeant Lionel Comstock came back into focus.

"Stephen *Ivan* Dumbrowski," I read.

I tried to furrow my brow. To look as if I was trying to place the name and the face. To search my memory. While deep inside the recessed gray matter, where no one could see, the frantic thoughts went round and round.

Had Anabelle told Randall what had happened to her at sixteen? What relevance did it have today? And what right did I have to tell Anabelle's story, if she'd chosen to keep silent all these years?

Slowly, I shook my head. "Stephen Dumbrowski definitely doesn't ring any bells."

This was semantically correct because the guy I'd met was Ivan.

"Sure took you long enough," Comstock said shrewdly.

I gave him a long, frank stare.

"I meet so many people in my job that after a while they tend to blur together. Even people I've never met begin to look familiar. And you're asking me to go back almost twenty years."

Comstock's jaw tightened. He pulled the laptop back.

"So what happened after Randall and Anabelle mopped up the spilled coffee?" I said, eager to change the subject.

Comstock fixed me with a moody look. "Apparently she went upstairs and looked up the Dumbrowski trial. Randall did a search history of her computer after she didn't come home."

"What do you mean, she didn't come home?"

"Awhile later, Anabelle came downstairs in workout gear. The mug shot had stirred up old ghosts and she needed some sweat therapy. She came home after midnight. Claimed she'd parked along a cliff after going to the gym and watched the surf for a while."

"Where do you think she went?"

"I was hoping you could tell me."

I shook my head. "She kept this all to herself."

"She kept a whole lot to herself. Randall checked. She never made it to the gym."

35

As I got back on the freeway, my head teemed with questions. Where had Anabelle been that night? Had she gone to confront Ivan after all these years? But how would she know where to find him? And what did that have to do with her husband's murder? Or Emily Mortimer's?

But most of all, why hadn't she told me?

I'd hoped we were drawing close again, erasing the passage of years, the estrangement. I wanted her to confide in me. As usual, I wanted to rescue her, to fix her and make it all better. Instead, I felt a familiar rush of disappointment.

When was I going to grow up?

"I'm home," I called, hanging up my jacket.

I was disappointed that no one answered. For all that she grated on my nerves with her smoking, her neediness, and her endless bossy advice, I'd grown used to my mother's presence. And compared to the disaster that reigned at Villa Marbella, my cottage was a haven of tranquillity.

What if my attacker had returned while I was gone? I sniffed the air. Smoke. It didn't smell like a house that had been closed and unoccupied for hours. The back windows were open. A pack of cigarettes lay on the kitchen table next to a dirty but empty ashtray. And from inside the trash can curled a spiral of . . .

I ran to the sink, grabbed a pot from the drain board, and filled it with water. The kitchen trash had caught fire. The plastic was melting along one side of the bin as the fire spread. Flames shot from the top.

I poured the water, then kicked over the bin as I ran for more water. Junk mail and Styrofoam cartons and cigarette butts with telltale lipstick spilled onto the tile, flames still licking the edges. I dumped another pot of water over the mess, flooding the floor, stamping on orange cinders. Then I ran for the pantry, grabbed a ten-pound bag of flour, and emptied that over everything.

Something exploded. I shrieked, convinced my attacker had chosen this moment to return.

"What on earth?" Mom stood at the kitchen door. The explosion had been our

549

screen door slamming shut.

She held a cigarette between her fingers. The smile on her face faded in alarm.

"Maggie, child, have you lost your mind?"

And then I did lose it.

"The one thing I asked when I took you in, Mom, was to not smoke in my house," I screamed at the top of my lungs, letting every ugly impulse from the past year rip loose inside me. "And not only did you disregard that, but you almost burned my house down. Thanks a fucking lot."

Mom hurried to the kitchen table and stubbed out her cigarette. "I'm sorry, hon, I meant to put it out before I came inside, but I —"

"It's not *that* cigarette," I said, picking up the ashtray and hurling it against the wall. It shattered, making a satisfying noise. "It's this one." I prodded at the sodden, floury mess with my high-heeled shoe, "and that one. And the other. You dumped an ashtray full of cigarette butts into the trash and one of them was still going and it ignited. If I hadn't come home when I did, who knows what could have happened? I have had it with you. You're worse than a teenager, sneaking around and lying about your smoking."

Mom's eyes darted guiltily from side to

side. "I'm sorry. I was sure I'd —"

"Well, you didn't. You're careless and disrespectful and ungrateful. I work like a dog to make sure we've got enough money to pay the bills and stay in this house, and you're trying to burn it down."

I tried to stop myself, but the floodgates were wide open and there was no turning back. Even though the irony of my next words made me squirm, I still spoke them. Perhaps my fervor was directed as much at myself as at her.

"Can't you see that you've got a problem? You're an addict. And you're stupid, Mom. Because smoking causes cancer. And if your cancer's back, it could kill you. And if it's back, then it's me who'll have to nurse you again, and if you don't make it, then it's me who'll have to scrape up the money for your funeral. You're going to die and leave me all alone. And I hate you for that, Mom. You're going to die. Do you understand me? You have to stop smoking. Now. Before it's too late."

Mom's face had gone from shame to anger as I spoke. Now something went soft and pained in her eyes and she hurried over and put her arms around me.

"We're all going to die sooner or later, Maggie," she said, so softly that I had to strain to hear her. "That's the one certainty that life offers us. Please don't hate me because I smoke."

"But it's going to kill you," I said with a sob.

"Stress and uncertainty will kill me too, and perhaps even faster. I'm sorry about what happened. I should have been more careful. Please look at me . . ."

She waited until I lifted my eyes to hers.

"Maggie, I give you my solemn word that I will never smoke in this house again."

"You'll just break your promise again. You've broken every promise you ever made to me."

"No." Mom's voice was steady. "This is one you can count on. But, Maggie . . . smoking relieves my anxiety. Of course I'm worried that the cancer's come back. It's killing me not to know. It's killing me to think that my body could be turning against me, that there might be these . . . cells inside me, growing, multiplying. You're not home all day and I'm by myself and it gets lonely. And I dwell on morbid things. So I invite Earlyn over to visit. She takes my mind off things. And she smokes and one thing led to another and I started up again. I knew I shouldn't. But please try to see things from my perspective for once."

My entire life, I'd been asked to see it from the perspective of others. First my parents, then my friends. And when I grew up, I'd chosen a profession where I was a perfect conduit, who existed solely to present the views of others. Our clients, who must be pleased and placated at all costs.

"I'm sorry about the fire," Mom said. "And I'm glad you reacted so quickly to put it out. But honestly? It probably would have burned itself out anyway before it did much harm."

There she went again, refusing to take responsibility for what she'd done and minimizing my concerns. Like I was the one who'd overreacted, just because she'd started a fire in my wood-frame house.

"There now," Mom said, running her palm along the side of my face, and I realized I was crying.

"I'll help you clean this up, then let's go visit Earlyn. That's what I came over to tell you when I saw your car in the driveway. Earlyn got a new cat. Bandit. You're going to love him. And she bought them each a six-foot kitty condo with ledges and hideaways and dangling ropes. They're very playful animals, you'll see."

But I was in no mood to be coddled and distracted like a child.

"No, thank you," I said. "If you like Ear-lyn so much, why don't you move in with her."

And I stomped out of the room.

In my bedroom, I changed into sweats, still bristling with self-righteousness, as I heard Mom sweeping and mopping the floor. I knew it hurt her knees to bend down, but I convinced myself that she'd caused this mess and it was her responsibility to clean it up.

For ten minutes, I lay on my bed and brooded as brooms and mops and dustpans banged. I'd just made up my mind to apologize for my outburst and offer to take over when I heard the kitchen door slam again and my mother's footsteps echo down the wooden stairs, headed to see Earlyn.

I remembered the sad, haunted look in her eyes as she embraced me and was touched by guilt. Why did we fight? What if she didn't have long to live? Shouldn't I overlook her faults and try to cherish the time we had together? I'd catch her when she came back, later tonight, and try to make amends before she left in the morning for Catalina.

I crept out to the pristine kitchen and got myself some hummus with crackers. Then I sat at the computer and typed in the names Stephen Ivan Dumbrowski and Heidi Magellan.

I got a lot of hits, especially from our hometown paper. The *L.A. Times* had still employed a large staff back in 1995, and they'd followed every lurid twist of the Magellan murder trial.

Stephen Ivan Dumbrowski was born in 1970 and raised in Carson, a blue-collar town near Long Beach. He was smart enough to get accepted into UC Berkeley and dumb enough to drop out after one year and return home. He'd held various low-level jobs, but his main income came from dealing drugs. He worked for a midlevel dealer with Mexican connections who supplied a lot of the surf crowd up and down the coast, a man named Barry "the Barracuda" Gibson.

I looked up, suddenly unable to read any longer. The letters shimmied on the screen, not making sense. My heart pounded against my ribs and I couldn't catch my breath.

The past burst through.

Barracuda.

Again, I saw the dissipated, aging beachboy in the hallway of the beach bungalow in Playa del Rey. Smoking and waiting. Lying in wait.

The sense of dread and menace emanating from him. The freakishly swollen gut. And later the streaky white fluid on Anabelle's thigh, the smirk on Ivan's face.

"The Barracuda got his taste."

I typed in Barry "the Barracuda" Gibson.

Almost immediately, a raft of stories popped up.

Barry "the Barracuda" Gibson had been murdered on November 13, 1995, killed execution-style with a shot to the head outside his car after a night of drinking at the Fisherman's Net, a squalid bar near the Redondo Beach Pier.

Slowly, my heart rate slowed. My fingers sagged on the keys.

The Barracuda was dead.

It was only then that I realized how long he'd inhabited my nightmares; a shadowy, sinister bogeyman all the more frightening because I'd glimpsed him only once and had no idea who he was.

The murder had never been solved, although rumors swirled that he'd been whacked by the Mexican Mafia, which was then in the process of consolidating its Los Angeles operations and eliminating the middleman. There was also a quote from a deputy district attorney who'd prosecuted Gibson on an earlier drug charge.

"It couldn't happen to a nicer guy," the prosecutor said. "He was a real piece of work, a true psychotic and sadist who took pleasure in corrupting young girls."

I shuddered, then toggled back to Stephen Ivan Dumbrowski. After years of low-level crimes, he had been arrested for the murder of his girlfriend, Heidi Magellan, a stripper who worked the bevy of "gentlemen's clubs" near LAX. The couple lived in a shabby apartment on 96th Street in Inglewood, right under the flight path. Magellan and Dumbrowski fought all the time. Even over the roar of the jets, the neighbors heard screams, thuds, crockery breaking. The cops would be called. The district attorney's office told the press the jury would convict.

Then at the eleventh hour, the defense produced a Mexican police chief who testified that Dumbrowski had been in a Tijuana jail the night Heidi Magellan was murdered.

The prosecutor suggested that the police chief had been paid off, but the jury believed the man in a uniform. They found Dumbrowski guilty of drug dealing but innocent of murder. He was sentenced to fifteen years and served seven.

I thought hard. Dumbrowski had been a drug dealer. Emily Mortimer had procured drugs for her boss, Senator Paxton. Could this be the connection we were all looking for?

I called Lionel Comstock, who'd grudgingly agreed to give me his number.

"I was thinking about our meeting, and I had a question."

"Look, uh, can I call you right back?"

"Sure."

I hung up and waited. He'd take precautions, not using his own phone.

Sure enough, when he called back, it was on a different line.

I said, "Did Dumbrowski go back to dealing drugs after he got out of prison?"

"His probation officer says he's clean."

"So he's not the one who sold drugs to Emily Mortimer? And it's just a coincidence that both Emily and Heidi Magellan were strangled?"

"That's what I was wondering too," said Comstock.

36

I tried to wait up for Mom to apologize, but my eyes closed around midnight and I fell into troubled sleep. My dreams consisted of one endless loop: I was having a screaming match with Mom. When she told me her cancer was back, I ran off crying and found myself in the beach house in Playa del Rey where the Barracuda waited at the end of a dark hallway, a cigarette dangling from his mouth.

When I opened my eyes, it was morning and I'd slept through the alarm. On those rare occasions, Mom usually woke me. Mom! My brain activated, flooding with data. Shame. Disgrace. Regret. Remorse. Love and fear. I reached for the Adderall in my bedside table. Fifteen milligrams. Just enough, at this point, to dissipate the fog. I had to get off it. But not today. Soon. I knew I couldn't keep this up for much longer. I was approaching mental and physical collapse.

On my way to the shower, I poked my head into Mom's room but her bed was neatly made. I looked outside. Earlyn's car was gone. They'd already left for the harbor.

Now I'd have to wait three days to say I was sorry. What if the ferry sank? What if their car crashed on the way there? What if she died, leaving me with only ugly memories of how I'd behaved the last time I'd seen her.

After breakfast, I called Faraday and told him I wanted to drive out to Villa Marbella and check on the Paxtons. He told me to go ahead.

Anabelle's family took my presence for granted by now. The house felt like a city under siege, and I thought they might welcome the insulation I provided from the outside world. Miranda said hello, brought me a cup of coffee, and told me Anabelle was upstairs.

Out back, Lincoln was having a tennis lesson. Each time he hit the ball, the nanny clapped her hands.

Anabelle was standing at her window, twisting the gold curtain sash around her finger and gazing down at her son, her face suffused with tenderness.

I lowered myself into the brocaded Regency chair with the carved wooden feet. We'd found it at Wertz Brothers on Santa Monica Boulevard for $175. I'd considered that a fortune back in 1992, but Anabelle had blithely handed over her credit card.

"How's Lincoln doing?" I asked.

Anabelle turned. Her face was pale and wan. "He keeps asking when his daddy's coming back from heaven."

"It isn't something any four-year-old should have to deal with," I said.

Anabelle was silent.

"I'm sorry if this stirs up painful memories," I said, "but I need to ask you some questions."

Her eyes grew wary. She seemed to draw into herself, then peer out.

"Go ahead."

Even years later, it was almost impossible to put the taboo subject into words.

"Did you ever tell Randall what happened . . . that night in Playa del Rey?" My voice petered out into an almost silent plea.

"He knew I was raped in high school and that I never reported it. But not the gory details."

Her cheekbones stood out. Her eyes were bullet holes in a white wedding dress.

"I thought it might have been part of your

recovery to tell him."

"It was. But neither of us wanted to dwell on it."

"It wasn't your fault. And it explains why you might have tried to blot out —"

"Please don't make excuses for me," said Anabelle. "I had free will. I made bad choices. That night had nothing to do with what came later. I've buried it so deep I barely remember, and when I do, it's like it happened to someone else in a long-ago dream."

I looked out the window, where a soft breeze was swaying the poplar trees.

Choosing my words with care, I said, "I understand that Randall was looking into a connection between the strangulation murder of Stephen Ivan Dumbrowski's girlfriend and the murder of your dad's aide, Emily Mortimer."

Anabelle turned. There was reproach in her eyes and a flash of something else — anger. I thought she might deny it, or play coy and ask who Dumbrowski was.

Instead, she said, "Who told you that?"

"It's not important. What's important is that we both know who Stephen *Ivan* Dumbrowski is. And" — I took a deep breath — "I think we need to tell Faraday. The police are probably going to ask you about it soon."

A wounded, accusing look came into her eyes.

"I didn't tell anybody anything, Anabelle. But apparently Randall told a colleague the odd way you behaved when you saw Ivan's photo."

"There's nothing to connect any of it," Anabelle said.

"Not yet. But maybe Ivan knew Jake Slattery. Or Emily Mortimer. Maybe he strangled both those girls. Maybe he and Slattery did it together. If they knew about that night, it might help the police . . . I don't know if you ever ran into him after —"

"No! There is no connection. And it's none of anybody's business. Please, Maggie, I spent ten years of my life blotto, trying to erase what happened that night. And I'm not going to have it dredged up and reexamined. This family has been through enough."

I was too much of a friend to point out that she'd just told me her addiction had nothing to do with her rape.

"I Googled Dumbrowski's murder trial," I said. "His alibi seemed highly dubious. He could have easily killed his girlfriend. And if there is something you know that —"

"I read those stories too," Anabelle said,

"but I can't help you. Nothing I know will solve anything. Besides, I can't go back to that . . . place in my head and relive it. It was bad enough seeing Ivan's photo. It was like a freight train slamming into me. I thought I might lose my mind that night."

"Anabelle? Where did you go, when you told Randall you were going to the gym?"

She looked shocked. "How do you know about that?"

I stood my ground, stared at her steadily. "I just know."

Her face softened. Her demeanor changed. She walked toward me, as if eager to confide in me. She sat on the bed and reached for my hand.

"I had all these emotions churning inside me. I needed to be alone. But I didn't want to upset Randall. So I told him I was going to the gym."

"But you never made it?"

"No. I drove through Portuguese Bend, up and down those rollercoaster streets, faster than I should have. Then I parked along the cliffs and listened to the surf."

"That's all?"

"You're starting to scare me. Where do you think I went?"

"I don't know. Maybe you went to confront Ivan?"

She drew back in appalled disbelief. "How would I know where he lives? Even if I did, wouldn't that be dangerous? I told you, I just want to forget that night ever happened. Please, Maggie, this is crazy. You sound like a cop, interrogating me." She drew herself up. "And I don't like that."

I said, "What happened in the past may be connected to this somehow. Cops are clever, they'll put all the pieces together and figure it out. We need to tell them."

"I forbid you."

I dropped her hand as if stung.

"Forbid me," I said softly, crossing my arms.

"I beg you," she quickly amended. "Right now, I'm struggling just to hang on. And it's so hard. The idea of going back to the house where Randall . . . I just can't . . . I've been clean a long time but . . ."

"Mommy?" said a small voice at the door. It was Lincoln. Behind him hovered the nanny. The boy was red cheeked and sweaty, dressed in tennis whites and clutching a tiny racket.

"Scott says I have a powerful backhand," he announced proudly.

"Darling," said Anabelle, kneeling and opening her arms wide. "How wonderful."

He ran to her with his awkward four-year-old gait, and the racket clattered to the floor. Anabelle wrapped her arms around her son and pressed her cheek against his damp blond hair.

"Where's Daddy?" Lincoln asked.

"Oh Lincoln, my bugaboo. I told you. Daddy went to heaven."

"I *know,* Momma. But when's he coming back?"

They remained entwined, and Anabelle's nostrils flared as she breathed in the boy's warm, sweet essence. Her hand reached out to caress his head.

"He *lives* in heaven now," she said, her voice muffled.

"But I still want him to live with us."

"I know, sweet boy. But he can't. He's in heaven."

Lincoln squirmed closer to his mother and as his head shifted, Anabelle's face was revealed, her eyes scrunched tight, her cheeks damp, clutching her son, both of them clinging to each other like they were dying.

37

When I got home that night, I lay on the living room floor under the fan, eating a candy bar and going over the day's events.

Secrets. We were all keeping secrets from one another. So many secrets that they threatened to overpower and drown us. Sooner or later, I would forget and tell the wrong person the wrong thing, and then the entire thing would collapse like a house of rotten cards.

The chocolate was soft from the heat and stuck wonderfully to the roof of my mouth. When it was gone, I licked the foil like a dog, then crumpled up the wrapper and went upstairs with a fashion magazine.

I found myself lingering at a spread of incredible punky-glam-Goth couture dresses by a couple of Pasadena sisters who called themselves Rodarte. Anabelle and I would have drooled over such dresses as teenagers — the ruffled, strappy, mesh, peekaboo, sheer, body-clinging Rococo over-the-topness of it all.

It didn't matter that I had nowhere to wear such an outfit, and couldn't afford one anyway; just feasting my eyes on these Goth confections kindled something magical inside me that I hadn't felt for a long time.

It was still hot and the ceiling fan only whipped the tired dead air around the room. Even at eleven at night, the city still felt like a furnace. Up to the north, the hills glowed a reddish orange. In its own horrible way, the fire was beautiful. Nature's neon. I made sure the window was open all the way to catch the breeze that would kick in before dawn and went to sleep.

Thud.

I awoke to something hitting my chest. Hard.

Startled, disoriented, flailing madly, I screamed.

Whoever had hit me was hiding in the shadows, waiting to strike again. I was on my feet now, panting, trying my damnedest to pierce the darkness. A pair of eyes glowed across the room, just above my head.

"What do you want?" I said loudly, groping for the police Maglite I kept by the bed.

There was no answer.

At the same time, I snicked on the bedside

lamp. As the bulb dispelled the shadows, I looked in vain for an intruder. Only Earlyn's cat Bandit, perched on my bookshelf, his fur standing up like a Halloween cat.

"Mrrrrrrreeep," said Bandit.

"Jesus Christ. You damn cat. Nearly gave me a heart attack."

For a moment, we regarded each other with equal resentment.

Then I put out my hand. "Here kitty, kitty."

Bandit hissed and darted across the room. With a flying leap, she was out the window. I heard her land with a thump on the deck and then she was gone.

Dawn was streaking across the sky before I finally dozed off. The alarm woke me an hour later.

I took an Adderall.

38

"I've got some news," Detective Delgado said.

It was the next morning. The Paxton brothers and I sat in the living room of Villa Marbella with the cops, who'd shown up unannounced. Miranda was out and Anabelle was upstairs with the bedroom door closed. The maid said she was indisposed.

Simon Paxton cleared his throat. "Should our lawyer be here?"

Delgado pulled his mouth back in what might have been a smile if it exposed less of his gums.

"That's completely up to you. But I'm giving out information today, not asking for it."

"Go ahead," the senator said in a resigned voice.

"Neither of you fathered Emily Mortimer's baby."

If either the senator or Simon felt relief to

learn that DNA testing had absolved them of paternity, they hid it well.

I found this interesting. Senator Paxton had always denied an affair with Emily, and Delgado's news certainly bolstered his claim. But Simon Paxton *had* been sleeping with the dead girl. Why wasn't he relieved? It struck me, then, that the brothers somehow already *knew* that neither one of them had fathered Emily's child. But how could they be so certain?

Henry Paxton leaned forward, hands clasped earnestly between his knees.

"Did your DNA testing determine who *did* father Emily's baby?"

"Yes," said Delgado.

He watched them, saying nothing, still hoping, perhaps, for some kind of tell, some twitch or eyelid flutter or spontaneous confession.

But the Paxtons sat politely and waited the detective out.

"The DNA matches samples from a coffee cup and a comb found in Jake Slattery's van," Delgado said, choosing his words carefully.

"So Emily Mortimer was pregnant by Jake Slattery," I said, making the link for him. "I wonder if he knew."

"We're going to ask him that, and a whole

lot else, as soon as we find him."

I glanced at Senator Paxton, who had finally permitted himself a look of suppressed triumph. Then he caught himself and his face became a grim mask.

Delgado said, "We've also collected DNA from Emily's body that might have been left by the killer. No matches with your office there either. Or with Slattery. We're running it through our criminal database, see if we get any hits."

"What's your theory, Detective?" Simon Paxton said eagerly. "If Slattery is the father, does that make him more likely to have killed her?"

"We're not going to speculate. What we do know is that Slattery threatened Emily. We've recovered long, rambling voice mails on her home phone. She saved them, maybe she had a bad feeling. The messages suggest that Emily was trying to break it off with him. Slattery was furious. He accused her of cheating on him."

"Did the voice mails mention who she was seeing?" I asked, forcing myself not to look at Simon.

Delgado hesitated. "No."

I wondered whether Jake Slattery had killed his on-off girlfriend in a jealous rage when he learned about her affair with

Simon Paxton. Or perhaps he thought Simon had fathered her child? My thoughts went round and round and stopped in an unexpected place: What if Simon Paxton had killed Emily when he learned she carried Slattery's child?

I kept this speculation to myself. Delgado stood up, shook hands all around, and left.

I called Faraday and recounted the good news.

"Draft a statement for the senator's approval," he said. "Once he signs off, e-mail it to me and I'll send it out."

"What about a statement from Simon Paxton?"

"Samantha George will handle it. Just worry about your end of things. I'll put everything together in my usual seamless fashion."

The statement I sent Faraday ten minutes later said that U.S. Senator Paxton was pleased that DNA tests and the LAPD's prompt work had exonerated everyone in his office. He would continue to cooperate fully with the investigation. His thoughts and prayers were with the Mortimer family during this difficult time, and he urged Jake Slattery to turn himself in.

Before I headed back to the office, I went

upstairs to say good-bye to Anabelle.

Her door was closed.

KEEP OUT, read a sixteen-year-old sign in Gothic letters framed by grinning skulls and bloodred roses. I hadn't noticed it on previous visits because the door had been open.

"Anabelle, can I come in?"

No response.

I knocked. "It's Maggie."

From inside the room came a sullen silence.

"I brought you something," I said.

More silence, as she considered it. Then the floorboards creaked and the door opened.

I was shocked at how her hair hung, lank and unwashed. Her eyes were dull and lusterless. Her skin looked sallow. She wore cutoff sweats and a T-shirt so faded I could no longer read the logo.

I extended an open palm. Inside was a glass perfume sample. I'd decanted it for her at home.

"It's Hermès." I gave her a lopsided smile. "Un Jardin sur le Nil. It smells like green mangoes and citrus and oceans and salt. Guaranteed to boost your mood instantly."

She took it like an eager child, sprayed and inhaled deeply.

"Mmmm," she said, in a voice rusty from

tears and disuse. "Thanks, Maggie. Very thoughtful. Come in."

I stepped inside and she shut the door. Then she retreated to the bed. It bore the hollow imprint of her body, as if she'd lain there, unmoving, for a long time.

I sat next to her.

"Did the cops interview you?" I asked.

"Yes."

"Did they ask about Ivan?"

"I said I'd never met him."

"That's too bad. It might have led them somewhere."

Anabelle shrugged one tawny shoulder. "It wouldn't have."

I stood up and walked to the window. High above the canyon, a hawk rode the thermals.

I cleared my throat. "There's something I've been thinking about for a long time. I owe you an apology. I should have stayed with you that night. In Playa del Rey. If I hadn't left you alone with Ivan, none of this would have happened."

Her head jerked up. Her eyes roamed the room like a cornered animal.

"I told you to leave," she said. "I practically begged you."

"I shouldn't have listened. I wish I'd had the courage to defy you. Do you know how many times I've gone over that night in my head, wishing it had been different? Wishing even that I could have . . . that we . . . that it had happened to me instead. Because then maybe you'd be okay now."

Her eyes widened in horror. "That is pure sick."

"I know. But I see how it's eaten away at you, like a radioactive half-life."

"Don't even think that. I know you like to take care of everyone and make it better but . . ."

"I can't help it. That's the way I'm wired."

She shook her head sadly. "There are things in life that can't be fixed."

Like her. Like me.

"Let me help you, Anabelle. I'm strong now. Not like before. I won't let you down. I'll help you get to the bottom of it and then we'll put it behind us forever."

"If you keep trying," said Anabelle, "you'll doom us all."

For a moment we sat there, locked in our private cages of pain.

Then I said, "Did you know there was a detective downstairs talking to your dad and Simon?"

Alarm flashed in her eyes until I explained the good news about the DNA results.

Anabelle scooted back on the bed until

her back pressed against the headboard. She pulled up her legs and wrapped her arms around her knees.

"It's so awful that Dad and Simon had to go through that. I hope they find the boyfriend soon."

"I'm not so sure that will be the end of it."

She gave me a sharp look. I sensed the mood begin to change.

"The feds are looking into Blair's dealings with your dad and other clients. There's a federal investigator who's contacted me twice now, wanting me to cooperate with him. So far I've told him no."

She gripped the edge of the comforter. "Does Dad know?"

"Probably. I told my boss about it the first time. But the second time . . . it's beginning to freak me out. I think you ought to tell the police everything. I'd sit in with you if it made you feel better. For moral support."

She looked at me coldly.

"Is this your professional advice on behalf of the Blair Company?"

"No. This is personal advice from me, your friend Maggie. To hell with Blair. I can always find another job. But this is killing you. And it's killing me to stand by helplessly and watch."

"You don't know anything about us, do you?"

"What do you mean?"

"The Paxtons don't do things that way."

"But, Anabelle, the lies are piling up and it's just a matter of time before —"

"Lies? I suppose that's something you know a lot about, in your business."

"We don't lie."

"You don't always tell the whole truth either. I've watched you on TV, speaking before the cameras. Nerves of steel. You're as cold-blooded as me, in your own little way. And you've had plenty of practice."

"What?"

"You were always a liar, Maggie. Even back in high school. That's one thing I admired about you. You made up your own reality, concocted it from whole cloth."

My palms started to sweat. "I didn't!"

"Maggie," she said patiently, "we all knew your dad wasn't a screenwriter. Luke had a friend whose dad ran a film noir festival in Hollywood and knew all about Monogram Studios. We asked him about your father. We were curious. We never said anything because we didn't want to embarrass you."

I laughed. "I guess I never told you he wrote under a pseudonym. He'd been blacklisted by Joe McCarthy and his red-baiters, see, and —"

She winced. "Don't, Maggie."

I picked at a loose thread on the comforter. What a stupid word, "comforter."

"And the big house in Encino?" Anabelle continued, trying to hurt me now, get me back for hurting her. "We tried to go there once, on your birthday. We had a cake and we wanted to surprise you. So imagine our surprise when we looked you up in the directory. Hard to believe a good liar like you didn't realize how easily your deception would be uncovered. Maybe you thought if you wished hard enough it would come true, like Cinderella and her mouse-drawn pumpkin."

"Stop."

"But the thing was," said Anabelle, "that in some weird way, it impressed us. That you'd go to all that trouble to concoct elaborate lies. For us! As if we wouldn't love you if you were poor and lived in a crappy part of the Valley."

Even now, I flinched.

"You were always so sure of yourself, so cocky and unassailable, and it made us realize how fragile you really were underneath the armor. It made you more, I don't know, *human*.

"But deep down, I must have sensed you

were a guttersnipe, and that attracted me. My life was so predictable and boring. Do you think I'd ever bought anything in a *thrift store* before? Mom would have died. The only time Paxtons went to thrift stores was when we donated our *own* things. I didn't have the eye to spot the Dorothy O'Hara frock and the Catalina vase amid all the junk. And the music? All those cool edgy bands. It was a revelation."

The room dissolved and I saw sixteen-year-old Anabelle holding a pair of concert tickets, asking if I was interested.

"But you liked PJ Harvey," I protested. "That's what first drew us together."

"My friend *Charlotte* liked PJ Harvey. I'd never heard of her. That's why it was thrilling when I found you. You introduced me to your world. And I loved it."

"Maybe you loved it a little too much."

"Whatever, don't overanalyze it like you always do. We each had something the other needed."

Her face darkened. "And on top of everything else, I had Luke."

I froze.

"You think I didn't know? Come on! We spent every waking moment together for two years. But you didn't understand about

Luke either. You saw what you wanted to see."

"I know he didn't care for me. You don't have to rub it in."

"That's not what I mean."

"I didn't use you to get to him."

"I know," she said softly. "And that's why I put up with it. But there's no denying that things began to change between us when Luke came home."

She sighed and rolled away from me, staring at the wall.

I stood to leave.

"Thanks for the company, Maggie," she said, her voice small and far away. "And the perfume. It did make me feel better there, for a little while."

"You're welcome. Next time I'll bring the whole bottle."

39

As I drove to the office, my thoughts drifted from Anabelle to the Emily Mortimer DNA results. Brothers had similar DNA, didn't they? What about parents and children?

I looked it up when I got to my desk, wondering what my brain was trying to work out.

The Internet told me that full siblings shared about 50 percent of their DNA. Children shared about half of their parents' DNA, and Y chromosomes were handed down intact from father to son. I found this reassuring, and it took me awhile to puzzle out why:

The DNA found at Emily Mortimer's apartment was not genetically linked to the DNA of the Paxton brothers. That meant it was not linked to Anabelle or Luke either, because the tests would surely have flagged any result that showed a 50 percent match.

In my darkest hours, as I tossed and

turned, my brain running down labyrinthine paths, it had occurred to me to wonder whether Anabelle or Luke might have killed Emily Mortimer. Though I couldn't find a plausible motive.

This brought me around to the one Paxton family member whose DNA had not been vetted by the police: Miranda.

And suddenly, I sat up straight and Tyler's words the other night looped like a refrain in my brain.

Miranda, with her strange fetish-art mannequins and her private fortune. Enough to hire ten hit men, if she didn't want to get her hands dirty. Not that she seemed to mind, I thought, recalling Anabelle's description of her mother in the desert, pumping her mannequins full of holes in the name of art.

How much further would she go in the name of protecting her family? Miranda wasn't a typical politician's wife, content to sit on the sidelines. Oh, sure, she knew how to play the gracious senatorial wife, but her wealth and her standing in the art world gave her an independence and a flair that were unusual in politics. Only in a blue state like California, her supporters joked, would she be considered an asset to her senator husband.

What lay behind that exquisitely buffed and polished surface?

And how could I find out?

40

We were back at Villa Marbella. Faraday was on the sidewalk in front of the Paxton house, doing stand-ups with the media. I was drafting a news release at the kitchen table. Then Tyler walked in with boxes of pizza and green salads.

I'd spent the last two days conjuring him into a demon. Now the sight of his lanky form caught me like a left hook in the gut.

"What's the matter?" Tyler said.

"We need to talk." I looked around. "Let's go outside, where it's more . . . private."

I led him out back, past the swimming pool, into the orchard where the gardeners lovingly tended the fig, apricot, peach, plum, and lemon trees whose fruit no one in the family ever touched.

At the base of a gnarled old pomegranate tree, Anabelle's dog Bangs was busy digging a hole in an attempt to catch something that was tunneling away. When she heard us coming, Bangs stopped, butt poised in the air. Her snout was encrusted with wet dirt and her pink tongue lolled, flecked with saliva. For a moment, she regarded us hopefully, as if we might pitch in. Then with an enthusiastic bark, she went back to digging.

"Is this clandestine enough?" Tyler said.

He stepped closer. Around us rose the homely smell of nature decaying — dirt and mulched leaves.

"Are you still working on the JTM Financial account?" I asked.

For a moment, Tyler looked surprised. "That bankrupt firm Senator Paxton's committee is looking into?"

He ran his hand through his hair in that disarming way he had.

"I did a little work on that account when I first started at Blair," Tyler said. "If I recall, they were buying another firm and there were some regulatory issues that worried Wall Street. Mr. Blair was grooming me to do financial PR." Tyler laughed. "That was before he realized I'm not a numbers guy."

"How long did you work the account?"

"About five hot minutes." Tyler shot me a lazy grin.

"So you're not working it any longer?"

"I just told you."

"Does JTM Financial still use Blair?"

Tyler's eyes glinted as suddenly he understood.

"As a matter of fact, no. They didn't like our rates so they ran off to Sitrick or some other ambulance chaser a long time ago. And look where it got them."

"How do you know they didn't come back to Blair when their stock crashed? Maybe he assigned the case to someone else, like Faraday?"

"Anything's possible, Maggie. But I think I would have heard."

"How? We're not supposed to talk about clients, not even with other Blair associates. Need to know and all that."

"Sure, but with a clusterfuck of that size, word would have gotten around. So if you're envisioning some conspiracy theory here, with Blair screwing one client to protect another who's paying more, you can drop that crazy idea right now."

"I didn't say —"

"Yeah, you did. That's what you think. You're totally frigging paranoid from all the Adderall you take."

I made a noise of throttled indignation.

"You think I don't see you popping them all the time? You have to ask yourself, Maggie, at what point do the drugs stop boosting your brain cells and start destroying them. 'Cause I think you've reached that stage."

Many responses formed in my brain but failed to make it out of my mouth. Because another thought quickly overrode everything.

If JTM Financial Services was a Blair client, and they were doing exactly what Tyler said, then the best way to deflect it would be to accuse me of paranoia.

"What you're saying doesn't even make sense," Tyler said. "Look around you. Does it look like we're trying to set Paxton up? Seems to me that all of us are doing everything we can to help the senator and his hound dog of a brother. As soon as the cops catch that Slattery freak, the truth will come out."

"I hope so," I said stiffly.

He shook his head in mock disappointment. "And here I was hoping you'd brought me into the orchards to ravish me." He took a step closer. One hand rested lightly on my hip.

"Seems a shame to waste the opportunity," he murmured.

I knew if I looked into his eyes, I'd be sunk. Summoning my last shreds of strength, I pulled away. I still felt the warm imprint of his hand on my body.

"I've got to get back," I said, and ran all the way to the kitchen.

Faraday had finished with the media and was sitting at the kitchen table when I entered, a paper napkin tucked into his dress shirt as he served himself a slice of pizza. He looked pink cheeked and robust, a vampire that had just fed. Really, it was disgusting how jousting with the press energized him when it left the rest of us so drained.

Now Faraday gave me a shrewd and knowing look. "What's going on?"

"Nothing."

The front door slammed, and moments later Tyler walked in, hands shoved into his pockets, nonchalant as ever.

Faraday looked from me to Tyler and back again, but before he could say anything, Miranda walked in, trailed by Bangs.

She said hello, then got a tray and filled it with cheese, crackers, grapes, and a bottle of juice.

"What else?" she said.

"Pardon me?" I said.

"Anabelle's barely eating and I want to bring her up a snack. What else do you think she'd like?"

It said a lot, I thought, that Anabelle's mother was asking me to recommend her daughter's favorite foods.

"She used to like peanut M&Ms a lot," I offered.

Miranda gave me a grateful look. "Thanks, I'll check the pantry," she said and hurried off.

Bangs eyed the pizza hopefully and I tore off a piece of crust and fed it to her. She ate it with surprising delicacy, then lay with her muzzle on the hardwood floor, eyes flicking anxiously.

Miranda walked back in.

"What kind of collar does that dog have?" asked Faraday. "Can I see it?"

"Sure, it's just a regular collar. Come here, Bangs."

Bangs walked over, wagging her tail, and Faraday bent to examine her neck.

"Okay," he said, straightening up and showing no further interest in the dog. "I just wanted to make sure it didn't have a recording device around its neck. You have no idea what the paparazzi are capable of. They switched collars once on a dog who belonged to a celebrity client of mine. Paid one of the help to put on a collar equipped with a mini-videocam. Can you imagine?"

At that moment, my phone rang. The

caller ID was blocked.

"Is this Maggie Silver?" a man said, his voice nervous.

"Yes. Who's this?"

There was a pause. "My name is Jake Slattery."

I sat down, already beckoning Faraday over.

"Where are you, Mr. Slattery?"

"That's not important."

"I'm happy to hear from you. We have so many questions. Things that only you can clear up."

Keep him on the line, Faraday mouthed.

"I need your help," Jake Slattery said. "Here's how it's going to work."

When he hung up, my hand shook so much it took three tries to jab the Off key.

Faraday was on his own phone. "Never mind," he said, hanging up in disgust.

"How could you let him get away?" Faraday said. "The cops need time to trace these calls and I'd barely —"

"He wants to meet with me," I said.

"What?"

"Tonight. He says he's innocent and he'll bring proof. Ten o'clock. Just inside Union Station downtown. He says to come alone or he won't show."

"It's too dangerous," said Tyler.

Faraday's eyes had gone wide and dreamy. "It's the PR scoop of a lifetime," he said.

"Are you crazy?" Tyler shouted.

"You *want* me to do it?" I said in disbelief.

"Don't go soft on me now, Maggie."

"But he's wanted by the police. He could kill me."

"Why would he do that? You're the messenger who's going to tell his story to the world."

I considered this. The idea was certainly alluring. I struggled not to get seduced by it.

Faraday said, "Imagine the free publicity this would bring us! What an exclusive: Blair, the crisis management firm that exonerates its client by catching the real killer. Our phones will be ringing off the hook."

"Wait a minute," I said. "Who said anything about catching anyone?"

"I thought Jake had proof of who the real killer is?"

"He said he'd 'bring proof,' whatever that means. Are you sure we shouldn't call in the cops?"

Faraday cocked his head and pretended to think. He pursed his lips. His brow furrowed. "We can handle it," he said.

"You mean *I* can," I said sulkily. "You want it so badly, why don't you go? Or send Tyler."

"He asked for you."

"Then at least let someone come with me."

"We can't risk scaring him away."

"What if I get killed?"

Faraday looked as though he'd failed to consider such an insignificant detail.

He sucked his teeth. "That is not going to happen."

"I don't want to be out there all alone if something goes wrong."

"If he gets even a whiff that you've got a tail, he'll split. Look, Maggie," Faraday wheedled. "Slattery says he didn't do it. He says he's got this 'proof.' We need to hear him out, not jump to conclusions."

"But you're the one who's said all along that he's guilty."

"I'm willing to be proved wrong."

A wave of paranoia washed over me. Was Faraday setting me up? Would this provide a perfect opportunity to get rid of me because I'd asked too many questions? I didn't trust any of them anymore. Not Blair. Not Faraday. Not Tyler. Especially not Tyler.

Faraday liked the idea of meeting at Union

Station because it was a busy, public place with plenty of security. And even at night, the place would be well lit.

As I squawked my opposition, determined to defy him, Faraday put an arm around me and led me outside.

"This is just between you and me," he said. "But one of our clients is a biotech firm that's setting up a medical trial for a promising new chemo pill. They've gotten incredible results zapping breast tumors in mice. I can get your mother a slot on the trial."

I pulled away and stared at him.

I recalled how I'd surfed the Internet for stories about promising medical trials and sent Mom several e-mails with attachments of what I'd found.

Faraday's large eyes held mine in alert silence.

"Hmmmm?" he said at last.

I shook my head in disgust. "I see. But only if I go meet Jake Slattery, is that right?"

"A small token of gratitude. Yes."

I considered. We were still awaiting the biopsy. After that, if we had good news, she wouldn't need any of this. But I had to hedge my bets. I needed a fallback plan. I needed to be prepared.

"How do I know you could even swing

it?" I said.

"Think about all the different deals we cut at Blair."

"I want it in writing."

He grimaced. "I'm afraid I can't do that. These matters are sensitive for everyone concerned. You'll have to trust me."

I thought about it. If Faraday reneged, I'd have something unsavory on him. Again, I wondered how far up the chain of command the rot went. Did it reach all the way to Blair himself?

When this was all over, I vowed to extricate myself from the Blair Company and look for a new job. But right now, there was too much at stake to quit. My mother's health. Anabelle's sanity. Henry's senatorial seat. A budding romance with Luke.

"All right," I said wearily. "I'll do it."

I got to Union Station twenty minutes early and stood nervously inside the wrought iron and wood and beveled glass doors of the elegant Art Deco building. The place was nothing like Grand Central in New York, but a pretty good crossroads by L.A. standards, with a steady stream of people coming and going.

I didn't see anyone who resembled the photo I'd studied of Jake Slattery. I tarried a few moments longer, then sat down in a plush leather and wood chair where I could watch the flow of traffic.

Nothing.

At nine fifty-five, I strolled back to the main lobby and stood just inside, scanning faces and fending off taxi drivers and porters eager to help me. Ten o'clock came and went and Jake Slattery didn't show.

At ten forty, my phone rang.

"I'm glad you know how to follow directions," said Jake Slattery. "And by the way, that jade green blouse really suits you."

"Where are you?" I looked around, creeped out at the thought that he could be ten feet away or anywhere in the vast cavern of Union Station. He was obviously close enough to see what I was wearing.

"Never mind that. I had to make sure you came alone. Now, I've got some new instructions. Are you ready? Because after we hang up, you need to turn off your cell phone. No texting or calling anyone. I'll know if you've turned it on, see, and then I won't show. These precautions are purely for my safety. You've got nothing to be afraid of."

The moon was up by the time I neared the restaurant in Silver Lake where Jake Slattery had directed me. I'd been tempted to call Faraday from the car. How would Slattery ever know? But as afraid as I was of meeting Slattery alone, I was more afraid of Mom missing the opportunity to take part in that medical trial. And that kept my itchy fingers from the phone.

I wondered if Faraday had managed to set a tail on me. If he had, it was a pretty invisible one. But I didn't harbor any false hope.

I was on my own.

I drove by the restaurant twice, telling myself that if it was dark or deserted, I wouldn't risk it. I'd drive right back to the office. But there were tables out front, with people eating and drinking even though it was almost midnight. I found a good spot across the street and parked.

The restaurant was crowded with denizens of the night, artists and musicians who'd slept away the heat of the day and only recently woken up. I figured I'd join the throngs of people outside waiting for a table.

I'd just locked my door when I felt a gun in my back.

"Walk," a male voice I recognized said, propelling me forward.

Just then, a hipster couple rounded the corner and began moving toward me, leading a boxer on a leash.

I wanted to scream, but I was afraid that Jake Slattery might shoot me. Instead, I threw the couple an alarmed help-call-911-I'm-about-to-be-murdered look. But they were busy averting their eyes and dragging off their dog, which was trying to poop on the sidewalk.

Slattery slung an arm around my shoulder like we were a couple out for a stroll and I felt the gun move to my side. He was a little taller than I was and wore long sideburns, a trucker's cap pulled low, and dark sunglasses.

He maneuvered me off West Silver Lake Boulevard and onto a residential street.

"What do you want from me?" I asked, forcing my voice to sound normal and conversational.

I'd read once about a woman who'd been raped by a man who swore he'd kill her so she couldn't testify against him. Desperate to establish a human connection, she'd kissed him as he assaulted her. Despite all odds, it had worked, and he'd left her, bleeding and violated on the side of the road, but alive.

Slattery didn't answer.

"Why do you have a gun?" I said, trying again.

He snorted. "Wouldn't you, if you'd been

framed for murder?"

A numbness crept over me. I felt oddly disconnected from my body. My next words were cold and eerily calm.

"If you didn't kill Emily, maybe you should give yourself up. It only makes you look guilty if you hide."

Jake Slattery jerked me along angrily and the words rushed from him in a torrent. He seemed desperate to tell his story.

"Are you serious? The police framed me, man. They *planted* that porn in my trailer. I didn't kill her!"

"The cops say you left threatening messages on Emily's machine. She was afraid of you."

Slattery stopped abruptly. We'd walked a few blocks by now, past a nightclub called Spaceland where I'd once spent many happy evenings. We were in Silver Lake Park, hiking through the grass. There was no one around.

He turned, his face illuminated in the streetlight.

"I loved Emily," Slattery said. "That was my baby she was carrying. You think I'd kill my own child?"

"I don't know what to think," I said, wondering if he would shoot me if I ran. The swings wouldn't provide much cover.

Would bullets penetrate the plastic of the jungle gym?

I said, "Why don't you write a letter to the cops, laying out what you just told me."

"I did," he said bitterly. "Made no difference. You think they're going to take my word over a U.S. senator's?"

"So how am I supposed to help you? Do you know who killed Emily?"

He gave a short laugh. "Oh, no. I save that for the cameras. That's my insurance. When I saw you on TV, it gave me the idea."

Slattery's gun arm was starting to droop.

"What idea?"

"I want you to represent me. Get me on some TV shows. I can't pay you right now, but I'm good for it. I'm going to write a book, blow the lid off this conspiracy."

"What conspiracy?"

He wagged a finger at me. "You can't trick me."

I tried another tack. "My firm already represents Senator Paxton. It would be a conflict of interest for us to take you on as a client."

"You'll be singing a different tune once you hear my story. You're honest, I can tell. I'm a good judge of character. I'll give you just one taste. Those drugs they found in Emily's apartment? They were *planted.* She was no addict."

So Slattery didn't know that his girlfriend regularly bought prescription drugs for Senator Paxton.

"Maybe she bought them for someone else," I said. "Does the name Stephen Ivan Dumbrowski ring any bells?"

"Who?"

The gun rose, wavering in Slattery's hand.

"Could you please put that away? I wouldn't want there to be an accident."

Slattery regarded the gun. "Sorry about that, back at the restaurant. I just needed to get you somewhere a little more private."

"You could have tried asking nicely."

He snorted. "Like you would have done it."

But he lowered the gun.

"Thanks. So what's your proof?"

"I told you I'm saving it for TV."

He paused, cocked his head. "What's that noise?"

"I didn't hear anything."

His gun went back up.

"Move," he said, hauling me back toward Spaceland. Inside the club, a band was in full throttle. The music was loud, jangly, raucous. At least there were people here. Hundreds of them. But they were all inside.

Slattery led me to the back of the club, by

the parking lot. The music grew louder.

"That senator?" said Jake Slattery. "He's rotten through and through. It's —"

Shots exploded near my right ear. I shrieked and threw myself to the ground. A wave of cold, sweaty nausea washed through me.

And then Tyler was standing over me, breathing heavily, arms extended, hands clasped around a gun, ready to fire again.

But Jake had disappeared.

Tyler turned, the gun tracking through the parked cars and the darkness, looking for Jake.

"Did he hurt you?" Tyler asked.

"I . . . I don't think so."

With trembling hands, I felt my limbs to make sure. Everything was fine. I tried to get to my feet but my knees collapsed.

Tyler moved back and forth, shining a tiny flashlight on the ground, into bushes, between cars, looking for something. Then he walked back.

"Take my hand. We have to get out of here. Someone may have heard the gunshots over the music."

His fingers tightened around mine as he led me back to the street.

I have no memory of getting to my car, but

the next thing I knew Tyler was driving and I was in the passenger seat.

"Are we going to the police?" I said.

"I'm driving you back to the office. We'll tell Faraday what happened and he'll decide."

In my whacked-out state, this seemed eminently reasonable.

"What about your car?" I said.

"I'll have one of the security guys pick it up."

I slumped against the seat and hugged my elbows.

Tyler kept shooting me looks and asking if I was okay.

Right before we got on the freeway, with the on-ramp already in sight, he turned down a residential street.

"I thought we were going back to the office," I said.

Tyler drove a few blocks. The houses grew more run-down, with parched lawns and broken windows. He pulled over, put the car in park, and got out. Then he walked around to the back of the car. The skin on my neck started to crawl and I twisted around to watch him. I wondered where he'd put the gun and whether this was the moment at which I should jump out and run shrieking away. I didn't have many instincts left to trust anymore. Tyler had rescued me. And yet . . . He was around the car now and heading toward the passenger seat where I sat, still strapped in. Would he shoot me and leave my body in the car? But that didn't make sense. What would police think if they found me dead in the passenger seat of my own car? He opened the door and leaned in and unbuckled my seat belt.

"Get up."

"Why?"

"I need to make sure you're okay and I don't have to take you to the hospital."

He ignored my protestations that I was fine.

I let him pull me to standing. His eyes flickered up and down my length and he ran his palm along my side, turning me completely around. I thought I saw his eyes flutter with relief.

Then his arms wrapped around me and his hands caressed my hair. He laid his cheek against mine and I could feel him trembling.

"He's not going to risk your life again, Maggie. I won't let him. I don't care if he fires me."

I stood there, only partially registering his words, wondering why I felt so stiff and wooden.

Tyler pulled back, examining me with concern.

Unable to bear the intensity of his gaze, I turned away, blinking.

"Of course! How stupid of me, Maggie. You're in shock. Let's get back in the car now. I promise it'll be okay."

I thought about how people had said that to me all my life when things got bad and how it was never, ever true. Beyond that, I didn't think much. My brain was a vast, blank emptiness.

We were almost to West L.A. when an important thought finally dislodged from my subconscious and drifted to the surface.

"Tyler, how did you know where I was?"

There was a long pause. "Faraday sent me," he said at last.

"But how did he know? My phone was turned off. No GPS. Did you follow me from Union Station?"

"Too obvious. Slattery might have spotted it."

"So how . . . ?"

Tyler gave me a lazy smile. "Faraday put a tracking device on the undercarriage of your car."

I shook my head. "What a clever bastard."

"It was my idea."

"And what were your instructions?"

"To make sure nothing happened."

Now there was a comment that could be taken several ways.

"And he gave you a gun to make sure?" I said dryly.

"It's mine. Got a permit and everything. I told you that the other night."

Tyler fell silent.

For a moment we both pondered how far things had gone since that night. What a bad judge of character I'd been.

"When I saw him waving the gun, I was afraid he was going to kill you," Tyler said at last.

"What if you killed *him?*"

"He ran off. There was no body. No blood. I didn't even hit him."

"What if you did and he's wounded?"

Tyler gave me a sardonic look. "Even if he goes to a hospital, it's not like he's going to use his real name. He knows the police are looking for him. And hospitals have to report gunshot wounds."

I thought about this.

"I guess he can't exactly file a police report."

Tyler shrugged. "If it ever came down to that, I'd claim self-defense." He gave me a shrewd look. "You were there. You'd back me up."

I squirmed uncomfortably.

Then I thought about how Jake Slattery had heard something at the park.

"How long did you listen to us before you fired?"

"I'd only just found you."

"Did you hear any part of our conversation?"

Tyler hesitated, then shook his head.

"Slattery said Emily's murder was part of a conspiracy. He said Senator Paxton was crooked. He was starting to explain when you began shooting."

Tyler absorbed this news. He looked stricken.

"What exactly are you suggesting?"

I swallowed hard. "Nothing. I guess. It's just . . . Yeah, Slattery had a gun. And he used it to maneuver me away from the restaurant. But I don't think he would have —"

"He abducted you with a deadly weapon. That's some serious felonies right there."

"He was freaked out that no one believed his story. He wanted me to broker him a TV interview deal. He swears he didn't kill his girlfriend. And now we'll never know. He's not going to resurface. We blew it."

Tyler's mouth tightened, but he said nothing.

Unable to stop, I went on. "I mean, look, if you feared for my life, why didn't you just call nine one one when you realized what was going on?"

Tyler looked as if he couldn't believe my ingratitude. "They wouldn't have arrived in time. I had to make a split-second decision."

We were nearing the Blair Building now. It was one a.m. And suddenly, the last thing I wanted was to face Faraday.

I had nothing to tell him. Tyler had scared Slattery away before he said anything worthwhile. And with Slattery gone, so was all hope of getting my mom on board the cancer drug trial. I knew without having to ask that my deal with Faraday was off.

"I've changed my mind," I said. "Pull up in front and you can get out. I'm going home."

Tyler looked surprised but did as I asked. As I slid out of the car and walked to the driver's side, glad that my legs were once more following my brain, Tyler regarded me with concern.

"I think you're making a mistake, Maggie. He's been waiting all night to hear what you have to say."

"Then tell him what happened. I've got

nothing beyond that."

Tyler stepped closer, as if to kiss me good-bye, and I sidestepped him.

"Don't touch me," I said.

And without a backward glance, I got in my car and drove off.

The whole way home, I replayed our conversation in my head. And one statement kept coming back to haunt me.

"They wouldn't have arrived in time," Tyler said. "I had to make a split-second decision."

Maybe that was exactly why Tyler had tried to kill Jake Slattery. To keep him from spilling the identity of Emily Mortimer's murderer. How could I have ever deluded myself about this man enough to sleep with him? The thought of it now made me sick.

I turned my phone back on as I drove home, and it rang repeatedly until I switched it to vibrate. I didn't bother checking the calls. I knew it would be Tyler or Faraday, trying to coax me back, or make sure I wasn't driving to the police station to report what had happened. And maybe if I hadn't been so tired I would have considered it. But right now, all I wanted was to get home and crawl between the sheets.

The porch light was out at the house, which is unusual. Usually Mom leaves it on so I won't have to fumble for my key. But her car was there. Then I remembered. Mom was on her Elderhostel trip.

The lock on our front door is old and ornate, with an iron clapper you have to lift before inserting the key into the hole. In the dark, it took me three tries before I got it right. Almost crying with relief, I turned the lock and pushed the door open.

At the same time my phone vibrated again, reminding me of the messages piling up.

The house was hot and still.

I locked the door behind me, turned on some lights, and went into the kitchen to rustle up something to eat. The brutal exhaustion I'd felt driving home had ebbed into a more twitchy, keyed-up state. I realized I'd been looking forward to pouring out my heart to the one person I trusted utterly. Mom.

My stomach grumbled, reminding me of the pizza I'd never eaten at Anabelle's house.

I got leftover sesame Chinese noodles from the fridge, forked a generous portion onto my plate, poured a glass of barley tea, and ate.

Then I showered and got into bed, my thoughts floating on a sea of betrayal, murder, and conspiracy.

The sparks that had flared between Tyler and me had made me overlook the obvious: He was a company man who would do as he was told. Tyler's claim that he shot at Jake Slattery because he feared for my life was a clever way to justify what Faraday had probably ordered him to do from the start: Kill him so he couldn't reveal what he knew.

Tyler must think I was really stupid. What galled me most was that I'd wanted so much to believe him. When he'd pulled me to him and rubbed his hot damp cheek against mine, I'd felt that warm feeling start up in the back of my stomach. I could still feel it.

Then the gun went off again, *pop, pop, pop*. And Tyler was standing above me, and for some reason I flashed on the man who'd chased me the other night. He'd worn a mask and a bulky jacket, and it was crazy paranoid of me even to think of it, but he was the same height as Tyler. I tried to hold on to that thought, but it drifted away like a feather as I plummeted down, down to the scant few hours of sleep that awaited me before I had to be at work again.

41

Light streaming through the curtains woke me at six forty-five. Realizing I'd overslept, I threw back the sheet and ran into the kitchen. I am Queen Caffeine and need my morning jolt.

I squinted at the kitchen clock, looked out the window, and groaned. No wonder the light had seemed so muted. This wasn't the sharp white light of morning. It was six forty-five *p.m.*

I checked my phone, expecting to see a dozen progressively more irate texts from Faraday, but there was only one: "GLAD UR OK. PLEASE TAKE TODAY OFF TO CATCH UP. CU TOMORROW."

I read it five times. Faraday was tricky and it could be a grave mistake to take his words at face value. Was he being sarcastic? He'd sent the text at 9:05 a.m. I went to voice mail to see if he'd called.

Nothing.

For once, he must have meant it.

I didn't delude myself that he cared. But a sleep-deprived, nerve-rattled PR person was a liability who should not be allowed near clients, cops, or the media.

I was in quarantine.

I made coffee and showered. Then I poured a cup, got some cereal, and took my breakfast to the computer, where I scanned the wires for news of Jake Slattery. Nothing. If the police had found him, shot and bleeding, they were keeping it quiet.

The only noise was my bovine crunching.

The doorbell rang.

I put on my robe, tightened the belt, and walked to the front door.

"Who is it?"

"Hi, Maggie. It's Luke."

A warm, hopeful feeling came over me.

I opened the door, realizing too late that my hair was slicked back wet, my face had no makeup, and there were probably bits of shredded wheat stuck in my teeth.

Luke looked serious and worried.

"What's the matter?"

He craned his neck and peered over my head. It wasn't hard, I'm about five five in my furry lamb's wool slippers.

"Is Anabelle here?" he asked, his voice overly casual.

"No. Is she supposed to be?"

Luke's brow creased as if he was trying to puzzle something out.

At that moment, my manners came thundering back. I opened the door wide and stepped aside. "Come in, please."

He followed me into the kitchen, glancing around my modest house.

At once I saw it through his eyes. How shabby and cramped he must find it after Villa Marbella. In a smaller part of my brain, I wondered how he'd gotten my address.

"Sit down, please. What's going on? Can I get you something to drink?"

I patted my hair, willing it to dry in flattering waves around my face, wondering how I could excuse myself long enough to swipe on some lipstick. And pop an Adderall. I felt fuzzy and confused, like the world had slipped out of focus. Why was Luke here?

He took a step closer, then stopped.

"What's wrong?" I said.

"Anabelle's disappeared. I thought she might have come here."

He gave me a searching look, as if I might be hiding her inside the grandfather clock or the clothes hamper.

"I haven't seen her since yesterday."

A horrible thought occurred to me. Jake Slattery. He'd be seething with rage, figuring I'd set him up. What if he'd gone to the Paxton house, seeking revenge?

"Maybe she went back to Palos Verdes?"

Luke shook his head. "Lincoln's still at Villa Marbella. But Anabelle's car is gone."

"When did *you* see her last?" I asked.

"Yesterday morning before work. She was asleep. Miranda said she hasn't been eating. But apparently she got a call last night, after you guys left. The next thing anyone knew, she came downstairs and said she was going out."

"Where?"

"We don't know. She said she was meeting a friend for coffee. But Miranda doesn't think she came home. Her bed didn't look slept in."

"Have you called the police?"

"Dad doesn't want to get the police and the media all riled up again until we've eliminated all the obvious possibilities."

"Has someone been to Palos Verdes to check?"

An image came to me, a glowing white flower growing on the edge of a sandstone cliff, luminescent in the moonlight. Datura. What if Anabelle had gone home alone to commit suicide?

"I was just there," Luke said savagely. "I've been checking all her old haunts. That's why I thought perhaps you . . ."

A third ghastly image materialized: Anabelle relapsing and slinking off to score drugs. "Could this have strained her sobriety?"

Luke paused. "That occurred to us. I was on skid row just now, showing her photo around. No one would admit to seeing her."

Luke's phone beeped with a text.

He read it and grew pale. "Oh, God. I've got to go."

"What?" I craned to read it, but Luke was already texting and walking out.

"She's at Palisades del Rey. By the airport," Luke said over his shoulder.

Something roared in my brain and I pushed it back. This was no time to lose it. I remembered what I'd promised Anabelle the other day in her room. *You can count on me. I won't let you down.*

"Wait," I called. "Let me put on some clothes. I'll go with you."

"Hurry," Luke said.

Five minutes later, we were in his car.

"I hope she's not planning anything dramatic and stupid," he said as we zipped down the hill, taking all the shortcuts, gunning for the freeway. Anabelle texted back that she was okay, and she'd call and explain soon. Luke read the words out loud, eyes darting between the screen and the road.

A sense of urgency gripped me. The hot, dusty streets, where stray pedestrians moved in slo-mo along empty sidewalks, made everything strange and unreal. All around town, people were gathered in backyards and parks and beaches to throw meat onto grills and crack brewskis. Labor Day weekend. At a traffic light, I smelled *carne asada* juices dripping onto hot coals, the toxic bite of lighter fluid exploding against a match.

The scent memory walloped me with unexpected force: Anabelle and I huddled around a pit fire at Zuma Beach with friends, towels draped across our sunburned backs to ward off the night chill. Nirvana was blasting from a boom box, Kurt Cobain still alive as we roasted marshmallows on sticks, then smeared them between melty chocolate and graham crackers, Anabelle's face shadow-lit by flames as she lowered s'mores into her gleaming red mouth, all of us giggling with the munchies.

By the time Kurt died in 1994, the only thing left to write was the requiem.

Luke pressed harder on the gas.

"Take it easy," I said. "The last thing we want right now is to get pulled over."

Luke grunted.

"Did you text your parents?" I asked. "Have they called the police?"

"Calling the police is not something the Paxtons do lightly. Especially with Henry —"

"But what if something's wrong? It'll take us thirty minutes, even if we go eighty."

"They want me to check on her first. Maybe everything's okay."

Steering with one hand, Luke dialed, got Anabelle's voice mail, and asked her to call back immediately. He didn't mention we were also driving out to find her. He feared it might scare her off.

Luke put his hand lightly on my knee. "I'm glad you're with me," he said. "If I can't get through to her, maybe she'll listen to you. Plus I'm going to need your eyes; I've got terrible night vision."

We were past downtown now, approaching the long soaring riser of the Century Freeway that curved west to LAX and the beach. Soon it was shooting us through the concrete pipe, smooth as a luge run.

Luke's phone beeped.

"She's still there," he said, glancing down and almost hitting the cement wall. "She's waiting for Tyler. He's supposedly bringing her some info about Randall's murder."

"Tyler?" My brain buzzed viciously. "That doesn't make sense. And why would he want to meet her in some remote, isolated place? Unless? Shit, Luke," I said, fumbling for my purse. "If you don't call nine one one right now, I'm going to. He's lured her out there to kill her."

"Your colleague?" Luke said, disbelieving.

"There's something very strange going on at Blair," I said. "I don't trust Tyler."

Luke hesitated. I could see him weighing the consequences. If we were wrong, and the cops broke up some crazy but harmless drama, it would be yet another PR debacle for Henry.

I said, "What possible normal explanation could there be for Tyler wanting to meet Anabelle at dusk in such a creepy place? He's seen her at your parents' house. Why didn't he talk to her there?"

"Maybe there's someone at the house he doesn't trust," Luke said slowly.

"And who would that be? Your mom or dad? Your uncle Simon? Faraday. Me? You?" I laughed hysterically. "That's crazy."

Luke groaned. Then he dialed.

"Yeah, um, I'd like to report a woman in possible danger in Playa del Rey near LAX. In that ghost town between the airport and Dockweiler Beach. I think it's called Palisades del Rey. She's gone there to meet a man who might be armed and dangerous. You need to send armed officers there right away. What?" Luke's voice rose, panicky. "I don't know what the closest cross streets are. Wait! Yeah, um, okay, Vista del Mar is the main one, it runs along Dockweiler Beach and . . ."

Luke turned to me. "Do you know the cross street?"

I tried to remember. It was sixteen years ago. I could see the rusting chain-link fence, the KEEP OUT, NO TRESPASSING signs, the abandoned residential streets that even then were cracking as weeds pushed through the asphalt. How creepy and eerie and terrifying and oddly beautiful it had been, late at night, as the jets screeched by overhead. Like a portal into another world.

"Sandpiper Lane," I said. "I think that's it."

Luke repeated it into the phone. I couldn't hear the operator on the other end.

Luke said, "Anabelle, uh, Downs. My name? Uh, Luke. Yeah. Okay, bye."

He clicked off the phone and I wondered how quickly the cops could get out there. I hoped that the flashing lights and megaphones wouldn't precipitate another tragedy.

"Luke . . ." I said, noticing he hadn't used the Paxton name.

"Hold on, I'm texting her now. She's still not answering."

The car veered.

"Let me," I said. "We're going to have an accident."

"Everything is under control," Luke said.

Furrowing his brow, he spoke the words aloud as he keyed them: "Maggie says ur in danger from Tyler. Abort. Run ASAP down to Vista del Mar. Meet us by gate."

He pressed Send, then exhaled loudly.

The Century Freeway dumped us out at the beach. To our left were the glowing white lights of the Hyperion Sewage Treatment Plant, crouched on the dunes like an alien spaceship. He turned right as an enormous jet thundered over our heads.

The dark expanse of Dockweiler Beach was dotted with bonfires strung like coral beads along the sand.

The ocean might be eternal, but the rituals of our modern coastal tribes changed with the seasons. In summer, we bobbed in the waves and gathered around the cooking fires. In autumn, lifeguards hauled their boarded towers past the reach of winter storms. Winter brought the biggest waves and hardiest surfers. And spring was when we watched gray whales and humpbacks spout offshore, heading to the polar ice caps to fatten on Arctic krill.

I didn't tell Luke how Anabelle had brought me here to play chicken. Of the desolation and despair I'd seen in her eyes. I was frightened of what we'd find.

"Maybe by the time we arrive the cops will have Tyler on the ground," Luke said. "Or they'll find my crazy sister all alone, dancing in the moonlight." He sighed. "Either way, Henry will have a whole new scandal on his hands."

He paused, and wariness came into his voice. "Is that why you wanted me to call nine one one? More work for you?"

I shot him a disbelieving look. "How can you *even* accuse me of that?"

He slumped in the seat. "Sorry. I guess I'm a little unhinged. Sometimes I don't know who to trust anymore."

The sea was jet-black and sparkly. A flock of brown pelicans flapped in lazy formation over the water, their prehistoric shapes silhouetted against the purple sky. Higher up, improbable birds of soldered metal screeched west over the Pacific.

Inland, the dunes gave way to an eerie tableau: paved streets with streetlamps and fire hydrants and gaping concrete foundations where homes had once stood.

The residents of Palisades del Rey had been forced to leave their close-knit neighborhood in the 1950s and '60s to make way for the expansion of LAX. As they left, their houses were condemned and torn down, hundreds of people scattered where once a vibrant community had stood.

A tall chain-link fence surrounded the property. Luke drove slowly and we both scanned the ruined streetscape, looking for Anabelle. The place was deserted. At each gate along the way we stopped and got out and called, but our voices reverberated in the emptiness and were lost in the wind.

There was no sign of police cars.

We drove to the end of Sandpiper Lane.

Night had fallen. A light breeze came up off the water. In the distance, the giant lights of LAX lit up the runways.

Palisades del Rey was eerie and empty, a vast, sand-strewn City of the Dead. Beyond the fence topped with razor wire, nothing moved. The surf and the jets drowned out all thought.

"We should wait for the cops," I said nervously.

Luke opened his door. "My sister's in danger."

"She's my friend too. But we're not

armed. And he is. He's got a gun. He used it last night."

I started to tell the story but fell silent as Luke reached for the glove box. A small black bottle rolled out.

I caught it, turning the smooth glass in my hands.

Jules by Christian Dior, I read, trying to recall what it smelled like. "Didn't you wear that in high school!"

"This is no time . . ." he said, taking it from me.

He was right, of course, but I was trying to stall until the cops came. The more I thought about it, the crazier this errand seemed. Anabelle wasn't here.

Luke tucked the bottle into his pocket, rummaged through the glove box, then groped under the seat, face scrunched in concentration.

"Here it is," he said in an odd, thick voice, pulling out a gun. "Who says we're not armed?"

"Please," I said, shrinking back. "The cops should be here any moment." I twisted around, scanning for flashing lights. Maybe the shrieking of jet engines and the roar of surf drowned out the approaching police sirens? A darker thought emerged. Would they also drown out a girl's screams?

Luke got out and walked around to my side.

His eyes were huge and dilated, and his voice came fast. "Come on."

"I think I'll stay here."

"You're a coward, Maggie. You always were. That night in the Jungle, all those years ago. You left my sister alone, drunk, drugged, passed out. You left her to a horrible fate."

I was scared at the way his voice had changed. I wanted the other Luke back, my desperate crush from childhood, who whispered in my ear, whose lips parted in that enigmatic, knowing smile.

"Let's face it," Luke was saying, "we all abandoned Anabelle that night. There's plenty of blame to go around. But finally I get a chance to redeem myself."

"The police should be here any minute."

"To hell with them," Luke said. "We'll save her ourselves."

And still I held back.

"Come on, Maggie. Your old friend Anabelle needs you. She's always needed you."

And so I got out. The wind whipped my hair and clothes. I followed Luke under the chain-link fence and into the empty streets with their shot-out lights, their drifts of sand, their weeds growing out of cracks in the fifty-year-old concrete.

"Anabelle," I called with Luke, our voices spiraling into a wail before being carried off by the wind.

There was no sign of Anabelle. There was no sign of Tyler. There was just this suburban ghost town, the waves crashing on the sea, the smell of brine, the tang of pit barbecues burning down on the beach.

A voice whispered at the edge of my consciousness as the jets screeched and the tide sucked the pebbles. If only I could make out the words. But it was just out of reach, echoing with faint, faraway laughter, taunting me with secret knowledge.

Anabelle?

What if she'd crossed the highway to the ocean, swimming out until she drowned? I pictured her body carried on the swell of the waves, arms spread like wings, orange crabs crawling in and out of empty eye sockets, long blond ropes of hair floating like seaweed, a million microscopic sea animals clinging to her curves, illuminating her in a phosphorescent shroud.

I started to sweat.

Nothing but blue skies, I hummed an old song, trying to calm myself.

But the sky above me wasn't blue; it was a heavy-water immensity the color of a bruise.

Anabelle, I thought, as Luke shouted out her name. *Where are you, Anabelle?*

In the distance, a cloud of seagulls rose flapping from the dunes, disturbed from their nocturnal roost.

Below the circling birds, someone was running toward us. I couldn't tell if it was a man or a woman. The figure put hands to mouth and shouted at us, but the wind and the jets and the crashing waves drowned out all words.

The figure drew nearer, and I recognized the familiar stride, and then at last I could see him.

"That's Tyler," I said.

Luke looked confused.

"He's alone," I said. "Where's Anabelle? What has he done with her?"

Tyler was gaining steadily. In less than a minute, he'd be upon us.

"Does he have a gun?" Luke asked, his voice deliberate.

"I can't tell."

"You scum," Luke shrieked.

Tyler was close enough now that I could make out some of the words.

". . . away from . . ." Tyler called.

Luke gulped. "She got away from him."

"Please let her be safe," I said, scanning the rolling dunes, willing myself to see a small blond figure sprinting to safety.

Tyler seemed completely mad and agitated. As he approached, his arm went up. And now I could see it.

"He's got a gun."

"Get behind me," said Luke.

"Maggie," screamed Tyler. His mouth continued to move, but his next words were lost in the smash of surf. When the echo died away, I heard him clearly for a few seconds.

"Killer . . . Run . . . Maggie . . . He . . ."

Then the roar of an incoming jet drowned him out. The decibels rattled my teeth and penetrated to the marrow of my bones. I wanted to flee from them both, but I was paralyzed and helpless.

Tyler stopped running. He raised his arms to chest level and clasped his hands together, sighting us.

"Put it down," Luke shouted. "I'm warning you."

Tyler angled the gun to and fro. "Maggie, get away from him," he shouted.

"I'll kill you, motherfucker," said Luke and shot Tyler in the chest.

"No," I screamed.

Tyler fell to his knees, clutching his heart. The gun dropped from his hand.

"Oh, Jesus," I said.

I stepped toward Tyler, then froze as Luke's scared, urgent voice floated over.

"C'mon, Maggie, we've got to get out of here."

Ignoring him, I ran toward Tyler. His eyes were closed, his body splayed unnaturally on the sand.

"You killed him," I said.

Staring at Tyler's unmoving form, I didn't see the gun-wielding maniac who'd tried to kill us. A wave of memory washed over me: his lean, warm hardness, the entanglement of limbs and lips and fingers, how I'd opened like a flower to his touch.

"What was I supposed to do?" Luke sounded scared. "He was going to kill us."

Was that true? Why had Tyler told us to run? So he could pick us off more easily, one after the other? Or was he saying that Luke was a killer and I should run from him?

Because for one tiny second, I almost *had* bolted. Before reason seized the upper hand and I darted behind Luke.

"What about Anabelle?" I said nervously. "Shouldn't we look for her?"

Luke turned. "What?"

"Tyler was trying to tell us something important. Anabelle could be lying here

629

somewhere, dead or wounded. We can't just leave."

"Anabelle's not here," Luke said.

"What makes you so sure?"

Just then, my phone beeped with a text. I pulled it out.

"Who the hell is that?" Luke's voice was flat and cold.

I glanced down. "It's nothing important," I said, trying to shield it.

"Let me see." Luke lunged. A small bottle fell to the asphalt. Liquid trickled out.

I smelled sage and cedar. This time I recognized it.

Jules. By Christian Dior.

And then it hit me. And I understood everything.

I remembered where I had smelled Jules before. And I mean recently, not years ago on Luke's sun-bronzed skin.

I'd smelled it on Emily Mortimer's scarf.

Jules wasn't widely available. In fact, it was little known and rare. I hadn't smelled it on anyone in years. Certainly not on Emily's boyfriend Jake Slattery. What were the chances that the dead girl knew someone else who wore this classic, practically discontinued French cologne? Plus, a man had to get awfully close for his cologne to wear off on a girl's scarf.

And with that, I grew truly frightened.

"Well, well," Luke said, holding my phone. "A text from your old Corvy pal Rachel Billings. Let's see what it says."

Luke read: "SORRY I WAS SO VAGUE @COFFEE. NEXT TIME ILL TELL U THE REAL REASON LUKE & I BROKE UP."

Luke's eyes narrowed. "You've been asking questions about me."

"It's just silly girl talk," I said. "You know we all had huge crushes on you in high school."

Luke stared at the spreading puddle of scent on the asphalt. He shook his head. "I should have left that in the car."

He scanned my face. "You know."

I tried to keep my voice calm. "Know what?"

The sides of Luke's mouth turned down. "Anabelle told me you had a nice little visit with Rachel."

"Anabelle . . ."

"Is safe and sound at my parents' house, where she's always been. But I knew I could lure you out if I said she was at Palisades del Rey. Where she used to play chicken and wish she was dead. You'd come, because you'd fear she planned to kill herself.

"But turns out you're not so smart after all. Because there's one thing you never

631

figured out, Maggie. And that's what went down that night in Playa."

"I'm not smart at all," I said. "In fact, I'm quite stupid. But I do damage control for a living. I know how to keep my mouth shut. Whatever your secrets are, Luke, I'd never tell anyone."

"It was supposed to be you," Luke said softly.

"What?"

"That night in the Jungle."

My face must have betrayed my confusion.

"I owed the Barracuda money," Luke said. "He'd fronted me a quarter key to sell, but I partied too hard, blew it right up my nose. And the 'rents had me on a tight leash. Took away my ATM and credit cards. I couldn't pull another burglary, I was eighteen and Lambert wouldn't be able to fix it anymore if I got caught.

"So I came up with a plan. The Barracuda liked them young, and I told him you were a virgin. I offered to deliver you on a platter if he forgave the debt. You and Anabelle were inseparable, so we planned to give you both roofies. Then Dan would take Anabelle for a 'romantic walk in the moonlight,' and Ivan would stand watch while the Barracuda screwed you. But the deal was that *nobody* touched Anabelle. The Barracuda agreed."

The bleak landscape of Palisades del Rey mirrored the ruined world inside my head.

"I loved you," I said. "I was sixteen and I loved you so purely and completely . . . I would have done anything for you."

Luke shifted from one foot to another and looked away.

A memory flashed before my eyes, of Ivan walking into the bathroom and returning with drinks. Of the look that passed between him and Dan, of Dan nodding and saying that he'd "behave himself." Then Dan took me to the beach and kissed me before I passed out. I'd come to and run back to the house. Wet and scared but okay. Dan had kept his word because he thought I was Anabelle.

"What other choice did I have?" Luke said. "You were expendable. You'd never tell. You'd be too scared. You were so desperate to be friends with us. But then it went to shit."

Luke kicked a pile of sand and it scattered in the wind.

"I told the Barracuda what you were wearing, see, and he told his friends. But you stupid girls had to go and change dresses. It wasn't my fault. I'd planned the thing impeccably, and with you pumped full of roofies, I figured you'd barely remember.

"Instead, the Barracuda raped my sister."

He began to cry. "I pimped her out for a lousy quarter key. You think I like knowing that?"

I shook my head.

"When I saw you out on the beach that night, you were so messed up I figured they'd changed plans and taken you down to the water. I was glad I could be there to comfort you. I knew you'd cry and cling to me, but eventually I'd make you feel better. You were like a kid sister to me, Maggie."

He stepped closer and brushed my face, light as eiderdown, with the back of his hand.

I lowered my eyes and struggled not to flinch.

Luke shook his head. "Then I realized you were wearing Anabelle's clothes. That's when I freaked out and asked if you were okay. Remember how I grilled you about that and asked where Anabelle was?"

I nodded wordlessly.

"Because if you were okay, that meant Anabelle *wasn't*. It meant she was in that room with the Barracuda. Instead of you. That's when I dropped you and started running."

Luke's calm, almost hypnotic voice had a

strange effect on me.

The events he was recounting had happened a lifetime ago. But ever since that night, part of me had stayed frozen in time, in suspended animation, my heart encased in ice.

For half my life, I'd believed that Anabelle's rape was my fault.

But as Luke destroyed my last illusions about him, the ice around my heart began to shiver and crack.

Because his hateful words also brought a blaze of illuminating warmth.

I didn't need to blame myself anymore.

And with that, something shifted deep inside me and I was free of a burden that had haunted me since the age of sixteen.

"I hope you can see how you ruined things, Maggie," Luke was saying.

I met his cold, flat eyes without flinching. For the first time in my life, I saw him for what he really was, instead of what I'd always wanted him to be.

"Yes," I said. "I do see."

Luke gave a little snort. "I doubt that. You ruined things with my sister when we were kids and now you're ruining them all over again. Why'd you have to call Raven?"

Luke's voice had taken on a plaintive whine, like a little kid.

"That was a bad move, Maggie. Because after that night in Playa, I had a lot of anger inside me. So yeah, I used to play at choking Raven in bed. That's what she was going to tell you. And you would put it together.

"I didn't mean to strangle Emily. We were just fooling around and it got out of control. Henry had no idea we were hooking up, but we'd met at one of his fund-raisers and hit it off. When I realized she was dead, I went to Henry in a panic, and after he finished cursing me out, he said he and Simon would handle it. And everything might have worked out if not for that reporter whose dad worked at the Mission Inn."

Luke gave a harsh laugh. "Emily was with *me* that night in Riverside. Henry and Simon cooked up the affair to shield me. Good ole Uncle Simon was furious, but he stepped up, because, after all, he had an alibi for the night of Emily's murder and I didn't."

"And when Randall got too close to learning the truth, you killed him too?"

"That putz?" Luke paused. "I should have. Everyone in our family wanted him to fall off the face of the earth. Especially Dad. But I guess I lacked the guts."

Out of the corner of my eye, I saw movement.

I turned to face the ocean. Luke moved with me, his gun tracking me in lazy arcs.

"*Au revoir,* Maggie. In your next life, stick to controlling the damage, not digging it up."

"Wait," I pleaded. "Your dad wouldn't want . . ."

"Henry . . ." Luke said, throwing back his head. I thought he meant to laugh, but just then a thunderous wave slammed into the sand and his words were lost in a gush of blood.

Luke fell.

I turned and saw Tyler five feet away, crouching, half hidden, behind a sand dune, a gun in his hands, still aimed at Luke in case he tried to rise.

For a moment my brain wouldn't work.

I'd seen Tyler lying there unmoving and dead.

But now Luke lay sprawled and dead with half his head blown off.

And Tyler was alive.

Forcing my jellied legs to move, I staggered toward him.

Tyler had saved my life.

Laboriously, I made my way to him. It seemed to take a lifetime.

Finally I stood beside him, my heart beating madly.

Tyler's breath came sharp and jagged.

"I thought he'd killed you," I said.

Tyler grabbed my hand and placed it over his heart and I felt the thick cladding of metal over his chest.

"I knew this would come in handy."

"What do we do now?" I said, looking at Luke's body.

Tyler already had his phone out, pressing buttons. More than three.

"There's been an accident," he said. "Luke's dead."

I looked at the LED readout but it wasn't familiar. In a few spare sentences, Tyler explained what had gone down. Then a familiar voice rumbled at the other end. Faraday.

"Got it," Tyler said, and hung up.

He walked over to Luke's body and squatted, inspecting it with the tiny flashlight on his key chain.

He nodded and muttered, "It just might work."

Tyler retrieved Luke's gun and shoved it into his waistband.

Then he walked back to me.

"Any idea whether he was right- or left-handed?" Tyler asked, inclining his head.

An image came to me of Luke playing tennis, walloping the ball with his powerful . . .

"Left."

Tyler took off his shirt and carefully wiped down his own gun. Then, using his shirtsleeve, he placed his gun in Luke's left hand as I screamed, "What are you doing?"

Tyler didn't answer. Carefully, he manipulated Luke's stiffening fingers so that they left prints on the gun. Once he was satisfied, he slid the gun out of Luke's hand and dropped it on the sand next to the body. Then he pocketed the small bottle of cologne, which miraculously was still intact.

I turned away, unable to stomach it any longer.

And then Tyler was at my side.

"It's done," he said, a catch in his throat. "Let's go."

He took my elbow like a well-bred young man at a debutante ball and led me away down the empty asphalt streets, avoiding the drifts of sand.

"The wind will blow sand over our tracks but there's no sense tempting fate," he said.

"You told me your gun is registered. Won't the police trace it back to you?"

Tyler smiled grimly. "That one's safe at home. Faraday gave me a throwaway awhile back when we handled a case with some organized crime connections. I suspect they paid him partially in trade. He sent Sam and me for lessons at the shooting range."

"He gave Sam a throwaway too?" I said, seizing upon this odd fact.

"A girl needs protection in this town."

We hiked over the empty streets, small nocturnal animals scurrying away at our approach. I felt naked and exposed. Any minute I expected flashing red lights and sirens to order us to the ground — until I realized that of course Luke had faked the 911 call. The jets howled and the tide roared and we moved like silent ghosts through the empty streets, back to Luke's car.

Tyler's car was parked alongside. My colleague examined Luke's car with pursed lips.

"Did Luke drive tonight?"

"Yes. Why?"

Tyler got a towel out of his trunk. He scrubbed off the handle of the passenger-side door, then opened it with his towel, leaned in, and wiped down the seat and the armrests.

Then he turned to me. "Touch anything else?"

I shook my head.

"We can go now."

He opened the passenger door of his car. "Up you get," he said, helping me in because I was none too steady on my feet.

He got behind the wheel and we drove away.

"We're not calling the cops?" I said stupidly.

"Faraday wants to talk to us first. He's at the office."

In my state of numb shock, that made a strange kind of sense.

Twenty minutes later, Faraday met us in the parking structure.

He handed me a large plastic bag.

"Both of you, take off your shoes and put them in here," he said. "And, Tyler, give me that throwaway phone you used to call me."

We did as he asked. Faraday tied the bag into a knot, holding it away from his body like dog poop, and said he'd dispose of it. Then he reached into a satchel and retrieved a pair of tennis shoes, which he dropped into Tyler's lap.

"My gym shoes," he said. "A little grungy, sorry."

Next, he handed me a box. Inside were cheap pumps from a discount shoe outlet down the street.

"Hope they fit," he grunted. "I had Samantha run down and buy them."

"That's two new pairs of shoes you owe me," I told him, remembering my ruined pumps from when I'd scaled the fence.

Once we were shod, and up in Faraday's office, he was all business.

"Tell me exactly what happened. Don't leave out *any* details. You know how I hate to get broadsided. In order to draw up the best strategy possible, you need to tell me the entire story."

With a surreal jolt, I realized that Faraday was using his standard client spiel on *us.*

He'd embarked on the most difficult damage control operation in our profession — keeping the client completely *out* of the news.

"It was self-defense," I protested. "We didn't do anything wrong."

"We can get into that later, Silver," Faraday said. "Right now, I need the facts."

Tyler and I looked at each other. "You first," he said.

I launched into a recap of everything that had happened since Luke Paxton showed up at my door.

Faraday seemed especially interested in what Luke had said on the dunes and his motive for wanting to kill me. He made me repeat it twice, urging me to recall Luke's exact words. When I told him that Luke had admitted to strangling Emily Mortimer during sex but denied killing Randall Downs, Faraday gave a snort of disgust.

"A clever defense attorney might be able to convince a jury that Emily's death was manslaughter, but Randall Downs was pure premeditated murder. Maybe even 'lying in wait,' which carries the death penalty." My boss nodded. "Yup, I can see why Luke Paxton would deny he'd killed his brother-in-law."

"Are we going to tell the police we've solved Emily Mortimer's murder?"

Faraday gave me a pitying look. "How could we do that when neither of you heard the confession? You weren't there. Luke Paxton drove out to the beach alone and committed suicide."

For a moment, I digested this, worrying it like a dog with a bone, looking for things that didn't make sense. And anything that might tie Tyler and me to his death.

"But what if the police catch Jake Slattery and charge him with a murder he didn't commit?"

"There's no hard evidence. Everything's circumstantial. And we'll deal with that if it happens," Faraday said blandly.

He turned to Tyler. "Your turn."

"As I've mentioned repeatedly" — he

glared at Faraday — "I've been concerned about Maggie's safety for some time now."

Tyler turned to me. "After someone lured you out in the middle of the night and tried to kill you, I asked Fletch for some software so I could use your phone to GPS your movements. When the program showed you leaving Cypress Park this evening and heading toward Playa del Rey, I followed."

"Why didn't you call me, Tyler?" Faraday said silkily. "We might have been able to defuse the situation."

"I'm sorry. I was so focused on Maggie's safety that I couldn't think of anything else."

"And you didn't think to call the police either?"

"For all I knew there was a perfectly legitimate reason Maggie was there. I wanted to assess the situation before doing anything rash." Tyler looked up. "Isn't that what you always say, sir?"

But Faraday was staring at the far wall and drumming his fingers on the desk.

"And you wiped down the gun and the car."

"Just like I was taught."

Faraday winced and changed the subject.

"Maggie, are you sure no one saw Luke at your house? Or saw you leave together?"

"It was dusk. Our street is steep and winding, with bad visibility. And he parked a ways down — I can see why now — at the bottom of a hillside lot."

"Did you have any electronic contact with Luke Paxton today? An e-mail or text or phone exchange?"

"No. He just showed up. I thought it was strange he knew my address, but he acted so distraught that I never asked."

Faraday turned his large, intelligent eyes on both of us.

"Luke Paxton recently broke up with a girlfriend. I understand he's been suffering from depression. Perhaps it all grew to be too much, and he decided to end things. So he went down to the ocean, a place he loved, and shot himself."

"It wasn't exactly on the beach," I pointed out.

Faraday sighed. "Okay. There were too many people on the beach for his taste. It's Labor Day weekend. People go down there for barbecues and stay half the night. He wanted to be alone. So he found a desolate place within sight of the coast he loved."

Faraday looked around. "The story needs some work, but it's a start.

"Okay, you two, get out of here. Tyler, give the car to Viken and have him give it a good wash and vacuum. Neither of you was at the beach tonight. You both stayed home. Separately," he said, in a tone that made me realize that he'd missed absolutely nothing about our failed little affair.

"Then what?" I said haltingly.

"We wait for the police to find the body. Someone is bound to report it. They'll contact the Paxtons, who will call me. And our official damage control operation will swing into gear. I'll handle it myself if it breaks early. You two need your beauty sleep."

"Is this the end of Senator Paxton's career?" Tyler asked.

Faraday frowned. "That's not for us to say. If the police rule Luke's death a suicide, it might sway public opinion back to the senator. He's ripe for it, after the worst two weeks of his life. Of course there will be questions. People will try to connect the dots. But they won't be able to, if you do your jobs and stick with your stories."

"So we should go home and go to sleep like nothing happened?"

"That's right. And don't forget we've got the Hollywood-Graystone Hotel opening tomorrow night. We have to raise a glass to Magnus Rex for paying our mortgages this month. I want everyone there by seven p.m. Party starts at eight. Dress sharp."

I groaned. "I don't think I'm up for . . ."

"You don't have to actually *do* anything, Silver, just stand around and look pretty. We want to convey that it's business as usual. And make sure you try the mini-crab cakes. The chef came from Water Grill, they're delicious."

42

But as it turned out, the phone rang at nine a.m. It was Anabelle calling, completely hysterical, asking if I could come over.

"What's wrong?" I said, struggling up from narcotic, nightmare-plagued sleep. Then memory kicked in and I was wide awake.

Crying, she told me that Luke's body had been discovered in the condemned airport land above Dockweiler Beach. Palisades del Rey.

"What?"

It took her three tries to get the words out because she kept bursting into sobs. I felt bad for making her do it, but I had no choice. I wasn't supposed to know.

I told Anabelle I'd be there as soon as I could, then texted Faraday, giving him the "news" and telling him I was heading for the Paxton house. Then I took another shower to scrub away my sins. I'd showered as soon as I got home the previous night, but the Lady Macbeth taint clung to me as if I'd done it myself.

Outside Villa Marbella, the media vans nearly blocked the street. I punched in the security code and waited for the wrought-iron gate to swing open.

The acid-green lawn was almost fluorescent. The morning was in full swing, bees buzzing drowsily, flowers open to the sun, ruby hummingbirds darting past on vibrating wings.

Anabelle opened the door. Her skin was sallow and her eyes swollen and ringed in red. She held a handkerchief under her nose and squinted at the merciless sun.

"Will it never end?" she whispered, pulling me into the house's cool, shaded depths.

We moved toward the kitchen, passing Henry's study. He looked up as we walked by, and I tried not to show my shock. He'd aged ten years overnight. There were violet pouches under his eyes and deep creases on either side of his mouth.

"Hullo, Maggie," he said. He tried to say more, but his lips trembled and nothing came.

Bernstein emerged from another room. He said, "The Blair people are on the phone, sir." His face grew puzzled as he saw me. "And another one has just arrived."

I took a deep breath. "I'm here today as Anabelle's friend."

"Right." Bernstein turned back to the senator. "Well, sir, the Blair people on the *phone* would like a word, if you're up to it. Shall I tell them we'll call back?"

For a moment, Henry's eyes showed dull bewilderment. Then he reached for a framed photo on his desk. I'd noticed it before, taking pride of place. It was a fading Kodachrome of Henry and Luke, bronzed and wearing board trunks, on Will Rogers Beach just down the hill. The sun was setting over the glassy sea. Henry was young and virile, his arm draped around his handsome teenaged son's shoulders, both of them grinning for the camera.

Henry Paxton made a strange, whistling sound through his teeth. For a moment, his fingers stroked the frame. Then he placed the photo facedown and punched in the phone.

"Where's Miranda?" I said, after we sat down in the kitchen with coffee.

Anabelle said her mom was upstairs, lying down. The maid had the day off. Somewhere far away, a phone jangled.

Anabelle cursed. "I thought I turned them all off," she said, running out. She came back a moment later. "There. Peace."

"I'm so sorry for your family's loss," I said. "When did they find him?"

"Around seven. A bird-watcher looking through the dunes with binoculars spotted the body."

"What do the police say?"

"He had a gun. They think it matches the bullets. It was windy last night; there's always an offshore breeze, so it covered up any footprints. They'll be sifting the sand for clues, though, you can count on that."

"So they don't think it was . . . foul play?"

"I don't know. I keep asking myself, why Palisades del Rey? What would Luke have been doing out there, where we used to . . . where I . . . remember how I took you there, once?"

"Yeah. It was creepy then and it's creepy now."

She gave me a wary look. "You've been there recently?"

I shrugged disinterestedly. "I use Vista del Mar to get to Manhattan Beach when the freeway's backed up. Several of our pro athlete clients live there."

But she was watching my face. And damn her, she knew me so well. She used to read me like a book. I hoped I'd grown some covers since high school.

"Anabelle?" I said, desperate to distract her.

"What?"

Feeling like a horrible hypocrite — because I could never admit I'd been three feet away when her brother was killed — I said, "Are you finally going to tell me about Ivan? Because there's a piece missing to this story, and I think you've got it."

The name still made her blanch. She buried her face in her hands, and when she spoke, her voice was muffled.

"What difference does it make anymore? He's gone. It can't hurt him."

"Can't hurt who?"

"Luke," she said, her voice barely above a whisper.

"Tell me about it."

Anabelle stared out the window, seeing something far in the past.

"When I was getting high, I'd run into Ivan. When I was desperate enough, I even bought drugs from him."

"So Randall and his cop antennae were right."

Anabelle nodded reluctantly. "But I found it hard to believe he'd strangled his girl-friend. He wasn't that type."

"Really? I read that he used to beat her up a lot."

Anabelle looked incredulous. "She used to beat *him* up. She was one crazy girl."

"What does any of this have to do with Luke?"

"Luke blamed himself for what happened to me in Playa that night. He swore he'd find the guys who set me up and take care of them. I told him to forget it. I just wanted to blot it out." She gave me a sad smile. "For a long time, I succeeded. But when I read that Ivan's girlfriend had been strangled, I decided to Google the Barracuda. And I learned he'd been murdered. And then I remembered Luke's vow and I got scared. So I told Randall I was going to the gym and I drove to Luke's house and confronted him."

I thought my head might blow off. "And?"

"He admitted it."

"Luke admitted that he'd killed Ivan's girlfriend?"

"The Barracuda too." Anabelle shuddered. "He was proud of it. He said, 'I told you I'd take care of them for you and I did.' Like I should thank him."

"But I don't understand. Why would Luke kill Ivan's girlfriend?"

Anabelle smiled crookedly. "That was so

like Luke. He'd destroy what you loved best."

"What?"

She twirled a strand of hair.

"When I was five, I had a doll I loved more than anything in the world. Her name was Calista and I'd make clothes for her and tell her stories and tuck her into bed next to me each night. And one day when Luke was angry at something I'd done, Calista disappeared. Mom said I must have left her somewhere, but Luke walked around with a funny little smile while I cried and tore the house upside down. We couldn't find her. Then a few weeks later Luke and I were playing 'buried treasure' in the sandbox and my toe touched something hard. It was Calista's head. I couldn't stop screaming and the nanny had to give me a sedative."

"So Luke killed what Ivan loved?"

Anabelle nodded. "It must have been icing on Luke's cake when Ivan got arrested for his girlfriend's murder."

"Then why didn't Luke kill someone the Barracuda loved?"

Even sixteen years later, Anabelle still flinched. "That pig didn't love anyone but himself."

"Did your parents know?"

Anabelle shook her head. "They would have thought I was crazy. And I wasn't sure myself. What if it was just some revenge fantasy Luke had dreamed up?"

But what if it wasn't?

"Did you tell Randall?"

Anabelle pulled herself up. "We Paxtons keep things in the family. Besides, Luke was planning to run for Dad's seat down the line."

"How could Luke run for office if he had a juvenile record?"

"Dad and Lambert got that expunged. His record was wiped clean."

I shook my head in disbelief. "I remember the first time I saw your brother," I said. "He'd just come back from boarding school. I'd never seen anyone so beautiful in all my life."

"You thought he was at boarding school?" Through her tears, Anabelle tittered.

I thought she might be growing hysterical. First her husband, then her brother.

"That's what you told me," I said, my voice rising. "What else was I supposed to think?"

"Please don't be angry, Maggie. I couldn't bear it."

"Then please stop talking in riddles."

"Luke wasn't at a normal boarding school.

It was a place for disturbed adolescents. A locked facility. He couldn't leave. Mom enrolled him under her maiden name."

"Now you're really freaking me out."

"It was either that or a work camp. Whatever they call those places for juvenile delinquents. Dad called in some favors and Lambert worked a deal."

Anabelle sighed. "Poor Dad. He was always rescuing one of us. As soon as Luke straightened out, I'd do something. It was like we passed the baton. And maybe Luke had a special chip on his shoulder because . . ."

I wrinkled my nose. "What?"

"I found that box Mom took from the guest room. I know all her hiding places from when I used to steal stuff to pawn."

"Did you find a gun?"

Anabelle shook her head. "Nothing like that. It was all photos and letters. There was a photo of that old boyfriend Mom almost married, and he looked just like Luke. So then I thought about the whirlwind courtship Mom and Dad had always told us about. And I began to wonder if they *had* to get married, because Mom was pregnant. By the other guy. The one who'd jilted her."

Which would explain why the killer's DNA

didn't resemble Senator Paxton's. Luke wasn't his son.

"Did Luke know?"

"No. But maybe deep down he wondered. He was always pushing Dad, testing the limits of his love."

She smiled sadly. "But Dad always came through. He'd do anything for us."

"What about Miranda?"

"Mom had totally checked out by the time we were teenagers. Vodka tonics and her freaky mannequins and her tennis serve. That's all she cared about."

"What did Luke do to get sent to that school?" I whispered.

"Trespassing. Assault. Drugs. He hated Maine. Begged my parents to bring him home. Finally Lambert was able to arrange a court hearing and the judge sprung him."

Anabelle's mouth twitched. "Judge Reiner. His wife plays tennis with Mom."

She turned to me. "I loved my brother. But I hated him too. He was nothing but trouble. When he came back home, I warned him to stay away from you. I threatened to tell you everything if he didn't behave himself."

"Why didn't you tell me the truth?" I said, thinking back to my lovesick mooning. How they must have laughed at me.

"Why didn't you tell us the truth about you?" Anabelle retorted.

"I thought you wouldn't want to be friends anymore if you knew."

Anabelle nodded sadly. "I guess I could say the same thing about me."

Dear Lord. How much of the truth should I tell her now?

I had to tell her. I couldn't tell her.

Did she really not know?

Swallowing hard, I said, "You know I had coffee with Raven, right?"

"Yes," she said warily.

"Raven told me she's the one who broke up with Luke, back in high school."

"That's not true," Anabelle said, a touch too fast.

"She told me why," I lied.

"Raven was a fabulist," said Anabelle. "Even when we were at Corvallis, she wasn't very tethered to reality."

"She seemed plenty grounded the other day."

"She's fooled a lot of people."

"She says she broke up with Luke because he choked her during sex," I said.

"I don't believe it."

Anabelle was crying, the tears streaking saltily down her face.

I continued, "And I got to wondering. If

Luke tried to strangle Raven when they were teenagers . . . is it possible he knew Emily Mortimer?"

"No!" Anabelle said in a piercing cry. "It's not true. They never met."

"Think about it: Your dad the senator gets invited to parties and fund-raisers and dinners. Maybe Luke the up-and-coming prosecutor went along with him to one event. He and Emily met. They liked each other, but because of who your dad is, they decided to keep their affair secret."

Anabelle said, "Emily was sleeping with Uncle Simon. But she had a boyfriend, that guy the police are all looking for, Jake Slattery."

"Wouldn't that be all the more reason to keep her relationship with Luke a secret?"

Anabelle looked at me in pure fury. "You don't know that. He didn't tell you."

Ah, but he had.

"And there's another thing," I said. "Randall was inquiring into Emily's murder. Did you tell Luke about the mug shot of Ivan you saw on your husband's computer?"

Anabelle gave a reluctant nod.

"The next day, someone killed Randall in front of his house. You think that was a coincidence?"

Anabelle's hair did a macabre dance as

she shook her head.

"Luke didn't kill him. He was up in Palo Alto taking a deposition the night Randall was murdered. He came back the next morning."

"Did you check his alibi?"

She gave me a hollow look and her body seemed to collapse in upon itself. "They're both dead. What difference would it make?"

And then I made my decision. Let her have this one thing. It would rob her fragile eggshell mind of the last defenses if she had to confront Luke's final betrayal.

I scooted closer and put my arm around her. "I'm just grasping at straws," I said. "I'm sorry, Anabelle."

She looked up at me through her tears.

"I'm sorry too," she said. "But about Randall? You should know: I was getting ready to file for divorce."

I looked at her, flabbergasted. "But I thought you were totally in love. You told me that wonderful story about how he saved your life."

She gave me a sad smile. "He did. And I was. Maybe I'll always love him. But for Lincoln's sake, I had to leave before he hurt us both. Mom and Dad and I had even met with Lambert and gotten the name of a good divorce lawyer. But I hadn't told him yet. I was afraid Randall would fight it and come after me, or threaten Dad with embarrassing disclosures."

Anabelle stared at her hands.

"So now what are you going to do?"

"I'm going to do what we Paxtons always do. Let someone else pick up the slack. We stick together. That's what you don't understand. We're a family."

43

All too soon, I had to go home and get dressed for the Hollywood-Graystone party. I called Faraday on the way. For once, he sounded exhausted. He said one tabloid paper had asked whether a Kennedy-like curse hovered over the Paxton family.

When I started to tell him about my visit with Anabelle, Faraday cut me off and said in a firm voice that we'd discuss it after the Magnus Rex event.

No talking on notoriously insecure cell phones, I muttered to myself.

I knew I was slipping. My mind was starting to disintegrate. How long could I continue to function?

Then Faraday hit me with some upsetting news: The police wanted to interview me.

"Why?" I said, feeling panicky.

"They're talking to everyone who knew Luke," Faraday said soothingly. "I told them you were tied up with clients today but set it up for eleven tomorrow morning. Is that okay?"

The unspoken questions reverberated in my ear. Would I hold up under questioning? Would I stick to the script? Could he count on me?

"I guess so. I don't have any particular insights for them."

"Then that's exactly what you tell them," Faraday said, his voice full and triumphant. "I'll see you soon."

After we hung up, I rehearsed what I'd done the previous night: I'd slept all day, showered, put some dinner in the microwave, and crawled into bed with a good book. But the police wouldn't ask me about last night. They had no reason to suspect I'd been out at Palisades del Rey with Luke.

And I had to keep it that way or else the whole damn house of cards would collapse. I flashed to Anabelle in her parents' kitchen today, trying to put up a brave front. If she could, then I could.

After showering, I slipped on a flowery dress and strappy sandals and selected Annick Goutal's Eau du Sud, a peppery, lemony Mediterranean concoction, perfect for a summer night. Mom was due back anytime from Catalina.

To my surprise, I found I missed her. Part of it was wanting to tell her I was sorry I'd lost my temper, and that she could always count on me, which would make me feel better. But I'd also grown used to having her around, cranky and misguided as she was. The last two days had almost undone me. Somehow I'd lost my true north, veered off the path. She could help me find it again. Leaving her a Welcome Home note saying that I'd be back by eleven, I left for the party.

Driving along the Sunset Strip, I pulled down the mirror and tried different faces, looking for one that matched my party frock. The wide boulevard was ablaze with neon lights and sports cars. Traffic inched along, allowing me to study the oil-painted billboards of young, svelte, impossibly beautiful people hawking vodka and jeans and new movies. I even liked the superbillboards on the sides of buildings whose moving images looped arty commercials. It made me feel like I was in Tokyo or Hong Kong or inside the world of *Blade Runner,* whose sci-fi noir had captured L.A. like no other.

The Hollywood-Graystone was a regal hotel whose Art Deco curves, sumptuous ocean liner lobby, and Tinseltown glamour drew well-heeled tourists and cutting-edge jet-setters from around the globe. From now on, it would also draw the macabre fans of Magnus Rex.

I handed my car off to the valet, put the ticket in my woven straw pursette, and strolled into the hotel, whose air-conditioned chill was fragrant with orange blossom.

Faraday was already there, resplendent in a tux. Tyler was looking somber in a seersucker suit. A bevy of starlets frolicked at the edge of an azure, underwater-lit pool while black-clad waiters circled discreetly, offering drinks and hors d'oeuvres. In one corner, Elmore Leonard held court, telling ribald stories. In another I saw members of Oasis, Guns N' Roses, an *American Idol* judge, and several reality TV show contestants.

I circled the room, giving Tyler a wide berth, fearing that the careful façade I'd constructed might shatter if I got too close. But no matter where I went, he hovered at the edge of my vision. Whom was he protecting me from now? Did he want me to break down in hysterics in the middle of the party?

I needed to chill.

Grabbing a glass of champagne and some eel sushi from a passing waiter, I drifted to the palm-fronded entrance of the hotel.

Every few seconds, a strobe flash went off as some new starlet or musician or celebrity stepped out of a limo. The explosions unnerved me and I jumped sky high, sloshing my drink, but slowly I got used to it.

As the crowd inside grew more dense, I strolled out back to the pool, where the desert air enveloped me in its hot, dry embrace.

The tiny bubbles waltzed into my bloodstream. I drank another flute of champagne. Hotel personnel were handing out tickets for tours of the haunted room. They began to lead groups upstairs with flashlights. On a makeshift stage, a tribute band played Magnus Rex's greatest hits. Long banners of raw linen with Warholian silk-screened images of the dead rock star hung from the stamped tin ceiling.

Suddenly I was exhausted. My limbs were lead. I hoped I wouldn't crumple into a heap on the marble floor before I managed to get home. I said good-bye to Tyler and looked for Faraday but didn't see him. Oh, well, I had put in my time.

The world began to close in as I drove home, the shutter clicking tighter and tighter. The champagne had left me with a throbbing headache. The world outside seemed garishly lit but also more deeply shadowed.

The Adderall was wearing off, leaving me with screaming nerves and a crashing tidal wave of exhaustion. I'd taken a whopping thirty milligrams this morning, then another fifteen milligrams at Anabelle's to goose me through the evening, but my tolerance had grown too high. My body felt heavy and tired, my thoughts sluggish and gluey. Soon, I'd be a zombie.

The porch light was on. A warm, welcoming yellow glow seeped from behind the closed living room curtains.

"Welcome back," I called, unlocking the front door.

Silence greeted me.

"Hi, Mom. How was your trip?"

My words echoed and clanged dully inside my head as I walked into the kitchen.

Someone had replaced my lightweight sandals with lead snowshoes. I set my purse down on the Formica table and blinked.

Jack Faraday stood in my kitchen.

"You're home early," he said.

I'd last seen him at the Graystone, holding court, and my syrupy brain took a minute to process that he was no longer there. He must have slipped out of the crowded party without saying good-bye.

He'd also changed and was now dressed completely in black.

"What are you doing here? Mom?" I called. "Where's my mother?"

"Your mother's fine. We were just visiting. Amazing woman, I can see where you get your spunk."

I made a sort of bleating sound deep in my throat and tried to dart away, but he was too fast and I was too sloppy.

There was a gun in his hands, with a strange appendage on its muzzle.

My synapses sizzled like a Fourth of July firecracker. Even though I'd never seen one before, I knew it was a silencer.

"Stu blew it the other day when he managed to take out only your windshield," Faraday said.

Stu. The Plumber. Faraday's black ops guy. The one he used for special projects.

Faraday marched me to the study, where my mother sat, tied to a chair with a gag in her mouth.

"Talk to your daughter," he said, removing the gag.

My mother coughed, spitting and retching.

"Maggie," came her wavery voice.

My brain skipped a beat.

"Mom! What has he done to you?"

I'm sorry I yelled at you. I'm sorry for everything. This is all my fault.

"Don't worry about me, Maggie. Save yourself. Run . . ."

"Shut up." Faraday hit her across the mouth and her head flew back as she moaned.

A moment earlier, I'd barely been able to move. Now I scanned the room for something to use as a weapon.

"Don't move," my boss said calmly.

He bent to retie my mother's gag, the gun dangling carelessly from his hand. He knew I wouldn't leave her.

"How did you get in here?" I said.

"Your mother *invited* me. I showed her my Blair ID."

I glanced at my mother's eyes, which beetled in hatred toward Faraday. I'd warned her about trusting strangers, but I'd never warned her about colleagues.

"She doesn't know anything. Please untie her."

Faraday shook his head. "I can't take that chance."

"What chance?"

Faraday inspected me. He chuckled. "So you've finally developed a poker face."

"About what?"

"Don't bullshit me, Maggie. I know Luke

669

Paxton told you before Tyler blew his brains out."

"Told me what?"

Most of my brain was in lockdown. But a tiny corner that still functioned now flashed to a recent memory. Of Anabelle complaining about Luke selling stocks in a down market. Why would anybody do such a thing unless he was desperate?

Then I remembered bringing my boss coffee and finding him on the phone. And Luke's voice on the other end, pleading.

"You've got to do something."

Faraday had fobbed me off with that explanation about angry neighbors. But what if that wasn't it at all? Luke had denied killing Randall Downs. Maybe that was true.

Maybe Luke had hired Faraday to do it for him, because he was terrified his brother-in-law was getting too close to discovering that Luke had strangled Emily Mortimer.

That would explain Faraday grilling me about Luke's exact words at Palisades del Rey. He feared Luke had told me and he was petrified, knowing that the cops were about to interview me.

"You killed Randall Downs," I said.

"I didn't kill anyone," Faraday said. "My hands are clean. But honestly? That family should give me a medal. Senator Paxton often wished Randall Downs would go away. I guess God finally answered his prayer."

"Did he wish Emily Mortimer would go away too?"

"That was an accident. Why should the senator's career be derailed and his son's life destroyed because of an accident?"

"Luke killed her."

"Luke was a good kid. With a great future ahead of him."

"A future bought and paid for by Daddy Dearest."

"They had it all planned out, you know. In two years, Henry hoped to get nominated for vice president and Luke would run for his father's Senate seat."

I shook my head. "There's not a crisis management firm on earth that could pull off that kind of miracle."

"Plenty of American political dynasties weather scandals. The Kennedys. The Bushes. People have short memories."

"So Henry knew and he protected his son?"

"It's no different from how he helped his daughter avoid arrest when she was on drugs. And getting her rehab instead of jail when he couldn't fix it anymore. What kind of favors do you think got called in there?"

"You can't compare that to murder," I spluttered. "Anabelle hurt only herself."

I paused.

"I promise I won't tell the cops. And I'm a lot more useful to you alive. The Paxton account is a cash cow, they'll be needing crisis management for years to come, and I'm your conduit into the family. Like you said, they love me and trust me."

"Clever girl," Faraday said. "I've thought about cutting you in. We could split the money. Blair would never know."

"He's not a part of this?"

Faraday hesitated a moment. "No."

"Let's do it," I said. "You and me. Partners."

He seemed to consider it.

"I won't let you down. I'll do anything."

An evil glint came into Faraday's eyes.

"You're a girl after my own heart, Maggie, and that's how I know you're lying. You'd do anything to save your skin right now."

His legs moved apart, as if to brace himself for what came next.

"You're going to get caught," I said. "The phone, the gun, the forensic evidence you leave behind."

Faraday pinched his wrist and I heard rubber snap. "These are gloves. The gun's a throwdown. My car's still with the valets, I drove here in a rental. It's parked down the street and I took off the plates. I'll change back into my tux and be back at the party in twenty minutes. No one will even know I was gone."

He tsked. "You really shouldn't live in such a bad neighborhood, Maggie. Two women, all alone, vulnerable to burglaries and break-ins. You're easy prey."

There was an explosion behind me. Faraday's chest splattered with blood and he slumped to the floor.

"But I'm not," said Earlyn, advancing into the room, rifle trained on my boss.

"I thought I heard a man's voice when I came through the backyard hole looking for Bandit.

"That no-good varmint," Earlyn said, examining the body on the ground. "Have you seen her?"

I opened my mouth to reply.

Then I fainted.

44

I awoke in the hospital, tethered to tubes, Mom at my side, dabbing my temples. I sniffed.

"You brought the good stuff," I said.

"You're awake," said Mom, pleased. "How do you feel?"

"I must be okay, if I can smell Chanel Sycomore."

Cautiously, I flexed and moved different parts of my body. Everything was accounted for.

I pressed my temples, trying to think. The smoky vetiver scent wafted through the room.

"The last thing I remember is Earlyn shooting Jack Faraday," I said.

"You fainted," Mom said. "Then Earlyn untied me and we called the police."

"How many hours have I been out?"

"Hours? Try two days. The doctors said you were run-down and near collapse. And you've got the beginnings of an ulcer. They apparently see that a lot with Adderall abuse. The doc says the dosages you were taking were dangerous."

I'd barely been awake two minutes, and she already was lecturing me.

Some things never change.

A righteous spark of anger went through me, all the more annoying because I knew she was right.

"Let's kick together, Mom. My pills, your ciggies. Deal?"

Mom pursed her lips. Then she gave a terse nod.

"Your Mr. Blair has been marvelous," she said. "His assistant keeps calling to see how you're doing. He's going to pay for us to stay at a fancy clinic near Palm Springs once they release you."

"Clinic? I'm fine."

"It's more like a luxury spa, apparently. He said we need to hide away from the media. He's a fine man. When he learned about my cancer scare and the long wait for a biopsy, he paid out of his own pocket for the procedure."

I thought I was hallucinating. "What, in the last forty-eight hours?"

Mom's eyes grew shiny.

"And we got the results immediately." She

squeezed my hand. "It's benign. A cyst. The cancer hasn't come back."

"Oh, Mom," I said, thinking I must still be dreaming. "That's fantastic."

For the next few days, Thomas Blair was in constant touch, running a smooth, textbook-perfect PR campaign while keeping Mom and me sequestered in Palm Springs. Tyler drove out to visit me, saying the police had come by the office. They were eager to interview me and we wouldn't be able to put it off much longer.

Tyler said the police had found a disk in Faraday's office containing a recording of my conversation with Thomas Blair in his rooftop garden, where the company founder had brought up my suspicions about Faraday.

They'd also found a file cabinet at Faraday's home stuffed with documents indicating he'd run a rogue operation from inside Blair, taking on black PR for freelance clients.

One of those clients was the disgraced JTM Financial Services, Inc., for whom Faraday had done a series of unsavory jobs including blackmail, break-ins, and intimidation. The files would be a treasure trove for federal investigators for years to come.

But some of Faraday's private clients were giving law enforcement trouble, including a company called Tune, Inc., that seemed not to exist.

At this, I let out a strangled cry.

"That was our pet name for Luke," I said excitedly. "Anabelle and I used to call him 'Tune' because of the way he swaggered around like Neptune, the god of the sea."

The police believed that someone at Tune, Inc., had hired Faraday to kill Randall Downs, and they'd resumed questioning drug lords who might have vowed revenge on the police captain.

"You're not going to enlighten them?" I asked Tyler.

"Me?" said my colleague, looking steadily at me. "I already told them everything I know."

I rolled my eyes.

Tyler walked to the window. "How about a walk, now that it's cooled off," he said.

He turned, giving me a significant look, and I knew we'd discuss it more outside.

The desert air smelled of baked dust and nocturnal flowering shrubs.

As shadows fell and warm winds blew, we strolled through the tranquil grounds of the resort spa and I finally began to understand Tyler's lies and evasions.

While courting me in vain, Oliver Goldman and his feds had also approached Tyler
for help with their investigation. And my
colleague, who'd grown increasingly uncomfortable with Faraday's black operations,
agreed to wear a wire.

Tyler had also befriended Faraday's dirty
tricks operative, Stu Nicholls, and gotten
him on tape after a night of drinking, boast-
ing that he'd killed an LAPD cop in Palos
Verdes. Faraday's man was now sitting in
jail awaiting trial for murder. The police
suspected that he was also behind my at-
tempted murder. They figured that when
Nicholls botched that, Faraday decided to
do the job himself.

To this day, I still don't know whether
Faraday was really a rogue agent or whether
he acted with the full knowledge and support of our founder. When I recalled my
boss's daily meetings with Blair, the nervous
way he'd finger his tie and mutter to himself, how shrunken and chastened he
seemed after each visit upstairs, I had my
doubts he'd acted on his own.

But I was also thankful to Thomas Blair
for everything he'd done for Mom.

Faraday never intended to get her a slot
on a medical trial if her cancer returned.
He'd said that only to buy my compliance.

As Tyler and I strolled through the landscaped grounds and the San Jacinto Mountains cast purple-blue shadows, Tyler hit me
with one last surprise.

Blair wanted to send us on a weeklong
fact-finding missing to Ireland to collect af-
fidavits from friends and former employers
of Marie Connor, the onetime Holloway au
pair. One family outside Limerick had accused her of stealing jewelry two years earlier.

"Since when does Blair send two associates overseas on expensive junkets?" I said.

"Maybe he figures he owes us some R &
R, after all we've been through," Tyler said.

"Is he going to pay for separate rooms
too?"

Tyler's face assumed the cherubic look of
a choir boy. "If that's what you want."

There was a message waiting from Thomas
Blair when we got back to the spa lobby. It
was for both of us.

When we called him back, Blair explained
that he'd decided to divide Jack Faraday's
senior vice president position into separate
jobs. He was looking for two good people.
Were Tyler and I interested?

We told him we'd think about it.

Was this a bribe, a way to ensure that we

stayed with the company and didn't question things too deeply? Tyler and I batted it around all evening over our five-star spa cuisine dinner but failed to come to any conclusion.

When it was time to leave, I walked him to his car.

"Could we start again, Maggie, from the beginning, and you give me a real chance this time?" Tyler asked.

I told him yes, and he kissed me under the hot desert moon.

45

The day before I met with police, I visited Villa Marbella to see how Anabelle was doing.

A black town car was parked in the driveway when I pulled up. A uniformed driver stood by the back, loading designer suitcases into the trunk.

Senator Paxton emerged from the house, carrying a briefcase, a trench coat slung over one arm.

Congress was going back into session and he'd soon be a busy man — making backroom deals, holding hearings, finding consensus, pushing bills through.

He looked as dapper as ever in his hand-tailored suit, monogrammed white shirt, Italian loafers, and silk tie. But his eyes were sunk more deeply in his sockets, his jowls hung loosely, and his skin was the color of mushrooms.

When he saw me, his facial muscles pulled

together, trying but failing to muster a smile.

"Hullo, Maggie."

We shook hands and he told me how much Anabelle cherished my friendship and how he and Miranda appreciated my efforts on the family's behalf.

We were about to say good-bye when I blurted it out.

"Henry, when did Luke and Emily start seeing each other?"

Horrified, I clapped my hand to my mouth, but it was too late, the words could not be retrieved.

He regarded me gravely. Then a look of paternal concern beamed from U.S. Senator Henry Paxton's large brown eyes.

"What are you talking about, Maggie? My son didn't know Emily."

Then Senator Paxton patted my arm.

"These last weeks have been a nightmare for us all. I think you should get some rest. Good-bye, Maggie."

He climbed into the town car. Immediately the tinted window rolled up, sealing him back inside his private world.

The luxury car glided down the long driveway until it disappeared.

And I thought: All the long hours and sacrifice. The lies and half-truths. The sleepless nights. I'd put my personal life on hold and my career and even my safety on the line because I'd believed in him and his family. Somehow I had suckered myself into thinking that the end justified the means, so long as it was for a good cause.

And because of that, I found it inconceivable that Senator Henry Paxton could look me in the eye and lie with such earnest conviction.

But now he'd finally shown his true hand: Henry Paxton didn't care about anyone but himself. He was narcissistic, cold, and predatory, unmoved by the suffering and death his family left in their wake with their indulgent, reckless, and destructive behavior.

In his exalted world, family and position were all that mattered, and the rest of us existed only to do his bidding. The most basic human decency eluded him. His charisma was chameleonlike. It changed depending on what he needed from you. He had no sincerity or depth. He was hollow inside.

It had taken me almost twenty years to see this basic truth, and it had almost gotten me killed.

I felt mortified by my naïveté and humiliated by how they'd all played me for a fool and manipulated my old loyalties. And not only the Paxtons. Faraday had read me from the beginning, correctly gauging my infatuation with this family, my desire to get close to them again in the hopes that their glamour might rub off on me.

When I entered Villa Marbella, Simon was standing at the picture window in the living room, staring out at the driveway.

He dipped his head to acknowledge me, and as he turned away, his lips curved into a tight smile.

I vowed to tell the police everything.

Anabelle was out back with Lincoln, filling a basket with aromatic white peaches that clustered so thickly the tree branches drooped almost to the ground.

Bangs was romping with them, and Lincoln screamed with delight as the dog found a bruised peach and ate it, a puzzled look in her doggie eyes.

"Did you catch Dad on his way out?" Anabelle asked, brushing specks of dust and bark off her face with her shirtsleeve.

I told her that I had.

"I'm so glad," she said, hugging me.

Lincoln held up a half-eaten peach.

"Try this one, Mommy. It's juicy-sweet."

"I've got an idea," Anabelle said, clapping her hands. "Lincoln, why don't you get

Bangs and bring her over to Aunt Maggie and I'll take a picture of the three of you."

Then it was time to take one with Anabelle too.

We squatted alongside the child and his dog and I held the cell phone at arm's length and took the photo.

"It came out great," Anabelle said, peering over my shoulder.

There we were, smiling bravely into the camera on a golden September afternoon, when the evening breeze brings the barest butterfly chill to remind us that winter draws near, even here in L.A.

I looked closer. The cell phone image had captured a change in Anabelle that I had missed.

She was as beautiful as ever, but the tragedy of recent weeks had burned away everything superfluous. What remained was a more elemental, haunting beauty, like a drift of wood the sea has tumbled to smooth white sculpture.

In the photo, Anabelle stood behind Lincoln, pulling him close, her hands clasped in a garland over his chest. Her eyes were sad, and her lower lip, caught between her teeth as she forced a smile, concealed a tremor.

But she was alive. And she was determined

to survive.

And at that moment, I knew that despite everything her father and brother had done, I wasn't capable of betraying her. I'd take her secret — all their secrets — to my grave.

Let the voters choose whether to keep Henry Paxton in office.

Let them decide whether the black cloud of tragedy and suspicion that swirled over the Paxton name made him unfit to govern. It's the eternal dilemma with politicians, isn't it?

And so I pledged my loyalty not for or against Henry but to his daughter, Anabelle.

I wanted to be a friend to her, the friend I hadn't been able to be at sixteen when she suffered a terrible injury that had been meant for me.

I owed her a karmic debt I could never repay.

I know I can't keep her safe. Life doesn't work that way.

But maybe I can control the damage.

ACKNOWLEDGMENTS

I would like to thank Anne Borchardt, Anna deVries, and Susan Moldow.

Maggie Crawford helped me work through the plot and Cynthia Merman, Marcell Rosenblatt, and Kathleen Rizzo caught my mistakes. Any that remain are mine alone. Thank you to Chika Azuma for doing the cover design.

Alan Mayer regaled me with stories and lunch.

The fine folks on MUA offered fragrant companionship.

David, Adrian, and Alex provided love, encouragement, and support. Thanks, guys.

ABOUT THE AUTHOR

Denise Hamilton has written for *Wired, Cosmopolitan, Der Spiegel,* and the *Los Angeles Times,* where she currently writes a perfume column. She is the author of the Edgar-nominated *The Jasmine Trade,* as well as four other acclaimed Eve Diamond novels, which were all *Los Angeles Times* bestsellers, and is the author of *The Last Embrace.*

The employees of Thorndike Press hope you have enjoyed this Large Print book. All our Thorndike, Wheeler, and Kennebec Large Print titles are designed for easy reading, and all our books are made to last. Other Thorndike Press Large Print books are available at your library, through selected bookstores, or directly from us.

For information about titles, please call:
  (800) 223-1244

or visit our Web site at:
  http://gale.cengage.com/thorndike

To share your comments, please write:
  Publisher
  Thorndike Press
  10 Water St., Suite 310
  Waterville, ME 04901